Pelzmantel

And Other Tales of Medieval Magic

Pelzmantel

And Other Tales of Medieval Magic

K A Laity

IMMANION PRESS
Stafford England

Pelzmantel and Other Tales of Medieval Magic
By K. A. Laity
© 2nd ed 2010
Introduction by Elizabeth Hand © 2010

Cover Art/Design by Ruby
Interior Layout/Design by Storm Constantine

Set in Garamond

IP0096

An Immanion Press Edition
8 Rowley Grove
Stafford ST17 9BJ
UK

http://www.immanion-press.com
info@immanion-press.com

ISBN 978-1-904853-74-9

Dedication

To all the girls who dream

Acknowledgements 2010

My grateful thanks to Storm and everyone at Immanion Press for breathing new life into this story. Thanks go, too, to the determined readers who sought out the original small printing and kept it in their hearts. Special thanks to Ruby for a cover so gorgeous, it made me cry.

Gracious thanks to fellow fairy-tale lover, Liz Hand, for a kind and insightful introduction.

Acknowledgements 2002

Big thanks to Lorna Tedder and everyone at Spilled Candy for midwifing this little book, improving her weaknesses, and burnishing her strengths.

Thanks to Wendy Goldberg for kind words on reading the first few hesitant pages, and to Mildred L. Perkins and Becky Thacker for reading the first draft and suggesting various helpful improvements.

Thanks to Clive Barker for the first words of encouragement I heard (and thanks to all of those whose words of encouragement I could not or would not hear).

Thanks to Betty Louise who was there when it began and to Freya who finished it up.

Thanks for endless support from Lillith, Kali, Louhi, Sekhmet and Hecate, not to mention Bast and Ganesha.

Thanks most of all to my sweetie Gene, my Greenman, my cheerleader, without whose help and love and support I would have given up a thousand times in despair—I love you.

Contents

Introduction

Elizabeth Hand

There is one story and one story only/That will be worth your telling, wrote Robert Graves in "To Juan at the Winter Solstice." *From woman back to woman...*

Here is another telling of that one true tale. It has had many names over the centuries — "Catskin," "Mossycoat," "The Princess with the Golden Hair," "Cinderella" — these are just a few. Charles Perrault called it "Peau d"Aune," "Donkeyskin," in his 1697 collection *Mother Goose Tales,* but it was an old tale even then. Not always a fairytale, either — the Irish Saint Dymphna shares much of Donkeyskin's history, including a royal father determined to marry his own daughter after her mother's death. Now K.A. Laity has made it her own and titled it *Pelzmantel,* "Fur Cloak," because, of course, every true sorceress knows the importance of a name, just as every sorceress knows there is nothing so powerful as a good story.

And Laity is a very remarkable sorceress indeed. Her lovely tale draws on all the classic elements of the versions mentioned above, and weaves them into an intricate pattern that draws deeply on the folklore and legends of the middle ages —Laity is a noted medievalist, and her knowledge and love for this period illuminates every page of *Pelzmantel.* The result is as dazzling and detailed as a panel from the Unicorn Tapestries.

Too many contemporary retellings of traditional tales are set in a generic Olde Europe that owes more to Sleeping Beauty's Castle in Disneyland than to the richer, darker, stranger landscapes that inspired them. *Pelzmantel's* world feels lived-in and startlingly *real,* with its beautifully-observed details of kitchens, herb-gathering, and dressmaking. It's a world recognizable to us from history, as well as from myth. There are references to the *suomi*, northern magicians who are in fact Finns, who were renowned and feared in medieval times for their sorcery; and to the Celtic countries of the British Isles, whose women, especially prized for their beauty and wisdom, were captured as slaves by Scandinavian raiders.

Nanna, who recounts Pelzmantel's tale, is one of these women, now trusted friend and confidante to the wise young queen Gunnhild, who rules over a kingdom (similar to medieval Denmark) where descent is matrilineal, much to the advantage of those who live within its borders. "There are always differences, what with women wanting to make life easier and men, it seems, always wanting to have the advantage over somebody. Power— why is it always their biggest concern?"

And so, as in all the best fairytales, *Pelzmantel* begins in strife and sorrow: Gunnhild has died in childbirth, leaving her husband so bereft he can't bear the sight of his only daughter. The child, Hallgerd, is raised by Nanna, who ensures the girl knows of her matristic heritage and its sigils:

> *The bobbin for guidance through wisdom and sense,*
> *The spindle for drawing out all excellence,*
> *The ring for binding the oath to this land*
> *To love and protect and be at its command.*

Despite Nanna's efforts, betrayal follows — would there be a tale otherwise? — as well as dark enchantment and wondrous shapeshifting, a love story and tales within tales; also the very best kind of magic, that which comes from knowledge of the human heart. Of all the branching stories in *Pelzmantel*, my favorite belongs to Grima, the crotchety cook whose past is revealed by Nanna in a scene of lovely, understated poignancy.

And have I mentioned the talking fox?

"The truth isn't nearly so exciting as a real story," Hallgerd observes. "An enigmatic and beautiful young woman suddenly appears—and disappears before you can learn her name. Strange

gold tokens appear in your supper. A terrific story, Nanna."
Pelzmantel is that terrific story, full of marvels and everyday
wisdom, joyous and touching and thrilling by turns. "A matchless
storyteller once taught me, 'Nothing ever begins,'" says Nanna as
she works her magic upon the reader. "Thus stories, having no
beginning, can have no end. This story, too, goes on. Shall I tell
you more?'"

Yes, please.

Pelzmantel

1

I am very old, though not so old as the hills. Kings and queens have been born and grown and died, while still I go on. Perhaps I am only curious. But many will tell you that it is because I am a witch. It is true that I know many of the hidden ways. But I am a story-teller first, last and always. Many stories, too, have passed before me, but there is only one that I turn to again and again. I do not know, yet, how it shall end.

Once upon a time, there was a queen. She had hair of brilliant gold. It would shine like burnished metal in the sunlight, dance in moonlight spears. Her face had the radiant glow of genuine happiness, for she loved the land in which she dwelled, and she had found her own true love. Her king loved her truly and deeply, and nothing but death could part them. This is the end of one story that I know: a happy ending. But it is the beginning of this story, so of course something terrible is going to happen.

The queen's name was Gunnhild. I came to her land in the time of her great-grandmother—or was it perhaps her great-great-grandmother? No matter. Like all these women, she called me "Nanna" and became my charge. She was very special to me, this child, for Gunnhild was born small and weak, barely alive. The midwife frowned and sighed. The child's mother cried silently, clutching my hand with dread. But I looked into the baby's eyes and saw no nonsense, no fear. I smiled. She would survive.

It was never easy. Gunnhild's mother, the queen, never lost

13

her look of worry. There was the fever at one year, the pox-scare at two, a dog-bite once, and a strange sleeping-sickness that lasted a week. Each time a little thinner, and yet more radiant, Gunnhild would rise weakly from the pillows of her sick-bed and smile. The queen would clasp her joyfully and I would clap my hands with delight. The king would bless my healing salves—I would thank the clear, bright light, which glittered within Gunnhild's eyes.

But this is not the time for the child's story. All the triumph and the sorrow of her early years I leave for another time. Today I tell of Queen Gunnhild. The child is grown—though never strong—luminous and energetic. She is a useful and beautiful queen, as the best ones are. Gunnhild knows the spinning wheel and the wine-press, the library and the quill. She understands the people of her realm, their desires and their fears. More importantly, she cares about them too.

She has found a man – Kormac - she loves like no other. Her king, too, is a handy man as well as handsome. He can jest with the farmer and ride with the hounds. He has ventured abroad to return with stories of fantastic lands and incredible people. Together, Gunnhild and he ride across their land to visit their families and to settle disputes. At feasts, they share their laughter and a loving cup, to toast the brave warriors and gallant women.

But they have no child.

It vexes the queen. Her people expect an heir, she will tell me, her brow furrowing.

"Do they say so?" I ask her.

But she will only tell me they need not, for she knows her duty. The women of her line have always ruled here. She must not be the last. In a family older than the Ynglings themselves, to be the last of such a powerful lineage of women after so many generations is a shame too great to bear. Much as she loves Kormac, Gunnhild does not wish to have her realm pass to his hands should she die. She has seen what such power can do to men, what it has done to the war-loving dominions around her. Besides, she sighs as we spin, how the king, too, would love a child.

"Does he say so?" I ask her again.

But she only gazes sadly out the window, her hands carrying on the work her mind has forgotten.

But one day Queen Gunnhild comes to me with bright hope shining from her eyes of mossy green. "Nanna, is it true? Do you really know secrets to help me bear a child?"

I drop my fine needlework to my lap. "Who has been telling you such a thing, my dear?"

"A mage, a new mage, from your land, he has come to the king, he says it. Nanna," she repeats, "Is it true?!"

The blood drains from my face and I feel cold. "It has a price—all such wizardry does. Have you seen this mage?"

"Nanna! We must begin at once! A child, a child, a dear child of my very own, oh Nanna, today!"

"A child cannot be rolled and baked in an afternoon like a pie," I say crossly. But her smile does not dim and I can see that this desire cannot be turned away, whatever the cost shall be. Her stubborn will! It kept her alive through fevers and chills, against the wish of her flesh. The terrible price means nothing to it. But the king may feel otherwise.

I put aside my handiwork with some determination of my own. "Let us go see this man from my country. Is he with the king still?" Perhaps he can sway her stubborn heart.

"Nanna, Nanna!" Gunnhild tugs at my sleeve. "Can it be done?" Her eyes gleam dizzyingly, hope blinding them.

I look up into her face. "My queen, it can cost you your life," I say softly, hoping my own eyes convey the enormity of this risk.

But she merely laughs and pulls me into sprightly dance, circling around the floor. "Oh Nanna, my own mother thought I would never live out my first day. Each one after that has been a gift. You, of all people, should know better than to forecast gloom. I'm much stronger than I look."

"You do not know what it's like to bear a child. With even the healthiest and strongest women, it is often dangerous and difficult. A thousand complications arise, a thousand challenges to your body—and your body is not one made for birthing. It tries to tell you that."

"Nanna, listen to me." Gunnhild's face is gravely fixed. "I will have a child. You will help me."

There is no more to discuss. She is my queen. We go to the king, her strides purposeful and swift, my own solemn and slow.

In the great hall of the castle, King Kormak stands before his high seat, laughing with his counselors and a short dark man. I feel a chilly finger touch my spine as my gaze falls upon him. I know this one. And I know evil has come to this pleasant land—from my own.

The queen hugs her man happily. His joy in her radiates from his face. "My dear, you must meet my new friend. He tells many an amusing tale." The king turns to me. "Nanna! He is from your homeland too and says that he may know you." The king winks at me encouragingly. I hold my feelings close to my heart. This is no time to betray fear.

I summon a cheerful countenance. "I can always recognize a son of Bricriu, whatever shore he may walk upon." The crowd turns expectantly to regard the guest. His smile masks much from them, but its malevolence is clear to me. He has not expected to find one who knows him—and knows him so well.

"When last you were seen, was your hair not fiery red?" he asks. "Could it be so long ago? Or have the people of this land frightened the bonny color away?"

Everyone smiles at his japes. They have heard it is the way of our people to banter and jest. I decide to reply in kind.

I raise an eyebrow and regard him with careful scrutiny. "And you, friend, still no taller? I was sure you were going to grow a little. Never mind; here they say the measure of a man comes not from the length of his legs."

They all laugh, he loudest of all. I keep my bantering tone. "Is there a bark that can restore my hair color? For since my trip to the Sithe, it has lost all its fire—and you are so skilled in the secrets of the wood." He knows all too well that I see his true nature.

I itch to uncover his plans, his reasons for traveling so far. Why has he come? And what evil does he bring?

Later in the evening I get a chance to ask, but the answer is not to my liking. We stand on one of the balconies stretching out from the great hall, looking on the twilit-land below. It is the first warm day of the year. The doors and tapestries are thrown back to let the night air in.

"Well, Mná," he says with a self-satisfied grin, "you have taken the name of grandmother. Were you named by a child?"

"Yes I was. It is no shame to me. Indeed here it has other resonances. What evil wind blew you to this country, Maldachta, or should I call you Thomas as you have asked my lord and lady to do?"

"Ah, you remember me." His smile is a sneer. He need not bother to conceal his sinister heart from me. "Yes, we know one another's true name. No matter. I'm sure neither of us wishes to have them widely known. And we know one another's true self. Lord and lady! How like a slave you talk still, though I hear you have been freed long since."

"It is true I came here as a slave. But I have always been free. I own my soul, my mind. My lord and lady respect me and value my knowledge. I show them the same honor. In our land I was but one of many wise women—here I am unique."

His smile shows teeth, small and flashing. "You were unique. I think I may stay awhile. If a weak old woman like you can have so much, surely I can have more."

"Like so many men you confuse strength and power. Do not underestimate resistance." I can feel my face redden with the anger I wish to contain. "Why come here? Were there too many who called for your blood in the Emerald Isle? Like that village I once helped chase you from when your mischief brought those poor shepherds to near ruin?"

"There were inconveniences," he admits, waving them away with his hand. "I have had adventures here and there. But when I hear that one of my country women has taken this realm in hand as her own domain—how can I resist such a challenge?"

"It is not my domain. I find only peace and joy here. I do not seek to rule."

He barks with laughter. "You are too modest. I see how you have inserted yourself into this land. And it will be my pleasure to wrest it from your control."

I bristle at this. "You will not find it as simple as stealing a cow from your neighbour."

Hate burns in his eyes. "The sons of Bricriu are not cattle thieves."

"Nonetheless, you will not succeed in ripping this realm apart. I will not allow it."

"Do not stand in my way, woman. You'll find out just how much power I command. You who were captured as a slave— "

"Do not forget, too, that I have been to the Sithe. The otherworld taught me much and fortified me in ways I am still discovering."

"We shall see, old woman." He measures me with his eyes. "The daughters of Mná have had their way for generations. You may have stolen many secrets in the Sithe, but I know that the women of your kin have a geiss against thwarting the magic of the sons of Bricriu, so your pilfered knowledge is useless. You cannot stand in my way. And I swear by all that my people swear by that you will regret it if you try."

"Perhaps—but the geiss only prevents me from using my magic against yours. There is much else I can do." But my words are more confident than my heart, and I fear for this land and these people. Can he tell my courage does not match my words? For the first time in decades, I miss my sisters and my green home.

We do not speak together again for some time, but already his plans have been set in motion. The queen is adamant that I use my magic to bring her a child. I sigh, but pack my herb-gathering bags, put on my red cap and head into the forest, seeking this root and that toadstool, some bark from here and a little mud from the bottom of the stillwater pond, muttering all the while. My gatherings done, I stomp back to the castle, grumbling to friends who wonder about my secretiveness—the queen wishes no announcement until it is certain.

Back in my rooms, the mortar and pestle grind away, the rough tool of the cook grates roots in the little bowl. To raise my spirits, I sing the secret songs I learned in the otherworldly Sithe, but their magic eludes me today. The mud dries on the sunny window sill. A covering of fine silk keeps the restless winds from the powder. Still I mutter. "A bad business, a bad business! Such a risk to my pretty queen!" She knows my mood and does not allow impatience to compel her to watch at my shoulder, and though I fancy sometimes I hear her quick, light step in the hall, I am left alone in my workroom.

I pry apart the dry leaves of one of my oldest books to check and double-check the recipe so seldom used. Most of my skill is for helping nature along, not for rebuking it, denying it. The great mother of us all has a knack for getting her way in the end. She has patience. And she does not take kindly to headstrong little creatures' demands.

My poor queen! I see her fate in the bowl that cracked when I ground the cloudberry seeds, in the angel hair that drifted out the window on a mischievous breeze, and in the withered gnarl of the wormwood root. My heart hangs heavy as I slip down the corridors to her chamber, my basket under my arm.

Yet her face shines brilliantly, a bubble bursting to the surface that water cannot contain. "What must we do, Nanna?"

How eagerly she meets her fate. Ignoring the question for a moment, I put down my basket and cross to the window. The curtains flutter but slightly. The day is calm and beautiful. A raven sits in the linden tree outside and I feel my lips form an angry line: it is a bad portent. But it is only one: perhaps there is still a chance.

I turn back and she has already stooped for my basket and hands it to me. My solemnity quells the queen's excitement a little, but joy lights the eyes I love so well. I take a pouch from the basket and use its powder to draw a circle around the queen's bed. "Do not step outside this circle until the morrow's sunset, my lady."

She opens her mouth, but closes it again, and sits down, turning back the coverlet.

From the latticework above her pillows, I hang an amulet of rosy milkstone, carved by my brother into the shape of a horse when I was but a young girl. I take the cup from her table and fill it with my herbs, adding some water from the pitcher. It forms a liquid of a satisfying green, which my lady drinks speedily but not without a grimace. I rub her forehead with the oil of lavender but I know it is more for my comfort than for hers.

She takes my hand in both of hers and kisses it. "Thank you, Nanna. It will be worth it. I shall not die. I will be a mother."

I can find no words that sound like truth to my ears, but clasp her hands in mine, a mute return of her affection.

And then I leave. There is nothing more for me to do, tonight. As I ready to head back to my darkened chamber, the laughter of

Maldachta creeps along the corridor like a heavy spider. It raises my revulsion. *You will not win*, I think, I hope. *My queen will live and her beautiful child too.*

When I meet the king in the hall, before he hurries to his wife's room, he takes my hand and presses it to his cheek. I return to my stale-smelling room and sit in the darkest corner, pulling my grey web of a cloak around me. It will be a long three seasons.

Nine moon-cycles later I have begun to hope. Foolish, I know, but Queen Gunnhild has been so strong, blooming really, as a mother should do. I have succeeded in keeping her near the warmth of the hearth these last few months of coldness and snow and her face keeps a ruddy glow. It almost seems as if all could turn out well. Certainly she believes this. Her complacent smile betrays her confidence. The king shares the feeling, trusting his lady to know best. I, too, could nearly trust her hope, if it weren't for the ravens.

Three days in a row now they come. Six of them sitting in the linden tree. There is no battle, no plague, no reason for their presence here. But only six? Surely, if the queen were fated to die, would there not be the dozen to foretell such an event? Perhaps—I grasp at the hope. Perhaps there is still no certainty. I do all I can. I sing the powerful charms of the Sithe. My days are filled with work, gathering amulets and potions and powders, yet I cannot remember ever feeling quite so helpless. Soon, very soon now, we shall all know.

2

When the call comes, I am nodding in my chair of carved oak-leaves by the light of the quarter moon. The dawn is several hours away yet, but the queen's handmaid is at my elbow, gasping breath back into her hedgehog-shaped body. But she need say nothing. What else can it be? I have my trusty basket on one arm and her elbow in the other before she can draw enough air to speak. Together we rush down the corridors. With difficulty, the maid Unn huffs out that the pains began an hour before. The queen— so brave, my lady—said nothing until she was certain. I am old, I have said before, but the maid's clunky boots soon lose step with my soft leather shoes, her weight pulls on my arm until I slip away with an apologetic look and hurry on, in silence, alone.

The queen's golden hair lies wet against her pallid forehead and her face has grown almost ugly in its pain. The green eyes are flecked with red. Her skin too has reddened from the strain of denying her suffering, but behind it all the queen wears a look of ghastly determination. "Nanna! It's coming!"

The fire blazes already and the kettle bubbles. Unn, though looking ready to drop, joins her three companions who shake open the crisp white linen cloths around their regal lady. Many hours, many tears and cries pass, not all from my lady. The king paces outside the chamber and moans in fear. Surely all the people in the castle, perhaps even the land itself, lie awake, waiting, hoping, sending their own courage to join the queen's.

And the child is born. With golden hair like her mother and grey-blue eyes that will one day be like the ocean spray before a ship's prow in deep water: she is a joy, a beauty. Her pudgy fingers reach out to us all, embracing her new life.

If only her mother could remain beside her. "Nanna, she is so beautiful," my lady croaks, barely a whisper. Life drains from the eyes I have so long met daily, my herbs and potions have done nothing. "I will be fine, I just need to rest a little. When I am stronger, you'll see." Her arms implore me and I return the babe to her weak embrace, my own eyes stinging. My heart seems full of tears, but there is only joy and pride in hers now. Sadness has no time to creep into her thoughts, though fatigue overwhelms her. I put my arms around the baby still snuggled on her chest as her limbs fall gently to the sides. When the sun peeps over the window ledge, her pale face is at last cool and I kiss my dear friend good-bye.

As the handmaids begin to wail, the king rushes in to clutch his wife's limp hand. He sobs her name, endearments that do not reach her silenced ears. His tears fall into the palm he kisses. I can hardly bear his suffering, more painful than my own. It is some time before we can persuade him to move from her bed, so that we can begin the necessary preparations.

"It's not right, Nanna," he insists, tears glistening in his beard. "She is too young... I—"

"There is seldom a good time for a loved one to die, my king. She struggled mightily. And she brought forth this beautiful baby."

The king looks at the fidgeting bundle in my arms. There is no love in his eyes, only anger. "It would be better off exposed to the snows."

"I'll do no such thing!"

"Nanna, it killed her." Fury at his helplessness runs through his face leaving trails of red. "I don't ever wish to see it again."

Pity for his pain wars with indignation. Indignation wins. I, too, suffer grievously. "She is your daughter, my lord. You have a responsibility."

He only moans, unmindful of my words, taking the queen's lifeless hand once more.

I take a breath and try once more. "My lord, your daughter needs your love too."

He turns and snaps at me, a wounded dog. "Take it from here! I cannot bear the sight of it. Do not let me look upon it ever again!"

I look at him. I know he is unhinged by his beloved's death. All must grieve in their own way. I want to tell him that love only multiplies even when divided, that it is the only cure for such sorrow—but he has already dismissed us from his thoughts. "Very well then," I turn and go. He will return to himself soon, I am certain, and he will regret his harsh command.

That is my error.

The king does not return to himself any time soon. He does not repent of his cruel abandonment. Worse, I leave him vulnerable to the worst influence in these lands. Maldachta: what foul wind blew you here?

I swaddle the baby in ermine and take her to a small stronghold on the edge of the Hundrada forest. Though meant only as rest stop for visitors, it is soon comfortable enough, though hardly fit for a royal nursery. But it is only for a time, I tell myself, only until he returns to his senses. A wet-nurse comes to stay for some months, but she is a simple woman, nervous of my powers and the stories told of them, thus little company for me. Unn, the maid who had fetched me to the birth that night, visits now and then with news of the court and of the king.

The first time, she brought me a lock of my lady's hair. I wrapped it in a piece of silk, blue as a robin's egg, and put it away for the child when she is old enough. The king, Unn tells me this visit, carries a lock of hair too, in a large gold locket. "It's supposed to be his heart, but it looks like a big liver!" Unn exclaims and I smile. I am curious to see it, but I do not plan to do so any time soon.

"What do you call the little thing? She hasn't got any name yet, has she? Nor is she likely to, eh?"

"I have followed tradition and named her Hallgerd after her father's mother. If the council finds fault with that, they must change it themselves."

Unn balances the little girl on her knee, mimicking the child's happy patter. "Little princess Hallgerd, how do you like your name? You like it, don't you, little lady, don't you? Ooh, I remember the old lady. Nice enough, you know, of course. But a little, you know, everything-neat-and-tidy like. I always felt on the watch around her, like she was checking the folds of the bed linens after I'd gone."

Unn prattles on with various news and gossip and I listen with one ear and watch the baby battle fatigue, then gently surrender. We place Hallgerd in her cradle and watch her sleep, tiny fists rolled into balls.

Unn winds a thick red scarf around her neck and shoulders as she stands in the anteroom. "Well, lady, it's a comfort to us all, I'm sure, to know the princess is safe with you here. The poor king, he's bound to come around soon and miss his little darling, though I don't know with that one bending his ear at every corner."

"M—Thomas?" Who else?

Unn's nose wrinkles as if she were smelling simmering pitch. "Him, all right. I suppose he was nice enough at first and a bit of fun too, what with his ready waggery—why he reminded me of old Thorstein the Cod-Biter, that silly fool with his stumpy walk and that way of going—"

"What has he been up to?"

"Why, he's been dead fifteen years, lady."

"No, Unn. Thomas." I cannot help my smile, despite the growing sense of apprehension. "What has he been up to with the king?"

Grim lines deepen on Unn's otherwise youthful face and she answers gravely. "I'm not sure, lady, but none of us—her lady's ladies, I mean—none of us likes it a bit. The king's not been himself since our queen died, the gods keep her, but you know that. That one—I don't know—but he seems always on the king's heels, whispering who-knows-what into his ear, and it's almost—"

"Almost...?"

Unn's features wrinkle further with unaccustomed concentration. "It's almost like the king's getting worse. Farther away. Like he's drifting into the mists."

I can feel the blood drain from my face. Why have I not thought of this possibility? Too busy nursing my wounded pride: pride for my beautiful queen, for her tiny daughter, but most of all, pride for my position. I had become accustomed to being regarded with deference, despite my difference from those of this land. Shame brings the blood back to my features. It was the loss of this esteem—as much as the shock of my lady's death—that convinced me to quit the castle with my charge. And now the whole realm may be in danger from a threat they cannot resist.

"Lady?" Unn speaks with a sudden urgency, breaking into my recriminations. "Is he enchanting the king?"

"Very likely."

"Oh dear! Oh heavens! What can we do?" Unn covers her cheeks with her hands as if she were cold, though the warmth of her clothing has already made droplets of sweat trickle down from each temple. "Oh, if the king were to be lost too—"

"I shall come to court tomorrow. Give word to the king that I wish to see him. No doubt he will not want to discuss the child, but he cannot put me off completely if he is anywhere near his right mind, and I'll know better what can be done when I can see him eye to eye."

"Bless you, lady. Things are so very different now." Unn sighs. "I fear the sun left with our queen."

"The sun will return, Unn. This little girl needs it."

3

The next day I trudge through the snow, back to the castle that had been my home for so many years. In my basket I carry a glass augury ball wrapped in linen, an oak ring-box, and a small parchment packet of vervain, which I had ground to fine powder during the night. Perhaps the herb can protect the king, though he may not believe he needs such safeguards.

The welcoming cries of the guards on the wall and the sight of Unn and Thorbjorg waving energetically above help to warm even my snow-frosted feet. It is good to come home. As I enter the castle, I am swept into a circle of chatter: questions about me, the baby, the fortress on the rim of the Hundrada wood. But the laughter and good cheer are soon hushed by more troubled tones—a pall has covered the court and the land since our departure.

"We mourn our queen, of course," explains Thorbjorg's twin, Thorhalla, trying to keep her twin nieces away from the hot oven. Little Thorgerd and Thordis smell the berry cakes cooking and can hardly wait for them to be ready.

"But it's more than that," insists Thorbjorg, "There's evil in the air, like the smell of burnt bread. Death is merely sad—this is something wrong." Both sisters nod and others around them do likewise.

"It's good you've come, lady. We need your counsel," Thorhalla adds.

"I'll do what I can. It is difficult to see such burdens on faces of those whom I have always known to be lighthearted." As I remove my wet shawl and shoes and the others return to their posts, thoughts in my head become more agitated and I begin to feel fear for the very first time.

Unn comes puffing down the central stairs and squeals a

happy greeting. "Oh, bless my heart, you're here, you're here! And the king, he'll see you. Seemed eager to see you too, lady. Oh, your things are so damp! Let me put them on the hearth. We'll have you put to rights in a twinkling." And she bustles around me like a fidgety hen, chirping nonsense and tsk-ing at the state of the woolens. In no time at all, I am warm all-through. How nice to be fussed over once more.

I enter the royal chamber stiffly, a special friend no longer. The empty chair where my queen once sat has grown larger in her absence, as if daring me to forget her luminous presence. The king stares out the window, unconsciously fingering the gold locket on his chest. With a start, at last he sees me standing before him, awaiting his words. "Greetings, Nanna," he says without a smile.

"And to you, my lord."

"I have delayed too long to speak with you after—after that horrid night." He winces, the memory sharp as a pinprick on tender skin.

"Your time was needed by many in the wake of that sad day. I take no offense at such inadvertent neglect. I serve you, my lord."

"You would do well to remember that." Though he speaks them mildly, the words sting as sharply as a slap. "I realize that while my wife lived…" he clutches the locket protectively, "you became accustomed to a certain… liberty—"

"I have not been a slave for some time, my lord."

"But you are the king's subject! And subject to the king's rule. Do not forget this." His eyes flare with the first show of animation, but it seems wrong, as if the heat consumes him. "My dear wife allowed you a good deal of familiarity. Things cannot be so any longer. I do not need a nanny myself and have no childhood attachment to such a thing. When you are summoned, you will come. Otherwise, I have no wish to see you—here."

I am stung and cannot hide it. "I have not burdened you with my presence before this day."

The king shifts awkwardly on the high-seat. "There is also the matter of your role in my wife's—her…unfortunate…demise."

Only a very great effort keeps the temper from my tongue.

"I know nothing of your magic, your people's ways. But there is one here now who does—"

"You place such trust in him, my lord."

"I have no reason not to do so." But he looks away from my gaze.

"Have you no reason to trust me? After my years of loyalty to you and your wife, and to her mother before her, and to her mother before that—"

"Enough! I will not be questioned!"

"Yet you question my fealty. I must defend myself." I am resolute.

The tide has turned, however, and his sadness muddles the anger. The barely-concealed pain rises once more to the surface. I see it on his face and my own anger recedes.

"I miss her too, my lord. Every day." Ample tears rush in to testify to the ache in my heart.

His head sinks. "Forgive me, Nanna, I don't know how I could—why I—I apologize."

In the sudden silence I can hear the whisper of the late winter wind announcing its intention to remain and to thwart the first thaw. Its dismal dirge underlines our grief and I long to offer some comfort, however small. "There is healing in the love of another..."

His eyes fly open. "I could not countenance such a thing! How dare you suggest—it is not even a whole season since—unthinkable!"

What? "My lord, I did not mean to advise another match for you. Far from it. In the fullness of time, perhaps, when your heart has become—"

"Never! There is none to equal my lady."

"She was indeed singular, my lord," I agree.

"She made me promise anyway."

"My lord?" A small feeling of foreboding awakes.

"I cannot marry again, save to one equal in every way to her. She made me swear an oath to it."

"Surely, lord, it was in fun, a playful thing. Our lady was fond of such jesting."

"She had me swear." He drew up his mouth resolutely.

I could see her saying such a thing if accompanied by that sparkling laughter—but to jeopardize her realm with such a vanity? No, it cannot be. I will not believe it. She loved her land and her people too much for that. Was this fixation part of his devouring sorrow—or the sign of something worse? I grope furtively in my basket for the glass ball. In the presence of the king, it will be most accurate. "My lord, I came today to speak of your daughter. She too yearns for what she does not have—a mother, a father. I cannot bring back her mother. But you have the power to return her father." The tiny orb warms quickly in my grasp.

"No, I cannot, it cannot be." His hand sweeps across his face as if to remove cobwebs I am unable to perceive. "I—I cannot think of it as anything but the harbinger of her death. You may have what you need to care for...the child. But do not trouble me with its keeping."

"My lord, she is heir to this land."

"By law, by law. I know the entailment. But she cannot rule so young. It falls to me, as her—guardian."

I gaze down into the crystal depths of the ball. Shapes shift and change as I tilt it for the precise angle. There! It comes. I wish it had not.

A serpent turns and winds upon itself in the depths of the ball. With an effort I keep my composure. Danger and imprisonment! For me? For the princess? The king? I must know more. But first, I need to get what I have come for. I slip the ball back into my basket and address the king again. "My lord, I wish to take for the child remembrances of her mother, the little gifts that have been passed along their line."

"Take them, and trouble me no more now." He waves me away. "I am so tired."

I take my leave with a bow and prepare to hurry down the hall to my lady's chamber. Unfamiliar steps ring behind me. I turn. Thomas smiles gleefully.

"How does exile suit you now, Nanna?"

"Well enough. Better to be out of the foul air of treachery."

"Tsk, tsk, tsk, a lady with a temper." He shakes his head with mock dismay. "Why do you try to spoil my little game?"

"I have done nothing."

"Ah well, I guess I can't convince the king of your dangerousness—yet." His smile takes a wicked turn. "He very nearly did believe, though, that you killed his wife. How much I have done in so little time."

"What do you want here? What poisonous wind delivers you here?"

"My own! I can command the winds to bear me aloft or to rain destruction down on this land or to blow you out of my sight."

"You foul son of Bricriu! Namesake of misery and betrayal!"

"You feeble old woman! The daughters of Mná, with your herbs and your potions and your fortune-telling crystals! It amazes me you have been praised for so many generations."

"While the sons of Bricriu are rightfully scorned as miscreants and mischief-makers. You will not prosper here for long," I promise him.

"You can do nothing against my magic—you cannot thwart me. Even if you had the power, your geiss prevents you. Use your magic against mine and the gods will destroy you. Either way I win."

"Do not claim victory before the battle has been fought."

"Faugh! Leave your crone's advice for the misguided fools who seek your jabbering—in vain! For this land will fall and then—only then—shall you die, having seen it all laid waste."

"I cannot use my magic against you, that much is true. But the spirit that leads the daughters of Mná does not rely on magic alone. That is why I will defeat you in the end. You are one—we are many. And many others will join us when they hear we seek to save their land."

"Ha!" He waves his hand dismissively before him. "The king is nearly under my power now. I can be so charming when I wish it. You have no authority in this realm anymore; you are less than a servant, a stranger here after all this time because these provincial folk fear your puny witchcraft. How easy it will be to prey upon the prejudices of these backward people. With their superstitions, why, they'll burn you on a pyre to save the harvest. And I will roast an apple on the fire!" His face grimaces into an evil smile.

"You are prideful and rash," I say with a confidence I do not feel, "You will learn by and by. Do not forget that wisdom is the fruit of years, a fruit both bitter and sweet. I have eaten of it and have learned patience. I will not tolerate your idle foolishness."

"Foolishness? You will not think it foolishness when these walls tumble around your ears! Chatter on with your prating words—while you repeat your empty proverbs, I will rip this dominion out by its roots and shake it until the last clod falls. I swear by all my people swear by, it shall be so!" He turns and leaves with unhurried steps. I remain drawn up with anger until he has passed into the outer hall, and suddenly I feel as if all the wind leaves my body at once. I sag onto a nearby bench.

"Oh dear lady! What are we to do?!"

"Unn!" How much did she hear? Likely all, I fear. How to avoid a panic? "We are indeed in danger, my friend. But I will do what I can to protect this land."

"But what about the thing— ?"

"What do you mean?"

"The guess? Goss? " Her mouth struggles with the unfamiliar word.

"The geiss? I can do nothing about that. It is a curse on my line. None of the daughters of Mná can thwart the magic of the sons of Bricriu—at least not with our own magic—to do so means destruction. I do not care for myself, my life has been a long enough one. But I may be the only one with a chance to rid the land of this affliction. I must protect the princess."

"Oh dear! Such doings! What can I do, lady?" Unn draws up her shoulders, ready for any burden. "I'm not clever or quick, I know too well, but I've got two sharp eyes and a heart always true to our queen, ready to be friend to her daughter. I'll do whatever I can to help, my lady."

I am touched by her simple devotion—humbled too. How often have I discounted this straightforward woman? "Thank you, Unn," I reply with graciousness and a return of warmth. "You must be my eyes and ears here, while I am guarding the princess. Keep a close watch on Thomas and bring me any news of his doings."

"Oh, that I will, no doubt about that. And I ain't afraid of him, no, not one bit."

Her pale complexion suggests otherwise but I admire her brave words. I rummage once more in my basket, pull out the parchment of vervain, and place it in her hands. "Mix most of this powder with water and sprinkle it at your window and in a circle around your bed. Carry whatever is left with you everywhere; perhaps tuck it into your apron. It will help protect you."

Unn sniffs suspiciously at the packet but slips it into the folds of her dress. "Magic, is it?"

"Yes, Unn. I had thought to use it to protect the king, but I am too late, curse my days. I should not have left..."

"Oh lady, if I hadn't slept late this morning, the custard would have been saved, but we can't hope for what hasn't happened when it already has."

"True enough. Thank you," I feel a renewed glow of appreciation for my confederate. "It is a waste of time and I have so much to do. I need your help too. Come, we must go to the queen's chamber."

Together we march up the stairs to the room where I once unwound so many of my hours. The door swings smoothly open, and for half a moment I can almost believe she will be there. But the beautiful room is empty, though it sparkles still with something of her polish. It is immaculate. She would approve. "Unn, you have done well here."

Unn's smile shares the glow. "It is such a pleasure, my lady. The other girls have gone on to other duties, and the gods know, I have plenty to do, what with the kitchen staff being so young and that Katla, even if she is kin to me I'd sooner—well, you know. I have to keep it just so. It'd make our queen proud, knowing it's kept so."

On the oak dressing table by the windows lies the queen's jewelry case. It is carved from dark Eastern wood, big as a kindling box. Bright jewels cover its sides like rosy petals. I open the top and the bright confusion of gold, silver, pearls and splendid stones dazzle me, but Unn's quick fingers delve into the jumble and bring forth a soft red bag. With reverent care she shakes the contents into her palm. Three gold objects: a spindle, a bobbin, and a ring, all made by a singular goldsmith time out of mind ago and passed through the women of this line. Three little tokens: they are the symbols of a good ruler.

Together we speak the litany, unaware that our voices become reverent whispers:

The bobbin for guidance through wisdom and sense,
The spindle for drawing out all excellence,

The ring for binding the oath to this land
To love and protect and be at its command.

Our smiles meet. Simple words and our hope is restored. I put the trinkets back in their bag and enclose it within the ringbox in my basket. I can hardly wait for the princess to be old enough for these gifts—and for the story of her remarkable mother and the other queens before her.

Later, as we gather my now-warm woolens from the kitchen hearth, I say to Unn, "One more thing... Has anyone a litter of kittens lately? I could use one for watch at the outpost."

"For watch? Wouldn't a dog be better?"

"Dogs are noisy—they warn intruders as much as their owners."

"Well, you have a point there, lady. Hmm. Someone was saying the other day, wasn't it —Thorbjorg! Didn't your brother's wife have kittens?"

The young mother giggles into the flurry of grouse feathers flying from her fingers. "Well, ma'am, her cat had kittens, if that's what you mean." Her sister and the other girls titter appreciatively.

Unn grumbles something about respect for elders and I try to wipe the smile from my lips as she turns. "You know him, lady, the blacksmith. They'll like as not have a dozen of them to pick from."

"Thank you again, my dear. Be watchful—for yourself and for the king." Outside I take a long good-bye look at the castle. Every window opens from a room I know. Thankfully, the view from my old rooms is hidden from my gaze. At last I believe that it may well be many years before I return to stay. My throat feels tight and I pull my shawl more snugly, but it is not the cold I want to keep out. *You're an old woman, Carae Mná. The time will pass before you know it,* I scold myself, *and there is so much yet to be done. You have a child who needs your care and guidance, and soon a cat to keep you company by the fire, but most importantly, an enemy you must prepare to face.* Ah, this last thought makes me feel the weight of every minute of the long years behind me. How many more lie ahead?

4

But my morbid ponderings get lost in the shuffle of the busy days that occupy me. The new kitten, to whom I give the name Siur, is a bundle of inquisitiveness. Little Hallgerd takes to her at once and they spend many afternoons rolling on the floor with my spindle and thread while I try to untangle them all, helpless with laughter. By the time Siur has replaced her kittenish friskiness with the beginnings of feline dignity, Hallgerd chatters and runs stiffly around the big common room, her frequent falls cushioned by the soft, colorful Saracen rugs, which Unn ordered to be brought to our outpost from the linen chests of the castle.

My heart warms to hear a child call me "Nanna" again. I do not mind that she learned to say it only after she mastered "Kitty." I tell her my stories, simple ones to lull her into restful sleep and to give her pleasant dreams. But too little time passes before she begins to ask questions and to wonder about her unhappy fate.

When I narrate the story of Hans My Hedgehog, her eyes remain obstinately open and her tiny brow furrows. "Are you my mother, Nanna?"

"No, child."

"Why don't I have a mother—and a father?" Her gaze fixes upon me.

"You have a father, Hallgerd. He is not well."

"What is 'not well'?"

"Remember when Siur ate from my herbs and was not well?"

"Yes, on the carpet. Did my father eat some herbs?"

"No, my dear. But he is not well in his head. He cannot think right."

"Will he be well again?"

"Perhaps, though not any time soon, I fear."

She mulls this over with solemn concern. "Where is my mother?"

I sigh. Too soon. "She is dead, my poor child."

"What is dead?"

"Dead is when a living thing wears out, usually when it is very old."

"Like my shoe?"

Yesterday we had mended her miniature shoe with a length of leather and an awl. "Something like that, yes."

"Could we not fix my mother? Like my shoe?"

"Sometimes we can. That's just what many of my herbs do. But sometimes we cannot."

The wrinkles remain on her tiny forehead. "Hans' mother and father loved him a lot. Did my mother love me a lot?"

"Oh yes, so much that she did not fear to die. She wanted you to be born."

"What's born?"

"When you come to be. To die, is when you cease to be."

A yawn: she did not understand half of my ramblings. I still find no easy way to explain these truths, which I've had to tell over and over to my many charges. Death has no meaning until a child meets it face to face.

"Does my father love me?" Hallgerd asks with a cat-like yawn.

Ah! "Yes, child, though some days he does not even know who he is or where he is. But yes, he loves you, very very much."

"Good," she murmurs and at once she sleeps, leaving me alone with my troubled thoughts. Does he love her? Can he still feel? How can I break the enchantment without my magic?

Unn's reports are not favorable. "He walks in a daze, lady, when he walks at all. More often, he sits in the high seat, holding that locket, with tears in his eyes, muttering who knows what. Three years now, lady. People do talk. It's just not right."

Unn wedges herself into the smaller chair and pulls out her latest knitting. Her fingers fly with sure efficiency as she talks, though she stops now and then to check for dropped stitches. "There are so many rumblings about, why just the other day, Kormak the shepherd, just because he's named for the king, though he's no better than he should be, he actually said in that loud bray of his, no doubt with an ale or two behind it, that the king better look to the land right soon if he wants to keep it. Says he's heard the far villages feel very worried, why you never know who might come a-raiding before the winter falls."

"Has he not sent the troops around the lands?"

"Oh, well, yes, I think so. Not he of course, you understand, but his chief advisor, that one —"

"Thomas?"

"Oh yes. Very proper now, the king gave him a big medallion with a great red jewel in the middle, not a ruby, oh what is it—"

"A garnet, I am very sure. They are plentiful in our land and assure protection to the wearer."

Unn sighs. "I suppose it must be, for almost all seem to have fallen under his enchantment somehow. It's like people are afraid to even mention his name for fear he'll appear. But when he does, they find themselves unable to resist his charms. It's almost as if there some kind of music behind his words that rings in your head and makes you agree. Yet he, too, is hearing the murmurings of the people and I think he has ideas of something. He goes around looking deep in thought and not laughing to himself half as much as he used to do." Her hands pause briefly in their frenzied labor, as she attempts unsuccessfully to remove Siur from the now-tangled yarn in her lap. The cat welcomes her interference as a sign of play and twists and rolls within her bonds, the thick threads tightening around her limbs.

I stifle my laughter and join in the fray. "Hallgerd, will you take this mischievous cat from Unn and find some way to keep her occupied?"

The child gravely does as I ask, sternly admonishing the animal "to behave yourself and remember who you are, a Lady," before they both tumble onto the soft rug to play with a wooden ball. My friend and I exchange glowing glances, proud of our little princess.

"A natural lady, and no mistake," whispers Unn and I nod a silent assent.

Ten years pass—sometimes quickly, sometimes more slowly. Hallgerd grows and learns, and proves to be every inch the princess—though a princess who can most often be found climbing trees and fighting enormous dragons only she can see. In the castle though, affairs go on without us. Thomas has been able to charm or frighten most of the people of this realm into his plans, holding out treasures to some, beatings to others, doled out as he finds fitting. I will admit he can read spirits well and know the secrets of the common folk. The latest developments favour his ill-will, too. It has taken them long to gather their courage, but the council finally approached the king to say he must take a wife. It is his duty, they remind him.

"Oh he's completely gone away, my lady," Unn tells me later. "It's the councilors and *that one*. They've decided she's not a natural child! They say the king's got to take a new wife and have a real daughter, not..." She pauses and looks away. "Not a goblin child made by your magic."

Fools! When they lay eyes on the true queen, they will know her. Let him marry whom he likes. It will not matter. I quiz Unn about the council itself, with unexpected results. She had made sure she'd been the one to bring the wine and bread and cheese to where the council had sat with the king around his great oak table.

"And that's when he said it—he'd not marry again but to one as lovely as his queen in every way. Oh, they hemmed and hawed about that! But his Honor," here she purses her lips in consternation, "Mr. Thomas himself, said how he agreed and how it was our lady's last wish—wasn't! Such nonsense! We were there, we know, but does anyone ask?" She continues without a breath, "Well, so he says, and they look in the law books and find that it's so— "

"What is so?"

"That it's a legato or something..."

"Legato?" It is my turn to purse my lips. "Explain it to me."

"Well, the queen's dying wish, it seems they have to honor it because she was queen, for sure, and because it was her word, that makes it a law, being her people's land and all."

"I see." Ah, a legacy.

"Mostly because the king said it, I guess. He's a witness to it, that our lady said such a thing—not that she did! But he, well you know, he's like a lost little boy. He doesn't know his own mind. You could tell him swans were at the front gate and he'd smile and go down to meet them. Talk to them, like as not, too." Unn shook her head. "So, now it's begun."

"What?"

"Why, the search for his new consort—the woman perfectly like our lady. She's not to be found on this earth, no, not at all."

"I don't doubt that you are right, my friend." I don't doubt it at all.

And indeed, such a perfect bride seems not to be found: five years pass, the king's messengers spread to the farthest curves of the world, princesses from every land send tokens —drawings and paintings of themselves—but not one suits his desire. Each day carriages draw past here on their way to the castle's broad doors. They are gaily painted, the wheels gilded, brass handles gleaming in the bright sun. Always the horses are proudly arrayed, ribbons flutter from their manes and tails in a festive riot and their knees rise high in sure confidence of the lovely princess they carry forth.

From time to time, one of these magnificent coaches halts at our outpost to ask for fresh water, to make certain their direction, or even to cajole some extra bit of information that might win the day. Hallgerd always runs to meet them, eyes sparkling with curiosity, words of happy greeting spilling from her lips. "I am the Princess Hallgerd! Daughter of Queen Gunnhild and Heir to this land. Welcome!" And the fine lady stepping down from her coach with help from the hand of her driver or footman pauses, taking in the picture of this girl in her braids and breeches. Always her eyebrow raises: if a princess, where are her silks and brocades, her attendants, her jewels? But the raised eyebrow never manages to invoke answers to its many questions. Too soon even the most recalcitrant royalty succumbs to Hallgerd's charm and boundless inquisitiveness.

Where have they come from? How far is it? What are the sights to be seen in their lands? What wonders exist beyond the little world she knows? What can they add to the pictures of far off lands that she has in her many books and the three old tapestries that hang in the north hall?

The princesses and their ladies tell her of Mercia, of Orkney, of Thule and of distant Espange: of the unicorn, the phoenix, the skergipr and the mysterious hjasi. Hallgerd eats their careless words, hungry for knowledge, thirsty for experience. I feel a nip of sad guilt. Such a bright young girl! She should have more than this old woman for company. But the fine folk from the carriage cannot be stayed, and they hurry onward to the castle, leaving the two of us alone once more.

Tonight Hallgerd is unusually quiet. Thinking of the day's visitors, no doubt. Her hands are busy pulling the leaves from the stalks of mint in her lap, but her gaze is turned to regard the late summer sun only now beginning its reluctant descent behind the dark forest. Pink hues stretch across the heavens in delicate fingers. My princess sighs.

"Nanna?"

"Yes, my dear?"

"Have you ever been in love?"

"In love?! Goodness, what's brought this on?"

She lays aside her busywork and comes to lay her head in my lap. I smile down at her. This is "Tell me a story, Nanna." How many times we have sat here like this—though less often lately—her head in my lap, dreaming. How many times have her bright eyes glittered as the child demanded, "Tell me about the king who fought the dragon—no, no, Nanna, the one who fought the monster under the sea!" and how many times have I told the story of brave Beowulf, and all the others too, Thidrek, Brynhild and Odd, or Emer and Cúchulainn from my own land. No story this time though; Hallgerd wants truth.

"Yes, child, I have been in love." My hand plays through the soft gold of her hair, luxuriant in its freedom. "It was a very long time ago."

"Was he handsome?"

"Yes, what lover is not?"

She smiles. "And you were beautiful?"

"So he said."

The princess' eyes startle at her realization. "Not that you are not now, Nanna, beautiful, I mean. But— "

"It was long ago," I soothe, "my hair was red and I was spry and saucy."

"Was it true love?"

Such questions! "Yes, it was."

"How did you know?"

"Such questions you ask, my dear." I cannot tell her the pain still haunts me.

"You said I should always ask what I wished to know."

"True enough," I laugh, caught by my own teaching, and bless her inquiring mind. "How did I know? Well, the knowledge was always there in my heart. I needed only to unlock it. That took patience. And time."

Hallgerd's gaze confronts me, serious and thoughtful. "How did you meet him?"

I close my eyes. It has been so long since I turned my thoughts to him. But his visage lies behind only a thin veil, black though it may be. At once the winds of my will free him to stand before me again. Broichan: his wide flashing smile so white, his hair black as the deepest bog, his skin as pale as cream in moonlight. And his laugh! A sparkle of sunlight in the darkest night. "We met at dusk where the wood gave way to the shore in the land of my people. I must have been about sixteen winters then."

"Were you out looking at the moon?" she sighs.

"No, dear, I was out gathering moss for medicine. I had been trained in the arts for five seasons then, and sad to say, I had begun to think that I knew a thing or two."

"Why is that sad to say, Nanna?"

"It is always sad when one uses gifts for the wrong purpose— or thinks one knows anything at all. Something he and I had in common, I'm afraid."

"So did he serenade you, Nanna? With those special songs you sing sometimes…"

"Serenade?! Such silliness—that's a foolish modern custom. This was ages ago child, when the business of love was still just that, for the most part. I was fortunate to be taken in by the kindly ladies so I did not have to be married to some aged man for his pasture land."

"I want to be serenaded." Hallgerd sighs again with the prospect of such future foolishnesses.

"You may." I laugh, hoping that she does indeed get that and many other happy frivolities. There is chance yet. "I was not sung to—in fact his first words to me were jeering."

"No!"

"Yes, he hid behind a rock and watched me gathering my moss and thinking my private thoughts, humming a little tune my mother taught me at her knee. Then suddenly he shouted out to me, 'Fire!' I was so startled, I dropped my basket. I couldn't see anyone anywhere. Again he yelled, 'Fire!' This time I think I saw something moving behind—which rock? He moved around out of sight, but now he was laughing that crazy laugh that I so quickly came to love, and it was easy to find him. 'Why are you yelling "Fire!" at me, sirrah?' I demanded sternly. He could hardly speak for laughing, pointing at my head. 'Fire, fire' he kept repeating until he got a coughing fit so badly that I had to pound on his back to get him to stop. Finally, half choked by his merriment, he managed to tell me that from a distance he mistook my flaming hair for an errant traveler's cooking fire—"

"Oh Nanna, no!" Hallgerd collapses into giggles.

"—and thought he might sneak a free meal, since he would have missed his dinner already. At my look of dismay he only laughed all the harder. Oh child, I was so inordinately proud of my fiery locks, I couldn't conceive of someone laughing at them."

"Oh, poor Nanna! He hurt your feelings. Did he apologize?"

I smile. "Not at first..."

"No?" My princess lifts up her head to look at my grin. "Nanna, what did you do!"

"I pushed him into a bog."

"Full of mud?"

"Black with it!"

"Was he furious?"

"Well, first he was surprised, then he roared like an angry bear and leapt up quick as a salmon and chased after me." I laughed at the memory. "You should have seen it! Poor me being chased by this dripping, muddy, shambling man—just two blue eyes shining and his mouth never stopping from crying my shame. I laughed so much I could hardly run, but run I did, down into the water and when he followed me, I whipped around and knocked him down again. Oh he came up sputtering once more and I told him, saucy as can be, 'Well, at least this time you're clean!' And he went all quiet, looked down at his dripping clothes, which weren't really all that clean yet, and at once he began to laugh at himself. He fell back into the waves and splashed around a good deal until his clothes were more or less clean—and I was almost as wet as he. Then we went back to shore and I did start a fire and we dried our clothes and talked of ourselves and our people and our dreams and by midnight —"

"You were in love." Her face shines in the last threads of sunlight.

"Yes, we were. It was the beginning of the end too."

"But why?!"

"I had pledged to be with the ladies who taught the lore of the land. It was not a mantle I could throw off again, even had I wished to do so. And besides...he was not from my people at all."

"What do you mean, Nanna?"

"He was from the Sithe, the Underworld, the land of the fey, my dear, and there was no way we could stay together."

"But true love finds a way, doesn't it, Nanna?" Her eyes glow with the hope of too many legends.

I shake my head with regret and no small bitterness in my heart. "Only in stories, my little one. Real love is full of difficulty and of far more broken hearts than happy ones. We had one beautiful night where we fell in love and met the dawn in one another's arms. Only one. But it is more than many have."

"Love does not come to everyone, then? But in the stories...are they only lies?!" Surprise fights with anger in her mind. "Why tell these stories then?! All made up! Not one true?"

I snort indignantly. "Of course they are true! But one cannot be promised true love any more than one can be assured of triumphant fights with dragons and trolls. One must usually seek adventure to find it—and one must prove worthy of the quest. We tell one another the stories of those who succeed, for not all do. But the ones who triumph give hope to those of us who wish someday to follow their paths. It is they we remember."

Hallgerd ponders this for some time. A frown of pain disturbs her young forehead. I place my hand upon hers, knowing only time can ease the harsh distress of this discovery. She raises her head. Tears glisten unshed. "Do you have stories of my mother?"

"Oh, yes. She was kind and wise and beautiful—and very happy in love too."

Two tears roll down Hallgerd's reddened cheeks. "I wish I had known her, only a little bit, I wish there was something—something I could remember, or—" Many more tears flow now and the princess presses her palms to them, vainly trying to halt their fury.

"She too wished to have you remember." I rise from my chair stiffly—I feel so many of my years tonight—and cross to the cabinet where the little ringbox has lain these passing years, the gold tokens safely inside. I pull out the soft red bag and hear the symbols clink together. "To you, my dear Hallgerd, from your mother, to her from her own mother, and on and on, back as far as anyone can recall, these three tokens of responsibility have been handed, from mother to daughter to represent each woman's duty and to reflect the love and respect each held for the other. Your mother Gunnhild treasured these little gold pieces and spoke often with eagerness of the day she would pass them to you."

Hallgerd's tears are nearly dry as her rough-sea eyes open wide in curiosity. "What are they?" She leaps up to take my hands in hers. Releasing the treasures, I repeat the poem for her:

The bobbin for guidance through wisdom and sense,
The spindle for drawing out all excellence,
The ring for binding the oath to this land
To love and protect and be at its command.

We hug, our tears for lost mother, lost friend, mingling. Hallgerd repeats the rhyme to herself, etching it forever upon her memory.

"Your mother took these little gold tokens out very often to remind herself of her responsibility to this land and her promise to its people. She always told me it kept her sure of herself and of what she needed to do."

Hallgerd smiles at the tokens in her hand. "She was a good queen?"

"In every way. Gunnhild was a noble woman, but she knew every job in the castle, from the maid's to the brewer's, from the cook's to the councilor's. She loved her land and her people and did what was best for them, even if it was not what was most comfortable for her. When the harvest was lean, she went without to give more to the beggars who came to the castle in search of her grace. When times were bountiful, and they often were, the village squares rang with the happy music of festivals and wild holiday games."

Hallgerd's smile slips away. "It is not like that now, Nanna.

The people are not cheerful and the land does not prosper. I am not the only one who longs for a mother."

I smooth back her turbulent locks. "Until now you have been a child, and had the duties appropriate to a child. The land was entrusted to those whose duty was to care for it in your place. That trust has been mislaid."

"My father is lost, you have said. Others are less kind. They say he is mad." Hallgerd's face has a stubborn resistance.

"He does not know his mind. Your mother's death was a blow from which he never healed—"

"He might have healed with you to care for him." She speaks without rancor, but also without pity, her kind heart aching for the father she innocently loves.

"But I could not stay without sacrificing you." Better she know now, at last, I think—though no easier to tell. "In his sorrow for your mother, he saw you only as the agent of her death and could not bear to look upon you. I brought you here, safe from his wrath, to give you all the love I had given your mother, to find in your care solace for the loss of my friend."

Hallgerd sits down without a sound. I know no words to comfort her ache as she loses mother and father anew. Her face pinches from grief withheld, but my hand on her shoulder lays helplessly. Siur too ventures forth a comforting paw, and when rebuffed, mews plaintively, unheard. The princess mumbles "I must walk" and rises. The moonlight casts her form in blues and greys as she strides out under the stars. Left behind, Siur and I snuggle together for comfort. I cry.

5

Hours pass. I don't know how long I have slept when Hallgerd wakes me but the moonlight has changed from silver to blue. My princess' face seems so much older. It is not only the night sky that makes it so grey. But there is purpose there too, replacing the childhood joy. I mourn, but I rejoice too.

"Nanna, I cannot assume rule until I am twenty winters old—is that not law?"

"That is indeed what I recall."

"How much may I shape the rule before then?"

"I do not know the law that well. Your mother's mother took her in hand well before the coronation year and together they ruled the land. The ceremony was mere formality; your mother ruled alone only after your grandmother's death, then she had your father as companion to help shoulder the burden. It is not a thing to be done alone, if one can help it," I add, thinking sadly of Hallgerd's poor father.

"I shall go to the castle in the morning and find out what the law says," Hallgerd announces, "And I shall not leave until I make it well known that this land is my responsibility—and that I expect it to be well cared for whether I am ruler or not!"

In the morning, we rise after too little sleep, our hearts overtaken by a sense of thrill. Hallgerd dresses not in her usual breeches and jerkin, but in fine silk the color of robin's eggs, wound around her strong young body and held by gold clasps from the land of my birth. With the bear cloak thrown over her shoulders, Hallgerd looks very much like a heroine from one of my tales and I feel hope rise in my heart. I enter into the spirit and wear my brightest red cloak and a gold comb in my hair, for am I not attending the princess? But I do not forget that we have dangers to face and slip helpful amulets into the pockets of my dress and hers.

The sun has begun to think summer is here already and we remove our cloaks before we even reach the village in the castle's shadow. But there is no mistaking my princess: the villagers stop and stare, then quickly bow down before her. Unused to such treatment, Hallgerd reddens and nods quickly to acknowledge their respect. By the time we reach the castle gates she is quite flushed and laughing delightedly. Everywhere the whispers spread: "It is she! It is the princess."

Guards stand at the gate—a sight unseen since the last war, so many years ago. I open my mouth to speak but my little one steps firmly forward. "I am Princess Hallgerd and I am here to see my father. And his councilors," she adds belatedly.

The guards are young men unseasoned yet by actual battle. They blush at the princess, so young, so beautiful and so proper. Finally one stutters, "M-m-my lady, please enter," and the other joins him in an awkward bow. The princess nods gravely at them and strides through the doorway. I follow her steps, trying very hard to keep my expression serious.

At once I see Thomas and it is no longer difficult to be serious. A smile creeps across his face like a crack in black ice. "Your highness," he purrs while executing a stiff little bow, "How pleasant to meet at last."

Hallgerd examines him, her gaze direct. "I am here to see my father. Pray inform him of my wish." I am proud of her regal manner so newly acquired.

"Ah, but he is not well. Perhaps a little later..." Thomas' smile lacks warmth.

"I will see my father. Do see to it." Hallgerd meets his frosty gaze and she does not waver.

"As you wish, my lady." He turns sharply and leads us to the throne room. As we approach, the cacophony within becomes clear. Thomas' smirk is undisguised as he pulls open the doors.

I am unprepared for what we see. The councillors revel like a pack of workmen in an ale-house at the end of early plowing. A disarray of food covers the chamber's table, bottles of mead variously full or empty balance precariously or roll musically across the floor. Everywhere shouts and arguments ring from the walls and even snatches of bawdy songs drift toward us from a knot of men in the far corner. And in the midst of this rabble, discordantly silent, the king sits holding the golden locket, his fingers telling its burnished surface as they no doubt have these many years. His eyes, unfocused, gravely contemplate the floor while his thoughts fly away.

Hallgerd's mouth trembles and tears rise to her eyes—shame, pity, anger war within her. It is easy to see which wins. It is her mother's chin that juts out as she tosses her cloak to me and strides over to the table, grabbing a large gold platter and upending it so potatoes roll across the table and off its edge. With the other hand she picks up a hefty ladle and bangs the plate three times. The clanging draws the attention of the boisterous crowd, many of whose eyes pop at the sight of the beautiful young woman, not yet cognizant of who she is.

"I am the Princess Hallgerd! And I am here to see my father!"

Utter silence at last reigns and I am disconcerted by the shock, as if the noise of their revelry was a solid thing now sucked out of the room. The realization now dawns upon some of them, that it is she—the true heir—and their faces brighten with blooming shame. Hands go to their hair, their clothes, trying to smooth the disheveled appearance brought on by years of dissipation. Meekly now, they shuffle toward the table, righting bottles and straightening the piles of food, searching for their papers among the detritus.

Alone among them, the king does not stir. Now the locket is open and it is his wife's hair that he smoothes with his restless fingers. I know the feel of her hair too and without my bidding, my hand too reaches for a locket tucked in the depths of my pocket, the cold of its silver surface a shock.

Less certain now, Hallgerd approaches her father. He is far worse than even I had imagined—so completely lost. How can she have helped but to envision something better than this? Vain hopes in my heart had grown despite my stern admonishments; after all, when I had last seen him, King Kormak's mind was still with him. But now—

Hallgerd stoops a little—she's grown so tall the last two years—and lays her hand on her father's arm. "Father?" Her voice is strong but gentle, little betraying the tremble her lips show.

He looks up. There is no recognition on his face. Only pain, only sorrow, and I see Hallgerd's tears begin. The king reaches up to brush one away from her soft cheek and so touches one of the unruly curls which has slipped from its bonds. Suddenly his vision seems to focus. The golden hair wraps around his finger. He looks to his other hand, the locket, the matching flaxen strands. Then the king's eyes meet those of his daughter and his face glows. Her countenance swiftly matches it, hope reborn. Every breath in the room is held—he speaks. "You."

Hallgerd grins.

"It is you!"

"Yes!" Her nod sends the last of her tears down her cheek.

The king releases the princess' hair and catches her hand. "You are as beautiful as—she—" His stare hungrily searches her features, seeking imperfections, finding only beauty.

"Oh, father—" Her tears begin anew, this time with joy.

"You shall be my bride!" The king leaps up, clasping both her hands and the locket in his. His words rend my heart. The councilors gasp as one and Thomas—that evil Maldachta, that son of Bricriu—barks a laugh of genuine surprise and delight.

"No!" Hallgerd struggles to free herself from his grip.

"You are mine," the king insists and presses the point by calling "Guards! She must not leave—she shall be my bride!"

There are no guards in the chamber, but Thomas sweeps away to get them. My frozen feet at last begin to move, slowly, too slowly, but I reach my dear girl and help pull her from his hands. The king's confusion—why does his bride seek escape—holds him momentarily but then his anger rises. "Leave her be—she is mine!"

"She is your daughter!"

"She is my bride—Guards! Guards! Seize her!"

They have arrived, in a flurry of noise, and grab Hallgerd, ripping her from my embrace. I cry out and she reaches for me but there are too many of them. And they are obedient to their master—Thomas. He grins with evil pleasure; how quickly the surprise has been turned to his advantage. I mutter a useless curse against his birth, and try to think. What can be done?

King Kormak and his daughter are both flushed with anger and surprise. How proud I was to see her stride forth this morning—how little I knew it would become this tragedy. My only comfort is knowing she has his will—and her mother's strength. Hallgerd looks to me and grimly nods. She thinks now too, what can be done?

As the room begins to still, I hear coughs among the councilors. Here is our hope! They cannot allow such an abomination. The king must adhere to the law as it is recorded; he is after all serving only in stewardship for the future queen. Even in this barbarian country, there is law.

I try to steady my voice. "Councilors! It is your duty to put a stop to this wickedness. The law must be upheld—if there is to be law in this land. The people will demand it!"

"I am king," Kormak snarls, "And I shall do as I wish!"

I turn to Thomas. "Then the people will rise up and reclaim the land for its rightful heir—your soldiers among them." Dealing with the devil—may it buy me some time at least. He considers my words and his options, but before he can decide the oldest of the councilors, Gunnar the Greybeard, speaks.

"My lord, ahem, we must ah, protest, er—mention the possibility that this um—proposed marriage may not in fact be entirely, ah—legal." As he stutters out this declaration, the others try unsuccessfully to crowd behind him as if they had nothing to do with his words.

The king says nothing at first, bending over to retrieve the locket dropped in the melee, but his face is an ugly twist of fury. He walks to over to Gunnar who cowers before him.

But even more quickly, Thomas steps forward to lay a gentle hand on the king's arm. He speaks with all the charm that has made the sons of Bricriu so loved—and mistrusted—in our land. "Majesty," he purrs and Kormak's head snaps toward him, "Let the lawspeakers confer. We have all the time in the world, for surely they will find nothing to vex your plans." He turns to Hallgerd, watchful among the guards. "Your wife lives again, is it not true?"

The king's haunted eyes turn back to his daughter and like that, he is gone again, like a fish disappearing into a darkened pool. He stands uncertainly.

"Escort her to the queen's chamber," Thomas orders crisply. "You may go too," he adds, turning to me with a grand smile which I do not return. But follow I do, looking back one last time to see the king gazing toward the departing princess, again fondling the locket in his hand, and again, lost.

We are prisoners. I restrain my feet from pacing the floor like a beast's nervous tread, but panic hisses a thousand fears into my heart. At least the door remains closed so we have some privacy, but it is small comfort.

"Oh, by the heavens, what shall we do, Nanna?!" Hallgerd whispers hissingly, her eyes on door that hides the guards who stand at attention outside her mother's chamber. She paces before the door. "This is not at all what I'd—what I'd—oh, Nanna—" We reach for one another. It feels so good to hold her. "He is completely gone, isn't he? He is mad! That he could even suggest—oh it's just too horrible!"

I pat her shoulder. "It is, indeed. But surely the people will not allow it. The land is ultimately theirs after all."

"But the councilors—they'll put a stop to this. There must be a law against such a travesty." Tears make her eyes shine brightly.

"I have learned—to my dismay—that the councilors are seldom swayed by right or wrong, only by law. And law, my dear, can be interpreted in many ways."

"Feh!" She strides away propelled by anger. "This is my land! And I do not even know the laws. How much time I have wasted!"

"It is my fault—I should have been instructing you in the practical matters of your realm as well as the more esoteric knowledge, though I must admit—"

"Only you don't know the laws either, not like they do." She smiles wryly. "Why have the women of my line left the laws in the hands of old men?"

"Who else has the time?" We both laugh and it restores us a little. "And they have fought so hard not to have the laws inscribed on parchment. It was one of your mother's desires to have them written down. She too worried about her reliance on old men's memories."

Hallgerd looks around her. "This was her room." She runs her fingers lightly over the silver brush and mirror that sit on the oaken dressing table, peeks into the jewelry box. "I almost feel as if—" A commotion outside the door breaks into her musings. As

50

the sound of that voice becomes clear, we share a happy grin. It is our dear friend, Unn.

"I shall see my lady and don't you think you can stand in my way, Grim Eriksson, or believe me I'll tell your mother of it, now!"

We hear the guards mumble uncertainly amongst themselves.

The angry voice turns quickly to a persuasive wheedling. "After all, you weren't told to keep anyone out, now were you? Now, then. Let me through, let me through..."

The door opens and Unn flies to gather us both in an enormous hug. "Oh my lady, my Princess!" Her tears bring on ours and we all talk at once and laugh, leaving our hugging to wipe our wet cheeks and speak more coherently.

"Oh, lady—the castle is a-flutter with word of our princess—so beautiful! So elegant! And here where she belongs at last—but what has happened? Why the guards? Is it true the king has—"

"Unn, the king mistakes Hallgerd for his own wife come back to life. He wants to marry her."

The princess nods, her face sorrowful.

"The king wants...No!" Unn can barely speak for her indignation. "I knew he was troubled, but by the gods, such nonsense! The council will not allow it. Such trouble! Dear oh dear oh dear! The king is quite mad, quite mad, I had no idea just how bad. And no doubt that Thomas is in the thick of it, eh?"

"Oh yes. It was his idea to imprison us here."

"Nanna," the princess considers me thoughtfully, "Tell me more of this Thomas. I shall need to know if I am to protect myself—and my father. He too is a victim of that one's intrigues."

Unn sputters with indignation. "Oh, my Princess, how can you even worry about that terrible old man? He is not even the king anymore, just an old fool."

The princess regards Unn with clear eyes. "Fool or not, he is my father, and was my mother's husband. I will protect him if I can. Understood?"

"Yes, my lady," Unn declares, head bowed.

Hallgerd turns her gaze to me, questioning.

I bow my head too. "As you desire, my Princess. I shall follow your wishes—always."

She rests a hand on each of our shoulders. "Thank you both. I

51

must rely on you two completely—you are my only champions now. But I cannot dishonor my father, though he has dishonored me."

"Yes, my lady," Unn says, but cannot help adding, "though someone should give him a knock or two on the head lest he keep on this way."

Hallgerd can't keep a smile from her lips. "Come, let's sit on the bed and be comfortable and then you can tell me about this Thomas."

"Oh dear, I'd forgotten!" Unn breaks in, "Why, I've brought some delicious wine and cakes to celebrate your arrival. Thordis! Thorgerd!" She sweeps across the room and yanks open the door. The guards reluctantly move aside to allow two young women to thread through their ranks. Thorbjorg's twins—grown so big!—blush before the princess and Unn bustles around them, pulling out the one small table, setting the trays upon it, fussing with the many little cakes and the big serving horn of mead. The girls finish their task and, bowing repeatedly, awkwardly take their leave. "Such a thing! You'd think they'd never seen the princess before!"

I laugh. "But of course they haven't, Unn."

We all laugh, Unn loudest of all, her apron over her face. "True, true. And I must say, I've never seen her quite like this. Goodness, but you do look lovely, Princess."

Hallgerd grins. "Somehow I thought my breeches and jerkin wouldn't get me through the castle gates. Not that these flounces have helped all that much." She sighs. "Nanna, what can we do? We are really at the mercy of these councilors—and that evil man."

"Too true. Let us wait and see. Until they have reached their decision we have nothing against which to argue."

"Oh lady,' Unn says, "I'm sure they can't find something so terrible, so—so unthinkable in the laws. It cannot be so."

I sigh. "Well, Unn, I have noticed that there is not only the law but the interpretation of that law. And the two can be very far apart."

Unn shakes her head as if to deny it but she cannot. "Dear, dear, dear. That's no more than the truth. Those councilors—old Greybeard himself especially—they're all slippery as eels, happy to interpret the law according to whomever pays them the most. Why if I—"

Hallgerd breaks in gently, "Tell me about this Thomas, Nanna. You know him from the old country?"

I nod. "I wish it weren't true. I had not seen him for many years when he turned up here as your father's new advisor. But one cannot forget a son of Bricriu—or ever trust him."

"Who is Bricriu?"

"He was one of the Old Fathers. Some said a god, others that he was from the Sithe."

"Now lady," Unn says, "I've heard you speak of that place before, the sheathe, shithe?"

Hallgerd interrupts. "I know that one. I know it from your stories, from your beautiful songs, from your love story." We share a smile and Unn looks at me with eyes wide. "It is the mirror land, the land of the fey, the Underworld—though I must confess, I don't really know what that really means."

"That's all right." I say. "You don't really have the same concept here. Your underworld is for the dead but the Sithe is very much alive. The people there possess magic of many kinds— sort of like your dwarves, but more light-hearted. It is a wondrous land in many ways, but also dangerous. Time passes differently there."

"What do you mean?" The princess leans close, curious. "I don't understand."

I fold my hands together as I try to choose where to begin. "When I was there, for what seemed like three lovely days, I returned—after much difficulty—to find that several years had passed and few remembered me. Fewer still believed my story, though these things happen quite often."

"How terrible! What did you go there for?"

I can't help a rueful twist of a smile. "Oh, my dear, that is a story for another day."

Hallgerd leans forward. "But it was for your lover, was it not?"

I laugh but it sounds hollow even in my ears. "That is true, my dear. Or so I thought at the time. It is enough now that you understand the Sithe for its danger and its seduction. That pull is behind the spirit of Thomas, and all the sons of Bricriu. Bricriu was both celebrated and reviled in the stories of my people. When he chose to favor you, you swam in good fortune—but when he chose to malign you, you had little recourse but to run. Even the champions of the land could be set at each other's throats by his clever manipulations as happened at his famous feast where he nearly had the three tribes at war over who deserved the honor of the champion's portion."

Unn snorts. "That sounds like Thomas to the letter, my lady. Sweet as honey when he wants to be but sharp as an adder when he turns." She shudders. "Better not to trust him at all, that's what I say."

"You say the sons of Bricriu have magic too?" Hallgerd asks, biting into a dainty cake with relish. "Like yours?"

I consider this. "Well, as alike as men's and women's magic can be said to be. There are always differences, what with women wanting to make life easier and men, it seems, always wanting to have the advantage over somebody. Power—why is it always their biggest concern?"

The princess looks thoughtful. "I guess when you have it, you keep wanting more."

"I do not think his power is so mighty. But I cannot do anything to counter it, nothing magical anyway."

Unn pipes up. "I know, I know. It's that thingee, that thing he has against you, oh what is it, the guess? The goowse? The gouwse?"

I smile and nod. "The geiss. Yes, it keeps me from using my magic against his—or pay the price of destruction. I care nothing for myself," though I cherish the princess' quick touch on my arm, reassuring me, "but I am the only one who knows the nature of this one called Thomas. His magic is only part of the problem. The sons of Bricriu's love for mischief is the greater part. When I met him first he was raining toads upon a village just for the fun of it. I could not use my magic against his, but I let the people know who was causing their misfortunes, and they were quick to drive him out of their lands with torches, pitch and clods of dung." Hallgerd and Unn laugh at this, and the memory of his hasty flight even brings a smile to my lips.

"He has entwined himself so securely into the king's world here, we cannot simply chase him away," the princess says, tapping her chin. "And we do not have the military power to fight his control of the land's troops."

"It is my fault, my Princess. I abandoned the realm to a madman and his wicked advisor. Should have guessed the evil that would arise."

"Nonsense. You were right to safeguard me. This is my battle after all and one I mean to win. Nothing can take me from my land. I am here 'To love and protect and be at its command.'"

Unn breaks in. "But how shall we do it?"

Just then a commotion in the hall way grabs our attention. The guards eddy apart and expel Grim through the doorway. "You are summoned before the king. The councilors have reached a decision." We three exchange looks—what will this spell for our princess?

Unn and I put the tray of food back on the table. Hallgerd retrieves her cloak, takes a long look around the room and smiles grimly. We follow behind her as she strides through the door. Unn reaches up and snags the ear of the young captain of the guards who utters a very unmilitary squawk. "Don't you forget who's the real power of this land, young man. Give your princess her due!"

Hallgerd smothers her laugh and Grim massages his misused ear, but he walks behind the princess as we make our way to the Great Hall, keeping his troop at his heels.

I look around as we enter the Hall. Thomas is beside the king, his face guarded. They cannot yet know the outcome, or surely his countenance would betray more, whether it be anger or jubilance. The king leans back in his throne, eyes closed. At least the locket is nowhere to be seen. Unn hangs back by the door, uncertain. I am swept along in the princess' wake as she strides resolutely toward the councilors.

"What is your recommendation regarding this matter?" she demands without hesitation, eyes blazing.

The king's eyes fly open and he leans forward.

The old men cower ineffectually behind Gunnar's voluminous robes. He clears his throat twice without obvious effect. "My lady, we find...er...that is a, ahem, most thorough review of the law in the memory of even the oldest of our number—Odd the Traveler, lady, he is sixty-three winters—"

"Never mind the reckoning of years—what of the law?"

"Ur, ah, that is we can find nothing to counter such a possibility." Gunnar coughs, wheezing into the fold of his sleeve, while the other elders mutter in presumable agreement. Thomas grins with both jaws and the king rises with delight.

Hallgerd's face is a mask of revulsion and she sputters, "Nothing to counter the possibility? Surely custom alone dictates the, the distastefulness of such a union! This is unacceptable!"

Gunnar swallows noisily while regarding the princess with her fists on her hips. "My lady, there is precedent in the history of the gods of, um, marriage between close kin."

I hear Unn gasp near the door but I cannot make a sound.

Doddering Odd nods his head and points a stubby finger at the angry princess. "Royal blood flows in a direct descent from the gods, as we all know from the ancient stories."

"Then we shall be wed, my dear." The king quickly takes her hand. She stares at him. Her mouth forms a small o. I cannot believe this is happening. He kisses her hand and she pulls it swiftly from his grasp.

"When shall the wedding be?" Thomas asks gleefully, rubbing his hands together with delight. "No need for a long courtship, eh?"

King Kormak smiles at his bride, who now looks wild-eyed to me. I must do something! If nothing else, I step forward to place myself between the king and Hallgerd and turn to face the king. "Are you not forgetting that you need to secure permission from your bride?"

The king beams. "But she is mine—it is fated."

Thomas has been quietly conferring with Gunnar. Now he says, "The time for objecting is past. Is it not true that the betrothal has been implicitly accepted by her appearance in the Great Hall before the king?"

The old man emphatically agrees, his shaggy grey head bobbing up and down. "We have precedent."

The evil one bares his abundant teeth in a counterfeit smile. The princess sobs. These cursed councilors. It breaks my heart. If I could kill them all now I would. But I cannot. I walk quietly to Thomas—Maldachta!—and spit out a promise, "I swear by all my people swear by that you shall rue this arrogant act and your evil shall return upon you threefold."

"Ha! I'll see you cold and dead first, old woman. You are powerless against me." He meets my glare with an insolent smirk.

But I have no time for him now. A ruse has come to mind. I turn to the king. "No wedding plans can be laid until the betrothal gifts have been delivered."

Kormak looks upon his intended wife contentedly. "As you wish."

Hallgerd moves away from him, taking my arm and searching my eyes with her own. I know she wonders—have I given up? I squeeze her arm to assure her that I will never give up. But we need time.

"The Princess Hallgerd shall make a declaration in the morning of the desired gifts," I say. "Allow us to withdraw now. We have had a tiring day."

The king sighs. "Until tomorrow then, my sweet."

Thomas cocks his head at me. "What do you have up your sleeve old woman? Not that it matters. You have lost."

I merely smile and silently follow the princess out of the hall. The guards follow upon Unn's heels as she trots along behind us, but they do not encroach upon the two of us walking ahead. Nonetheless, we do not speak until we are within the chamber. While Unn admonishes the guards with the princess' need for privacy—and the unlikelihood of her jumping to freedom, not that she'd survive the fall—I gently take the cloak from Hallgerd's shoulders. She sinks into the soft bedding, bows her head in her hands, and quietly sobs. I sit down beside her and wrap an arm around her waist.

"Oh Nanna," Hallgerd rasps and then, only tears. Anger, shock, pain—all flow in a torrent from her eyes, blue-grey sea waves stained with the red of blood and tragedy. I cannot pretend I do not suffer too. My own weeping joins hers.

Unn returns with a bustling commotion, a large tureen between her strong hands. "Here's just what we need, my dears. Good hearty broth—lots of spear leeks in it too, my princess, the way I know you like it, and lots of fresh bread to dip." She ladles it into bowls as she speaks, thrusting warm crusts into our hands. "And I have rich Frankish wine to warm up your hearts and give us all spirit." Cheerful as she sounds, I can see that Unn's eyes too are as red as the southern wine, but she fusses around us as is always her way and has us heartened in no time. Blessed be, my friend, I think as I catch her eye with a smile. We are lucky to share your spirit.

"What are we to do?" Hallgerd asks at last, refusing any more broth and leaning back on her elbows. They both look expectantly at me.

"We ask for the bridal gifts. We need time. The moon is waning and I am at my weakest. A couple of weeks and I can plan and work and come up with something. To be sure, I am not entirely certain what we can do."

Hallgerd turns her face away and swallows. "So I might have to go through with this?"

"No. That is unacceptable. But you might have to leave your land for a time."

"Leave the land! No. This is my realm. These are my people. I have a responsibility, an oath—"

I put my hand on hers. "We cannot fight them, not with law—the law is against us. And not with magic either. We are too few. We need strength."

"What about the people?" Unn asks. "Sure enough, the folk of this land are behind the princess, before the king."

"But how do we organize them? We will not be allowed to leave the castle now—and though we may escape, we cannot ride freely from town to town, farm to farm, and gather the people."

The princess nods. "Thomas will raise an army and be after us in no time and we will be back in the castle—and probably not in this lovely room but somewhere more secure."

"Oh dear." Unn's hope crumbles and she chews sadly on a crust. "I suppose you're right. But if they only knew..."

"No doubt they would indeed help, Unn. And it will help if you and your faithful compatriots help spread the word of what evil there is in the castle. Many, I know, already guess that things are not what they ought to be and are eager for the princess' rule. But to face an army—we cannot expect them to risk so much. It is our task to do that."

Hallgerd begins to pace before the big bed. "Can we not send to one of the realms friendly to us and ask for support? Would not one of our allies defend my right to rule?"

I consider this for a time and reluctantly reply, "Perhaps—but

I do not know that we should trust entirely the fate of the realm into the hands of another king. Though many of the neighboring lands are friendly, this region is a constantly changing map. Kings like to acquire. And a vulnerable land—with leadership in dispute—may be seen as an ideal target for adding to a king's own domain. It is a definite risk."

Hallgerd rolls the little gold bobbin in her palm. She flushes and smiles at me when she notices my gaze. "I'm hoping it helps me realize what is indeed wise and sensible. It is not easy to know."

I see her mother so clearly in her face and smile. I cannot halt the tears that spring up. Why why why? —I know better than to ask, but still my heart cries the word. How could things get into such a muddle? Maldachta—you are so well-named. If only I could use my magic to put him into a long sleep, to wake the king from his madness, too—but it does not matter. If wishes were pies, we'd never starve. If I could be certain the princess would be all right, I would willingly risk myself. But that one has wormed his way into so many aspects of the realm, such a trusted advisor, ha! Would that those villagers had killed him all those years ago.

"Nanna? What do you mean to ask for as the betrothal gifts?"

"It is tradition to ask for a wardrobe for the three nights of celebration, and a cloak too, so you can hide the dresses until the ball begins. But we must make the gowns special—difficult that is—so they cannot be sewn in a day or two. And the cloak, hmmm." I get my crystal orb from its hiding place deep in one of my pockets and roll it between my palms until it is warm. I peer into its milky depths and see—

"The sun, the moon and the stars." I smile. That won't be easy. "We shall ask for a dress as golden as the sun, another as pale as a full moon, and a third as brilliant as the stars. That will give us a little time."

Unn claps her hands together. "If they can do it at all! They'll be asking Astrid from Djupa to make the gowns, surely, there's no finer needle in the world, but where they'll find fabrics is hard to say. They'll be sending couriers to the far off lands, for sure. You are so wise my lady—and wily too!"

Hallgerd already looks much happier. "What about the cloak, Nanna?"

I look into the ball again and see a confusion of signs—animals, one after another, some I do not even recognize, hundreds, maybe even a thousand. "This is odd. All these animals." I close my eyes and at once before them is the vision of a long, dark cloak—made from the fur of them all. "Ah! I see now. A thousand furs! The cloak shall be made of a thousand furs."

Hallgerd frowns. "I don't like to think of the slaughter of so many animals just for my sake."

"Even better! We can make it a condition that no animal die. That way they must capture each animal and remove some fur to weave into the cloak. That will take much time!"

Unn giggles. "I can just see them trying to catch a great shaggy bear and shave a wee bit off her side. Better hope they can find one without a cub to protect. Oh, land's sakes, this could take quite some time!" We hug another in relief. A respite has been achieved, hope kept alive.

Unn finally tears herself away to attend to her late night duties and keep a stern eye upon her charges—"Goodness knows, they'll have forgotten to set the bread out to rise and as far as cleaning the kitchen, ah that Katla, even if she's my own sister's child!"—and Hallgerd and I ready ourselves to sleep in the soft bed on which she was born.

As we snuggle down under the thick coverlet of swan-down, she reaches up to touch the amulet of rosy milkstone, carved so long ago by my brother into the shape of a horse, still hanging from the latticework above the silken pillows. "What is this, Nanna?"

I untie the golden thread that holds it and drop it into my princess' open hand. "It is an amulet for fecundity. It helped prepare your mother for your birth—well, as much as she could be helped, poor dear."

Hallgerd considers the amulet for a minute, then closes her hand around it. "She fought hard to bring me into this world. I must not let her down."

"We won't."

The next morning the princess, completely composed, makes her declaration. "It is the custom for a bride to be outfitted properly. I wish to have one dress as golden as the sun, another as pale as a full moon, and a third as brilliant as the stars. And I shall have a cloak of one thousand different furs—and because I am so kind-hearted, you must swear that not one animal's life is taken."

The king merely nods, looking at his intended bride tenderly, and says "As you wish."

Thomas grumbles irritably about the necessity of such a requirement but the council firmly agrees to the tradition, though I see eyebrows rise at the peculiar specificity of the designs. No matter. It will give us time—time to plan, time to work, time for magic.

A flurry of activity besets the castle afterward. Messengers ride out across the land and into neighboring ones, seeking the special requests of the princess: the fabric like the sun, the moon and the stars to be sewn into the celebratory gowns. They will not find them anytime soon.

The finest hunters in the land set forth upon the delicate project of capturing, unhurt, all the fur-bearing creatures of this realm. It is against all for which they are trained. It is a game that requires great patience and care—and courage. Unn was right to wonder at the capture of the great brown bear—or the ghostly wolf, even the cunning fox, or any beast—for the animal who fights for its life, fights to the death—they cannot know they will survive their capture this time.

Meanwhile the queen's chamber has become our home. Unn even sends to have Siur brought here and she arrives, hissing and spitting after her trip in Thorgerd's basket, immediately hiding under the bed for hours before finally creeping out to look over her new domain and determine the most sunny spot. It almost feels like home, but for the fact that we cannot leave.

I spend my time thinking and planning, sending Unn off on secret journeys to gather herbs and roots and berries, hoping against hope she does not sting herself on the nettles nor run into the five-finger ivy. So far, luck has been with my friend. She waves away my concerns anyway. "I need to get a little fresh air now and then, my lady," she tells me as she arrives huffing and puffing from yet another foray into the woods. "Why, I'd be getting no air at all and getting all het up about that no good niece of mine who today burned half a dozen loaves—half a dozen, can you imagine it! Oh dear, it makes my blood turn just to think about it—" and off she goes grumbling to herself, refusing my words of thanks. She is good hearted, and I thank whatever forces have led her to my aid.

The princess spends her days reading her mother's books. The collection is not large, though; I have seen that the people of this land do not put as much trust in the written word as those of my land. It has always seemed curious to me. My teachers often consulted written instruction and jested about their poor recall. But here, the law is kept in memory, just as recipes are passed from mother to maid. I remember Hallgerd's grandmother saying that written words cannot be trusted, that they take on a life of their own. It is a different way. Who can say which is better?

Hallgerd reads voraciously as is her wont. New books are a treat enough, but she reads hungrily too because they are her mother's. Often annotations appear in Gunnhild's own hand. I have seen her run her fingers over the marginalia, as if touching them she can almost touch her long-gone mother. She sits in the window-seat when it is sunny and in the big rocking chair when it is chill, next to the tallow lamp. Often Siur curls in her lap, comforted once more, as if she is home. Sometimes the princess reads aloud to me as I furtively grind herbs or braid long vines into a rope—after all even the story-teller needs new stories from time to time.

Meanwhile tales filter back to us of the hunt for the bridal gifts. Many messengers return empty-handed, but at least one or two have returned with rich fabrics from the far eastern world, where magic has been done with gold and silver to make them resilient and flexible enough to bear the pressure of the loom. And the hunters too have been patiently gathering their bounty. Many a beast bears the mark of their encounter, forever scarred by the strange request. We have bought time, but it will not last forever. I follow the progress of the moon each night and consider our fate.

There are so many uncertainties. Surely I can arrange for the princess to escape, but where is it safest to go? What will happen to me when I am left behind? And to our faithful friend Unn?

"Oh, don't you worry your heads about me," Unn says when I express my fears and misgivings. "Like a cat, I am. Always land on m'feet."

"Unn," Hallgerd admonishes, "They'll know you helped us and they'll punish you. We have to think of something. And for you too, Nanna. I cannot leave you behind. You'll simply have to come with me."

"Thomas will never allow such a thing. If you escape, it is no real matter—he will see you as powerless outside your realm. But if we are both gone, he will know we have plans and will not rest until we are caught—dead if he can manage it."

"But I need you with me!" Hallgerd reachs for my hand and clutchs it tightly.

"And I shall be—but we must cover our tracks so he thinks himself safe. The easiest way is if Unn betrays us."

"Lady!"

Unn's face turns white as dough. I quickly put my hand on her shoulder. "My dear, we have to make certain you are not suspected. The best way is if you seem to betray us. It must look real. Though of course it will be a part of our plan, they cannot know that, they cannot even suspect. It is the only thing that can assure your safety—and ours."

"I don't care two hoots for my own safety. 'Tis only the princess's and yours of which I think."

"I care, Unn."

"So do I," Hallgerd adds at once, "And as your future queen, I shall have need of your services, so you must be safe in the meantime."

"We have to be able to understand—and predict—how Thomas and his agents will respond to each move. If you, Unn, tell them the princess is going to try to get away, what will they do with us?"

We all ponder this for a bit. Finally the princess says, "Well, I think he'll have us put in a more secure area, where we can be watched, rather than simply add more watchers. With the tapestries across the door, we could be doing just about anything in here."

"True, true," Unn agrees. "The cells below the main floor would be a good guess—dark, horrid, tiny windows for air and only one door on each. They're mostly used for storage, but in war times, I remember—"

"They made very good prisons," the princess adds bitterly. "My mother writes of the great wars against the Geats in years gone by. I wonder if under the reign of Thomas the cells have not already been put to such use."

"It is likely," I sigh. "But I think Unn is right. They will consider it the most secure place. So we must be prepared to get you out of there at night. I will be able to follow soon after, but I will have to escape in a quite different manner, so they do not realize that I am gone."

Hallgerd looks at me curiously. "Whatever do you mean, Nanna?"

"I cannot explain, and it would be safer if neither of you knew." I cannot hide a smile though and say, "Be prepared to see me in a most unexpected light."

Unn shakes her head. "I trust you know what you're up to, lady, but I confess I fear greatly that infernal one. I tremble to think he might guess our plans, why sometimes, I can't help but think he can see the insides of my head, knows what I'm thinking. And I don't like it, not one little bit."

"That is our greatest danger—for he has ways of magic too and will be trying to catch us in our plans."

"If he is not too busy taking over the land," Hallgerd adds with a grimace, "and destroying my people. I swear, when I am able to, I will make sure that one pays. I can hardly bear to think of him and all the cruelties he has perpetrated. I will not forget."

"Use that anger for your resolve. Difficult times lie ahead of us, much danger and much delicacy. It would be so easy for something to go wrong."

"When will our plans be acted upon, lady?"

"When the bridal gifts are ready—probably next week, if my guess is right. There shall be a new moon about that time—propitious. And helpful for you to escape in the night."

"A week," the princess says, her thoughts far away. "I shall be ready."

7

And it is about a week before we hear news of progress. Thomas himself comes to the queen's chamber to impart the news that the presents have been completed and would be offered by the king himself on the morrow. The princess for her part accepts his message cordially, if coldly, and nods her acquiescence to his suggestion that she appear in the Great Hall the next morning to receive the gifts. He lingers a moment to appraise this quiet grace—even he cannot believe she will welcome the gifts that spell her humiliation and defeat—but he find nothing helpful in her calm demeanor. Thomas has a smile for me as I sit in the big chair, placidly carding wool.

"You are too quiet, old woman," he hisses quietly. "I know you are planning something.".

I look up at him with sheep's eyes. "I see no alternative but to let the princess marry. Perhaps then she will have the power to fight you."

"Ha! She cannot rule until her twentieth winter. By then she will be dead."

"Do not bury the corpse before she has stopped breathing."

"Do not think you can outwit me with your womanly words and your knitting. I have power and I have strength—and control of this land."

"And I have friends—and peace in their love. How do you sleep?"

"Bah! Sleep all night, Mná, while I bring this land to ruin and destroy it to have my fun. You cannot understand the pleasure it gives." He leans toward me. "Chiefly because I know it breaks your faithless heart. That is pleasure enough for me."

"Pleasure? Is that why grey hairs take over your black? Why so many more lines cross your face and palms? Do you wake in the night fearing a knife in your back or poison in your food? It is indeed good that you are so trusting of these barbarians."

"Barbarians—you are so right. I cannot understand how you came to love them so. Their music is so dull—their tales even duller."

"It is not like the music of our land."

"Our land—" He sighs.

"But they have a charm of their own. It is merely of a different kind from ours. In time you may come to appreciate its beauty."

"I have been here far too long as it is," he says, idly running his hand over the silver brushes on the princess' small dressing table. "If I did not have such matters to occupy my time, I hardly think I would have stayed." His voice trails off but, as if aware he has showed some kind of weakness, he eyes me sharply and continues, "However, things have become so entertaining of late, I am quite content. This will be a fine wedding."

"And nothing like the village where they chased you from their midst with fire and dung," I add, my voice demure.

Thomas flushes. "You spoiled my fun there, but I was young and foolish then and you, fresh from the Sithe with a reckless abandon."

"You are not so young now," I tell him, my voice quiet but my anger still vibrating through the words, "and you have had time to mend your ways."

"Fool!" he spits at me. "You thwarted me once and it taught me to be careful, to plan and to savour the dissolution of fools. We who are born to greatness need not suffer the lesser beings of this world. That is the mistake of the daughters of Mná; you look fondly on those who would hate you for your magics and steal them if they could. People do not thank you for being their superiors. They hate you."

"How sad it is that you see the world in such terms. It is not a bowl of fruit where each piece I take leaves you without," I tell him, an urgency fueling my words. "Life is a stream; every drop adds to the whole. When we drink, new rain falls to swell the tide again. Nothing is gained, nothing is lost."

Scorn flashes from his eyes like a roaring fire. "You simply will not admit that you love the same power I do. You pretend it is all about fairness and friendship—but only because you are accustomed to making things go your way. When your power is gone—as it is now—suddenly you want things to change. I am not fooled. And no one else will be either. Lay your plans. It will do no good."

So full of hatred and despair! I say nothing and he bows a good-bye to me and then to the princess. After he has left the room, I let the revulsion I feel rise to my face. How can one take such pleasure in the misery of others?

"Nanna, what do you speak of with Thomas? Anything that might help us?"

"Perhaps. He certainly suspects that we are planning a ruse, but I have tried to lead him toward thinking that we will do nothing until after the wedding."

"Do you think it will work?"

"I don't really know. When it comes to the sons of Bricriu, one cannot hazard a reasonable guess—that is not the way they behave."

The princess frowns. "How predictable then are we?"

"We must appear to be absolutely predictable. That is the only way to trap him—in his own unquestioning prejudices, that I am a foolish old woman and you, a simple young girl."

"Simple!" Hallgerd laughs. "I'll try to remember that."

"Our safety depends upon it."

"Does he really think so little of your abilities, Nanna?"

"Yes, and to his own regret it will be too. He thinks because I use my skills for health and happiness that it is all I can do—cure a cold or soften an ache. They are merely the most called-for services. But I know great magic—and I will use it as it is necessary." And possible—I have not forgotten the geiss.

"I am glad of it," Hallgerd says, coming to lay her head on my knee.

I run my fingers through her luxurious golden glory and swear again to myself to keep this girl safe from all harm, regardless of the cost. She shall be queen—and not by marriage to her father.

The next morning we rise and dress in our finery for the solemn ceremony in the Great Hall. Unn brings us breakfast and good wishes for the ordeal. Thordis and Thorgerd help by acting as handmaids for the morning, brushing the princess' hair and helping to select from her mother's jewel box the most appealing gems and brooches. I feel quite the drab in my simple dress, but that is all for the best. Unremarkable, I will be for the most part unobserved. All eyes will be on the princess and her fabulous gifts. All eyes but mine.

Hallgerd carries the milkstone amulet. It is not much, but it may help a little and as it was carved by my brother, it is safe from the penalties of the geiss. But it is not so much magic I fear just now. Brute force is enough. Everything will have to run smoothly and according to our predictions if we are to make our escape.

The soldiers shuffle impatiently outside the door, but even Grim is hesitant to breach the layer of tapestries that afford us privacy, so he coughs unconvincingly to let us know it is the time we are expected below. Hallgerd makes a last inventory of her costume and smiles at the twins.

"You're every bit the ruler today, my lady," Unn glows appreciatively. "All who see you will be struck dumb in wonder."

"Thank you, Unn. This is still a bit odd for me, like playing dress-up. I miss my breeches and climbing trees."

"You may have them back sooner than you think," I whisper as we prepare to head out. The princess twists her face in a wry half-smile then returns to impassive nobility as the guards all straighten up at attention. Without a word she leads the way down the corridors to the Great Hall.

Inside the vast room there is a hushed sort of bustling. The seamstress—Unn says it was indeed the skilled Astrid—is there in a marvelous, yet understated gown of alder green, standing nervously behind the king's throne. If this is evidence of her skill, the choice was indeed made wisely. Attendants of all kind—many I have not seen in the many years since the queen's death, many more who are new to me—fuss around the large tables, carrying trays of delicacies, horns of mead, and flagons of foreign wine. The councilors no longer look like drunken, war-weary fighters, but men of learning and of distinction. They stand in a loose knot before the king, talking quietly and turn at our arrival, bowing low before the princess. She repays their respect with a cool nod and I remember her vow to replace them with written laws when she is ruler here.

Thomas beams, rising quickly to greet the princess and lead her before the king who sits bolt upright, an eager smile stretching cheek to cheek. Hallgerd curtseys stiffly, her large skirts hampering her movements, but she does not allow it to upset her. She stands expectantly, arms folded in front.

Words roll grandly from Thomas' tongue. "The great King Kormak wishes to offer his best greetings to the Princess Hallgerd and hopes that she finds herself in the very finest health and prosperity this morning."

"I am well enough," Hallgerd answers in her clear, loud voice.

Thomas, clearly a little peevish that she refuses the subterfuges accustomed through time, continues, "The requested betrothal gifts have been secured. I—the king, that is, is certain they will meet your desires in every way."

Hallgerd merely nods. It is no matter to her what the clothes look like. We have either bought enough time—or we have not. Only her escape matters now.

The king nods to Astrid. Her workers bring forth a large wardrobe on wheels. It is draped in rich red tapestries. Thomas steps forward and pulls a long golden cord. The tapestries fall to reveal the rich maple wood. He throws open the door and motions to Astrid and to her assistants who try, shyly, to hide behind their teacher.

The first dress comes out and it is indeed a wonder. Like a beam of light directly from the sun, its golden color brightens the entire room. I hear a gasp—whose I cannot tell, it could be any one of ours—as they carry it to Hallgerd. The princess cannot disguise the pleasure she feels at seeing, at touching this masterpiece. "Lovely, lovely," she murmurs to Astrid, who blushes hotly, her wrinkled cheeks burning crimson.

But the second dress, too, is a revelation: glowing as silvery-white as the full moon, casting a radiance quite unlike the first, yet just as bewitching in its power. Hallgerd can only shake her head. It is astonishing. Artists have a magic all their own—I could not begin to go about making such a wonder.

The third is quite impossible. We all draw around to stare at the shimmering stars—how can they blink so? Truly this is enchantment. I steal a glance at Thomas, but he is as entranced as the rest of the court. Astrid alone must be responsible for this miracle of fabric and metals. Hallgerd runs her fingers over the soft, twinkly white of the cloth. I can hardly wait to see the cloak. I do not have to wait long.

Astrid herself—with a little help, for it is bulky—holds the cloak out for the princess' inspection. It is like a living thing, the thousand furs rippling and billowing in unison like some newly created beast. The lives spared animate the warm mantle. Thrown over the princess' shoulders, it seems to wrap closely, protectively around her. I look more carefully at Astrid's proud face—is there more here than the skill of the expert seamstress? Is she too a practitioner of the arts? Her joyous countenance reveals nothing to me. For her sake, I hope Thomas does not suspect anything. But why should he? The arts of women have long been dismissed as magic by most men; that is, they are incomprehensible but the men remain incurious—it is only women's work.

Hallgerd hugs the wizened seamstress. The fur envelopes the tiny woman, flushed with pleasure and dazzled by such royal acclaim. The king too shows his delight by leading the councilors in enthusiastic applause. And I thought Astrid could blush no redder!

When the happy tempest finally abates, King Kormak speaks. "I must take this merriment as a sign that you approve of the gifts."

Hallgerd reluctantly shrugs off the cloak into the hands of others. "They are indeed all I asked for—and a good deal more. Your seamstress has a gifted needle."

"And you accept the gifts?"

"Yes," Hallgerd says simply, aware of the import of her word.

"Then the marriage shall be held in three days time!" Kormak leaps up with excitement. "Let the preparations begin!"

Even though she is prepared for the announcement, Hallgerd's expression clouds with anger and despair. But she says nothing. Secrecy means all our lives now. She tries on a smile. "Where is the reward for this fine needlework? I wish to show my appreciation for her accomplishment."

The king waves old Greybeard forward, who carries a cushion upon which sits ample recompense: a fine yellow-gold arm-ring, a red-gold brooch and good size whetstone. The princess steps beside the old man and holds her hands out to Astrid, who takes them and kneels. Hallgerd helps her to rise again. "Thank you for your fine needle work. I have never seen its like before and doubt that I ever shall again. Let your gifts be rewarded with equal generosity." She reaches over to the cushion. "This gold ring for the dress like the sun," she declares and slips the ring on the woman's arm. "This brooch for the magnificent moon." With some difficulty Hallgerd pins it upon Astrid's simple shawl, smiling at her own awkwardness. "For the shimmering dress of stars, this whetstone. May it keep your needles sharp." Hallgerd then reaches up to her shoulder and removes one of the gleaming stones. "This emerald, which was my mother's, for the cloak of a thousand furs. It suits me particularly well—may the emerald please you likewise."

"Bless you, my lady! Bless you! You are so like your dear mother, it was such a pleasure to sew for you too."

Tears add to the radiance of Hallgerd's smile. "You knew my mother, too?"

Astrid nods quickly. "I rarely saw her, but for a fitting each season. She was gracious and good and so very generous every time. We all would do anything for her—as we will for you too, my lady," she adds, nearly whispering.

Hallgerd grasps her hand tightly in both her own. "Thank you, Astrid. Your loyalty will always be well-rewarded by me."

The older woman, overwhelmed, smiles shyly at the floor.

Hallgerd returns to the king. "In three days time, we shall be wed. I too must make preparations if the feast is to be laid to my liking—I believe that part of the celebration is in my sphere of control?"

"Yes," agrees the king with relish. "Decide your menus for the feasting. Your wishes shall be carried out to the letter." He takes her hand. "Please make your desires known to me and I will see that they are met. The kingdom awaits your commands."

"The realm," Hallgerd corrects him, "has all my concern and good wishes as my duty requires."

But the king is oblivious to the significance of her remark. Thomas smirks. The councilors shift uncomfortably on their feet. Hallgerd pulls her hand from the king's grasp as gently as she can do so quickly. I hasten behind her as we lead the entourage to the queen's chamber, where we may examine the wardrobe at greater length—and in private.

Surrounded by the splendor of the dresses, we are dazzled. In the midst of such despair, who could guess that we would have such wonders over which to coo and to rejoice. Hope may come in many ways—a feathered thing or furred.

Hallgerd races back and forth between them, running her hands over the smooth surfaces and the rich embroideries. "Oh, it's very frivolous of me, but do tell me, Nanna, that I won't have to leave these behind when we escape from here. I don't think I could bear it!"

"Never fear, my dear. They are very much a part of the plan, not merely a distraction while we worked. They will be needed when your true station is revealed. Who could not believe they were the trappings of royalty?"

Hallgerd claps her hands together, a child still at heart.

"But how?" Unn asks, always the practical one. "It's not going to be too easy to get away—and with this giant wardrobe as well? You must have quite some plan, my lady—not that I doubt you!—but how?"

I reach deep within the basket on my lap for the secret. "Are you certain no one listens at the door?"

Hallgerd steps quietly to the tapestry coverings, threading her hand through their abundance. The view assures her and she nods furtively to me.

I pull out the walnut and present it on my palm.

"A walnut!" Hallgerd exclaims

"What, that little thing?!" says Unn.

I grin foolishly at their surprise, savoring it. "Trust me, there is a way." Magic is so very useful, but it can also be fun. I rise and step before the dresses arrayed upon the bed. Picking up the gown of stars, I show how neatly it folds itself into the small brown nut. Hallgerd and Unn jump up with squeals of delight.

The princess takes the nut and, opening it gingerly, takes the dress back out. It shines just as brightly without a wrinkle to be seen.

"Oh, the gods!" Unn cries. "I've never seen such a thing!"

"Nanna, how perfect it is!" Hallgerd hugs me. "How can you? It's so clever!"

Unn chuckles. "My goodness, I wish I'd had one of those when we were washing the winter linen—all those trips back and forth up the stairs, I tell you—"

Their delight warms me like a mellow wine and I treasure again these dear friends. How soon we will all be in danger. But for now, it is so good to be together and happy. Much like the old days it seems, when Gunnhild and I enjoyed an evening's talk. Which reminds me—

"Unn, do you know this Astrid, the marvelous seamstress who made these gowns? Do you know much about her? She sewed for Gunnhild, yes?"

"Yes, though I never saw her much. Quiet she was, very timid-like, it seemed. I hardly ever heard a peep out of her, though you know the way I ramble on, it's just possible she didn't get a word in edgewise." Unn laughs loudly at her own foibles.

Hallgerd looks at me, one eyebrow arched. "What is it, Nanna?"

I purse my lips. Maybe I shouldn't stir the pot. But I can trust these two—as can Astrid, whether she knows it or not. I get up and walk over to the cloak and run my hands over the soft fur for the umpteenth time. Yes, it must be. "I think she too knows the arts. I think there is magic in this mantle—and likely the gowns as well. They are not only brilliant but truly amazing." I look to the princess, "I have seen skilled needles before, but never anything like this."

"Do you really think so?" Hallgerd jumps up and strokes the fur too.

Unn crowds behind us, almost afraid to touch it. "Is it good magic?" she asks hesitantly. "Can you tell?"

I nod. "I am quite certain it is good. I saw the way it enveloped Hallgerd, almost protectively. I feel strongly that there is good here."

"More on my side," Hallgerd smiles to herself.

"Goodness," Unn shakes her head, "It's getting so there's a witch on every corner! No disrespect, of course, lady." She reddens.

"None taken, my friend. What wife is not a conjure wife when she can be? The little tricks passed from mother to daughter to make life richer, a little easier, more lucky. These little rituals are magic too. It's a pity your land has so long taken a dim view of our powers. Many hide their abilities rather than face torment or cruelty."

"Ah, but you don't know how it was, with the wily Suomi to the north," Unn says protectively, "They were—ha—I don't know what, causing storms and drowning innocent people—lightning and thunder and snow! Weeks and weeks of snow and ice without let-up. Hard times they've caused, lady. Hard times indeed." Unn shivers at the recollection.

"On the other hand, were they not fighting back against the ships of your country, carrying men who went plundering their lands, attacking the women and children when the men were on hunting missions?"

"Well, I don't know about that, lady. I suppose it might be," Unn adds doubtfully, picking at some imagined lint on the dress of stars.

"I know, like the story of Arrow-Odd," Hallgerd pipes up. "Doesn't he do just that? Or was it his men? And he warned them away from it? Yes, I recall that story."

"I was never there," I say, "but I met a woman from Suomi on the ship that brought me here as a slave. We had much to talk about. Unlike the people in the surrounding lands, they do not go plundering their neighbor's lands in the warm season. Instead they herd deer and traverse their plains gathering food. Their magic is great, but they seldom use it, save only for fighting enemies—enemies who seek them."

Unn sighs. "Well, no doubt you know better than me, but you'll have a hard time changing the people of this land. We're old and set in our ways and won't be changing anytime soon, I can tell you. Much as you have been so good to us—and I know that, and many others—there's still that other one, and he's not making many friends this way."

"When I am queen, things will change," Hallgerd says, arms crossed. "I have seen the value of this knowledge first-hand. I will not tolerate superstitions and prejudice—understandable though they may be," she adds with a smile to Unn, unfolding her arms to put one on the old woman's shoulder.

"Well, first," I say, "we have to make sure that you do become queen—and your escape will have to come very soon. Tomorrow,

Unn, you'll have to do what you've been dreading."

"Oh dear!" Unn swallows like a startled chicken.

I want to smooth her fears away, but I must be sure she will not quail. "Be sure to tell Thomas that not only am I planning to spirit the princess away, but that we have already stolen away the dresses—which will be easy enough to convince them of."

Unn wrings her hands. "Oh, but lady, what if he doesn't believe me?! I'm not sure he'll trust my word that I would go against the princess."

"Well, I think the best thing is that you voice your concern for the princess getting hurt in an escape. Make that convincing and he'll believe you. He has to believe you—for all our sakes." I lay a gentle hand on her shoulder. "Remember Unn, if he suspects anything he'll punish you as well. And we can't afford that, my friend."

Unn sighs. "I know, I know. But I hate to think of everyone believing I'd betray the princess. Not possible. No, no, not in three lifetimes."

She is so good, I can hardly bear her pain. "That's why you have to be so convincing to Thomas. He's going to find it difficult to accept. You must believe your own words as you tell him, as if they were the truth."

"I know, I must. It is hard, lady." She sighs again, fumbling in her pockets.

Hallgerd lays a hand softly on her arm. "And you know, when I am queen you will be amply rewarded. This I vow."

"Pish posh! As if I needed for anything, my lady. No, no, I lack nothing in my life in the castle. Maybe a little extra rest now and then, which I can never get with that devilish Katla causing fresh disasters—"

Hallgerd hugs her friend warmly. "I'll have a comfy chair carved just for you from an old ash tree, with big soft cushions and a thick coverlet to keep your legs toasty."

"Thank you, my princess. It's more than I deserve, I'm sure, but welcome all the same. Now I'd better be on my way before I start weeping like the old woman I am. Good-bye. I will do what is necessary. But I wish to the gods I didn't have to." Her eyes seem to darken with the weight of this sorrow. How can we bring such suffering to those who love us most?

But I take her hand in mine. "Good night, Unn. I'm sure you'll still be able to see us tomorrow, when we shall be imprisoned. If not, good-bye my friend. We will all be together eventually. I swear by all my people swear by to make it so."

We embrace, uncertain of what the morning will bring, hoping against hope it will go according to our expectations. There is no way to know for sure. But I trust we have prepared well. It is difficult not to keep Unn here a little longer, to enjoy her pleasant company as I did on the long days and nights of exile, when she was my only link to life here in the castle. But the kindly old woman takes her leave, turning at the doorway for one last look at us both before continuing on her way, muttering of all the things she must do as if it were any other night. Hallgerd and I hang on each other, sobbing quietly.

It will be a long night.

Though we are expecting it, the clamor of the rushing soldiers awakens us to fright and we cower quite convincingly in the bed, though Siur courageously spits and hisses at them. The knot of soldiers parts and Thomas steps forward. His eyes blaze angrily. My spirits immediately rise. We have caught him by surprise! I am sure of it.

"Search the wardrobes!" Half a dozen of the men begin pawing through the beautiful clothes, unmindful of the way they tear through delicate fabrics, thoughts only on the hunt.

"Stop at once!" the princess demands.

The guards don't even pause. Thomas has been their only authority for far too long. When Hallgerd attempts to rise, two soldiers swing their halberds over her. She angrily crosses her arms and waits for the search to end. It does not take long. For a queen, Gunnhild was never all that interested in clothes. There are only the two wardrobes, huge though they may be. The searchers return to Thomas, shaking their heads.

"Where are they?" Thomas hisses.

"Gone," I say simply.

"Gone where?"

"Burned."

"You lie, Carae Mná, I know you too well. You would not destroy such beauty."

"Don't be too sure. They are presents wrongly given and therefore cursed. We are all safer now that they are gone."

He still doubts, rightly. "Then is it also true that you have plans to spirit away the princess? As if such a thing could be done, sheer madness."

"Well, as you declare it to be impossible, I should think you wouldn't worry about it. If it cannot be done, we shall not do it."

"And if it can—?" He glares at me, his face only a handspan from mine.

"We shall."

His eyes flash and I know he would like to strike me.

Hallgerd slips her hand over mine, the slight pressure of it conveying all her fear but I know it is important to push Thomas a little now.

But he does not wish his anger to be so clearly seen—and impotent. He turns away and brushes something undetectable off his arm. Looking out the window he commands, "Take them to the cells in the lowest level. Keep them separate! Your life may depend on it. This wily witch will see to that."

"Can we not dress?" the princess asks harshly. "Do not forget who I am—if only that I am the king's chosen bride."

Thomas barks an abbreviated laugh. "You would do well to think about who I am. You don't seem to realize that I am a very important and influential person in this land and that you owe deference to me. The king may be lovesick, but he will not take kindly to those who plot against him. There is still the code of warriors—even love cannot go against that."

Hallgerd laughs. To her credit, it sounds genuine. "Are not the legends of this land proof of just the opposite? You should spend more time with the bards."

Disgust radiates from his visage as Thomas turns to the soldiers. "Let them take their clothes. They can dress in the cells below. Do not let them talk or come near one another, on the harshest penalty! Do not test my wrath on this. You will be severely disappointed."

Hallgerd gathers up her clothes, surreptitiously scooting the walnut into the folds of her dress. Her sleight of hand is not seen. I fold my own dress carefully, so many useful things in its pockets. Will Thomas search me? Some necessities are carefully concealed, but many other helpful items are simply thrust deep into the pockets. I avoid his gaze and cloud my thoughts. Perhaps it will not occur to him.

But as the guards prepare to conduct us from the room, Thomas walks over to me and snatches the dress from my arms. I do not betray my anger as he shakes the garment and my herbs and amulets and gems and hairpins rain upon the floor. With an evil grin he hands it back to me. I take it without looking, my gaze holding his. "Burn these!" he barks to one of the guards, who begins to try to pick up the litter that has dropped.

"Can I at least keep the hairpins?" I ask, my voice haughty with irritation.

Thomas—Maldachta—narrows his eyes. "No. I don't think so. One never knows with you." He turns to the guards. "Beware this one, my friends. She may turn you into a newt if she so desires." Pointing to the items gathered in the soldier's hands, he continues, "These are her weapons, harmless though they may seem. She must not be allowed to have them. If you see her doing anything suspicious, inform me at once. Is that understood?"

"Yes, sir" they all agree, eyeing me nervously. Damn these superstitious folk! If only—

But it does not really matter. So far Thomas has done exactly what we predicted. He must have believed Unn enough to trust her word. Now to set the hook. "How did you find out our plans?"

His lip curls into a smile. "Your faithful servant, that dim-witted Unn."

"She shall be repaid for her work today," the princess promises fiercely—and, we hope, truthfully. We exchange looks that we hope appear to be grim. Unn, you have done your work well. Now if only everything else goes as smoothly.

We troop down to the lowest level of the castle. The walls feel cooler to the touch and little of the sun's light makes it to this place. Two doors stand open, one after the other. They were ready for our betrayal. How many occupants have perished here in recent years? These were formerly used for food storage in times of abundance and to ferment the mead after honey harvests. But the doors have been altered since that time, a peep-hole cut in the wood so that a keeper may watch his prisoner.

The guards force me into one cell, the princess into the one beyond it. The doors slam shut behind us and heavy bars ensure that they will stay that way. The cell is almost bare, the floor cold, hard clay. There is a wooden bench, a barrel of rain water, a chamber pot and a small window to the outside. Though high on the wall, it rests at ground level. A cat might slip through—but not a woman such as I. I slip my dress on, furtively feeling along the seams for the reassuring bulges. Still there!

As I try to braid my long locks into a manageable rope—cursing Thomas' spite—I cast my eyes around the dim cell. There is nothing else here at all—not even old grains of the harvest. The guards have been most thorough. Still, it will not matter if things continue to go as we have anticipated. It is unnerving though not to see my Hallgerd and be assured of her safety. My hair coiled and tucked around my head, I creep toward the peephole in the door to see what I can see.

The guards are still in the hall, though they circle around Thomas who gives them curt instructions, which I cannot quite hear. I take the chance to speak, hoping I too cannot be heard. "Hallgerd?"

"Nanna!"

"Shh! We have so little time—if I cannot get out when you do, head south, sleep high in the trees. They won't look there."

"Nanna, I—"

"No talking!" A club strikes my door, jangling my thoughts. The burly back of a guard completely blocks my slight view of the hallway. All is darkness and the muttering of the men outside. I sit on the bench and compose myself to wait for Thomas to decide to come speak with me, for our only hope now is that the king will insist on the marriage regardless of the treasons believed to have been wrought.

But it is nearly evening by the time I hear the voice of my nemesis in the corridor. His steps pause outside my door. Will he talk to me first? Or to the princess? Will I be able to convince him to treat the princess according to her rank—at least enough to make our plan work?

After a moment his steps continue on and I hear the door to the princess' cell swing open on its screaming hinges. I rush to the entrance of my own cell, but I cannot hear any of what transpires between them. A short time later, Thomas emerges with a curse and a crash behind him. Hastily, I step back into the darkness. The door to my cell is flung open and Thomas enters, a lantern in his hand.

"Well, well, well. Do you like prison better than exile? Or is it the more comfortable? Hmm? Cat got your tongue? Oh that's right, no cat down here is there? Hard to work without a familiar spying on everyone for you?" He sits down on the bench, completely at ease, a huge grin across his face. I know it is a sham, but I feel his confidence gnaw at my own.

"I do not care for myself, but the princess needs a servant. She is not accustomed to having to do for herself and—"

"The spoiled brat!" he breaks in. "She simply cannot conceive of what a situation she is in. Ordering people about as if she were still somebody. If it weren't for that addled king…" He makes a fist, then gets control of himself once more. "Ah well, the follies of kings must be borne by those who rule in their stead. It is a small price to pay."

"So the king still wishes to marry his betrothed?"

"Pah! Love is indeed blind—deaf and dumb too. He will not listen to reason. He is far madder than I'd even planned."

I stare at him. My wonder grows. "How can you be so cold, so cruel? That poor man!"

"What are they to me? Amusements, games. I killed your beloved queen—even better," he sneers, "I made you kill her. That was the real fun." Yet he sighs. He has become so entrenched in the business of this land; it is no longer just a game, much as he boasts.

I soften my tone. "Why bother? There are so many other worlds out there to amuse you. Why stay here?"

"To spite you, for one thing. The ancient enmity between our people makes I my duty to thwart your careful little home. Besides, it charms me to see you so troubled—though I must admit it is not much sport. Your fabled powers are nothing against mine. I can hardly credit the centuries of praise the daughters of Mná have received. Power! Ha—the weakness of women infuses their magic, too. I am not impressed."

"Do you forget the geiss? You have seen almost nothing of my powers for I cannot use them against your paltry magic."

"Paltry! My abilities have made me as good as king here." Thomas preens. "The fabled daughters have no right to be mentioned in the same breath as the sons of Bricriu. My triumph here will be added to our legends. We are conquerors of kings, while you are merely their servants. My exploits have assured my fame."

"And brought you much trouble besides. Why you have stayed here, I cannot fathom—surely there can be little to interest you in political maneuverings and such, unless you have become so much less energetic in your old age."

"I am still very young, why, much younger than you." He grins at my grey head.

"But we live longer. And you cannot hope to fool these people forever—already glimmerings of revolt spark in the farthest reaches of the realm."

Thomas waves these concerns away. "They cannot fight me. I have too much control."

"But you are tiring of the game."

Thomas stands. "Not enough to let it go, not yet. Not while you can still suffer. Or perhaps it would be simpler just to have you killed." The coldness of his threat kindles fear in my breast. How dangerous the scorned may be.

Yet I keep my voice even. "We shall see."

"The day of the wedding I think," he says as if from a daydream. "Your precious princess will be too busy to raise the alarm, and when she does—well, I think the king will not care too much. He'll be thinking of the wedding night."

"You are a foul one, Maldachta." I spit the words from my tongue like trail dust.

"Yes, I am." He yawns and turns toward the door. "These simple fools can keep an eye on you here. You'll get some food and your princess will get her royal attendant, but I'm afraid I don't trust you with a lantern after all. Who knows what magic you might work? You'll have to sit in the dark, old woman." The door creaks to a close behind him and my apprehension rises. I sink to the bench and cover my face in the dark.

The dawn's glow edges through my tiny window before I hear another sound. Light, hesitant steps creep down the corridor, as if alarmed by their own sound. Surely not Unn, but one of the maids to attend to the princess. At last our plans can continue—wait! Another step behind hers now, just as surely Maldachta's tread. Murmurings outside her door before it is unbolted. I am uncertain what transpires within and must wait to see when once more they emerge. A few steps echo and to my surprise, my door is opened almost at once and the evil one strides in.

"Morning, old one! You'll be pleased to know that I no longer wish to have you killed." Thomas sits himself comfortably on the bench next to me.

"Well, well, I hardly know what to say," I remark dryly, as if I had never feared such a thing happening.

"Truly! I have thought about how much more fun it will be to watch you suffer, year in and year out. Watch your precious little princess be crushed into submission with this unnatural marriage to a mad king. Watch your beloved land laid waste and its people starved and killed. Yes," he adds, stroking his chin, "I think it will amuse me greatly."

"You are easily enough amused."

Thomas glares. "Anything that causes pain to a daughter of Mná brings great joy to my heart."

"Does it? Why hate me so?"

"The sons of Bricriu have always hated your kind and always will. For centuries, your praises have been sung without reason, while the sons of Bricriu have been treated with distrust. Your evil ways always twist the stories and the songs from the time your grandmother's grandmother's grandmother first spited the great Bricriu."

I sigh. "What do you even know of the feud? Why was it begun? Who invoked the geiss?"

"Every child knows the story of the feast," Thomas spits out. "It was Mother Mná who turned Cú Roí into that monstrous hound and thwarted Bricriu's plans."

I laugh with surprise. "Only to stop Bricriu from turning all the great warriors of Ulster upon one another!"

"What a wonderful sight that must have been!" Thomas says with a genuine smile. "They Cú Chulainn killed fifty of his own men."

"That is the shame of Bricriu! How can one glory in such slaughter, the destruction of the best champions who ever lived?"

"Foolish woman. What does it matter? That magic is the power we all crave. Admitting to it is what makes me strong and you weak. Makes me hate you and you hate me."

"I do not hate you. I loathe you. I despise your hatred and cruelty. I will continue to fight your evil as long as I am able. But

84

you are not worth hate."

"Words, words, words! And people think Bricriu the weaver of useless utterances—it is you and your kind who babble on needlessly."

"Words have great power—great magic. The sons of Bricriu seem to only realize that in lies. There is much else words can do."

"Well, I have had enough of your words today, Mná," he says, wiping his hands and rising from the bench. "Your precious charge will be married tomorrow. Enjoy the anticipation."

A timid knock interrupts his words. Thomas crosses the cell and flings the door open. "Come in and care for this old bag of bones! She needs some tidying up." He smiles mockingly one last time at me and bows exclaiming, "Please, enjoy our hospitality, dear friend," and disappears chortling.

The maid enters, head bowed, and closes the door firmly behind her with her foot, carefully balancing the bowl and pitcher in her arms. She sets them down on the bench and only then throws back her hood.

It is my princess.

Silently we hug, but oh, so tightly. Though I can clearly see through the glamour that makes Hallgerd resemble young Thorgerd, few others should. Thomas is the only other one likely to see through my little trick, but as expected, he pays no attention to those he considers his inferiors.

"Thorgerd said she wanted only to help, but I'm so afraid for her," Hallgerd whispers. "Poor girl, she too is in danger now."

"She and her sister both wished to assist us. Unn said they drew straws to determine who could stand in for you. If you blew the dust on her, Thomas will recognize it for the glamour it creates. It may not keep him from punishing her, but perhaps he will not feel the need to kill her."

Tears well in the princess' eyes. "I could not bear that anyone should die for my sake."

"We may not be able to help such a thing. If it should come to that, let us make certain, at least, that no one dies in vain. We must restore you to the throne and rid this land of the evil one."

Hallgerd nods. "I guess this is the beginning of my responsibilities. They weigh very heavily. But I have an oath." She reaches into a pocket and pulls out the walnut. "The dresses, my cloak and the tokens from my mother are all safely stowed in this wondrous nut. I will protect them with my life."

"I know." I smile, feeling tears on my cheeks.

"Nanna, how will you join me? You assured me I would not be alone. I need your help."

"It may not be so easy. Once you are gone, Thomas will be very angry—there's no telling what he might do. But I will find a way to follow you, so keep to the plan; head south, sleep high in the trees. The farther you can get before morning, the better. They will track you as soon as the disappearance has been noticed."

"But how will you catch up with me? How will you be able to elude the soldiers?"

"Hush. I have a couple of possibilities up my sleeve, quite literally," I show her the bulges where they have been sewn into the hem. "I may not look like myself, but you shall know me. For now, you need not worry, but hurry on your way. You must get very far before the dawn and cross through the market square and as many streams as possible."

We hold one another for a long time, too long my feverish thoughts keep telling me. She must go. Though I fear for her safety, I know the princess is brave and wise beyond her few years. I kiss her hands. "Be safe, be careful, be watchful."

"I love you, Nanna. Let us be together again soon." Hallgerd's eyes are glittering with unshed tears, so I do my best to hold mine back too. A few steps to the door, one last look, and she is gone, her soft steps swiftly retreating into the silence, leaving me alone, quite alone, and I can hide my misery no longer and weep silently, steadily. Have I done what is best?

All the day I have left for lamentation and doubt. Have I condemned us all? Unn my faithful compatriot, young Thorgerd and her sister too; they have all been so willing to help, eager even. But I doubt my abilities, my plans. Perhaps Maldachta is right and I am only a foolish frightened old woman after all. It is so difficult to think reasonably when those one loves are in danger. My learning has been for healing and helping—now I must turn it to trickery and lies. Oh, I am no pure spirit of goodness. I have played tricks and told lies. But unlike my nemesis, I do not make a practice of it; I have not honed the skills. Yet, I must remember that our lives, most importantly the princess' life, depend on my ability to fool this Thomas and escape this dark cell.

The waiting proves most troublesome. When will he discover the switch? For her sake, morning will be best. Poor Thorgerd, waiting all this time to find out how the cruel one will react—he may ask for her head without a second glance. Poor Hallgerd, running through the woods, fleeing the land she has always known, fearing capture at every turn. I must join her as soon as I can, but that will not be easy.

At nightfall I slip my meager bowl of stew outside the small window, cursing my short frame. I can barely reach up high enough, even standing on the bench. I wait. One hour, almost two, then I hear a hesitant step. A wet black nose shines in the moonlight, sniffing suspiciously but boldly. A rusty red face peeps at me, his eyes black pools reflecting my face. I reach out my thoughts to speak to the fox. "You are safe here. Please eat my food. I'd like to barter with you."

He looks at me, curiously impassive, and continues to snuffle toward the bowl of stew. A dainty tongue flicks out. He seems to consider whether the taste is to his satisfaction. It is. He moves closer, eyes still on me. "I do not trust your breed," he says at last, inside my head. "You are always dangerous—never more so than when you seem to be kind."

"True enough. But I offer no tricks or traps tonight. Here are my hands, empty and harmless." I hold them up for him to see.

He sniffs the air. "Just the other day I was caught by several men in a giant spider web. They took a piece of my hide but I escaped." He turns his flank toward me so I can see the healing wound, keeping his gaze upon me.

"They were gathering fur for the princess' cloak—consider it a tribute. They chose you as the fox with the finest coat."

"Perhaps." He licks another taste from the bowl. "What do you wish to trade with me?"

"Your skin for mine," I tell him, adding hastily, "—only temporarily. While you are in here, you will be fed like this every day—no hunting."

"Hmph—and no running either."

"But comfortable sleep—fearless. Safe from enemies, the humans won't recognize you for what you are."

"How can I be sure? I do not trust your kind—for good reason."

"I understand. But I am no hunter—"

"You are an eater though, so someone hunts for you."

"Yes, you are right. But I need your help. What can I offer you? Food is all I can think of that I have and you would want. That and comfort from the cold. These I can offer you." A glimmer of hope stirs in me. "You can learn the ways of humans here too, understand how they are, how they think. Perhaps it will aid you and your family in eluding them."

The fox pulls a piece of meat from the bowl, daintily eating around the gristle. "Summer will be here soon enough, though it blows cold now."

"It will be cool down here. Why, it's the reason we store our food in these cells. It stays fresh."

The fox almost seems to smile. "Are you food, then?"

"No, but I am captive."

"And you want me to free you?"

"For a time. I must take care of my princess who escaped earlier. I cannot steal away as I am. I must be disguised."

"Your princess, she is the head of the den?"

"Yes, though there is a struggle for control with an evil human. She too would reward you greatly—she already owes you for your coat. You could ask her for any favor and she would grant it."

"I shall have to think it over," the fox says while carefully cleaning the bottom of the bowl. "Perhaps I will see you tomorrow." And with that he runs off, disappearing into the darkness almost immediately.

I sigh and reach for the bowl. Tonight I feel so old; must be all this stretching to reach the window. I rub my arms to ease the stiffness. Another dark night alone here. I have not felt so abandoned since the lonely days after my return from the Sithe, when I found that all my friends were old or dead—or worse, that they had forgotten me. It seemed I had passed only three days there, yet when I returned to the land above, many years had flown away. It was not until a child referred to me as "Old Woman" that I realized my hair had turned completely white. I was wretched indeed. Is it any wonder I let the men capture me for their slave ship? I wanted to be as far from that land as I could be, away from the absence of familiar faces and my memories of the other world. Of course, my exile has only fixed them permanently in my imagination, as I should have guessed.

Giving in to my melancholy, I sing myself to sleep with songs from the Sithe, whispering melodies of ethereal joys and empyreal sorrows. Tomorrow will come soon enough and it will be a trying day. Best to sleep now. I will need my strength.

9

"Stupid, stupid creatures!" Thomas' howls of rage wake me early on the wedding day. "How could you be so easily fooled?!"

I rush over to listen. I can hear the guards mumbling apologetically and Thorgerd crying. Thomas throws something across the small cell—a bottle, a bowl?—which smashes noisily into shards. A few of the men sidle out the door into the hallway, trying very hard not to look as if they are trying to escape his wrath.

"It was magic! It was magic!" Thorgerd screams. She fights for her life now. Will he believe her? I hear Thomas growl in response, then Thorgerd's voice again; halting, tearful, desperate. Surely he must see the powder, know the magic. Then he will come to me—and with luck, leave her be.

Something must have happened. In a flurry of confusion suddenly two guards pass by, a frightened and sobbing Thorgerd clutched tightly between them. She just has time to catch my eyes in the darkness and give a fleeting smile before her keepers wrench her arms painfully and carry her on to captivity.

I step back just in time to miss the heavy beamed door as it flies open and a very angry Maldachta charges in, his face a red blotch of anger.

"So clever, aren't you!" he snarls, spitting like a cat, his face less than a handspan from mine. "So damned clever! You will pay!"

I merely blink back. Careful, I remind myself, you don't want to make him so enraged that he kills you despite himself. I try to betray no emotion whatsoever. Anything could rile him.

He kicks the door, hissing his anger like steam from a fire. The remaining guards shift uneasily but wait for a command of some kind. Glowering at me, Thomas stalks back over. Quicker than I can see, his hand is at my throat.

"I hold your life in my hand, old woman. You seem to have forgotten that." He increases the pressure. "And it ends when I say, whenever I so wish it. Do you understand that?"

I do my best to nod my head without too much movement. His eyes are inhuman, full of the lust for killing, for death. I have no desire to be his revenge. His stare burns like a black thunderbolt and the thought comes to me that this is the closest I have been to death in a very long, long time. I have no time for death just now, though. There is too much to be done.

At last, the dark eyes regain some of their equanimity. Though he does not take his hand from my neck, it loosens ever so slightly. The nearly perpetual smirk returns to his lips. "But it wouldn't do to kill you, Carae Mná. I would lose so much entertainment—why, I wouldn't be able to watch you rot in this damp cell year after year as I crush your precious friends." The smirk twitches. "The Princess, however, could not have gotten far. Your little inconvenience is just that, an inconvenience. We shall track her down and bring her back and she will be wed today, make no mistake. If she is a little worse for wear, perhaps the king will not notice—it is not his first bride after all, and he is so besotted with her—if his wife is not untouched. I shall not give the soldiers any particular orders, I'm sure they can handle things in their own ways once the trackers have found her, which ought to be quite soon. She can't have been gone all that long, now can she, hmmm?" At last Thomas deigns to notice that he still grips my throat a little too tightly. With an impatient push, he shoves me backward and I stumble, half-landing on the bench.

My hand flies up to where his held me. I feel the indentations left by his fingers, and a ghost of their pressure lingers. Still, it is good not to be so near him, even if his fury has relented.

"You have sealed your fate, old woman, with that feeble glamour. A sprinkling of the fey dust—a modest charm, even by your standards. A pity it will be your last. You will never be free. Here is your grave." With a wave of a hand he indicates the walls of my cell. "Commune with your death and your gods—you'll have no other company. No maid, no friend, not even me, unless I am in the mood to torment you. Alone. You women need company. I know you suffer alone." He smiles and then just as suddenly frowns. "Get used to it. This is your life." He turns on his heel and strides out the door. I hardly flinch as it crashes shut.

I exhale the breath I do not realize I have been holding. The darkness gathers around me once more and I enjoy its quiet peace. The princess is away! If she follows the wise path, chances are with her that she shall not be caught. I must get away so I can help her. The fox—will he help me? I have tried to make life in the castle's cell seem luxurious, or at least easy. Food brought on a platter or in a bowl—what could seem more splendid to a creature who hunts every day for his food? But to convince any creature to relinquish freedom, ah, that's the difficulty. I'm not sure, if I were he, that I would ever do such a thing.

But there is nothing to do save wait until evening. Above me life in the castle goes on as it must—how many preparations were laid for the wedding? How is the king's great councilor handling the disappointment of his liege and the questions of all the rest? I have no way of knowing. When my food comes, I do not even glimpse the face of she who brings the dish. Furtive hands scoot it through the little panel in the bottom of the door without a word. I eat a little of its contents, saving the rest for bartering and meditating over what else I may have to offer the fox.

When at last evening comes, I have had no new ideas. I am not confident that the creature will agree to the trade. I can only hope. I tear the amethyst from my hem and hold it between my fingers. It may not help see the future just now, but at least it may sharpen my wits and hold evil thoughts away. I am comforted by its smooth coolness. Perhaps it is only the stone's soothing effect but I feel the future is hopeful, though I admit I see nothing clearly. Let it be so.

Darkness falls. I slip the dish out my tiny window, stretching to my full height and teetering on the bench. The gods help me if I should fall! I step back down with care. It will likely be some time before the fox returns—if he does. I cup my hand and drink a little water from the barrel. My nose wrinkles. Already it tastes a little brackish, like a still water pond. I have little assurance that anyone will care to change it, so I might as well get used to it.

Less than an hour has passed by my reckoning when I hear a soft bark at the window. The fox has returned! He noses a bit of fowl on the dish and tears some flesh off the bone. "Good food," he says licking his snout.

My spirits brighten at once. "You'll consider the trade, then?"

"Well," he says, worrying the bone clean, "I have faced many seasons in this land and evaded many a hunter. This is not the only scar I bear." He waves his head toward the missing patch on his haunches. "My mate died this winter and I am getting too old to look for another. Perhaps it would be pleasant to rest a while in safety."

"Oh thank you, thank you! You don't know what this means to me."

"I ask one thing, though. Before I left the castle last night I thought I heard a most glorious bird singing. I crept closer and found that it was you."

I blush. "I sang myself to sleep with songs from long ago, songs not known in this country."

He nods. "They reminded me—" his gaze grows thoughtful. "They reminded me of watching my first kits be born, when my mate—when we were both young and spirited. They were like the first smell of green buds under the snow. And like the terrible day I saw my mate fall in the drifts, only to be ripped apart by the dogs." He pauses, regarding me gravely. "They must be magic, I think, to make those moments return to me so clearly."

"They are."

He regards me a little apprehensively. "You are a woman of magic, then?"

"Yes."

"Like the male they say brings misery to all who dwell in this land?"

"No. He is my enemy. I would gladly bring about his demise."

"Is it he who captured you and holds you here?"

"Yes. He wishes to keep me alive so he can watch me—he imagines I suffer."

"Do you not?"

"I wish to be free to help the rightful princess of this land, who will restore it to balance when she has power. It is no great hardship to dwell here."

"Hmph—but no great joy either." The fox sits down, casting a look over his shoulder now and then. Can't be too careful. "If while in this cell, I can rip the evil one's throat out—"

I smile at the thought of my body doing such a thing. "I think you'll find my teeth are not entirely suited to such an endeavor." I show him my teeth.

"Well, one never knows. If I see the chance, I may take advantage of it."

"So you'll do it?"

"If you sing those songs to me again."

"I shall. Tonight and when I return, and every night after that if you care to hear them."

"Well, not every night. The grapes taste sweet because they fall but once a year. I should be ill if I ate them every day." He scratches his ruff with a hind paw. "What do you have to do to trade our skins?"

"I have an ointment. It will take me only a minute to prepare."

"Do so then, before I change my mind." He yawns. "And take the food back in. I shall want it when I am in your skin. So much bigger—it will need a lot of food."

I laugh and turn to my work. Chasing the pouch out of the hem—ah, hems! So useful, so invisible to men like Thomas—I pour its contents into the palm of my hand. After a moment's consideration, I scoop half back into the pouch and put it back on the bench. With my other hand I dip some water from the barrel and mix it into the powder, until the mixture becomes sticky. Using two fingers I spread some of the ointment in a circle on my forehead. I climb once more onto the bench and reach out the window to the fox who has been watching all my movements attentively. "Here, I need to put this on your forehead so we may exchange skins."

He sniffs at it and sneezes. "What's in that?"

"A great number of things, my friend, but we do not have time to go through the ingredients." He inclines his head cautiously toward me and I gingerly smear the mixture in a circle on his head above his eyes. "Give me your paw," I ask quietly, reaching my hand out the window as far as I can. As we touch I close my eyes and I feel the shock as if lightning courses through our bodies and bright lights burst and pop like shooting stars.

"Did it work?" I hear my own voice say, my vision clearing to reveal—me. I am looking at myself and I'm bewildered to see how tired and old and small I look in the darkened cell. I gasp as my eyes open and then flash wider in mute surprise, staring at me. "It did! My goodness, is that what I look like? I'm quite handsome still, I must say, a little grey here and there but not so old!" The fox looks out through my eyes then abruptly turns to look at his new self. "Dear me, I can hardly see in this murk. Your eyes aren't very good, woman. Mmm—that bird smells good though." He clambers down rather unsteadily, unaccustomed to the dimensions of this frame. He noses the bird, trying to figure out the best way to use his mouth.

"Here, you should sit like this," I say demonstrating as I balance on my haunches for a few seconds, before dropping my forelegs back to the ground. "And use your paws to eat—it'll look more human that way."

The fox considers this and flexes my hands in wonder. He reaches for the bird's wing and the dexterity of the fingers delights him. With great relish he chomps on the meat, tearing off pieces with ease. "Your teeth are not so good," he says between bites, "But these paws! They more than make up for it."

"One more thing—you need to hide that pouch again."

He picks it up and sniffs at it. "Hmph—your nose isn't all that good either. How do you creatures survive?"

Ignoring him, I continue, "Try to put it back in the hem—yes, there where I got it out—that's it, that's it. Good. That should keep it for a time anyway. I can always make more, but it would be easier to have some handy." I look up at the moon. "It is time I were going. I must be on my way and find the princess."

"All right. I hope I shall see you soon. I think this place will lose its charm. But do not forget—you must sing me one of your songs before you go."

I had forgotten. "Do you know which one you would like?"

"I do not know which is which. Sing one that will make me think of summer and warmth."

I sit down in my new skin and hum a little to test my new voice. Then, eyes closed, I sing the song of summer love from the Sithe, bright with its clever enchanting. Looking down into the cell when I finish, I see tears on the cheeks of the fox. He reaches up in surprise. "What is this water?"

"We call them tears. Whenever we feel more than words can

describe, they fall from our eyes—happy, sad, or sometimes both at once."

"Yes, yes, that is what it is. Who knew your kind were capable?" He wipes the tears with the back of my hand. "Thank you, thank you for the song. I look forward to your return for another reason now."

"I do not know how to guide you to live amongst my kind. You have my voice, my body. But I cannot pass my memories to you with any ease."

The fox shifts on the bench. "Must I know anything? I am caged. I can be silent. Or growl if need be."

I ponder this. "Well, there is one who will question you, the enemy of my people. He will not expect silence. Growls might confuse him. But I suppose if he thinks me mad, it will not be the worst thing." No, I think to myself, the worst thing would be his killing me with my spirit in exile.

The fox tilts my head at me. "You are worried."

"Indeed. But I do not know what advice to offer. Keep your wits about you seems needless advice for a wise creature like you, but it is all I have."

My chortle sounds the same coming from the fox. "My kind have earned a reputation for our cleverness for a reason. I will be wise."

There is nothing more I can offer except the obvious. "Good-bye and thank you."

"Good-bye!"

I run off into the night. Patches of late snow still lie on the ground here and there and I run through them exhilarated by the sharp coldness of it on my fur. Everywhere are scents! I can recognize many of them but not all. I can still smell the dampness of the dark cell, even the unevenly cooked fowl on the dish. The pungent aroma of the ointment overpowers my senses and I stop at one of the irregular piles of snow to wipe the bulk of it from my forehead. Better but still the scent lingers, amazing!

I scramble across the courtyard, fearless, easily, my four legs flying with the easy joy of it. It is difficult to pull my mind back to the task at hand. I want to run and run and run. I have not felt this energy for many a year, maybe not since childhood. And he called himself old! He does not know age yet. I admire the play of my muscles—musical!—and jump whenever I can, over bushes, over logs, over snow banks.

Skirting the village itself, I head out toward the south, casting around for the scent of the princess. It distresses me, though I am not surprised, to find that I pick up almost immediately the smell of the hunting dogs. They were tracking her after all, though surely since night fell they had to return and wait for morning light. I don't need it.

I follow the dog tracks for some time and finally, as the pack spreads out, beneath their odor I sniff the beautiful scent of lavender and rose—the princess! It is unmistakable. Unfortunately, the tracks of the hounds continue to follow her too. Surely, I scold myself, if they had captured her Thomas would have come to me to gloat. They cannot have caught her yet.

At the first stream I can see where she has waded downstream to try to throw the dogs off the scent. Many tracks line the banks in a wild riot of smells and confusion. But a trampled area shows that they found her trail again and hurried after it. Too bad. But my princess is wise. At the next stream, she wades even further though surely that night was very cold and she must have suffered for it after. I hope her mantel has kept her warm, a good gift to have and no mistake. But then I discover that the dogs eventually discovered her track far down the stream and made off once more in pursuit. Again I feel a stab of fear. Has she made it, is she still free?

At the third river, I lose her entirely. So too did the dogs. Footprints of the dogs and trackers wander for miles up and down the stream…and then turn back. They lost the trail! Hurrah! But now I realize that I have as well. And despite my initial elation, I am beginning to feel tired and cold. No warm fire to keep the chill away tonight. Where did she go? I wander up and down the river for some time. What should I do? Find a place to sleep and begin again in the morning? Ah, but the scent is already faint, perhaps it would be gone by then and if it should rain, ah, then what?

I sit down on the bank and curl my tail around my paws. It does help to warm them. I look around the banks of the river where I last smelled Hallgerd's scent. What did she do to foil her pursuers? It seems an unremarkable stretch of land, if anything the banks are rather steep and the trees are old and tall, their branches spreading across the sky, hiding the moon's new face. A glimmer of an idea pops into my head. I look up and down both sides of the brook. A ha! A likely one over there. I splash through the cold water, convincing my toes that this is essential work and that we will soon be with the princess and warm. On the opposite bank, I look up. Yes, with a desperate jump, she could have made it to that low-hanging branch. But how to tell? My body is much too small now to make such a leap. If only I could be sure—maybe? Is it only a wish furthering the hope that I catch a slight whiff of rose?

I walk around the mammoth tree which must be at least as old as I am. If she did climb up there, where did she go next? I look around to the big oak's neighbors. There—that one, surely. Not quite as huge, but sturdy, a low branch that she could easily have reached, intermingled with the oak's own branches. And from there? Nowhere to go but into that thicket of pines. Certainly though, they could not hold her weight, nor even mine, little creature that I am now - and yes! There! Broken branches and the lovely perfume of lavender and first roses. Clever girl!

Nose to the ground I run on along the trail, my energies restored both by elation and renewed fear. If I could figure out her path, no doubt the hunters might do so too. Best to find her tonight if I can, or tomorrow if I cannot. If we are lucky they will search up and down the river first, and only afterwards think of more unusual solutions.

More rivers, more confusion, more tricks from my princess but surely now I am gaining on her. She could not have run all night. She must have taken refuge some time as fatigue overwhelmed her, frightened as she must have been. Eventually, I find the place. I cannot reach it, high in a rough old tree, but with my new senses I can clearly smell the truth: a little tuft of fur from the cloak that kept her warm while she slept, the apple cores from her furtive meal, still wedged in the arms of the tree, and more faintly now, the perfume of her favourite flowers. A few hours, no more, she slept. Uncomfortable, I am sure, and no doubt, fitfully, but a little rest before she headed back out, risking the daylight.

And then? I cast around once more and find where she dropped from the high limb, the track much fresher than before. But now it is time for me to rest a little, before I go on. My legs are more tired than I can ever remember, though my heart beats evenly. I cannot help smiling to myself—I could not have gone so far nor so fast in my own body. I look around the small clearing for a place to hide and settle on a wildly chaotic growth of gorse. No one is likely to bother me beneath its protective spikes. Using both paws I dig into the soft ground, mercifully unfrozen, and uncover a few chewy roots. They are not very tasty, but they will provide me with enough energy to continue my search. My last thought before I fall to sleep is to wonder how the fox is enjoying my warm meal.

The dawn already throws its greeting across the dull grey sky when I awake from strange dreams. I try, as always, to run together their disparate threads before they unravel. I suspect they are not prophetic visions, but the attempts of my spirit to comprehend its new home. I stretch my four legs and attempt to shake off the dirt that has crept into my pelt. The roots have left my mouth bitter and dry. I lick some dew from the gorse leaves, but it does not begin to slake my thirst. For now, though, I must bear with it and return to the hunt.

Fortunately, my princess' track soon leads to yet another brook and I drink deeply—and not without difficulty. I am unaccustomed to lapping up the water. Though yesterday gave me some practice, it seems to take so very long to drink as much water as my need demands. How different to live in this skin— and a male one too, and ah, the youth of it! He spoke of himself as old. Yet so strong and hardy—but that is necessary for all wild things. I suppose if he weren't, he would be long dead. Such a difficult life. I hope he is enjoying the warmth of the cell, if not the cramped confinement.

But I must turn my thoughts back to the pursuit. The trail is colder now, but still fresher than it had been yesterday. Perhaps if I hurry I will be able to find her by dusk today. I do not like to think of her fending for herself so long, alone, though I must say I am very proud of the way she has managed. I smile inside to think that all those adventure stories I spun through the years have served a good purpose.

Nose to the ground, running through the snow and mud—for the sun has come out today, trying to bring the first hints of the new season—I follow her track, decipher her tricks and gain steadily. The trail gets fresher. She is tiring. I must catch up to her soon. She needs my protection. Her wiles have kept her far ahead of her pursuers, but a little magic would help even more. I worry so. But maybe I trouble too much—she has not needed me yet!

By the time night's twilight fingers stretch across the canopy of trees over my head, I have come close. By my nose, it would seem I am upon her—but she is still several leagues ahead. There is much mud here, further south than I have ever been in this land, if indeed we are still in the land of Hallgerd's foremothers. Easier to follow the trail—water fills each footstep—but slower to run through. My fur is caked with the heavy muck. Drying as I trot along, it makes me itch fiercely. I keep my hopes up for another river, where I can bathe away this grime. I almost laugh at the thought—some wild animal I am.

Abruptly, the trail ends. I anticipate the princess' usual subterfuge and look up to the trees above me. It is not long before I find traces of mud that reveal her hiding place. She had tried to wipe them away, but I know what I am looking for, so it is easier to see the well-disguised marks. I am so happy! I have caught up at last. In my excitement I bark, frightening a busy squirrel who gathers acorns nearby. I then try again to speak, struggle though it is to get this mouth and tongue to emit the speech of her land. "Hallgerd! Hallgerd!"

Nothing moves in the leaves above me.

"My dear, it is I. I have come to you." In the deepening dusk I can just barely make out stirrings in the tree above. She does not answer. Of course—she does not recognize my voice, so changed.

"My Princess! You will not know my skin. I come to you as a fox, he who gave up some of his pelt for your mantel. It was the only way I could get out of the cell." More stirrings above, slight sounds that might be only the whisper of leaves if I were not sure of the truth.

"Nanna?"

In my name I hear her fatigue and fear plainly. My girl! "It is I, though I do not look like myself."

"How can I trust you?" Despite the tiredness, I hear her resolute firmness.

I sit patiently, head tilted up to where I know she waits. "Perhaps if I told you a story? Hmm, let me see—how about Odd's journey to Permia?"

"Oh Nanna, it is you!" Her face, so pale in the shadows looks down at me, her smile radiant. "How did you find me? How did you become a fox? And are they chasing me still?"

"I found you with my nose, which is much keener now. I cannot begin to tell you how I changed skins with the fox and yes, they are still after you as far as I know and they will not likely quit until they are ready to face the wrath of Thomas."

"Let me come down—"

"No, dear, don't. You've got a good spot to hide. I will try to get up there with you."

"It is good! I think lightning must have hit this tree. It is all black and burned inside. The fire hollowed it out. But Nanna, how can you get up here?"

"I'm not sure. It is a long way." How high can I jump? Farther than I could before, yet I am so much smaller, it will not be as far as I need.

In the end, Hallgerd clambers down part way and I clamber up into her arms, half jumping, half clawing my way up. Hallgerd laughs and grabs the scruff of my neck—a convenient hold, though it gives me a rather strange sensation.

Presently we are snugly secured in the hollow of the tree, the mantel wrapped around us both. Soot covers Hallgerd's cheeks and her tears leave little paths in the black. I did not know that foxes really could cry too. I rub my face against hers and our tears and soot and mud mingle. Such a mess! But a happy one.

"You look so funny, Nanna. But how clever! I never knew one could do such a thing, but then what do I know of your magic, really? You have many tricks—where do you hide them? Up your sleeves?" She chuckles.

"I have no sleeves now, child," I return with my own laughter. "Nowhere to hide my herbs and roots and paraphernalia. But the knowledge is still there. And after all, I am sure the fox could use as much protection as possible while he dwells in my skin and my prison."

"What happened after I escaped? Is Thorgerd all right? When did you get away? Was Thomas furious?"

"Of course he was. He completely lost control for a while. But then he tried to make me believe it was nothing to him—though he vowed to let me rot until the end of my days in that cell while he destroyed the land around me."

"He must not! Now that I am free, I will stop him. He must be stopped." Hallgerd's eyes of sea-storm waves flashed in the dark nook, a promise of her retribution. "And if he has done anything to hurt Thorgerd—" She buries her face in her hands.

"Do not think of it. Until we are in a position to effect change, it is better. He did not immediately seek her death, that I do know. But as for what happened after I left…well, we have no way of knowing just now." I reach a paw up to her gentle face. The tough pads no doubt feel less comforting than my old finger tips, but I cannot think of another way to convey my sorrow and fear too. "We need to concentrate on what can be done and not be distracted by what sorrows we bear."

Hallgerd hugs me tightly. When at last she speaks again, her voice is rough and tired. "I know. But it is very hard."

We sit in silence for some time, safe in the black belly of the old, dead tree, exhaustion overwhelming us both. Tonight I have no strange dreams and awake only once, to the sound of Hallgerd's regular breathing and immediately fall back asleep once more. How very strange our lives have become—how changed. And this is only the beginning.

60

It is little past the first light when I hear a sound. At once my whole body is awake, hair bristling in response to the smells that come faintly, but unmistakably—men! And dogs! The whole of my heart cries out that it is impossible. Unless they have followed me and closely too. But surely not! No one knew what I would do, how I would escape—not even Thomas. I cannot believe I have somehow betrayed my princess through foolhardiness or blind confidence. But I cannot mistake what I smell, and now, hear too, so very faintly.

"What is it?" My alert tension has awakened Hallgerd, who senses my fear though not its cause.

"Men with dogs."

"Oh no—"

"It cannot be! They could not have tracked you so quickly—and listen! No, the sounds come from the south too." I relax immediately though I pitch my ears eagerly toward the sound. "Must be a hunting party. I believe we have passed into the next realm, the one to the south of yours. Perhaps it will pass us by. The dogs are in full cry. They must have already found their quarry."

"I hope so," says Hallgerd, wiggling a little to dispel the night's stiffness. "Shall we wait until we can no longer hear them?"

"I don't know. At present they seem to be headed in our direction."

"I hear nothing."

"My new ears are quite keen," I remind her, trying to find a way to smile. "But it is hard to smile."

Hallgerd laughs. "It looks rather like you're about to take a bite out of me."

"Never fear. I am still myself, changed though I may look.

103

Which makes me wonder yet again how the fox is doing in my skin."

"It must be difficult for him," Hallgerd muses. "How did you get him to agree to such a thing anyway? Especially to be cooped up in that dingy cell?"

"It wasn't easy. He was tempted by the food, but of course didn't want to give up his freedom, despite the warmth. But he heard me, by chance, sing the songs I know from the Sithe and asked me to sing them for him. That was a payment to which he could agree."

"The songs you only sing when you think I'm not around."

I nod. "They are not just songs, my dear. They are also forms of enchantment, with a great power, not to be taken lightly. They can have unexpected results. I did not mean to tempt the fox with them, but now he will have an endless appetite to hear them always."

"Perhaps that is why I long to hear them, and I cannot even recall any of the tunes."

"That is part of the enchantment—" I break off as I hear the sounds of the hunting party approach more closely. Several people, many dogs—horses too, I can hear now. They must have come quickly while we chatted.

And they're heading right for us.

"Can they have heard?" Hallgerd asks. Panic flashes in her eyes.

"No, surely not. They are chasing something, something that happens to be coming our way." I poke my snout out of the tree and sniff the air. "It's probably another fox—that seems to be the popular thing now. Either that or a hart. I cannot tell yet. But if they have that many dogs, it is large group of nobles, out for an entertaining day. Perhaps even the king of this realm." I pull back into the safety of the tree. "The young Prince of this realm—who has since probably become king—your mother once thought would likely be a good match for you, because he was the younger son and would be without his own realm."

Hallgerd wrinkles her nose. "Such foolishness. I need to take care of my own realm first. I have no time for princes."

"However, my dear, he may well be a good ally in your fight."

Hallgerd mulls this over. "But can we trust him? He does not know us. I may indeed be able to prove what I am, but that does not mean he will not consider it profitable to turn me over to the king—or to Thomas."

"True enough. I think we should be very careful."

"And we do not even know if it is he."

"But we shall find out very soon!" Indeed the baying hounds have come quite close and we can hear the stampede of the horses' hooves with remarkable clarity. The prey seems almost to be heading right toward us. In the riot of smells suddenly filling the forest, I can smell—a fox! In the very next moment I hear its labored breathing. It has been running for its life for some time. In no time at all, she runs past our tree and splashes through the nearby river and away. The dogs approach and halt momentarily, confused by the two tracks, raising a cacophony of howls and yelps. The first of the hunting party arrive on their heels, the shouts of the master of the hounds and the whistling of his riding crop adding to the hubbub. Some of the pack decide to pursue my scent and gather at the foot of our tree, crying the hunt's success.

I can see the party now. The men and a few women show all the wealth of this land, clothed in fine furs and silks from the Eastern world. The horses have glossy coats and their manes and tails are braided with gay ribbons. Such sumptuousness! It is far beyond the simple tastes of our realm, an ostentatious display that both dazzles and dismays me. What value will these people place in my poor princess?

"What is it, Karl?" a young man asks, his voice full of good humor. The forest green cloak around his shoulders does not cover the purple ribbon of royalty. "Have your hounds given up the game?"

"No, my liege. There are two trails." Despite the man's neutral tone, I could sense his hostility. All was not well in this court. This intrigues me. I turn my gaze back to the young man who must be the king—a very young king! He cannot be that much older than Hallgerd.

"Ah, and did one of them climb a tree?" Several voices join in the laughter. "Do we have a new race of flying foxes in the land?" The other nobles laugh and I feel disapproval form in my breast. What kind of king ridicules his servants? A very poor king indeed.

Beggars, however, cannot choose what horse they ride.

Karl clears his throat. "I have seen foxes to be surprisingly nimble, particularly when their lives are at stake."

"What will we do, Nanna?" Hallgerd whispers fiercely.

I whisper back, "I do not know, but I think it would be best at present to pretend you are no one important. We must get to know this king and his court before we can decide whether he is trustworthy."

"I suppose you're right. Let us hope—but he seems a rather foolish young man. I'm not sure that we will be able to trust him for much help."

The commotion reigns below. The hounds continue to bark, though now some of the hunters shout at them to be silent and the horses stamp skittishly. Laughter continues to peal across the clearing. Amusement seems to be primary interest of this lot.

The young king yanks on their reins of his restive mount. "Well, send one of the lads up there to look for our fox, Karl. The sun is getting rather high and we're going to lose the better part of the day standing here and staring at a tree."

"As you wish, Prince Mord," Karl answers stiffly. Prince? Hmm, so he is not king after all. There must be a story there. Things are not as I expected.

Karl points at one of the beaters, "You, Freawine, climb up there and be sharp about it. Don't get your nose bit off in the process." Some of the party keep the eager hounds under control while the chosen boy scrapes his way up the tree.

"Hold me close, so they do not risk a shot at me in their haste for the quarry," I whisper to Hallgerd, "and stand now."

Hallgerd clings to me and raises herself gingerly. Blinking in the bright sunshine, she speaks uncertainly. "Hello?"

A gasp flies from the towheaded youth, who by this time is nearly up to the hollow's entrance; it is at once echoed by those below, who crane their necks to see Hallgerd emerge.

The young prince laughs yet again, merrily and loudly. "Good heavens, Karl! What is this strangely-shaped creature your dogs have harried into this tree? Ah, but look! She does indeed have a fox with her—and mark well, my friends, mark well! No bow, no club—why she's caught him with her bare hands! Come Diana, join our little party and share your hunting lore with us poor mortals." The hunting party joins in the young prince's laughter.

The lad below us stretches out his hand to help Hallgerd step from the hollow of the tree. She clutches me tight. I catch only the briefest glimpse of the lords and ladies gathered below, arrayed in their bright hunting clothes, before Hallgerd turns and makes her slow way down the trunk of the tree behind the nimble youngster. Reaching the soft ground, the princess faces the curious crowd, chin in the air and arms wrapped possessively around me.

The prince grins. "Well, well, quite a wily prey we have caught today, eh friends? Pray tell, Karl, what do we call such a creature? Is this a wood nymph? I don't know that I've ever seen such a pelt as this!" The smiling prince reaches out to Hallgerd's mantel and strokes the soft fur.

I growl as menacingly as I can and he pulls his hand back nervously.

"Goodness! Perhaps we should let the huntsmen take care of that creature for you, little one." He smiles as if to an idiot child.

Hallgerd bristles. "Never! You shall not touch her—him!"

Fortunately, the young monarch finds amusement in this sharp girl. "Do you know whom you address, my fine lady?" He turns to the hunting party with a sizable grin. They take their cue and titter appreciatively as he continues to scold Hallgerd, who remains sullenly—and wisely—silent. "Why, I am a prince of this realm. You do not wish to displease royalty, now do you, my dear?"

Hallgerd takes another tack. "This fox saved my life. I owe it protection."

That really makes the prince guffaw. "Such a noble lady! Whom do I have the honor to address?"

"I am no one of any importance...your majesty," Hallgerd adds with distaste. I notice she casts a discerning eye over his attire, an excess of finery seldom seen in her more practical world. I feel a smile try to rise as I sense her disapproval.

"No one of importance? Yet you are dressed so well. I do not recognize the cut of your coat, but it is a very fine mantel—surely you come from a dukedom nearby? Perhaps to the south, where they get more of the sun?" He brushes a very pale hand against her soot-blackened cheek. A couple of the ladies shriek with laughter at that, waving their handkerchiefs at his recklessness in touching such a vagabond child.

"I am no one and nothing but a poor kitchen maid," Hallgerd replies through clenched teeth, "this cloak my only treasure."

"But what are you doing in the woods, child? So far from home?"

"I—I ran away," Hallgerd says and I see the gleam of the story-teller in her eye. Go with it, my girl!

"Ran away? Dear me!"

Hallgerd continues warming to her tale, "My parents wanted me to marry a warty old man and I couldn't bear it because he was so unkind. So I ran away—many days—until I was nearly captured by evil robbers, but this fox—he saved me…"

"How did he do that?" the prince asks with a curiosity that seems entirely genuine.

"He—he ran at them, barking and growling. They thought it was a wolf, I believe, and they were quite frightened."

The prince steps a little closer but keeps away from my muzzle. "And this fox? Why do you think it helped you, child? Do you enchant animals regularly?" More laughter from the lords and ladies follows this suggestion. The young monarch, however, seems entirely captivated by this strange little figure.

"No, I do not. But he is one of the animals whose pelt is sewn into this cloak so we have special bond. We must protect each other."

"Fascinating!" The prince's smile grows broad. "What shall we call you, my child?"

"They call me Pelzmantel for my coat of many furs," Hallgerd replies, burying her face in my fur.

"Well, little Pelzmantel, your story has touched my heart. Shall I rescue you from your woodlands adventure and give you shelter in my kitchen?" He chortles at his gallantry to one so unlikely, but notices his fine lords and ladies murmur restlessly now. "I know my cook can always use a good kitchen maid. Are you a hard worker?"

"Yes, your majesty."

The prince already walks away, seemingly bored with this novelty—or at least chastened by the scorn of his compatriots. "Well, if you can keep up with the horses, follow us back to the castle and I'll put you to work in the kitchen. Come, ladies, gentlemen! Let us return to the castle and enjoy the fruits of the hunt." They turn away from us and mount their fine horses.

"It will be quite a trick to keep up with them," I mutter.

"Still, it seems our best chance. We'd better go," Hallgerd whispers back. "Though, I must say, that young prince! What a frivolous, empty-headed, spoiled—"

"Less talk! More running, or we'll never catch them!" I jump from my princess' arms, ready to run. She follows, far more reluctant, but her long legs stride effortlessly along. Nonetheless, the riders soon widen the gap between us. I am glad, for the dogs are farther away. They want to rip me to pieces. Still, we need to keep them in sight, if we want to make it to their castle.

Fortunately, it is less than an hour before we are there. I am a short way ahead of my princess, to keep the hunting party in sight, and I see the castle first. Though it is much smaller than the castle of Hallgerd's family, it is far grander.

Everywhere gold shines. Ornaments of all kinds perch on the beams and stones of the edifice. Great sweeping windows of colored glass glint brightly in the sun's rays. Rich red carpets from the far eastern lands cover the entrance area where the lords and ladies of the hunt now gather. Servants pass amongst them with trays of food and horns of drink. Lavish tapestries depicting hunts and mythical beasts hang in the entrance to the great hall. Heorot itself could not have been more impressive, I think, remembering old Hrothgar's famous med hall. With that thought, I remember at last that I have been here before. So many years ago: was it in Hallgerd's grandmother's time? I try to dredge up something useful from memory. The castle had been grand even then, though not quite this ostentatious.

Hallgerd stands beside me now, dumbstruck by the sight as well. While I am taken by the magnificent opulence, my princess has another reaction.

"What ridiculous waste! Think of all the people such nonsense could have fed. So this is the kind of ruler he is, the kind of life he lives? Ha! I should have guessed. He's trifling and worthless and weak."

"He may also be our only hope," I counter sternly.

"No," Hallgerd says, "There is another."

"What is that?"

Hallgerd speaks her words in a rush of desperation. "We can go back, raise a rebellion, talk to the people, get them united against Thomas—"

"And his army? Don't forget, he has control of the soldiers of the realm. The people, however angry or resolved, cannot defeat a trained army. Would you ask them to do so?"

Hallgerd hangs her head. "No, Nanna." Her cloak has come unfastened with the effort of running and her face has picked up a rosy glow, barely visible under the sooty grime on her cheeks. She looks tired and petulant, angry but exhausted. She has lost so much in such a little time.

"Let us go to the castle, hide ourselves within its bustle of activity. Learn the way to this prince's heart so we can persuade him to help fight Thomas—without jeopardizing control of your land. It will do no good to win the land back only to lose it to our ally."

"You are right of course. But I resent putting our fates into the hands of such an unworthy supporter."

"Do not judge by appearances, my dear! Do not repeat his mistake, my little kitchen maid, Pelzmantel."

Hallgerd grins. "I think I shall like being called Pelzmantel. Suitable name for an adventurer like me." She sighs. "All right, let's go join the household. It is time I draw out 'all excellence' and become the finest kitchen maid this kingdom has ever seen." We trot off, approaching the fine castle and its happy commotion in front.

"Nanna, what should I call you? I can't very well call you 'Nanna.' I already have trouble referring to you as 'him' instead of 'her.'"

"I am a wild creature. I do not need a name. Fox will certainly do."

"Is it very strange to be a fox?"

"Yes, it is. So different to run on four legs rather than two—and to run! And to be male rather than female, so much to learn! His frame is much sturdier than my old woman's bones. I wonder how he is doing in that cell." But there is no time to pursue my musings. We stand at the bottom of the great steps, waiting for the ruler to notice us. It is some time before he does so. The great lords and ladies do not seem even to see us, just as they do not see the servants who bring their drink and food. It is only when the servants try to shoo us away—and Hallgerd refuses—that the prince notices the commotion and comes to see who causes it. He smiles at once in remembrance of his little adventure in the woods and pats Hallgerd's head. I see the anger seethe in her stormy-sea eyes but she restrains herself.

"Well, my little woodland creatures! You have followed us home. Skapti!" He waves to one of the servants making his way through the crowds. Skapti immediately steps over to his ruler and makes a quick bow, carefully balancing the over-laden tray of breads. "Take this little creature to the kitchen. She is our new scullery maid. I'm sure Grima will be glad of the help."

"Yes, your majesty." Another bow.

"But be careful, Skapti! She may bite." Laughing Prince Mord returns to his guests, leaving us to our next step. Hallgerd's eyes shoot daggers at his back.

Skapti, after allowing himself the indulgence of a look that takes in Hallgerd's disheveled hair and clothes as well as my sharp teeth with disapproval, motions for us to follow him. He leads us around the outside of the castle where we cross vast expanses of carefully tended plants and bushes, their keeping far more meticulous than the crops of the most dedicated farmer. So much effort is put into appearances here. Pleasing as the final result is, like my princess I cannot help but think of what better uses to which all this labor might have been put.

"Wait here," Skapti commands when we reach the kitchen area. He steps into the voluminous clouds of steam and smoke and disappears from sight. From within the fog we can hear shouts and curses and strange clanking noises.

"My goodness, such a state of things!" I whisper.

"Surely it's not supposed to be like this?" Hallgerd asks, who has only seen our small, neat kitchen in our little fortress on the edge of the Hundrada woods. I have no time to answer her as two figures suddenly emerge from the white haze.

"Here's your new maid, Grima—and her companion," Skapti sneers. "Prince Mord commands you to make use of them here in the kitchen. Do try not to poison them."

Grima appears to be close to my age—well, the age I appear to be—but with a haunted look of resentment that speaks of ill-treatment. Though of medium height, she stoops, a posture that suggests a battered spirit as much as an over-worked body. The tufts of her hair fly out from her head in different directions and her hands look roughly red from her work. There is something not quite right about the shape of her head and the colour of her eyes. She stares suspiciously at Hallgerd, then turns her gaze toward me. Her eyes widen in fear. "A wild animal! Shoo! Get away!"

"He's perfectly safe," Hallgerd says with calm authority. "Not to mention useful."

"Wild animal like that. Bound to kill us all in our sleep," Grima insists, her dark brows beetling with consternation. In all my years I don't know where I have ever seen a more homely woman, though her ugliness arises as much from her sour expression as her pained and pinched face.

"Nonsense," Hallgerd declares firmly. "And we're both here by the prince's order, you know."

Grima looks to Skapti, who merely shrugs and departs, leaving all debate to others. The woman sighs mournfully, pulls at the three big hairs on her chin and stares at me. "Rip our throats out during the night, no doubt about it." She casts a nervous glance at Hallgerd's face then returns her gaze to me. Finally she spits and turns, mumbling under her breath, "Probably all the better you do kill us in our sleep, out of this mess then, past worrying." She weaves her way through the billowing steam.

After a moment, when it becomes clear she will not be invited, Hallgerd forges her way into the kitchen and I follow at her heels. I have never seen a more disorganized kitchen. Unn would despair! She would also put it to rights in a twinkling. Ah, my friend, how I miss your cheery laugh...

"Well, if you want to make yourself useful," Grima's voice wanders out from somewhere in the mists, "we need half a dozen chickens from the yard to boil for the dinner. Sure enough this venison won't go far enough, the way they eat. Ladies, hah! Not when you see them at table." The rest of her words trail off into indistinct murmurings of sound.

"Here's where you win her over," Hallgerd smiles down to me. "Surely a fox can catch chickens."

I nod and head out into the yard. Such a relief to get out of that stuffy place! The fowl are easy to find, wandering around the less-well-kept grounds behind the castle, scratching at the earth. Of course my bright fur warns them of danger, but I am too quick for them. I bring my first victim back to the kitchen, head held high. Weaving through the watery mists I bring the prize to Hallgerd, who immediately calls out to Grima.

"See what my pet can do?"

The old woman turns and her eyes bulge. "A fox in the chickens! A fox in the chickens!" She grabs a large wooden spoon and shakes it at me.

Hallgerd laughs. "I told him to catch some chickens for us." She takes the hapless fowl from me. "Go get some more!"

I run off, hearing Grima grumble behind me, something about dangerous animals and cooking not mixing. But by the time I have caught all the chickens she needs, I sense a grudging acceptance though certainly no trust.

Hallgerd has it much worse. Though she has been accustomed to helping me with the daily chores of our existence, it hardly prepared her for work in a busy castle kitchen. She draws the water from the rain-barrels, stokes the fires, sweeps the ashes, chops the vegetables, grinds the herbs (the few that there are—I sniff the air and disapprove—and all the wrong ones too) while Grima looks on, grumbling and growling, "The dinner will be ruined, no doubt about that, new help—never any good, train them for years and what do they do, leave you without so much as a by-your-leave, and bring vicious animals into the kitchen, like as not kill us all in our sleep…" She stays far from me and catches up her voluminous skirts protectively if I should come too close.

Evening's cloak has wrapped itself around the castle by the time the bustle in the kitchen slows to near silence. Most of the steaming clouds have departed and we can see one another again, even across the room. Hallgerd throws heavy logs into the cooking stoves. They ought to burn until morning.

"Well, I haven't much choice but to keep you," Grima sighs, "though the gods know I will most likely die in the night attacked by that savage beast of yours." She jabs a finger toward the Princess' chest. "Mind you don't let that hairy thing run round here at night. I find one dropping—just one, mind you—and I'll have to throw you both out or else everyone will lose their appetite. Can't have Prince Mord eating spoiled food."

"Don't worry, madam. My fox is very smart—and fastidious too."

Grima narrows one eye with suspicion. "Well, he may be fast enough to catch the hens, I don't deny it. There better not be too many disappearing in the night, though, in the dark when I'm not watching."

Hallgerd steals a look at me, hiding her smile from the cook who mutters on.

"Now, since the prince is so eager to risk our life and limb here, I have to put up with you, but you'll stay here in the kitchens. I don't want to find you wandering about in the castle. You'll frighten the good gentle people." She points to a shadowy corner. "There, under the stairs to the great hall, there's a little closet. You can stay there with your filthy animal. Mind you keep it clean, too," she continues, wagging a threatening finger at the Princess. "Not that it'll do any good. Fox hairs in soup now. The prince'll have my head, no doubt. Not that he's happy with anything, when he takes the time to notice it. Complain, complain! Why I bother—" But Grima is already off, trudging her way up the stairs to the accompaniment of her own grumbling chorus.

"Well, I guess that passes for welcome in this land," Hallgerd says lightly, a wry smile on her face. "Shall we go examine our new sleeping quarters?" She lights a small candle from the stove and, guarding its tiny flame with her hand, leads the way to the closet. It seems to have fallen into disuse; cobwebs obscure its outlines and Hallgerd cannot easily open the door, but has to set the candle down and seize the handle with both hands as I stand by helplessly. On the third try, it groans open—protesting almost as much as Grima—and we peer into its darker shadows.

"Home," Hallgerd laughs but she no longer smiles. The candle's slight light shows two empty barrels, each with some ribs missing. Hallgerd drips wax onto the more sturdy of the two and sets the candle firmly and sighs. She goes back to get her coat—discarded early in her duties in the hot kitchen—and I sniff around the small room. It has not been used for many a year and is barely large enough for the two of us to sleep in. I guess it's a good thing I am so small now.

"We can lie on this," Hallgerd says as she shakes the coat, laying it on the floor of the closet. "I'm so tired. Grima will have a hard time waking me in the morning." She lies down on the soft furs after checking her pocket for the precious walnut. "How awful not even to wash my face—I know it's quite black with soot—and the heat here could only have made it worse." She sighs. "No matter. It—it adds to my disguise"

"At least we are not running through the woods, afraid of the hunters and trackers."

"True enough," Hallgerd admits, "but I do not know how much better off we are." In the dim flickering light I can see tears roll down her dirty cheeks, leaving trails behind. "I wish we were home. I wish—I wish I knew for sure that Thorgerd is all right. I wish I were in my own bed and Siur were curled in a ball next to my head." More tears, too many to count. I put my paw out to her and she clutches it tightly. "I'm sorry, Nanna. I know I should be brave, be strong, think about the good of my people and not the state of my face."

"My dear one, there is only so much even you can bear in one day."

Hallgerd sniffles. "Tonight I will cry. Tomorrow, I will be a Princess again, but right now I am just a sad little girl, far from home, tired, dirty and afraid." She covers her eyes and weeps aloud. I lay my head on her chest and let my own tears fall.

ᚠᚠ

In the morning, Grima's grouchy complaints awake me early, but I let Hallgerd sleep on. I push the door open with my snout and slip through. Sniffing the air has become habit now—it tells me much. Grima has already lit the fire. The morning fog still lingers outside and the chickens have only begun to stir. Though the breeze drifts through, leaving cold fingers in its wake, the sun will come out today. The first signs of summer have gained a foothold and will not be shaken. I need to gather fresh herbs.

I scurry between the cupboards and out of the kitchen. It is good to be in the light and away from the sour smells of past meals and sweaty workers. Despite yesterday's exertion my lithe frame stretches smoothly as I bound across the clearing, waking the frightened chickens, who cluck their disapproval. My belly gets wet from the dew, my legs too. With a bark of pure joy, I decide to throw myself down and roll in the grass. It feels so good! Poor Hallgerd—if only she could bathe this way. I shake the dew from my fur and the droplets explode into a rainbow of colors in the early morning light. Tears in the evening, bliss in the morning—our hearts have amazing resiliency. Now—to work. I must find some spear leeks if nothing else. With luck I shall find more.

My luck abides with me. Some laurel leaves will help Grima's soup to great effect. A little fennel here and there will make her dishes palatable. The only difficulty is carrying all the herbs. All I have is my mouth and I try not to bruise them, but I can taste their blooming spirits. I must find a little basket I can use to carry the delicious plants. If only I had my mortar and pestle! I have not seen any in Grima's cluttered kitchen—such a staple! She must not have come to cooking with any will—or skill. Hallgerd and I shall help her, whether she wishes it or not. I need these herbs for

116

other reasons, too.

When I return to the kitchen, all is clamorous again. Steam has already begun to rise and Grima's shouts and curses echo in the darkened hall.

"Pelzmantel! Where is that wood?! The fire is going out and we'll never get the embers started again. By all the gods, child, move your bones or I'll give you what-for!" She waves a wooden spoon around for good measure, while a pot behind her boils over, bringing a fresh cry of alarm.

Hallgerd runs in, her face blushing pink, and unceremoniously dumps an armload of kindling into the stove. The clatter of the wood on the stove almost drowns out her irritated exhalation of breath, but Grima hears it and chides her further.

"You should be lucky the Prince took a likin' to you or you'd be out in the woods now, starved or eaten no doubt. There's bears in the woods, they come and get you and they don't leave anything behind. Now stir this pot while I make the biscuits and don't let it boil over again or we'll be hearing of it."

When Grima turns her back, grumbling, I tap Hallgerd's leg with my paw and she looks down and smiles. "Good morning, Nanna. I see you've been busy too." She bends down to take the herbs from my mouth. "Mmm! Fennel! Just what this needs," she crushes the tender leaves and drops them into the pot. "And spear leeks! My favorite—this will improve things quite a bit."

"Save the laurels for the soup tonight. You'll be appreciated by the guests if not by our surly cook."

Hallgerd smothers a laugh and lowers her voice further. "I think she puts salt in everything. Imagine!"

"Sure sign of a bad cook. My goodness, it takes all my herbs to get the salty taste out of the winter stores."

"They must go through an incredible amount of ale— especially if last night is any indicator. Three empty barrels! I guess they needed something to wash down the food."

"Pelzmantel! Are you watching that pot?!" Grima eyes her suspiciously from the far end of the kitchen, white up to her elbows with flour, a few misshapen loafs encircling her bread-making mound.

"Yes, ma'am," Hallgerd answers brightly. "I feel like poor Aschenputtel," she says more quietly to me, "and Grima is both my evil sisters." Her smile is wry and I feel a stab of sadness and doubt.

"Who are you talking to, child?" Grima asks irritably.

"My fox," Hallgerd shouts back.

Grima jerks unpleasantly. "All the lords and ladies—must you have that filthy beast in here?" She stomps over to glower at me.

"Look, he brought herbs for the cooking. Clever little thing, isn't he?" The Princess grants her most appealing smile.

Grima sniffs suspiciously at the fennel, one mismatched eye on me. "Don't want to find you've gone and poisoned the Prince. It'll be my head as well as yours. Not a thing I want to part with, you hear me, child?"

"Yes ma'am," Hallgerd answers dutifully, hiding her smile with a bowed head and stirring the pot carefully. Grima takes a spray of fennel and chews it slowly, ready to spit the weed out. "The seeds are the best part," Hallgerd adds brightly without looking up from her duty, "And it keeps evil away." She sneaks a look at me. "Good for digestion too, to keep you from getting windy."

Grima chews and finally swallows. "Well, we'll see if I live until midday…" she says, but does not forbid Hallgerd to use it. She looks from the Princess to me and back again. "I can't really decide," she says at last, shaking her head in sorrow, "Are you a blessing or a curse?" Hallgerd smiles in return and I try to wag my tail. "No doubt I'll be losing my head directly. Bread won't rise right, funny smells in the sauce, and big red hairs in the soup too." She frowns down at me but then turns and stomps back to her bread-making, muttering all the while, "Relief when it comes really, no more worrying, head off, nothing more to trouble me."

Once the cook is out of earshot, I say to Hallgerd, "I need a basket so I can carry more and not bruise the leaves so much It is difficult to be without the use of my hands, I must say."

"Want to trade?" Hallgerd asks, wiping her beaded brow, but smiling. "Have you ever had to do cooking on such a scale? I can't imagine how it all can get done."

I sigh. "Grima needs more help. This realm is certainly prosperous enough. There is no end of idle lords and ladies—yet so few servants. Badly managed."

"I could just hear Unn, faced with this mess. How she'd scold!"

"And set to work," I add nodding. "She'd have this place humming in no time—be out rounding up youngsters to help out and learn the skills."

Hallgerd stirs the pot thoughtfully. "Do you suppose Grima can't do that? Or won't?"

"We need to find out. If the prince forbids her, we must know his reasons. It is the only way we can begin to figure out how to make him help us."

Now it's Hallgerd's turn to sigh. "Must we? He doesn't seem at all likely to help or—nor does he seem likely to be of much assistance. Silly, spoiled young man."

"Nonetheless, we don't have that many options. It is a long way to the next realm—and our prospects there are no more certain."

So, we must spoil him further with good food?" Hallgerd sulks but goes about her work efficiently, turning now to chop vegetables with a sharply-honed knife.

"Perhaps it is the best way to win him over," I argue in my most agreeable tone. "Good food calms a wild spirit."

"I thought that was music," Hallgerd says, but the crossness is only in the words and she hums to herself while dicing the turnips.

I leave her be. I need to look into a few things. We need to find out a lot more about this realm.

I was here before, long ago, during the reign of this one's grandfather. Some kind of festival was going on—whatever might it have been? Ah, the vagaries of memory, that most untrustworthy faculty. The castle was not nearly so grand then, that I do remember, nor were its people. Fun-loving to be sure, like people anywhere at a celebration, in their new clothes, eating special treats. What was it? A wedding, maybe? A coronation? Why indeed was I there, when I usually stayed at home? No matter.

As I run quietly through the corridors toward the big hall, I see one or two things that might be from long ago—a large tapestry of a great battle, a great set of golden horns carved with runes of charm and portent. But most of the items I see are new, gaudy and carelessly strewn without regard. Who maintains the order of the castle? Where are the staff?

I hear the rumble of the great hall before I reach it. Wild songs echo down the room to me, and a ragtag assemblage of musicians tries to keep pace with the drunken singers. Raucous conversations go on in every direction, voices raised in joy and in anger. Just as I am about to reach the entrance, I flatten myself against the wall to let a trio of servants pass, heading to the kitchen to collect the next meal from Grima. They look exhausted and speak bitterly of the lords and ladies they serve.

Peering around the corner of the doorway, I see the feast that has gone on for some time. The smell is overwhelming, especially to my fox's nose. It does not seem to bother the fine crowd who gather here that food well-past its prime litters their tables with a pungent ripeness. Their merriment rings from wall to wall, unchecked, the din of a hundred shouted conversations.

Two women talk together, more quietly than their neighbors and with frequent, secretive looks at the head table where Mord laughs and shouts. Here, surely, I will find news of the castle's keep. I wiggle between the legs of people and tables, unseen it seems by all, to catch the drift of their conversation.

"They ought to have figured out by now they'll do no good," hisses a woman in green silks, her eye spitting venom at the usurpers around the prince. "He may flirt and smile, but he will not go against the prophecy."

A woman caped in brown fur nods a quick assent, watching the two finely-robed women on either side of Mord try to feed the prince some dainty morsels from their fingertips, their reddened lips twisting in carnivorous laughter. "I've seen plowherds more decorous!" she growls.

"If not for the prophecy, he surely would have married me," grumbles the first woman into her cup. "I've got the hips of a real queen."

Her friend slams down her own cup. "Not after the way he always looked at me, why last Oimelc—"

"Last Oimelc was a year ago, my dear," the first reminds her friend bitterly. "He has forgotten us now."

"Curse the heartless!"

"Well, at least they'll get their turn in sorrow too, make no mistake about it." A malicious grin lights her face briefly. Upending her cup, her friend makes no reply and they both sink into silence.

A useful bit of information, that—what could this prophecy be? That should be no trouble to find out soon. I hope for other useful snippets as I wind around the revelers' benches, but there is little talk other than of last night's pleasures or today's carousing. Here, I dodge a spilled cup of ale—there, a leg of fowl thrown to emphasize a point. Such waste! How my Queen would blanch; my Princess too. I shall probably not mention it to her, as she will no doubt—

Oof! A rough arm scoops me up and drops me on the table before the prince. "Here's your wily opponent, my lord," Karl guffaws, "Shall we make him run for us again today?"

Prince Mord laughs in reply, one arm flung around the shoulders of the young woman on his right, the other hoisting a carved drinking horn aloft. "Now, now, Karl, let's not forget that this fox has magical qualities—or so its charming keeper thinks." His cheeks swell with laughter and ale, and his companions join in twittering. "Tell us the future, Mr. Fox! Give us a prediction!" The nobles nearby join the ruckus, shouting likewise "Tell our fortune! Read the future!"

I sit before the prince and look up at his face. Swollen as it is with drink and too much food, it yet has a kindly aura—it shows the man he still might be. He has indeed been spoiled as Hallgerd so rightly complains. But he must not have been always so.

"Ah, the creature is dumb, of course. Magic cannot give it the power of speech."

"Aye," says Karl, "But it understands us, I think. See how it marks our words and attends to the speaker."

"Ask it a question," suggests the disheveled young woman to the prince's left. "Perhaps it will devise a way to answer."

The prince considers this. "Hmm—tell me, magic beast, is my future consort in this room today?" Everyone laughs but the two women at his side, who both find somewhere else to look in their discomfort. I make a show of turning to look around the room quite carefully, conscious of the attention upon me. As my gaze travels around the tables, an uncomfortable silence follows in its wake. Hope and distress flare in the eyes that I meet. I consider my best course.

Returning my gaze to meet the prince's, I gravely shake my

head 'no.' Behind me I hear furtive whispers, but Prince Mord refuses to be concerned. He laughs with gusto and admonishes the woman on his right to "Beware the wild predictions of woodland creatures." She seems not to be amused however, sulking over her empty cup. Her counterpart on his left presses her lips into a thin line, her eyes brimming with unshed tears.

"Well, then Mr. Fox," the prince continues, unmindful of his callousness, "Tell me, shall I meet her soon?" A handful of his nobles titter appreciatively. All lean forward to catch my reply. I stare up at the arched ceiling for a moment—I cannot resist delaying the suspense—then nod three times in quick succession.

At once the hall reverberates with the many breathless comments. Who could she be? When will she come? How will he know her? Only the prince is silent. He regards me curiously, weighing the truth of my prediction. His smile now glimmers, eager and shy—he believes.

"Perhaps at the next midnight dance," calls an older nobleman, a crafty grin on his face. No doubt he has a daughter or cousin that he has not yet introduced to the monarch.

Others join the speculation. "Surely, the dance!" shouts another, enthusiastically waving his leg of hart in agreement.

"Yes, when the minstrels return, she will come."

"Don't be foolish—it's only a fox," gripes the woman in green silks.

"I'll bring my sister to the dance—a fine fresh lass she is."

"What, that lumpy little girl-child marry the Prince?! Why he's more likely to marry my mother though she's blind in one eye and gimpy as a log-hauler."

"Fie on you, Thorstein! I'll teach you to make fun of my sister—"

"Pipe down, youngster. Have another mug of ale…"

I take advantage of the confusion to jump down from the table and slip away down the hall. The arrival of Skapti and the other servants, laden with trays of further dainties helps to distract them even more as the horde vie with each other for the choicest morsels. What a scene! So much bounty wasted on excess, while the castle molders unkempt around their banquet.

Returning to the kitchen, I find both Hallgerd and Grima bent over their tasks. The old cook springs back and forth between her loaves baking in the oven and the pies she shapes on her counter. Hallgerd busily stuffs spear leeks into a large roast, rubbing the pungent cloves all over the rough surface, turning to stir slowly a large kettle of gravy beside her. The kitchen smells so much better today!

I tap Hallgerd's leg as she stops to wipe her brow. She smiles down at me immediately. "Hello, Nanna!" She glances quickly at Grima but she seems to have heard nothing. "How much better the kitchen is already! This roast will make their mouths water."

"I found out some useful things, my dear."

"Anything that will get us away from here?" Hallgerd asks as she stirs the gravy, sniffing it with care, then reaching for some laurel leaves.

"There is some kind of prophecy about the prince's marriage, something that hinders his choice—or at least the plans of others," I add, thinking of the two unhappy women. "We must find out what it is. Grima should probably know."

"Perhaps—do nobles confide in their cook? I've yet to see any of them step down here. Who manages this castle?" Hallgerd lashes the roast to a small spit and places it over the cooking fire. "So much waste! No one seems to keep track of the stores but Grima—and she only notices when she has nothing left."

"It is very haphazard. Perhaps Skapti is in charge—he seems the one most ordered about by the prince."

"Perhaps his is the only name the prince knows. Imagine!" Hallgerd shakes her head in disbelief. "You are so right Nanna. I remember how you always told me that we each need some occupation, to make some contribution. Idleness must be as tedious as too much work. I cannot imagine such a waste of time. How long will he reign surrounded by such chaos?"

"Not for long. It may be that the prophecy has something to do with it. It does almost seem as if he is avoiding something."

"I expect Grima shall know—we just need to find the right time to approach her. After her pies are done—or later. Though I fear to wait until she is too tired. No doubt she collapses in exhaustion every night. She really should have a bigger staff."

I smile to myself at this. My princess has learned her work well. But has she learned strategy? "I made a prophecy, too."

"What?" Hallgerd looks down from her spitting roast. "A

prophecy?"

"Yes, the prince saw me when I was eavesdropping and made me answer questions for him, as I am a magic beast."

"Oh Nanna, what did you say?"

"He asked if the woman he would marry were in the room. I said no."

"I bet that made you unpopular with a lot of noble ladies," Hallgerd chuckles.

"Oh yes. But I also said he should meet her soon."

Hallgerd turns at once and addresses me, hands on her hips. "Oh dear, Nanna, you're not thinking—"

"Why not? If you intrigue him, he may desire to help us."

"Intrigue him? Intrigue him? I'd sooner have the itch!"

"Often sacrifices must be made: 'To love and protect—'"

"And be at its command.' I know, I know," Hallgerd jumps as the fat from the roast pops loudly in the fire. "This is not what I had imagined would be necessary to protect the land. You're telling me to act as bait. Bait! I hate the idea of being a trap."

"Better live bait than a dead princess—and a lost realm. Besides, it will be chance to wear your lovely dresses."

Hallgerd laughs out loud at this. "So, like a child playing dress-up, I am tempted with grown-up finery? What's next? I get to stay up to see the moon rise?" Hallgerd chuckles into the gravy pot and stirs the thickening sauce.

"You are very close. Apparently they have midnight dances—I have heard it done—around the full moon. The nobles were saying the minstrels return then. I can imagine this court lavishes rewards upon them that make their travels worthwhile."

"How shall I get away from Grima? Surely she will not allow—"

"Pelzmantel!" We both jump at the old woman's sharp voice, suddenly behind us. A dusting of flour clouds her apron, and her hands are raw and red from the work. Grima's eyes quiver, bloodshot, and the three hairs on her chin waft slightly in the billowing heat from the roast. "Jabbering with that animal of yours again? Hair in the gravy, mark my words. Heads chopped off the next morning. You know what happened to the last cook?"

Hallgerd meekly meets her gaze, "No ma'am."

"Dead!" Grima blinks in righteous dismay. "Not drawn and quartered, mind you, not that. I should be so lucky."

"Dear me! How did she die?"

"He!" Grima corrects her.

"How did he die?" Hallgerd asks, chastened.

"How should I know?!" Grima says her lips bunched up in an unpleasant knot. "But dead is dead! And I don't want to be killed dead, young lady. I'll not have you be the cause of my too-early demise. Hair in the soup! Why, he was but four and twenty, much too young, much too young." She shakes her head with disapproval of such promise lost.

"Ah, but surely he was much older than you, Grima," my Princess says innocently into her gravy.

"Older than me!" She narrows her eyes, weighing the question's intent. "Older? No, no—not older. Thirty-two winters I've lived, all of them hard."

"Thirty-two! Surely not," Hallgerd turns to her mistress, her eyes as wide as any young fawn's. "Why, it must be the good cooking."

"The good cooking?" Grima glares suspiciously.

"That keeps you so hale and hearty. My goodness, thirty-two winters. No wonder you are so wise too."

I can barely keep back a bark of laughter at my naughty princess' teasing, but her expression remains free of guile. Thirty two winters! I would have thought her twice those years. They have not been kind ones. It moves me to pity.

Grima considers this unexpected compliment. "I know a thing or two, missy. A hard life teaches you much." Knowingly, Grima taps her nose with her finger. "That's why I've survived so long here. That and my good cooking."

I cannot help it; I bark with laughter and Grima jumps nervously into the air, while Hallgerd spins hastily to hide her smile, carefully turning her roast on its spit.

"We need water," Grima sputters, uncertain whether to trust Hallgerd or not. "The rain-barrels are empty—a bad sign that, hasn't happened for years—you'll have to go all the way down to the stream, round to the south of the castle, beyond the tournament grounds."

"Yes, Grima," Hallgerd murmurs, setting the gravy off the fire and positioning the roast just right over the crackling lick of the flames.

"The pole and buckets are in the corner." Grima points to the spot, once more in command. "Perhaps your little pet can carry some water too."

With Grima's eyes glaring into our backs, we go about our task. Hallgerd picks two sturdy poles and checks the buckets for possible leakiness. "Here, Nanna, here's a little bucket." She looks over at Grima but the pie-making once more absorbs the woman's attention. "It won't carry much water, but if we come across some useful herbs…" I clench the offered handle between my teeth and we set off.

Despite the last winter chill—not all that long until the Beltane fires will burn, back in the land of my birth—the promise of summer to come helps us have a pleasant walk to the stream, though it will be less so trudging back with the buckets filled. But for now, myriad birds brighten the winds with their joyous colors and their blissful songs, as if the fresh air weren't enough itself after the steam and heat of the kitchen. Hallgerd grins, again the smile of a young woman who responds to the newly-budding life all around her and to the hope of better days ahead. My bright fur glistens in the midday sun as I trot along, swinging my bucket into the air. Hallgerd, inspired perhaps by her jangling load, breaks into a song. How little we really need, just the land, to restore our spirits when we slide into despair. Its luscious smells and vibrant colors intoxicate. Hope takes wing once more in our hearts.

The stream proves even more delightful than the dew-bath I had yesterday. Cool and crisp and lively, it bubbles and chuckles its way along. I lap the water greedily and it chills my tongue and throat. Hallgerd too bends low to the stream, cupping the cold wetness in her hands and gasping with sudden shock as it splashes her face and mouth. Fresh water, not from a barrel—a simple treat but so delicious, and treats are few these days.

"How it catches the light! See—brighter than the stars," Hallgerd cries in joy. "If only one could divert the stream, have it run right to the castle itself."

"Like a millhouse?"

"Yes, why not? Or perhaps not so elaborate. After all, you

only need a little bit of water, not as much as turning a grindstone. Just enough for cooking and washing. A small brook even." Hallgerd uses a stick to carve a tiny path in the bank, thinking of the possibilities.

I examine the banks carefully. Laurel grows here. Willow too; its bark makes an excellent headache cure. It is early yet to look for dog's tooth, but there may be dried remains of last year's bounty in the meadow. Other plants are not as hardy as the spear leek and the hop cones, which hang in the thickets across the stream. Soon the plants that have waited out the winter's grip will begin to sprout anew, and the now-struggling vines will bloom again and bring the meadows alive with delicate colors.

"Phew! Nanna, what's this stinky plant?" Hallgerd pokes at the drooping leaves of a hairy plant growing out of the sandy bank.

"Goodness! Don't touch that, my dear—"

"Too late!" Hallgerd grimaces and shakes her hands rapidly.

"Wash your hands at once," I order sharply. "That's hennebelle. A poison."

"Eww!" My princess complies at once, picking up a small stone to help rub her hands clean. "How strong a poison?"

"Depends on the plant, how long it has been growing, what kind of soil in which it has sprung." I trot over to take a closer look. "This is definitely been here a few years. Hmmm." I look around for inspiration. A ha—the thick moss growing on the rock by that big willow should do the trick. "We can use that moss, over there. It will protect your hands and allow you to pick some of the leaves."

"But I thought you said it was poison?!"

"Yes, but carefully handled, it will be safe."

"I trust you, Nanna," Hallgerd assures me, "but why do we need poison?"

"It has other uses too, my dear. Not only is it a good sleep aide—one never knows when that might be handy—but it can also help one to achieve visions."

"You want visions?" Hallgerd asks as she peels the soft moss from the stone's surface. "Visions of the future?"

"No, visions of the present actually."

Hallgerd carefully wraps the moss around a few leaves and tugs them off.

"Here," I say, "put them in my little basket and cover them with the moss. We'll need to dry them. Shouldn't take too long—we can have them ready by the new moon, just a few days hence."

"I don't understand," Hallgerd says, her brows furrowing as she gingerly sets the basket before me. "What do you mean by visions of the present?"

"There is a way to induce a trance with hennebelle wherein your spirit may travel without hindrance of your body. It is rather precarious magic, but it can prove useful to know things one might not otherwise know, glimpse things while cloaked in the invisible of spirit-form."

"I can imagine spirit traveling without your body could be dangerous," Hallgerd admits, beginning now to fill her buckets and fasten them to the poles.

"Yes, certainly, though there are ways to safeguard your journey. But hennebelle itself is a perilous plant. Too little and the trance will not free your spirit—too much and you will never awaken."

Hallgerd looks up, eyes wide. "Nanna, you cannot consider such a thing then! No—I cannot allow it," she decides. "You are far too important, I cannot permit you to risk yourself in that way."

I smile - I have the way of it now, fox jaws or not - though I am proud of my princess' concern for me and of her decisiveness. "My dear one, I am quite experienced in this magic and well-acquainted with the dangers. I will not be putting myself in much danger and I will carefully ascertain the potency of the leaves before using them. We need to know what has happened in our absence, how fares the land—and what Maldachta is doing and planning. Would you not feel better knowing what has become of our friends? What has become of the poor fox in my body?"

"Yes, I do wish to know – but not if it means risking your safety."

"The only concern I have is that I am not in my own body. My spirit will of course be drawn to its true home and not as surely to this flesh."

"Then it is risky," Hallgerd scowls.

"Risky, but with your help even that risk shall be minimized. We need information, my Princess, and this is our only way to get it at present. Our minds will be set at ease and we will be able to work with clearer purpose."

Hallgerd bends her knees and lifts the poles onto her shoulders, straightening up with some effort beneath the weight of the buckets. "You will have to tell me everything, Nanna. You have to convince me that we can safely control your journey. I must know exactly what I can do to keep you from harm or from wandering too far."

"Don't worry, I shall certainly want your full cooperation. In fact, I will rely on it. Our first concern will be to get these leaves dried—without having any of them end up in the soup by accident."

"Oh Nanna, don't even joke about a thing like that!"

"Come, let us go back before Grima loses all patience with us."

Our trip back is far less jolly and myriad thoughts run swiftly through our minds. Mine I know—Hallgerd's I can tell by the shifting expressions of her face and the solemn looks toward me. I will convince her. Only a few days until the new moon, but it should leave enough time to make the preparations for that optimum time. I feel a thrill of excitement—it has been so long since I've done any real magic; it is not so easy to inhabit a fox's body and do without the use of my well-trained fingers. How much I took them for granted! But this sensation of titillation is not good. Magic must always be undertaken with a clear and balanced mind and body. Only then can one focus the will and achieve one's aims. Lay out the plans, prepare—only then attempt the magic. I think back to my teachers, the women who taught me carefully and compassionately, to whom magic was more than science, more than art—life itself. I strive to reach their perfection one day, though it may take me many years yet.

62

Most of the preparations have been made; we are nearly ready. Two nights from now will be the time for magic. We await only the rising of the dark moon—and a chance to elude the notice of Grima.

It gets harder for us exiles to escape notice, however. Today Skapti makes a point of talking to Grima about the changes in the kitchen. At midday he pauses before herding his meager troops up the stair to the great hall. Though he addresses the old cook his eyes fasten on Hallgerd. "Grima, the Prince has noticed a distinct change in the fare lately."

Grima sighs heavily and stabs her knife into the counter. "Don't need to tell me—he wants our heads no doubt. Feared it so long, almost a relief after all, not to say that I don't blame this one!" She growls at Hallgerd, "Fie on you and your coarse little, mangy—"

"Actually, Grima," the steward continues with what nearly wants to be a smile, "he was quite complimentary."

"Complimentary?" Grima regards him through one squinty eye.

"Yes. Said things seem to be improving, at least now they're almost edible." The smile becomes manifest and, though malicious, genuine. Holding up the largest bowl, Skapti continues, "He's especially fond of this bread soup. Guess your little companion has brought good luck." He says no more but heads his crew upstairs amidst a rattle of trays and bowls.

Grima gapes at his retreating form, unable to digest this bit of news all at once. At long last, she finally turns back to her work-counter and pries loose the knife, an effort that requires both hands. For a long time the cook says nothing while she chops the turnips into small cubes. Throwing the vegetables into an already simmering pot, she turns to face Hallgerd. Gone is her rambling melancholy—replaced with a vivid anger. "Make no mistake child, you will not have my job. If it means I must get rid of you myself, I shall do so. I cannot lose this position and be left a beggar—I will not!" Her eyes blaze with fury and reflected fire and she points at the princess with the well-honed knife.

"Grima," cries Hallgerd, "I plan no such thing and would not take it should it be offered."

"Liar!"

Hallgerd sets down her ladle and walks slowly over to the cook. "I would never repay your abundant kindnesses with treachery. You took me in. You gave me work and a warm place to stay. I try to do the best work I can for you to do you credit and if it should ever be in my power to do more, I shall reward you with all manner of goods and praise." Hallgerd bows low before the homely woman and doubt suffuses the pinched, angry face. "I offer you a secret, a chance for a wish."

"What? What are you talking about?" Grima says irritably, but much of her anger has already drained away, leaving her cheeks an angry pink.

"My fox." Hallgerd looks back at me hopefully. I nod, as I can see where she must be going with this. "My fox is capable of magic. Perhaps he can grant you a wish of some kind."

"Magic? Good magic?"

"Yes, no evil. Is there something you wish for, Grima?"

"Foolishness!" But I can see there is something rising up through her thoughts, something that makes her soften with sadness.

"Tell us, Grima, no, better yet..." Hallgerd turns and scoops me up, "tell him. He will give you an answer and tell you whether it is in his power to do what you desire."

Grima, who draws back from me immediately, considers the offer. Hallgerd places me on the counter—far from Grima's work space—and takes a few steps away. Grima squints at me, not without some rancor, but hesitates.

"Go on, Grima. What have you got to lose?"

"My nose, no doubt," the cook snaps but without too much venom, "Be lucky if I don't lose an eye too." But she meets my gaze before turning her eyes back once more to Hallgerd. "Mind you, if this little beast—"

"Just ask, Grima, ask him." Hallgerd picks up a broom and idly sweeps around her feet. The cook returns to her contemplation of my face and there is no mistaking the wistful hope in her look. I try to project my desire to be helpful, but stop short of a grin for fear the teeth might provoke more fear than comfort.

"I feel a right foolish woman," Grima mutters mostly to herself.

I cock my head to show my attentiveness and she glances with haste once more toward the princess, then wets her lips and whispers, "I want to know...I want to know...what happened to Gizur."

It is my turn to look to Hallgerd. I nod. She runs over to join us, still holding the broom in her excitement. "He can do what you ask! Hurrah!"

Grima clearly does not believe this; she stands arms crossed, lips meeting in a thin line. "Well?"

I sigh. Impatience is always the way with us humans. Hallgerd opens her mouth to speak, but I beat her to it. "Can you keep a secret?"

Grima shrieks, dropping her knife and backing into the counter. Her elbow upsets the careful stack of bowls, which crash loudly to the floor and makes Grima jump yet again; this time her flailing arms nearly upset the pot of simmering turnips, which Hallgerd manages—just in time!—to catch before it splashes us all, burning her fingers in the process, but saving us all a nasty scalding.

"Butter! Butter on your fingers!" Grima commands.

"Cold water," I countermand, startling the poor woman once more.

"By the eighth leg of Sleipnir! I never—"

"But cold water does really work better," I offer and Hallgerd runs over to plunge her hands in the bucket. The relief shows immediately on her face and in her sigh. "Hold them in there a few minutes, my dear, then we'll make a poultice."

Grima still stares at me, amazed. "I'd not be more surprised to see the Hooded One himself. How is it you can talk, beast?"

"It is a long story—not all of which is safe for you to know.

But we wish you only good and we seek only help—and in return, I can answer your question."

"How can I help?" Hallgerd asks, binding her hand in a wet rag.

"First, we should finish the preparations for the evening meal and get a poultice for your hand—"

"Oh, it's not that bad, it feels better already."

"Nonetheless, we want to prevent scarring. Then we must try the hennebelle—this is good, it gives us a chance to determine how strong its potency is."

"Hennebelle!" Grima says, suspicious once more. "That's poison."

"Not in the right hands. Trust me, and I will give you the answer you've been seeking so long." She quiets at that, saying no more, but turns back to her duties, occasionally stealing surreptitious glimpses of Hallgerd and me, as we prepare a poultice of day's eyes' leaves for the burns.

Once the preparations for the next meal are done and the clattering dishes and bowls from midday are cleaned and scrubbed and left to dry, I fetch the little basket of herbs from our closet under the stairs and we three head out to the roasting fire. It has not been used in many a week, but we need only start a small fire to burn the leaves.

"It would help if I had some item that once belonged to this Gizur, anything at all, even a lock of hair," I say as Hallgerd arranges the kindling.

Grima nods and reaches up her sleeve with her left hand. She draws a silver ring from her arm and holds it before her. Though plain, it is finely worked and glints in the settling twilight, reflecting the blue, red and grey. "He gave me this before he set out that last time, fifteen years ago." Her eyes are shiny but she resolutely fixes her expression. "Mama always said he found a handsomer bride across the sea in the Northern lands, but—"

"We shall know the truth soon, Grima," I tell her softly, "And I cannot believe the young man who gave you such a beautiful arm-ring would forget your love so easily."

Hallgerd gets the tiny fire roaring in no time and once the coals glow red and white in the deepening gloom; we are ready to begin.

I move toward the fire. "Now, you two fan the smoke toward me when I lay the leaves on the fire. It is not likely to happen, but if I should begin to be overcome by the fumes, dunk my head in the barrel a few times until I am wide awake again, but don't worry my dear," I smile, catching Hallgerd's concerned look, "I've done this before—and it's not as if it were a full trance. I need merely to open my mind to the spirit roads."

The bitter smoke of the hennebelle leaves assaults my nostrils. Fox-sensitive, they rebel, but eagerly I draw the ghostly fumes into my lungs. Not too much—these lungs are much smaller than my own, but deeply I feel the unaccustomed sting and the rising flutter of my heart. Hallgerd and Grima fan the smoke with gentle flaps of their skirts. Breathe again, deeper even than before, and I sense my eager spirit desire to fly from its fleshly confines. But I must hold it here, and instead open myself to the other spirit beings. I close my eyes, the better to concentrate.

"Are you okay?" Hallgerd asks, her voice heavy with concern.

"Yes, my dear, it is all right. Don't worry until I fall over," I chuckle—a fox chuckling!—and continue opening my mind. Gizur, I call through the silence of my mind, Gizur who once gave this ring to Grima, where did you go? Why did you leave her pining from your silence? What happened on that journey?

A spark, firelight glints off the ring. A vision springs up, as clear as if I am standing in the snow that day too. A gaggle of men on the hunt for some time—their clothes are torn and dirty—talk a little amongst themselves while they trudge on slowly through the early winter.

"A band of men, hunting, far far to the north," I murmur. "Winter has come, and come early, but still they press on." Grima's sharp intake of breath shows I am in the right place. "Your Gizur—he is not so tall but very broad of shoulder, he hums a tune as the men walk on, something about Volund the smith."

"His favorite!" Grima cries.

I inhale deeply once more. "Their hunt has not been too successful. They seem to have but few skins and no one has wanted to return with so little. They press on north. In a clearing ahead, danger! What is it? I see white and red...oh! Two great white bears savage a reindeer. It is their first success in days too.

So hungry! They fear the men—fear they will take their meal. The men pull out their broadswords and long knives. The bears roar, rise on their hind legs, mouths and paws stained red with blood. The men split ranks—three on the bigger bear, two on the other. Screams! Blood!"

"Oh! I don't know if I can listen!" Hallgerd holds her hands over her ears—loosely enough, I notice, that she can hear just fine.

"The smaller bear swipes at Gizur, he ducks low and stabs at her side with his knife. The bear shrieks in pain and clasps him in her powerful arms. Gizur fights to loose his weapon, but with a terrific roar the bear seizes his left arm in her powerful jaws and rips it from him." Grima moans at this, but I cannot stop. "Suddenly she drops him and spins to menace her other attacker who has come upon her from behind. One horrible swipe and his neck is broken and she turns back on Gizur who struggles on yet with his knife. Stabbing desperately at her neck as she bends low, he opens a mortal wound, but it is too late. All will die today—hunters and hunted though Gizur holds on as long as he can. Hope sustains him, but the cold creeps in as the warm blood blanketing him cools and his heart beats more and more slowly. He has thrown away his knife and clutches instead something small, something round. What? An egg? It looks like an egg. And with his last strength he laughs—a sad laugh, but merry—and he whispers 'Dear one, I got you a lovely fur coat' as the final breath leaves his body and the snow flakes begin to fall, softly, almost at once hiding the gruesome tableau under successive blizzards. They are never found."

I draw away from the fire, my thoughts woozy and wandering. But I must not slip into a trance tonight, so I turn away and gulp hungrily the crisp night air. "Cover the leaves with other kindling and move away from the fire, don't want you two to start having visions." My head clearer now, I look back at my friends. Hallgerd throws ready sticks on the fire as she mops her wet brow. But Grima has fallen to her knees beside the roasting fire, hands covering her face as tears fall streaming into the pit. Hallgerd wraps one arm around the cook and bids her walk away from the smoke. We move to a grassy rise outside the kitchen entrance and sit on the cold ground. I begin to cough, my lungs rejecting the imposition of the fumes. Hallgerd jumps up and fetches a bowl of water and I gulp down half its contents at once and then cough some more. I am very glad I don't need to do this often—I couldn't!

"True, it's all true, oh my poor Gizur!" Grima sobs her heart's ache and all the lost years of bitter resentment well in her eyes and flow down her cheeks. I hope they take some of her festering anger with them—painful as it is—for her back has bent beneath the weight of it all the time since then. "How terrible, how awful! The way he died! The way I doubted him!" Loudly her sobs ring out into the stillness of the night, frightening the chickens who fear it may already be day despite the dark. "Why did I not believe? Why did I let her poison my thoughts?"

"Who, Grima?" Hallgerd asks in her most gentle voice, clearly not quite sure if she should put her arm again around the prickly woman.

"My mama, the old wretch. She always told me I was too ugly, too mean to keep him." Grima wipes her streaming eyes defiantly. "But I wasn't, not then, not with him. Oh, could he make me laugh! He had the funniest way of pulling faces at me, he always made me spit up my ale or whatever I was drinking—or make it come out my nose!" She sighs happily at the remembrance, but just as quickly the smile slips away. "All alone! He died all alone—without me, I mean," she adds, perhaps afraid we'll misunderstand. "I know, there were others there with him, but I wish I could have been too. To tell him how I loved him, how much he meant to me, to die with him. I would have been happy enough. Oh, all these bitter years, thinking he'd left and didn't care and…and…never loved me," Grima covers her face with her hands again, harsh sobs racking her body in mournful waves.

"Grima ," I ask, more to distract her from her pain than anything else, though I am quite curious, "What was the egg Gizur had in his hand?"

"The egg?" She looks up and I see the copious tears have reddened her eyes, but brightened them too and years have come off her face. Her heart breaks anew and yet a lingering pain now begins to heal. "Oh, it is very silly, but I love him even more for having it still. I was all of eight when I gave him that, not even an egg, just a little rock, but it was blue and speckled like a robin's egg. I was sweet on him from the moment I can remember, and I found that one day and I don't know, it just seemed so special to me—I was just a child you know," Grima reminds us hastily, terrified that we were about to laugh, "But I thought it a wonderful gift. Just a boy—I was certain he would lose it of course but years later he showed it to me, after our first kiss." And now Grima smiles shyly and I see the young girl she was, in all her awkward beauty, "And I knew then that he really cared, that to him I was special...whatever my mother might say. And he held it there, in his last moments, and he thought...of me." More tears, but tears of joy, of relief, and Hallgerd and I join her, telling her how lucky she was to have had such an extraordinary man love her.

"A valiant man," Hallgerd assures her.

"And handsome too, such a cheerful face, and a ready wit," I add.

"Fur coat! Silly Gizur, oh my dear." Grima cannot decide whether to laugh or cry. "Oh, but if he had not gone—he was so determined to get some furs and other spoils to buy us some land. He didn't want me to be a kitchen maid forever, but I would gladly have done any grubby work to have him back by my side again."

"It is a shame, I wish it too," Hallgerd wistfully agrees.

Grima pats her hand and turns to me. "Thank you, little fox, thank you for bringing him back to me forever. I can never thank you enough—and after I've been so cruel to you. Can you forgive a foolish woman?"

"Nonsense! You took us into your kitchen and gave us shelter. It is we who are grateful."

"Still, I owe you much," Grima puts the ring back on her arm, stroking its simple interlace design, "And I shall not forget it. I do know that you two are not what you seem—a fox that tells fortunes! A little lady, who though very capable in the kitchen, has golden locks worthy of a princess—much as she tries to hide them." She reaches up and grabs a curl which slips from Hallgerd's kerchief and the Princess blushes. "I will not ask your secret, but I will help you as much as I can."

"Thank you, Grima," Hallgerd says, the warmth in her voice doing much to convey her gratitude. "We will tell you more by and by as it becomes safe. But be assured, I will one day have means to repay you for the abundant kindnesses you show us."

"Pish posh! Let no one say Grima is kind or cheerful." The cook laughs and struggles to rise on legs grown cold, "After all, I have a reputation to maintain! Kind, indeed! Come, let us finish the late meal, Skapti will be here in no time and will grumble like a grandmother if everything's not to his liking, though why I bother…" She is already putting her apron back on and throwing wood into the sluggish fires.

Hallgerd and I stand too, shaking off the cold of the grass and the lingering smoke of the fire. My princess leans down to hug me fiercely, whispering "Thank you, Nanna, thank you so much."

"But it was so little—"

"Not for Grima," Hallgerd looks to our new friend, "You gave her back her heart."

"Hope—it is what saves us all from despair."

"But love too, Nanna, it is so very important. I did not realize it when I was a sheltered exile," - she smiles down at me - "surrounded by love. You and Unn gave me all the love you could. I thank you, again."

I put a paw on her lap. "It was so very easy to do, my dear."

"Perhaps, but I see now how devastating its lack can be. Not just Grima, but Thomas too. There seems no love in his heart."

"But great ambition has a hold there, like an enormous tree casting a killing shadow on the other emotions which cannot take root."

"Well," says Hallgerd standing to brush the debris from her skirt, "if we cannot cure him, we still have to stop him."

"We shall." Feeling full of hope and love, we go inside to help Grima with her tasks.

63

This will be so much more dangerous, but I dare not tell Hallgerd how much so. There is not merely the hazard of the hennebelle, but the questionable strength of my spirit's tie to this body; too thin, and I might not be able to return. Not only do I risk getting stuck once more in my own body—uncomfortable enough with an old fox in there too!—but I gamble too getting lost in between. Without a path to follow back to this flesh, I would have only my sense of direction to rely on—in a strange country, with few landmarks to guide me.

But it is the dark night of the new moon and that is best for our kind of magic, when women like me feel at our strongest. I must be confident. Doubt weakens one and I cannot afford to let my princess down. We need to know how things are in the land we left behind.

Near to midnight, we slip away. Better Grima not know too much of our plans—and she has her duties after all. The revelers upstairs in the castle may well still desire some refreshment, so she naps in the little room with the other servants who can get away from their duties for a time. Hallgerd and I carry kindling, a coal, the basket of hennebelle and a bucket of water as we trot through the quiet darkness. We cannot risk being disturbed, so we must not be too near the castle—but the woods are full of creatures every bit as dangerous as any human interference. So we must choose our place carefully.

A giant oak spreads welcoming arms across the blackened sky. This is the place. The massive tree has cleared the ground around its base through its cast darkness. Split early by lightning, it not only survived its youthful trauma, but grew around the damage, forming a hollow that no doubt has provided home to many a bird or small creature over the years. Hallgerd pushes back the sleeve of her mantle and reaches up into the cleft.

"Careful!" I say. "You never know, but someone might be at home."

"It's all right," Hallgerd replies. "No one's lived here recently." She pulls out some dried grass. "Look, an old eggshell. And here, some acorn hulls."

I smile to myself; it is as if my princess were only six winters old again. She is after all, still so young. Too young for all the danger and ill-will we have had to face—but is one ever old enough? I have lived so very long and yet, I am no more ready than she to face the evils of this world—or of any other. "This is a good place," I say. "We'll build the fire here. With the tree at our backs and a fire before us, we should be safe from any wandering predators."

"This is an amazing old tree," Hallgerd says, admiring its reach before she turns to building the fire. "I have the most pressing urge to climb up into its limbs and see how far I can see." She laughs.

"I know what you mean. It calls to the child in me as well—"

"Child—or kit?" Hallgerd giggles.

"Very funny. Tonight it is imperative that I remember I am a woman in a fox's body if I am to return to the right flesh."

The kindling smokes as Hallgerd lays the coals on top of it. She leans forward and blows on the coal which glows brightly red. Hallgerd throws the dried grass from the tree hollow on the pile and a small flame immediately shoots up, followed by cracks and pops. The fire is going! It takes some time to get it burning strongly, but we two stare silently into the shifting tongues of orange and yellow as they flicker and chase another. So much to think about, yet nothing to say, for we have already decided our course.

The flames consume their fuel with voracious licks, stifling their own heat in the dizzying hunger and leaving behind skeletons, red under white. The time has come for traveling.

"Throw the leaves on the coals."

Hallgerd leans forward. The heat has forced her to shed the coat of many furs and formed a shiny patina of moisture on her brow. She grabs a handful of leaves from the basket and tosses them on the pyre. Smoke rises at once.

"More."

She complies, coughing on the already abundant vapors, and wisely moves away from the brunt of them to the other side of the fire. Her eyes on me, my Princess waits.

I breathe deeply the acrid clouds and feel once more the sting deep inside. Now is time. Eyes closed, deep, deeper and I feel my senses rebel briefly then succumb. The tug of freedom pulls my reluctant spirit from its shell and I am floating—a handspan, five, ten, then I am in the branches of the old tree. What a relief to see that a fine, so very delicate gossamer thread ties me to my body. My body—the fox's body, that is, for as I float I once more have the outlines of my former shape. I delight to see the shape of my hands, old friends. But flesh is the trap—I am only spirit and must remember it.

I look below. Hallgerd regards my slumbering form intently, one hand on the bucket of water, ready to use it if my breathing should stop. I try to give my shoulders a shake and I see the fox body respond ever so slightly below. Good. Taking a deep breath, I open my thoughts further to receive the call from my other flesh. It remains the only beacon which may lead me back to our land. I reach out with all my senses—there! I feel its pull. Slight, distant, but it is also unmistakable. The force drags me, imperceptibly at first, then with greater speed as I fly through tree branches, unable to curb my habit of ducking them for some time.

Once I stop short, sensing danger. A wispy tail of greenish-white, like the color of something too long underground, whips past me and I draw back. Nathair! Though it cannot see me, the beast senses my presence and pauses in its flight. In the gleaming talons of its huge forepaws the wyrm grips an armload of treasures, more gold for its hoard. A dragon! So near to our land, yet never sighted? Perhaps it has been asleep atop its riches—I have heard they may sleep for centuries undisturbed, but oh! The gods help he who disturbs them. Seeing no danger, the dragon turns once more toward its lair and, flapping its membranous wings, departs.

I too continue on my journey. Faster now, I soar high over trees and I begin to recognize the landscape. In no time I am passing quickly over the little fortress on the edge of Hundrada wood—too quickly, for a shadow of sad longing covers my heavy heart at the sight of it—then right through the surrounding village and, in a wink, right into the castle. The close greyness seems almost suffocating after the freedom of the night woods and I find it far more disconcerting to pass through the thick stone walls than the spidery branches of the trees.

Spiraling down from the grand entry hall, I finally reach the dark lower cells where we were once imprisoned. In a flicker I am through the door of the same darkened chamber and curled on the floor lies my body! The fox wakes at once, sniffing the air. I cannot help it—I laugh to see my old flesh acting in such an alien manner. But the next instant I panic and only just avoid being pulled back into my body.

"Who's there!" the fox cries in his own tongue.

"It is I, the one whose body you occupy."

"I see nothing. I cannot smell you, though with this poor nose that is little wonder. I hear you though, inside my head. Not with my ears."

"I am spirit only, that which animates the body," I try to explain.

His alarm shows on my face. "Where is my body?!" the fox demands.

"Fear not. It is quite safe. It is merely faster to travel without it."

The fox stretches my body elaborately, from the neck on down each bone of my back. "It worries me nonetheless. This body is not so much good. No sense of smell, little of taste—and the eyesight, well, the eyesight is tolerable enough, but only just so. And no fur! It gets cold at night without my brush to warm my nose. I don't know how you manage, your kind."

I grin. It is a most unusual sensation to listen to my body complaining to my spirit—in a fox's voice. "Otherwise, how have you fared in this prison? Not too uncomfortable? Plenty to eat?"

"Oh yes, that is certainly true, though I fear it makes me quite indolent." He laughs. "Not that it will be my trouble to get this body active. You are very old, though not so old as you seem."

"I am not like the others, quite."

The fox narrows my gaze. "That has become quite apparent. You have vexed the evil one."

Oh dear. "He visits?"

"From time to time. I pay little attention to his rantings. I cannot answer in his tongue anyhow. He becomes entirely incoherent, and not only because of my lack of interest."

"Anger?"

The fox considers this, tilting my head to one side and squinting one eye. "A part of it is surely anger, but more...confusion? He cannot fathom what has happened to you. Frequently he loses his temper altogether and shouts at me. Calls me mad."

"Good. If he has not figured out my trick, he cannot seek my true self. We are safe."

"Safe or not, I would like to be back in my own skin. I can smell the first buds of crocus. The thaw will not be far behind."

"Soon," I entreat. "We must be free of this evil one. Our plans to thwart him must be laid down carefully. There is much work to be done yet. Please—can you hold on a bit longer? You will be amply rewarded and the Princess will herself protect you."

The fox, propped up on my arms, shudders briefly and sighs. "I am not meant for your human life of close contact and small spaces. My spirit pines to be free again, to walk beneath the mother moon and smell the secrets of the night. It is very hard."

"I know, I know. It is so much to ask. But our lives depend on your help, your generous sharing of your flesh."

He stares silently at the floor, my face puckered with sadness. I feel the pain of his trap, this wretched prison, and feel a burst of shame for my abundant liberty in his body. How can I convince him of something I cannot believe myself?

The fox looks up to where my spirit hovers. "There is one thing. One that might be enough to feed my spirit which hungers in a way my belly does not. A worse way, more painful. Please, if you can sing one of your songs, your magic songs, one that might...I don't know—help me feel hope? Feel free? With a tune like that in my head, perhaps I could bear this prison a bit longer. Your songs of beauty still echo in my ears. Do you know one like that? One of hope?"

"Yes, yes I do." The very one pops into my head unbidden, a gift. Emer's song of hopeful longing for her absent champion will surely lift this fox's heart, a tune full of hope for her absent love and certainty that soon all will be well. I pause to run through the melody then, parting my spirit lips, bring it forth in ethereal tones reminiscent, as far as possible, of the elderly woman I first heard sing it long ago and far away. As the words fill my head, I too feel a renewal of faith and assurance that our good will triumph, that beloved ones shall come home. Hope lightens my very being; I float higher.

When I open my eyes—open? How have I closed eyes I do not have in this spirit body, ah, how the habits of the flesh stay with us—I see the fox and my face shows me the success of Emer's lay. The tracks of tears trace my old cheeks, forming clean rivulets in the grime of my imprisoned body.

"Again this water that pours from my eyes," the fox says in wonder.

"Tears. I suppose it might be more natural for you to express strong emotion—grief or joy—with a howl or bark."

"Of course." The fox flicks my tongue out to capture one of the drops. "Hm, salty, like the first taste of blood, but not so earthy." His gaze meets mine and I stare into my own eyes. The sensation is quite disconcerting. I am torn between laughter and despair, and my spirit feels the pull to its own body. A queer look distorts the lines of my face as the fox tells me, "Go, go now, while the song still echoes in my ears. It will bear me up a while longer. But this cave crushes me a little every day—do not be long."

"Thank you, thank you. We will hurry our plans as much as possible and free you from this torment. Good-bye." I hasten away, out of the sight of the suffering beast whose pain I must share. It is so hard to be the cause of such distress—I am accustomed to healing, not hurting.

I seek my friend Unn. She is not in her usual room. As I float through it, I can see other women, young girls really, most of them unknown to me. Where are the twins? A gloomy foreboding takes hold of me. Grave changes have been implemented—by Maldachta, no doubt. But how grave? I reach out with my spirit, feeling for sign of my friend. There! I head in the direction that pulls me to a small room on the ground floor, very near the king's chambers—and undoubtedly too, those of Thomas. Mere invisibility may not be enough of a cloak with that evil one on guard. If he is—perhaps his apparent success has caused him to relax his vigilance. I can only hope.

I look down upon the sleeping form of my friend. Siur dozes, curled behind Unn's knees, one wary eyelid already twitching at my presence. Even the solace of sleep has not removed all the care from Unn's countenance. Worry has deepened the many lines defining her kindly face and she stirs, restless, in her dreaming. But it brings me such joy to gaze once more on her familiar features and it seems almost a pity to wake her and renew the anxiety, but I must. "Unn," I whisper, hovering near her ear, "Unn, wake up!"

"Wha—? Time? Oh dear, is it time already, goodness, but it's dark—"

"Unn! Unn, it's me."

She gasps and sits up abruptly. "My lady!" But her smile disappears almost at once and she shakes her head firmly. Siur stares up at my unseen face and purrs.

"It's a not a dream, my dear friend. But you cannot see me at present, I am spirit only."

Unn gapes at this. "Not dead! Oh please say you're not dead!"

"No, no, never fear. They have not caught us. I am alive and the Princess is well. I have come back to check on matters here."

"Well, that's a relief to be sure, though it's hard hearing a voice of someone you can't see—puts me in mind of ghosts, I must say, quite startling."

"I am so very sorry, but I couldn't come all this way and not stop to talk with you, my friend."

Unn, more awake now, looks a little shocked. "Then you're not down there in that cell? I didn't think so—but that one, he just thought you'd gone round the bend for sure this time, old age, whatever, so he said, but I didn't believe it, no, not for one minute."

"I haven't been in my own body for some time. I made a trade."

"Trade? With whom?"

"A fox."

"The gods you say!" Unn claps a hand over her mouth to contain her mirth. "A fox! Well, that explains a few things, it does.

Like your eating habits these days!" I join her quiet laughter eagerly. It feels so good to do so. "So you go about on four legs these days? I can't see it. No, not at all."

"It's true, nonetheless. I have become quite used to it." Unn shakes her head, giggles still shaking her body. "I cannot say the same for the fox. He is rather unhappy cooped up in the darkness. He longs to wander the forests again. I can't say that I blame him."

"No, I'm sure, it must be very hard." Her brow knits and her giggles die away. "It's a wonder that Thomas hasn't figured it out—not that I think he cares much, mind you. He does really seem to believe that you've lost your faculties altogether—"

"Due, no doubt, to his nefarious plan."

"Oh yes, and your inherent weakness," Unn says with a twist of a grin. "I remember how you said it, that our plan would work if we kept him thinking we were 'just women.' You were right."

"He still believes it's me in that cell?"

"Yes. Though he wonders sometimes—stays there and rails at you. Calls you mad—and all manner of other unpleasantries, too. But not so much lately, he has too much to worry about, what with rebellions springing up in the land here and there, and soldiers deserting him."

"Deserting him? Hmm, that could be good."

Unn sighs. "If only it weren't for that Grim Eriksson."

I cast my memory back. "The captain of the guards? Why?"

"He's determined that this is the path to prosperity for his kin—they are all solidly behind Thomas and work desperately to keep their ranks filled. Their cruelties have become the stuff of nightmares—maimings and hangings and worse. Even if every soldier deserts that evil one, he'll still have the rest of Grim's family and they'll support him to the end."

"They have to now—they'll never be trusted for anything else." What a sad day has come to pass in this pleasant land. Hallgerd will redouble her efforts to reclaim it. "Is Thomas actively pursuing the hiding place of the Princess?"

Unn shakes her head, reaching out a hand unconsciously to stroke the purring cat at her side. "He has posted a reward for the return—safe return, he says—of the Princess, but he's not really doing anything much, at least as far as I can hear. I hover over the soldiers when they're fed in the great hall—such a mess, I can't tell you, it's shocking, would never have allowed in the old days—I pick up a lot of the news that way. I keep my eyes and ears open too, as you bad me, my lady. Thomas keeps me close because he doesn't trust me. But I hear much because of it."

I wish I could lay a reassuring hand on her arm. My friend is so courageous! "You are so very brave, my friend. Hallgerd will know what you do for her and for the land."

"Pish posh! I want my comfortable life back, that's all." But she smiles and blushes all the same. "Things won't be so easy for you, though. Thomas does his best to stir up great hatred for you. He has made many believe that you are the one who has bewitched the King, made him so…wrong."

"I? How has he spread such foul rumors! Why are they so believed?"

Unn shifts uneasily. "Your kind have always been looked upon with suspicion, I know you know that. Times have been harsh, the people feel the pinch. Everyonr likes a scapegoat. Thomas hasn't really helped that matter. He's only rubbing the sore spots our people already have, raising the foolishnesses they harbor in their hearts for those who seem to have uncanny abilities—now, I know, I know, there is so much more to magic, it's learning and thinking and a lot of work, that much you have shown me. But others don't know you as I do, don't know that you are the kindest woman in the world, one who loves all people and our Princess most of all. They're cruel, cruel and ignorant—and blinded by their fear."

"What has he told them, Unn?"

"That you imprisoned the spirit of the king—that you put it in a little bottle and hid it somewhere and that's why he seems so lost. He lies in his chamber all day as if in dreams—or nightmares really, for his sleep is not easy. Your witchcraft, that one always tells us."

I wish momentarily that I had a foot to stamp. "Ridiculous!"

Unn looks thoughtful. "I've seen a bottle, a peculiar one that is, in his quarters when he had me run there one day to fetch something for him…ah, his walking stick it was. A movement on the shelf caught my eye. I dared not touch it, but I stared at it for some time. Sometimes it looked like a thing, sometimes like light moving in water. I had to run off because he was waiting, but I've never forgotten it—and I couldn't help thinking it had something to do with what he claimed to be your crime."

"Wisely said. It is very likely just as you imagine it. Such magic does exist, but its repercussions are tremendous. One should not undertake it lightly. I wonder at Maldachta's recklessness."

"Can we rescue it and free the King?" Unn asks, excitement lighting her face. Unsettled by her movements, the cat regards Unn with candid resentment, stretches and moves off to a corner of the bed to begin her ablutions.

"It's not as simple as that," I say, but already the possibilities turn over in my head, "but that is good to know. It will be useful—though perhaps not immediately. We must do nothing to make him suspicious yet."

"Well, I suppose not. Yet it is hard, my lady, to live day in and day out so close to that one. Your coming here has renewed my hope—even if I can't see you," Unn adds with a wry smile. "And it's odd, I hear you in here," she taps her head, "and not in my ears."

"I have no mouth with which to talk, so I must use my spirit. It talks directly to yours."

"Goodness! If any one would have told me such a thing just a year or two ago...well, never mind my wonderings, lady, just tell me the Princess is well and you have plans to return her to her throne."

It is hard to meet her eager gaze and for once I am glad she cannot see my face. Things are so uncertain yet. "The Princess is indeed safe, in disguise, and we are working on an effort to bring her back to power in this land. But we need to make powerful allies, and that takes some time. But we have a plan." I realize that I do indeed have a scheme hatching in my thoughts, but it will all depend—but later. I must concentrate now. There are still matters to which I must attend. "Any other news I ought to know, my friend?"

Unn considers this. "There's one thing, a very little thing, but somehow I feel it niggle at me and that makes it seem important."

"A good sign. What is it?"

"As I said, it's not much of anything, but odd all the same. I'd always see him looking at his hand, Thomas that is. I thought maybe he had something written there as I recall the King once used to do, to remind him of things he wanted, well, to remember I guess."

I smile at the memory too. "Yes, I remember the Queen teasing him about his cheats, as she called them. Would forget his own head if it weren't written down, he'd tell her and she'd laugh and agree."

Unn laughs and many years fall from her face only to creep back much too quickly. "Such a happy home this was then. So changed now! Ah, but I was telling you. So I see him doing this time and again and finally I get to where I can peek at his hand and what do you know, it's a little mirror. My first thought was, well, getting vain in his old age no doubt with all his fancy clothes, but then on the other hand he's not nearly so good about dipping his hair in the blacking as he once was—ridiculous silver roots! He looks like a badger, I must say."

I chuckle at this, but set to wondering what this can mean. "Thank you my dear. I don't know at present what it might mean, but no doubt it will prove important. He is up to some mischief as always. It could be many things—I will have to ponder the question. But I must be going, I can feel the pull. I have one more quick question—please tell me, are the twins all right? Did he punish Thorgerd?"

"Banished her at once—though she pleaded with him, said she was enchanted. He seemed to smell something on her clothes, or so I heard much later. Believed her enough to spare her life, anyway."

"And probably he thought that left alive, she might still be in contact with the Princess."

Unn nods. "Had his spies onto her, hanging about, I'm fairly certain. Not that it did him any good. You and the Princess could have vanished into the air for all he could tell. Oh, but he was so sure he'd have her with his hounds and his trackers, but she was too smart for that one! And you, my lady—but you need to be going, I know, I know. It is so hard to let you go, but that if your leavetaking means it will be that much sooner that you and the Princess may return, I shall say good-bye. Take good care my lady, of yourself and she whom we all miss. Tell her so—you will, won't you?"

"Of course, my dear friend. The Princess knows already what friends she has in this land and she has great faith in you all. We shall strive to make our plans work quickly—for your sake and our own. Good-bye my friend, keep hope alive."

"Good-bye! All the blessings of the gods upon you and the Princess. Come home soon!"

After one final look at my old friend and her happy but tired face, I give in to the pull that is all but tearing me from the spot.

My return journey to the little fire under the oak is much swifter even than my flight to our homeland. I have no time to dodge the branches that flash through my spirit body. Most disconcerting! But there is no time to fight it. The effect of the hennebelle wears off more quickly than I had anticipated—or have I spent far too long in the land I have missed so? I admit this could be true, but it is so hard to resist comfort, familiarity and a friend.

With an effort, I try to halt my downward spiral. I know I am only spirit, but somehow I imagine that the impact of hitting a physical body again will be quite jarring enough without the factor of speed to consider. The pull of the slight silver cord remains strong, insistent and the effort of fighting it soon tires me. Still, I manage to hold on long enough to break my "fall" and uneasily, I slip back into the fox's body and gasp my first breath.

"You're back!" Hallgerd greets me, jumping to her feet. In her excitement, she sheds the fur mantel she had huddled beneath, waiting, and embraces me whole-heartedly.

"Water!" I manage to wheeze as I try to take in great gulps of air. The flesh is so heavy to wear! I forget the weight of it when I am gone mere minutes—good thing I was not gone longer.

Hallgerd, misunderstanding my cry, throws a good bucketful over my head and I sputter under the deluge, licking a few drops with my tongue, choking and sneezing all at once. I try to clear my throat but Hallgerd has already run for more water. Before she comes back, I am able to compose myself enough to ask to drink from the bucket.

"Oh dear." Hallgerd complies at once, thrusting the bucket before me and watching anxiously as I drink. "I hope that's better, I just thought—well, you had warned me to be ready—"

150

"Never mind, my dear," I finally wheeze between swallows, "it was really quite refreshing."

Hallgerd stares at me, her eyes betraying worry. Her expression changes to amusement when I wink at her but she cries out when I decide it is time to shake my fur dry from the deluge. "Thank you so much! Now I'm going to freeze."

"Not with that coat around your shoulders. Come, let's get back to the warm kitchen and a bite to eat. I shall sleep well tonight. Tomorrow, I'll tell you everything."

Hallgerd sighs, but pours the last of the water on the dying fire and tests the coals with her hand. Finding them cold, she gathers our belongings and we walk back to the castle. I can feel the shroud of sleep stealing over me already, and it is only with an effort that I can keep my eyes open. I will sleep very late. I hope Grima will not miss my help too much.

♭♮

"But Thorgerd is safe? Oh, I am so happy," Hallgerd throws her head back with a deep sigh. "I could not bear the thought that helping us should bring her harm. I will sleep a bit easier now, though from what Unn has said, we have much to worry over." She turns her attention back to the bowls soaking in the warm tub of water. "I fear even more for my father. Thomas will not let him die, will he? Surely he cannot."

"No, he needs the authority of the king—even if he is not wielding himself. But we need to move quickly to secure aid. A powerful ally is our only hope, for Maldachta has many warriors on his side. We cannot face that alone—without my magic we have little with which to counter such brute force."

Hallgerd shakes the water from another bowl and adds it to the stack beside the tub. "I have never asked about this geiss that keeps you from using your magic against this Thomas. Can you explain? For I must admit I do not really understand how it works."

I look up and meet her gaze. Hallgerd's eyes look troubled, but resolute. How to explain? She knows so little of magic but what she has seen—though the Princess has seen more than most. But our ways are so alien to her society, as is our magic. I think with some bitterness of the prejudices that evil one has stirred up against me in the land I have served so long, but no mind. It is not the people who ask for an explanation: it is my dear girl. Still I sigh. This is not one of the tales I love to tell, but a story is a story. As she busies herself with drying the bowls, I unravel the history of my people's grief.

"Long before, when the world was younger, a wise woman took a fancy to a young king. She had seen in the scrying of bones that it would be possible to begin a great legacy of fine daughters

152

if she chose the right man. The crystal she carried day and night sparked brightly in the presence of this king, so the woman knew he was the one.

"But it is no easy matter to marry a king. He may kiss a woman who catches his passing fancy—as many kings have indeed done over the years—but to form a more lasting relationship, well, she must be something special. The wise woman considered what might be her best opportunity, studying the king's habits while a guest in his court. He was not a wild man as so many kings are, but thoughtful, restrained. She could not win him with a comely face alone, though she was not short of glamours that would make her irresistible. He would never ally himself with a mere pretty face, a pleasing form.

"The king had a weakness though—horses. He was proud of his fine steeds, the swiftest, the most beautiful and elegant animals in all the green lands. If she could offer him an even better stallion for his herd, that would be temptation enough to secure his affections, share his world. But where to find such a horse? For all agreed the king's horses were without equals in the land, and our land was known as the finest for breeding incomparable horseflesh. What could she do?

"At the next new moon, all the wise women gathered to sing their songs and share their stories. She confided her troubles to one of the oldest ones there, asking her help and advice. The aged woman, her face a matrix of laughing wrinkles lit by sparkling eyes of impossible black, smiled quietly but admitted she knew only one possibility. 'They say that the wily Bricriu Nemhthenga can become a horse under the full moon if he takes a fancy to do so. Many times he has sired fine colts on the mares of this land and that is why we have such glorious herds, sought for the world over.'

"'Could he help me win my desire?' the wise woman asked her elder eagerly.

"'Perhaps, my child, perhaps. But Bricriu is not one to be trusted, as you ought well know. Dealings with him invariably lead to sorrow and dissension.'

"But the seed of the idea was planted in her head and her eyes were focused on the prize she hoped to win, not the consequences of her actions. After all she was a wise woman and

she would use her skills to persuade the mighty one to help her—
or force him to do so. Much had to be considered: how and
where this could all take place. After some considerable time, the
woman decided she had a perfect plan and by the time of the full
moon, she put it into action.

"First, she bought the largest pig she could find and roasted it
for three days, basting it in thick honey and her special
combination of rich herbs until it was sizzling and succulent.
Then she cleared the area around the spit and furnished it with
fine cushions and gold tableware and lit jeweled lamps of fragrant
oils, calling forth to no one in particular, 'Such a fine feast, here
for the taking, if only a champion worthy of such a feast were
here—why Bricriu himself would not be insulted by this feast, and
a true honor it would be to serve him too.'

"No sooner had these words left her mouth than the trickster
himself appeared before the woman. 'How could I resist such a
pleasing offer?' he said. 'Too often my name is mentioned only in
curses. To what do I owe this generous banquet, my lady?'

"She smiled and bowed before him, answering 'I desire only to
serve you. If you are happy with the feast—and only if—perhaps
I shall have the courage to ask a small favor.' He smiled warily but
she pressed on as if she did not notice. 'Sit, please! Let me lay the
repast before you.' And he did as she bad him, sitting on a low,
flat rock piled with soft cushions and she brought him generous
portions from the roast, sweet new potatoes and warm golden
bread. The woman poured him frothy ale from earthen jars,
mixed with herbs to bring out the rich flavors of the malt, an
exotic treat Bricriu much enjoyed.

"When at last he could eat no more, Bricriu leaned back on the
natural chair, a hand patting his full belly. 'Well done, my dear,
well done. I have not feasted half so well at the tables of kings in
many a year. And your roast—well! I cannot keep from thinking
there is more than the usual culinary skill involved. This must be
magic.'

"'Thank you, my lord. Your compliments carry great weight. It
means a good deal to me that you praise my humble skills,' she
answered him gently but her mind was racing with the thrill of her
daring—and the fear that the wily one might see through her
scheme. But he appeared to be merely happy with the fine food

and drink—and in a generous state of mind. But she waited.

"'I think you well deserve the boon for which you wished. Come, woman don't be timid now, tell me what it is you hoped to win by currying my favor?' He smiled and beckoned her closer.

"The woman returned his smile shyly and pretended to hesitate. 'Oh you will think it silly, my lord, a foolish and vain desire.' Her hair, ringlets of midnight, hid her crafty look from him, but he took it only as more of her humble servility. Delighted by her manner, Bricriu pleaded return for the meal, certain such a bashful soul would ask but little of him. At last she relented and in doubtful voice she asked her boon.

"'I have heard it said, lord, that at the time of the full moon you have been known to turn yourself into a fine steed, the finest ever to exist! And that you roam this great land at wondrous speed, traveling from one end to the other and back before the sun rises.'

"Bricriu rubbed his chin, looking carefully at the woman now, but she made her eyes reflect her expectant hope only. He considered her words for a time and at last answered simply, 'It is so.'

"She swallowed and found her throat dry. So much depended on this! 'I—I have long desired to ride with you on such a night. I have seen none but the smallest corner of this land and have pined to see the wonders told of in the songs of the bards. Would you carry me on your back through your night journey, show me the far corners of this land? This is what I desire.' She bowed her head as if sadly, expecting the answer 'no.'

"Bricriu laughed and slapped his thigh. 'Is that all you wish, my lady? That is easily done! Why, the moon rises as we speak. We can be away at once.' And with a hearty chortle he began to throw off his clothes, while the woman looked modestly away. 'Come, let's away on your ride' he cried, and when she looked again he was indeed a horse, a fine stallion of ruddy chestnut as if formed from the very earth, stamping his foot with eager impatience.

"She clapped her hands with a delight she did not need to feign. 'Climb up!' he called and moved nearer to the rock he had formerly sat upon. She obeyed as far as standing upon the rock and grabbing a handful of his mane, but then she paused. 'You go at great speeds do you not, my lord?'

"'Yes, yes, of course,' he said, ready to be off. 'Just throw your leg over—'

"She delayed. 'I fear, lord, that inexperienced as I am, I might fall off.'

"Bricriu snorted. 'Well, dear woman, I could deign to go more slowly' though he did not seem enthusiastic about the idea.

"'Ah, but then we would not see the whole land. I do so wish to see it all. But with no saddle, no bridle—I fear I would fall and be hurt.'

"'Unaccustomed to riders, I am not in the habit of carrying either,' Bricriu rumbled, now clearly losing his temper with the woman's fussing.

"'I do have an old bridle, hasn't been used for years, not sure it's all in one piece and hardly the thing for Briciru to be seen wearing...' she trailed off as if uncertain of what to do.

"'None shall see us, woman, I shall not be insulted. Fetch it with all haste, and let us get on with the ride!' She ran off to get the bridle from behind the rocks where she had hidden it earlier.

"Coming back, she distracted him with further questions of his deeds. 'Is it not true, my lord, that once you set all the heroes of the Ulaid against one another at a great feast?'

Bricriu laughed with pleasure at the memory and began to regale her with the tale as she walked up and slipped the bridle over his head. All of the sudden he fell silent. The woman smiled.

"The bridle I have placed over your head was crafted with magic to bind you to your present form and silence your voice. I have need of you as the finest horse in the land. When I am done I will set you free—if you swear by all my people swear by not to hurt me or those I love.' She could see his anger, but his powers were bound by her spell, and he had no choice but to obey."

Hallgerd interrupts at this point, doubled over with laughter. "Oh Nanna, I can just imagine his face! He must have been enraged! And such a clever woman too! She certainly got the better of him—not difficult either, a little flattery goes far!"

"True enough, but she did not think about the consequences of her actions. To degrade such a one as Bricriu—he was not going to forget such an insult soon."

"But she made a bargain, right? Didn't she make him swear to it, not to hurt her or those she loved?"

"Yes, but she didn't think of every possibility—who can? She used him to interest the king and it worked like the charm it was. No one, in the memory of the oldest man in the kingdom, had even seen a horse so beautiful, so swift. The king—already attracted to her wise ways and her lively conversation—asked for her to join him as his wife and share her steed with his mares. For a year the stallion ran free with the mares and many fine colts were born in the spring. And born to the woman now queen, a fine young girl with hair fiery red and a wise look for a child.

"At the end of the year, under another full moon, the wise woman took Bricriu into the woods again, near where that feast had been prepared. She told him she would let him return to his natural form provided he swore by all her people swore by to not harm her nor those she loved. Bricriu nodded his head silently and she removed the bridle. Instantly he became a man once more, rubbing his arms and shaking his head with relief. The wise woman produced his clothes from a pouch. They were clean and neatly folded and he took them without a word, glaring at her until she turned away. While her back was turned, he began to speak.

"'You have managed quite a deed, fooling old Bricriu. Your name will become famous for it.'

"She shrugged. 'I have no desire for fame. The secret may remain between us two if you so desire.' He grunted as if it were no great matter. 'I only wished to fulfill a prophecy that I could begin a line of eminent wise women if I sought the right partner. To woo this king I needed the finest horse in the land—there's none finer than you, dear Bricriu.'

"'Why did you not ask me the favor?' he grumbled, now fully dressed. 'I may have been persuaded to offer it.'

"'Truly? I had not thought it possible. One is always warned against dealing with the cunning Bricriu. This way I was certain.' But she felt herself tremble when his dark eyes met her own.

"'In doing so the only certainty was that you would have my enmity—'

"'And your word that you will not harm me nor my loved ones!' She sounded far more courageous than she felt, for she realized too late that there were other things he might do.

"'True enough.' He scratched his beard for a time and then a wicked smile broke out across his face. 'Daughters, eh? Well, I shall spawn sons and set them up to thwart your wise daughters and I swear by all my people swear by that a geiss shall be upon your daughters such that they cannot use their magic to thwart my sons—or they shall perish.'

"The curse!" Hallgerd cries. "I see now. How did she take it?"

"She was aghast of course. All her plans for naught, or at least in great danger. She fell to her knees and begged him not to make it so, but he remained obdurate. All her tears could not move him, and sadly she resigned herself to the fate. Since that time each of her daughters has told the sad story to her children to keep them from repeating her mistake and to warn them of the sons of Bricriu."

"Has anyone ever disobeyed the warning?"

"I'm afraid so." I shudder with the memory of it. "In desperate times, people take desperate measures. My grandmother's sister ignored the geiss, used her magic to frustrate one of the sons of Bricriu—she was trying to save her village from a conflagration started in anger by one of the sons of Bricriu in retaliation for an imagined slight. The fire threatened to engulf the entire town, its fields and woods. She called up the clouds to bring down a rainstorm. Lightning struck her almost at once and there was nothing left but some blackened bones."

Hallgerd gasps and covers her eyes in horror. "Oh Nanna, I can see now why you did not use your magic. I would never ask you to do so. You are too important to us alive." She bends down to give me a quick hug. I feel the tears spring to my eyes—how I love this young girl! Her story will be a much happier one—if I can do anything about it.

"So what are we to do, Nanna?" Hallgerd says, stacking the bowls back on their proper shelves. "As you say, we cannot face Thomas without an army."

"We need to get one—through a powerful ally."

"Oh dear, not Prince Mord?"

"Prince Mord, of course."

Hallgerd's snort reveals her complete contempt for the spoiled young monarch. "Even if we could get him away from his hunting and feasting, what on earth would make him want to help a little kitchen maid and her fox?"

"We shall have to make him desire very much to help the little kitchen maid." I try not to smile—this is serious business and we have so little time left—but Hallgerd's grumpy face draws out my grin.

"So what exactly is your plan, Nanna? I dread to think of it."

"Oh, it is not so bad. You may even have some fun playing the role."

"Oh dear," Hallgerd says wiping her hand on her apron, "As if I weren't having enough fun playing kitchen maid!"

"Playing? No playing in my kitchen, nothing but hard work, missy!" Grima comes up behind my princess, her face an exaggerated scowl which immediately breaks into a shy smile.

"Grima, tell me something about these midnight dances Prince Mord has around the full moon. What all takes place there?"

"Oh, all kinds of foolishness," Grima sighs, "And a lot of work for us, I can tell you, no doubt. You think we have elaborate meals now! It is double the work for the dances—dainties for the visitors, special trays to pass amongst the dancers—and even more ale to refresh them from the reveling. And the minstrels! By the gods, no one eats more than they. I've seen the smallest lute player, barely more than a boy put away half a hog himself—and two chickens besides"

"Goodness!"

"And the Prince always wants a bowl of soup before he retires to settle the stomach—no doubt he'll want your special bread soup this time, he's gotten so fond of it—so we have to stay up as late as he does, or at least someone has to do so, and that usually means me. Never before the morning dawns, I tell you, never. And there's some that get up early for the hunting next morning, so like as not, you're up three days straight, four if you think of the day preparing before it all starts."

"That's an awful lot of work, Grima," Hallgerd says, somewhat daunted. "But now you've got us to help you."

Grima tries to hide her smile, but I can tell she is pleased. She has changed so much since the night I was able to reveal the fate of her true love. I try to reassure her. "We are happy to help you in every way possible for this busy time. But in return we may need a little help from you too, my friend."

Grima purses her lips but answers, "Well, I don't know how

much I can do for you, but whatever I can, I will. You have done so much for me, I...I owe you a deep debt of gratitude. I know you would not endanger me unless absolutely necessary," she adds with a little nervous cough.

"No danger will be necessary, just a little subterfuge."

Her eyebrows raise in alarm. "Eh? What's that?"

"A little scheme, a little deceit—actually the deceit has already been practiced. Soon we will reveal the truth of who we are."

Even Hallgerd is surprised. "Oh, shall we? When?"

"Why for the party, of course. You will attend."

"I?!"

"She!?" Grima shakes her head. "I can probably find some cleaner clothes, a little nicer than what you've got, but no fancy ball gowns, I don't know how. Unless we were to steal them from some lady here but oh, they take a dim view of such things here—hanging is not my idea of a way to go!"

Hallgerd clasps the woman's hand in both her own and kisses it. "Oh Grima, we would never ask such a thing. Never fear, I have clothes suitable for the finest ball in this land or any other."

"Will you need to send for them? We have so little time—"

Hallgerd laughs. "Not necessary, either. We have had them all along. Do you think it's safe to show her?" As if she could resist!

"After that dinner," Grima says, "no one should be wanting anything for a good bit of time. And they've wine and ale a plenty—should last them several hours even at the rate they choke it back."

Feeling sly, we three pad noiselessly over to the little closet under the stairs and Hallgerd swings open the door—the door which once squealed and moaned as one dragged it open.

"My goodness!" Grima has not seen the insides since the first night Hallgerd and I slept here. Since that time Hallgerd has brightened it considerably, removing extra shelving and boards, throwing down straw to soften the floor, though we still sleep on the great cloak of furs at night. "It looks almost homey in here. Why, I would hardly recognize it."

"It's still a closet," Hallgerd says, not unkindly. "But we do have it to ourselves." We all laugh at that. She reaches under the far edge of the cloak and pulls out the walnut. "Here's my wardrobe!" The Princess is enjoying her fun.

"What? That? A little nut?" Grima narrows her eyes. "You're having fun with poor old Grima now, aren't you?"

"No, no, it's all true! See here?" And Hallgerd opens the nut and pulls out the first dress. At once the little room is as bright as midday.

Grima gasps with wonder. "It's like the sun come down from the sky and sewn into this dress! I've never seen such a thing."

"Or like this one," Hallgerd cries pulling out the next dress.

"It's just like the moon when it's full, so delicate, so silver!" Grima leans closely to get a good look. "I can hardly believe it's real." She reaches out gingerly, afraid it might not be.

"Sometimes I think this one is my favorite," Hallgerd says stroking the shimmering fabric. "But then I remember this one!" With a calculated flourish, she pulls out the last one of twinkling starlight. Grima is speechless, only holding her hands to her cheeks and looking from one dress to the next, shaking her head in wonder. The gowns seem to ripple and glow in the shadows of the tiny room and I find myself thinking of Astrid, the enchanting seamstress who made this magic. How she should bask in the praise of our admiring gazes!

Grima sniffs suspiciously at the little nut that held the dresses. "This magic is quite remarkable." She looks down at me. "Yours, I suppose. Quite remarkable, indeed. The uses I could put something like this to!"

"Perhaps when we no longer need it—" I suggest.

"Oh heavens, you misunderstand me, I didn't mean to suggest—"

Hallgerd laughs and hugs Grima. "Never fear, Grima, when I have returned to my land as Queen you will be showered with wonderful gifts of thanks, more than you can imagine—and no, I won't hear any complaint from you!"

Poor Grima has turned beet red. "I hardly know what to say...milady?"

"Please, Grima! Until I am returned to my land, I am only humble little Pelzmantel—with a few tricks up her sleeve!"

"And in her fox!" I put in. Even Grima joins the laughter. It feels so good! To have another trusted friend is gold beyond measure. Though this once-grumpy cook has been overwhelmed by magic and wondrous secrets, she has not flinched nor run in fear. How many would believe our tales? How many more would fear my powers?

"A queen! By the gods, such news! But I knew something wasn't as it seemed—no serving maid ever had such hair of spun gold," Grima says fingering one of Hallgerd's loose curls. "And a talking fox! You are under an enchantment, no doubt."

"One of my own making. Our enemies believe me captured still. They have no idea a fox inhabits my skin as I do his."

Grima gasps and shakes her head.

"But he yearns to be free and a fox once more. And dangers grow in the land. We need allies and we need to return. Grima, we think to make an appeal to Prince Mord. He is a convenient choice because we are here—is he trustworthy? What can you tell us of him?"

Grima taps her chin, thinking, and I notice for the first time that she has plucked the three long hairs that once grew there. I remind myself to tell her later how much nicer she looks. She looks so much happier, which has a more profound effect. She finally says, "Well, I don't know everything about him, just what gets told, you know, one servant to another, and what I sometimes see with my own eye. Trust him? I think so—if you can interest him in it. He seems a real layabout, I know. You'd hardly believe it, but he was once quite the adventurer."

"Him?" Hallgerd snorts with contempt. "With his fancy balls and hunts?"

"When he was but fifteen he went off on his first voyage with thirty men. Though old Bjorn was supposed to be in charge—he was the most trusted companion of King Mund, Mord's older brother, the ruling king of this land—and like I said, he was supposed to be in charge but Mord actually took command and quickly earned the loyalty of all aboard."

"Where did they go?" Hallgerd asks eagerly. I smile to myself, thinking of the Princess' love for all the exotic places she had imagined from my stories and her books. Perhaps Mord will hold some interest for her after all.

"All over! From the northern lands to the lands of the reindeer, the Suomi and the giants—"

"Giants! He really saw giants?"

Grima shrugs. "I have no idea. I'm just repeating the stories told. He sailed out to Iceland and to the Orkneys and to the lands of the Saxons and the Scots. They went south too, to Brittany and Espana and I hear, all the way to Constantinople."

"Constantinople!" Hallgerd's eyes shine with pleasure. "Oh, how I have always longed to visit that city—so many wonders, so many people, so many books, such learning! Constantinople!"

Grima nods. "I remember because it took me so many times to learn that name." She reddens. "I thought it would make me sound quite intelligent, but I haven't actually had the courage to say it until just now."

"Well, you say it exactly the way I learned it," Hallgerd assures her.

"Thank you, lady, you are too kind."

"Please! Just call me Pelzmantel, Grima. We can't let our secret slip too soon."

"Oh, yes, of course. But I must say it makes me rather uncomfortable to know that you are so much more—and then to treat you as a mere serving girl. But I will try."

"What else? What else? Where did he go? What did he see?" Hallgerd can hardly contain her excitement.

"Oh dear, I can't remember all the places, but he did go just about everywhere I'd ever heard of and a great many more places."

"But what happened to him? To make him change so?" I ask.

"Yes, why has he become such a frivolous young man?" Hallgerd agrees.

Grima frowns with concentration. "Well, on his third voyage, I think it was—yes, just two years ago—they were battling a man Egil in the Orkneys, a very fierce warrior, seldom equaled in battle. The two groups fought one another very evenly matched for quite some time, but in the end, old Bjorn fell in the battle, valiantly protecting Mord from the assault of the Orkney chieftain. His death enraged Mord and he fought like a berserker, killing the few remaining on the ship—only Egil himself escaped by swimming to the shore. When the crew returned home, the news sent Mund into a fury of his own, for he had prized Bjorn's friendship and counsel and even more, envied his brother's growing comradeship with the man."

"He blamed Mord for the death? Surely, death could have

come to any of them just as easily," Hallgerd argues, "After all, that is what such adventuring to leads to, sooner or later."

Grima nods and sighs. "Surely, but one cannot convince a king of what he does not wish to believe."

"What did he do?" I ask, certain that here lay the mystery of our idle young king.

"Mund stripped his brother of his ships and crew and sent him here, to guard the border."

"Guard the border?" This puzzles me. "But the border here is with the land of my lady's people. It has been peaceful for generations."

"Exactly. There is nothing for him to do. He is exiled from the center of his country, where decisions are made, where visitors come: musicians, bards, kings and queens. And his younger brother is being groomed as successor to Mund, so there is little hope that his luck will improve in the years to come."

"So Mord has given up," Hallgerd muses, not without a little contempt. "He feels trapped and without hope, far from any power or culture. Hmph! He knows not how bad things could be!"

"Lady!"

"Well, he is not alone, in disguise, and in fear of his life."

"My princess speaks truly—we are indeed in dire circumstances. The prince would do well to have a little perspective on his troubles. Perhaps we can help."

"What is your plan?" Grima asks nearly whispering, her eyes surreptitiously scanning for anyone who might overhear.

"I'm not entirely sure," Hallgerd confesses looking my way, "Though I know I shall be wearing my fine gowns at the moonlit dance."

"Indeed, and you shall be trying to win the attentions of Prince Mord in order to bind him as a trusted ally who can help us defeat the powers of Thomas."

"The powers of evil, that is," Hallgerd assures Grima.

Grima draws a breath sharply. "The sorcerer! Stories have come to this land already of the evil one who works great and terrible magic. All obey him or are destroyed. By the gods, you cannot battle such a one! They say grown men die of fear before him—women lose the children in their bellies with just one look from his evil eye!"

"I have looked him in the eye and lived to tell of it," Hallgerd says firmly. "I will not quaver before him. He has magic," she puts her hand on my head, "but so have we. And even more importantly, we have something he will never have—trustworthy friends." She takes Grima's hand and holds it to her cheek.

The plain face of the cook glows with pleasure. "For you, my lady, anything I can do is not enough. And for you too," she smiles at me, "All my trust, all my pitiful abilities. You gave me back—something, my heart? My self? My love! I am happy to know it was all real, I was loved. You need only ask and I will obey."

"Thank you, friend Grima," I say. "Your help and advice will be key. The Princess will need to slip into the dance without being noticed—and even more difficult, she will need to slip back out at the appointed time."

"Why will that be more difficult, Nanna?"

"Nanna? You are a woman?" Grima breaks in.

I chuckle. "I am afraid so."

"And yet," Grima looks thoughtful, "I had known. I had. I am not sure why, but I am not so surprised after all."

"Our spirits do not change with our flesh. It is merely the home where the spirit dwells."

"I suppose, but heavens, it does frighten me, the thought that my spirit might just fly out of my body without a by-your-leave!"

I cannot laugh at her fears, it is too unkind. "Don't worry, Grima," I assure her, "It takes a great deal of effort to make one's spirit leave the confines of the flesh. You have nothing to fear."

"Well, I'm sure it's as you say, but I don't know that I won't be thinking of the possibility in my nightmares! Enough though, you need to know about the dance. Well, it should be an easy trick to get the Princess," here Grima smiles at Hallgerd, still delighted to be in on the secret, "into the dance. There is so much hustle and bustle and people everywhere. Easy as pie. But once the prince catches sight of you in any of your gowns, dear me! He will never let you go."

"I can't believe Mord will take the same notice of my clothes as we do," Hallgerd muses. "Likely as not, he won't pay the slightest bit of attention to them. He notices so little after all."

I disagree. "Perhaps not—but he will see their beauty as a part of your own, though he may not realize it. But Grima is right, it will be much harder to get you out of the dance than in. We must think of a diversion."

"Yes, it will take quite something to get all eyes off those dresses of yours. Those dresses! Oh my, all the lords and ladies, the prophecy!" Grima claps her hands to her cheeks as we stare.

"What prophecy?" Hallgerd asks breathlessly.

"The prophecy for the prince! Oh heavens! It must be, must be, couldn't be anything else."

"But what is it, Grima?"

"Years ago, when Prince Mord had been here but a short time, a prophetess passed through and the nobles all delighted in asking their fates: who they might marry, how long they would be happy, how wealthy they might be. The prince asked, so they say, to know of the woman who would be his queen. The story got around to everyone in this part of the land, so it was never really any secret, not that anyone really tried, most people took it as nonsense of course, and anyway, who wouldn't try to marry a king if they could? Every woman who stood a chance would try—"

"But what was it?" I ask.

"Yes, what!" Hallgerd has even less patience.

"The seer said 'Under the sun, moon and stars, a woman would win his love and he would lose his kingdom.' He has always laughed at the prophecy—but he has not married. They say he fears it to be true."

"Sun, moon and stars—"

"My dresses!" Hallgerd whispers in awe.

"I know!" Grima wails. "What is to become of us?"

"What do you mean, Grima?" I ask while Hallgerd tries to comfort the crying cook.

"He will lose the kingdom and we will all be turned out! I am too old to be hired on by some other kitchen, no one will want me! I will have to turn to begging and thieving and I'll be hung, oh I just know it!" Her words dissolve into incoherent sobs. Hallgerd pats her shoulders and tries to make soothing sounds, turning her eyes to me in mute appeal.

"Hush now, dear. There'll be no such thing." I try to soothe her fears. Old! She is not so old, but her fears make it so. It would indeed be a terrible thing to be turned out.

"But the prophecy! The prophecy!"

"Prophecy is nothing without understanding. It is only raw materials, like vegetables" I say, seizing on a metaphor in desperation, "They have to be cooked and seasoned and blended before they can be eaten."

Grima wipes her eyes. "Seasoned?"

"With interpretation," I assure her. "We need not assume the worst."

"Yes, yes, of course," Hallgerd soothes. "It could be interpreted in so many ways—not all of them tragic, you know."

"I suppose," Grima admits, wiping her streaming eyes on her apron, "but what else could it mean?"

"Perhaps he will not so much lose his kingdom as relinquish it."

"Oh dear," Hallgerd says.

"What?" Grima looks back and forth between the two of us. "What?"

"If he should fall in love with our Princess here, he will no doubt want to join her in the realm of her people, help her battle for its return."

"If! Only if," Hallgerd says. "We don't know that he's likely to do any such thing. Or whether one should want such a thing to happen." There is a stubborn look to her face that suggests this princess has no need of help from a prince, particularly one like Mord.

Grima stares open-mouthed. "Heavens! This is your secret, your plan. Why—why I hardly know what to say." She shakes her head. "Mind you, it could surely work. After all, the Princess is so extraordinary and those breath-taking dresses and well, Prince Mord, he's a man after all!"

"Grima!" Hallgerd laughs.

"And true too, if he were to leave the kingdom, it would go to Sæl, his sister, who got his ships when Mund took them away. Surely she would take up the reins of command if he were to leave, and you know, that might not be so bad...." Grima strokes her chin.

"Well, don't marry me off already!" Hallgerd says, crossing her arms decidedly. "I may not think much more of this buffoon, even if he has been to Constantinople."

I can't help laughing. "We shall play it by ear, my dear. Nothing is certain—except the fact that it is not only your freedom that hangs in the balance."

Hallgerd sighs. "I know, Nanna, I know. But it appalls me to be used as bait to attract a man I don't think all that much of. He may have been an adventurer, but he seems little more than a spoiled child now."

"Perhaps he misses being an adventurer. You may awaken that impulse in him. Think, my dear, how many nobles like yourself are raised as carefully pampered as a Yule goose—though not for slaughter in most cases."

"Hmph. True enough—though I certainly run the risk of just such a fate." She sighs again. "As do my people. You do well to remind me, Nanna, I do not work just for myself, but for the realm and all the people in it. I must think of them. I have thought in the past only of the advantages of power. Now it is time to consider the responsibilities."

"It is not so terrible. After all, nothing is certain at this point. We shall see. One never knows what possibilities lie with the morrow. Tonight's nightmare may be tomorrow's dream."

Grima glances out into the main kitchen area. "We'd better look sharp, I think that's Skapti's step I hear."

We scurry to our places as the steps get louder. The meal must be over. While Hallgerd hastily puts the dresses back in the shell, Grima steps out to the boiling kettles, wiping her hands on her apron as she goes, ready for the deluge of dishes to be cleaned. I scamper over to the open area of grass outside, out of the way, but ready to help. As I run our plan through my thoughts, I feel doubts creep in like cold, little beetles. Is this really the best solution? What if it doesn't work? What if the prince will not be persuaded?

65

The time draws close before we know it. As Grima predicted, we have been so busy preparing for the dance that we can hardly stop to think. Three nights of feasting—and such feasting! Huge boars caught wild in the forest, packed in herbs, covered with honey, ready for the roasting, stuffed with nuts, spear leeks, earth apples and more herbs are lined up side by side with pheasants and ducks; should the bounty run low, mundane chickens will supplement the more tasty fare. Hallgerd bends, perspiring, over the stock for her special bread soup, adding the herbs I have taught her to use. The prince will be even more pleased with his favorite treat after it has simmered for three days. Casks of ale the size of royal chargers have been rolled up from Skapti's special subterranean cell along with barrels of wine from the southern lands. It is all quite overwhelming!

Outside, the clearing before the castle is being readied for the festival. Tents and pennants of every color imaginable have been hoisted at the edges of the woods to provide lounging areas for the dancers and a platform for the musicians. The once green scene is a riot of exotic colors: royal purple, saffron orange, the gold of finches, the red of late summer sunset. Everywhere one turns, someone is at work making the outdoor setting look as fine as any room in the gilded castle: there a woodworker assembles impromptu benches, there a seamstress covers them with rich satin and brocade, there another servant weaves bright banners through the lower branches of the trees circling the clearing. No wonder the fine ladies and noblemen look forward to this celebration. No wonder too, the servants dread it! So much to be done.

Poor Grima jumps startled at every harsh word from Skapti, who seems to take the preparations as his own personal trial, one where his life hangs in the balance. He barks out orders like a ship captain in high winds, terrified lest the least thing go wrong.

"You'd think it was his very own party," Hallgerd says, running off on yet another errand, this time with a pot of honey. Last time it was more kindling to get the roasting fires started. Such a hullabaloo!

"The first ball of the summer is always a fright," Grima assures me between the growing mountain of breads and sweet buns. "Everyone looks forward to it so, all the long winter, waiting to see when it will be warm enough to manage it. Some years we've had to wait as long as Odal or Dag before the cold departed fully. It's good when the summer comes early—everyone seems happier and gay. Except Skapti, of course," she finishes, scowling.

"When does he finally relax?"

"Oh dear, not until the dance is over. For the next three days he'll be as tightly drawn as a lute string—not one you'll want to pluck!"

"I'll be sure to stay out of his way. We don't want any last minute changes around here to spoil our plans."

Grima lowers her voice. "Have you come up with an idea for a diversion in case the Princess can't slip away easily?"

"No, I'm not certain at all. But I think I shall stick closely and watch for the opportunity. It should be easy enough to cause some kind of distraction."

"Perhaps if you run off with a chicken—or some lady's fine silk purse."

"Easy enough. But we need to be careful not to arouse the princes's suspicion too soon. He must not guess there is a connection between this little fox and the Princess. We must keep her identity a mystery for the whole three days at least if we hope to intrigue him."

"Do you think he will really fall in love with her?" Grima blushes.

"I can't say, but it is important that he admire her enough to wish to come to her aid. From all that you have told us, Grima, I think he may do so. Perhaps her plight will awaken his spirit of adventure."

Hallgerd rushes in, her face flushed from her scurrying—and no doubt too from the excitement. It is contagious! The superfluous energy from so many people busy at their tasks, full of thoughts of what the night shall bring. For it is not only the fine ladies and gentlemen who will be enjoying themselves. Once the dance begins, there will be less for the servants to do and they will receive their reward: time to relax and treats to eat. Earlier Grima pointed out a small cask of ale secreted here in the kitchen: "by Skapti himself, no less!"

Our Princess of course nearly bursts with excitement. "I can't wait to waltz into the party with my beautiful dress," she says, hastily chopping vegetables for the special bread soup. This morning I gathered all the herbs necessary for the King's favorite treat and they perfume the whole cooking area, though it is already redolent with the baking breads and cooking sauces.

"You will need to bathe well before you attend the dance, my dear, or you will smell only of the kitchen—lovely though that may be. But we want him to think about you, not about food!"

"I doubt that will be a problem," Grima says with a countenance of mock seriousness.

We are all so busy running hither and yon, that it seems no time at all until the sun slips away toward the far ends of the earth, painting the sky crimson with its passage. The cooing of the day birds gives way to the chirping of night creatures. The nobles begin to arrive in small groups, their horses clad in brilliant hues that challenge their own attire's gay profusion of colors. Happy chatter fills the air and soon, the first squawks and plucks of the musicians as they prepare for the evening's revels. The evening sky still holds onto a purple tinge when Prince Mord descends the castle steps and an expectant hush falls over the eager crowd. He nods to Skapti, who in turn gestures to the musicians. They begin to play and the ladies and lords all clap their hands in delight. The dance has begun!

"Quickly now!" I say, but Hallgerd has already started to shed her kitchen clothes. "Grima, can you bring that tub of hot water—"

"Already got it," Grima grunts as she tries to keep it from splashing too much, "Where to?"

"Our little closet?" Hallgerd suggests.

"Best place—no one will be too likely to see you in there. Scrub well! All evidence of Pelzmantel must be gone."

"It will be a welcome relief. Oh, to be clean and pampered again! If only for three nights," she adds ruefully, following Grima into the tiny room.

"Soon enough, if all goes well, we will be able to go home—though pampering may not be first on your list of things to attend to."

"I know, I know. But in the mean time, I will make the most of this dance. I shall feel like Amleth tonight, hiding my true face behind clever inventions."

I chuckle. The Princess has listened well to my stories over the years; may they provide her with the hope and inspiration she needs to pull off this masquerade.

The preparations are many. First the scalding bath from which Hallgerd emerges pink and shining once more. Then she rinses her hair with a willow and chamomile infusion which leaves it shining like spun gold. Grima's fingers prove far more nimble than mine ever were when she helps turn the Princess' crowning glory into the elaborate nest of braids that seems to be the fashion in this land.

"Such a work to get a lady ready for a ball!" Hallgerd says slipping into the dress of brilliant sunshine. "I don't think I could do this every day—nor would I wish to do so. I miss my good old breeches!"

"This fuss will be worth it when you see the astonished faces of the court. They will be quite overcome with amazement and curiosity. Everyone will be whispering, wondering who you are—and no one will know!"

Hallgerd grasps handfuls of the shimmering gold cloth and swirls her skirts around, delighted with the play of even the meager lights of the kitchen on the rich folds. Under the sparkling torches of the night, the display will draw all eyes and our little Pelzmantel will be the Princess we know her to be. Even if it weren't necessary for me to sneak into the big party, I would go just to see her spectacular debut.

Astrid's handiwork has put a huge, lopsided grin on Grima's face too. I cannot believe now that I once thought her to be the homeliest woman I had ever seen. With the weight of her sorrow and anger lifted, she is becoming once more the earnest, kind-faced woman with whom Gizur fell in love. Shyly she pats

Hallgerd's hand and wishes her luck. "I cannot see how the prince—or any man—could possibly keep from falling at your feet. I hope all goes well."

"I am confident now that it will," Hallgerd says. "Somehow this dress seems to radiate great determination along with its sunny beams."

"I think that may be a glamour of Astrid's weaving. We are fortunate indeed if that is the case. Every little bit of help is to the good."

"Well," Hallgerd says, smoothing her sleeve, "I guess I'm as ready as I'll ever be."

"Let's go!" With a last glance around for possible onlookers, Hallgerd and I duck out of the kitchen area and into the surrounding darkness, making our way through the woods, circling back to the front of the castle. The creatures of the night run from our rustling passage. With my fox's nose I can smell the damp greenness fighting its way up through the detritus of the long winter months and it fills my senses like the scent of an exotic wine. Such a night! So many hopes. May they all come to fruition! If luck is with us—and I think it is. Just look at the Princess, her face pinkly aglow from the trot through the woods. She has never been more beautiful—or more sure. All the confidence of youth, of a heart with few disappointments, shines from her eyes and quickens her step.

"Here," she whispers to me, pausing to take in the revelers' movements as they whirl hand in hand. We are behind the tent covering the sweet roasted boars. The pungent aroma makes my fox's mouth water and my too empty belly grumble heartily. But it is a wise choice. All eyes here are on the dancers and will not mark my Princess as she slips into the festivities.

"Go! Do well! Have fun!"

She smiles and folds her skirts tightly round her as she passes between the brightly hued tents. Within the circle, Hallgerd smoothes the golden fabric so it once more floats and ripples in her passage. Head held high, every inch the Princess, she strides across the clearing to join in the dance.

From my low vantage point I can see only that surprised faces gyrate in her wake. Now that she has been noticed, it will be that much harder for her to sneak away later. But I do so enjoy seeing my little charge turn the heads of such fancy ladies and gentlemen. If I move around to the other side, perhaps I could see more. I circle through the darkness toward the edge of the trees facing the castle. It is dangerous, but I think I can pass unnoticed this far from the torches. After all, these fine folk are looking for amusement, not foxes.

I seem safe enough, but I can't see anything! Too low to the ground. I'll have to wait to hear Hallgerd's version of events—unless I hear a cry for help. In the meantime, maybe I can sneak some of that succulent boar.

16

The revels have gone on several hours with no sign of disturbance—apart from the little fight between the two pipers who both wanted the very same roasted chicken and were neither willing to give up, until placated with tastier fowl—and it is now the midnight hour, our assigned time for a diversion. Though the question perturbs me for a time, the answer is quite simple: I shall run off with a tasty meal!

I slip between the legs of the happy dancers, listening for Hallgerd's voice. Ah, at last, over here, near the darker side of the clearing, under the deeper shades of the comforting oaks, she speaks softly with a man. I look up from behind his feet, trying to catch my princess's eye and that's when I realize it is indeed the prince's feet I stand between. Well, so far so good!

I whip my tail back and forth. The movement catches Hallgerd's attention and her eyes meet mine. She smiles—no, smile is too mild—she grins. Already curiosity burns me. I turn and run over to the roasting carcasses. Biding my time carefully, I leap up on the next cranking turn and sink my fangs into the one remaining leg. I growl loudly and pull at the appendage with all my meager strength. Well-roasted, it pops off. Oh, the flavour! The aroma nearly makes my hungry senses swoon. But I have to keep my thoughts about me.

"Ey! You! Get away from there!" The roaster has just noticed the crime. He waves his arms at me, fearful to get too close. I charge at him, growling, and the man backpedals so quickly he loses his balance and falls, shrieking his fear. Heads turn. Skapti comes running with a look of exasperation stretching his features. Enough pandemonium seems to be loose. I turn tail and run with my prize. A number of people give chase, but I have the advantage of size and darkness. I am in no danger, unless they loose the dogs. And surely that will be too much trouble this late—even Skapti cannot worry that much.

I circle around cautiously. No one seems to be in pursuit any longer. I catch a movement in the dark. Approaching silently, I see with my fox eyes two shapes. With a sigh of relief, I realize it is Hallgerd and Grima. I slip up behind them. Wisely, Grima has brought the fur mantel. Its kaleidoscope of patches hides the princess well in the mottled gloom under the trees. In no time at all we are back in the warm kitchen. Hallgerd whisks off the cape and soon the dress follows. She slips on her filthy kitchen clothes and bundles up her hair.

"You'd better cover it," I say between mouthfuls of the savory roast. "It's just too pretty."

Grima smiles broadly. "It was such a sight, you with the Prince in all your finery! Not my little Pelzmantel, but a real to life princess. Beautiful!"

"Well, well, not so busy after all," I tease our friend.

Grima laughs. "Busy, yes, but I couldn't resist. Curiosity, it's Loki's curse."

"My only regret is that I could see so little! I am too low to the ground now," I grumble, "So we must wait for Hallgerd to tell us her adventures."

"But first the soup!" Hallgerd reminds me, a kerchief now wrapped tightly around her head, though her apron is still askew. She tries to tie it one-handed while stirring the soup.

"Here, let me." Grima steps over and ties a big bow as Hallgerd bends over the steaming pot of soup. "It's only bread soup after all. You've made it dozens of times."

"Yes, but it has to be special tonight."

"It will be."

"I know, I know, but it has to taste just right."

"It will," I assure her. "But that's not the only reason it will be special."

Hallgerd looks down at me over the spoon from which she had been sipping. "What is it, Nanna? What have you got up your sleeve?"

"Hmph. As a fox, I have no sleeves, my dear."

"Very funny! You know what I mean."

"You'll drop one of the tokens into the bowl so he'll find it."

Hallgerd turns very pale at this suggestion. "What? Oh, Nanna, you can't possibly mean that! Give up one of the tokens? Never!"

Grima looks back and forth between us, catching Hallgerd's fear. Before I have a chance to answer, Skapti clatters down the steps. His face looks very sour.

"The prince would like his bread soup now! Take it up at once."

"So soon?" Grima wonders aloud without thinking.

"Yes!" His glowering eyes burn the poor cook for her impertinence. "And look sharp about it, no dawdling now." He turns without a further glance at us, knowing none would dare disobey his barking.

"By the gods, I'd like to…" Grima mutters to herself.

Hallgerd ladles soup into the prince's special bowl but she has not forgotten my comment. "Nanna, you can't be serious. Give him one of the tokens?"

"Before we are through, we'll have given them all. Oh do not fear, my dear. He will return them to you when all is said and done." *If he is any kind of a gentleman,* I add silently. "Quickly now, we have no time to debate."

Hallgerd's lips meet thinly but she turns and walks to the little closet to fetch the walnut. Returning, she opens it and selects the bobbin and, with a heavy sigh, drops it into the bowl. Grima looks full of unasked questions, but she says nothing, whisking a cover over the bowl to keep it warm and handing Hallgerd the Prince's golden spoon.

"Keep your head down, my dear. Best not to take any chances."

Hallgerd nods, wiping a dirty sleeve across her face to help mask her beauty while she holds the bowl in the crook of her other arm. Swiftly she disappears up the steps.

Grim is clearly worried. "What if he recognizes her?"

"It won't be the end of the world," I say with a confidence I do not feel, "but it would be a bit premature. We shall have to have confidence that a prince overlooks things he considers to be below his notice—like servants."

We two potter around the kitchen area until Hallgerd's return minutes later.

"I'm back!" she cries. "He didn't even look up, so I was in no danger at all." Nonetheless, she breathes heavily, as if she had held her breath the whole time and then had run all the way back here. "He was staring out the window, frowning. Skapti was speaking to him, but it was clear Mord didn't hear a word he said."

"Thinking of you?" Grima grins and blushes.

Hallgerd looks thoughtful. "I don't really know. He looked far too serious. Perhaps more weighty concerns occupy his mind at present."

"We shall know more, no doubt, when he finds the token."

"Nanna, why? Why must we give him the tokens?"

"They are a pledge of certainty. He may believe you are a comely maid under the rags and kitchen grime, but he must be assured of your royal blood too. The tokens will assure any that their keeper is who she claims to be."

"What are these tokens? May I know of them?" Grima's curiosity can barely be contained, though she tries vainly to quash it.

"They are the legacy of my family," Hallgerd says gravely, the walnut once more open in her palm. "Passed from mother to daughter, mother to daughter, they remind us of our responsibilities, our sacred bond to the lands we rule. Each one represents a quality of excellence." She holds up the remaining tokens and recites

The bobbin for guidance through wisdom and sense,
The spindle for drawing out all excellence,
The ring for binding the oath to this land
To love and protect and be at its command.

By the final words, her tears are falling. Tears of pride, tears of sorrow, tears of anger, tears of hope; all fall, the rivers make furrows in her newly begrimed cheeks, then roll off her chin to splash on her outstretched palm.

"Everything will be okay, please trust me," I say, choked by my own tears. I lay an ineffectual paw on her leg in mute comfort.

"Oh, dear Princess, please don't cry, please!" Grima entreats. "Trust your fox, do! She must be right, everything will be okay! Your enemies shall fall and you will be returned to your splendor."

Hallgerd laughs a little through her tears and puts her hand on the cook's shoulder. "Oh, Grima, it's not the splendor I miss, it's the friends. And I'm glad to say I am making new ones here. I know you are right."

"Sure, sure. New friends who'll do whatever they can to help you, believe me. I'd brave a Suomi sorcerer for you—oh, dear, here comes Skapti again!"

The rapid staccato of steps ring down the stairwell to our snug cooking area and in no time the producer of those sounds himself appears. "You! Girl!"

Hallgerd closes the walnut surreptitiously and curtseys. "Sir?"

"Come over here. What is this?" He holds up the glimmering gold bobbin so it catches the firelight.

"I have no idea, sir," Hallgerd answers softly, her eyes once more on the floor.

"It was in the prince's soup bowl." Hallgerd says nothing. "Well, how did it get there?"

"I have no idea, sir. Perhaps it was in the bread."

"In the bread? How would it get there?"

"I have no idea, sir," Hallgerd repeats. "I have never seen such a thing."

"What about you?" Skapti turns to Grima. "Did you put this in the soup?"

"By the gods! If I had found gold the likes of that—"

"Enough, woman!" Skapti scowls and turns once more to Hallgerd who still stands meekly. "The prince is most displeased."

Uncertain of the appropriate reply, Hallgerd curtseys again. "I shall endeavor to do better in the future," she manages at last.

"See that you do," Skapti replies coldly.

He seems about to leave when his eye lights upon me and then narrows unkindly. "Was your fox running around loose tonight?"

"Oh no, sir!" Hallgerd says.

"Indeed not," Grima adds. "I had to keep him out from under foot, so he was tied in the corner all evening. I just let him loose to do his business now." Taking the cue, I slip quietly away outside, though I stay within ear shot.

"Well…well, I shall be keeping an eye on you all. Something doesn't feel quite right. And when I find out what it is, I shall take care of it." He waits for no comment, but turns on his heel and clatters away, the bobbin clutched tightly.

"Well, now that wasn't so bad, was it?" I ask, returning inside.

Hallgerd and Grima both gape at me, appalled, then suddenly burst into relieved laughter. "I suppose not," Hallgerd says at last, "But I must say I was shaking in my shoes while he grilled me."

"I can't believe I said that! Said I'd take any gold I'd find? I must be mad!" Grima doesn't seem to know whether to keep laughing or start crying.

"He does not think you a thief, Grima, fear not. Skapti merely wants to solve the mystery. He recognizes it for an exquisite piece and he's sensible enough to know it did not fall from the sky."

"He suspects the source, though," Hallgerd worries. "What shall we do?"

"We go on as we have planned. Tomorrow the same. But first—tell us of your night! What passed between you two?"

"Oh my! Such a night! The dancing was delightful." Hallgerd smiles at the memory. "I have not had such fun ever! When I am queen, I shall have many dances."

"I see you have great plans," I say drily.

Hallgerd laughs. "It is frivolous of me, I know, but I cannot get over the simple pleasure of dancing. All those people, whirling and laughing, as if they hadn't a care in the world. And even though I had many cares, for a time they felt as light as duck feathers. It was…magical."

"Dance is often used in magic," I say. "Sacred rituals include its joy."

"I can believe it. But where to begin—yes, yes, Nanna, I have learned well, begin at the beginning. So, I swept in, pretending like I owned the place and had every right to be there. If I'd even stopped to think about it—well! I would have been terrified and tongue-tied. I hadn't gone very far before I could sense in my wake the eyes of others. My dress! It drew them, drew stares. The radiance of the sun shining in the middle of the night. I couldn't help smiling to myself—such fun! Someone offered me some mead. It ran down my throat cool and sweet. I took a bite from one of Grima's mince pies and it tasted so good!"

"Oh thank you, my dear!" Grima's pleasure spreads across her face.

"A young man asked me to dance but I waved him away, pretending I was shy—I wasn't sure I wanted to dance just yet.

He relented but he kissed my hand and asked if I might consider him later. I nodded, trying to blush. Can you blush on purpose, Nanna?"

"I have known it to be done."

"Well, I'm not sure whether I did or not, but he seemed to think me a fine young lady. And then, as if that had given them the right answer to a test, several other young ladies came over and began asking me all sorts of questions about my dress and my parents and such—they obviously thought I was the right kind of young woman. I managed to avoid telling them my name, always changing the subject—remarking upon the cunning hair style one had or the fine brooch of another. They all admired Astrid's handiwork and were eager to feel the gold fabric. I told them the truth, well, a sort of slanted truth—that the dress was a present and no, I didn't know whether they could have another such one made. I'm not sure I can avoid telling them my name for another night," she adds, her brow furrowing.

"You could perhaps tell them the truth, a little of it anyway— slanted as you say," I chuckle. "You are a Princess in exile, your life in danger, your secrecy a necessity. They'll be more intrigued than ever."

"Oh, that should work quite well! I shall do that. It will be ever so much easier than just rattling on to something new— 'Goodness, how do you braid your hair like that?' and other such inanities. I could hardly believe myself after a while. Still, I didn't have to do it for very long, for sure enough who should arrive but Mord. Curious to see what all the fuss was about, for by then I had many young ladies all around me, eager for a story. You're right, Nanna. People really do hunger for stories, new stories, anyway."

"New stories, old stories, it's all the same. What happens next? How does it turn out? Will they survive, love, thrive? Stories feed us as much as meat and wine. Without their richness, we starve."

Hallgerd giggles. "Telling them becomes intoxicating too! I'm afraid I shall have to invent many thrilling adventure stories tomorrow night to explain my escape into exile. The truth isn't nearly so exciting as a real story—I think I can make it more so. Dragons—there has to be at least one dragon in it, I think."

"Perhaps, my dear, perhaps. But remember not to stretch a

story too far, or it will slap back in your face like a willow switch."

"Yes, you're right, maybe not a dragon. But I shall think of something good." Hallgerd's face fairly glows with the anticipation. "Now, where was I? Oh yes, Prince Mord. He made his way through the throng around me and bowed a greeting—nothing like the real prince I have seen!

'Oh milady, I bid you welcome to my kingdom and to this evening's dance.'

"Pish! Where was the guffawing ruffian who taunted me in the woods? Ha! But I curtseyed to him, pretty as you please and merely said 'Thank you.'

'Would you care to dance?' he asked me next.

"'I would be delighted,' I replied and he led me out to the center of the clearing. Then came the hard part! I don't know how to dance! Not fancy anyway, just the way you and Unn and I cavorted around our little stronghold in the woods. Surely he would realize—but I did the best I could and perhaps out of politeness, he didn't say a thing about my hopping off beat or my treading on his foot at least three times. In my dress of golden sunshine, I guess I look much more the princess than in my kitchen togs. Still, he was looking at me rather strangely and I was starting to get worried.

"Mord finally said, 'I was certain we had never met when I first caught sight of you, but as we dance, I begin to find your face almost familiar.'

I laughed and told him 'Oh, everyone says that. I have such an uninteresting face. No one remembers it, yet at first sight, it seems well-known.' Of course he protested at that because he was still trying to be polite. 'Perhaps we have met,' I said, 'and I simply don't remember. Where could it have been?'

"Well, that turned into a guessing game—the object of which I made my name too. I told him 'Surely, you would recall it, had we met before.' He of course didn't want to admit to being wrong, so he was wracking his brains for every possibility, starting with nearby lands and then heading off for exotic locales.

'You're not from Alexandria?' he even asked me, teasingly. 'No no.' 'Perhaps from Burgundia?' 'No!' 'Vinland?' 'Ha!' 'Constantinople?'

"'Have you been to Constantinople?' I asked with a genuine

thrill.

"Well, it took very little to get him talking about his travels, all the learned people and stupendous architecture of Constantinople, the many treasures. I was truly enthralled—and fortunately it kept him from asking any more about my name or where I was from! Mord was just finishing a ripping good story about battling berserkers on an island when I caught sight of you under his feet. I must say despite what I feared, I had a most exciting night in my fancy dress playing the part of the secret princess."

"But my dear, you are a secret princess," I remind her. "Perhaps I should be blamed for raising you so simply but—"

"Oh never fear, Nanna. I am aware of my duties and responsibilities—and of the power I may one day wield. But I see here too easily the corruption such power can bring, a weakness that can come from its protective comfort, like wearing a cloak once the weather is warm. I do not regret being raised in simple benevolence. It would have done Mord some good. He has a worthy heart—courage even, but he has been too long protected from the harshness of life. He forgets that others suffer and that as their ruler, he could aid them." Hallgerd's eyes flash with sudden temper. "It is truly a waste to see such a young man with so many advantages idle away his days in frivolity—though I must say, for my own part, that a little taste of the frivolous now and then makes for great pleasantness indeed." Her anger has faded into a self-conscious giggle.

"Balance, always a balance," I say. "Work to give life purpose, play to lift the heart, music to soothe the spirit, love to give one strength. One cannot ask for more."

"Oh, you are so right, little fox friend!" Grima smiles, her face nonetheless drawn with regret. "No play, no love—then work poisons your spirit, breaks it. I know too well."

"Too much care is as bad as too little," I agree, laying a paw on my friend's skirts. "The heart needs to sing, to be free just as much as the spirit needs to be challenged with hard work. Celebrations warm our spirits, as does everyday love. We cannot be whole without it."

"And with nothing but celebrating, one loses the taste of it. I can see that in Mord. I think he would welcome a little work,"

Hallgerd says adding, almost to herself, "and it is about time he got some."

"Helping a princess regain her land would certainly be hard work—not to mention dangerous. But he may welcome it just the same. Lives need purpose."

"Well, right now, our purpose should be getting ready for tomorrow night," Grima reminds us with a little shake of her wooden spoon. "There will be even more hungry mouths to feed then."

On the second night, events proceed much the same. There are even more people—eager, excited, faces bright with expectation. They arrive in coaches decked with flowers, snowdrops, crocuses, other early bloomers, and with ribbons of every color, mid-summer hues exploding, whipping in the wind. The nobles alight from their conveyances and show themselves too to be decked in similar finery. The noise! The shouts and laughter—and the music rises even louder to compensate.

"It's going to be much harder to run away tonight," Hallgerd says as we take in the latest arrivals, a small but gilded coach of amazing delicacy drawn by a pair of mares equally delicate and golden. We are disappointed to see emerge from the gleaming doors no fairy beauties, but a rather dumpy pair of potato-faced royals. "And you'll need to come up with a different diversion."

"It will have to be good-sized to attract any notice," I agree, but I haven't the slightest notion what I can do. "There are so many more revelers tonight."

"And there'll be even more tomorrow," Grima says as she takes another quartet of loaves from the fire. "People think they won't bother to come this time, after all they went last year, then they hear all the fun their friends have had, and they're afraid of what they might miss."

It is the night of the true full moon. She rises glowing and radiant, a smooth silver orb freckled with blue and grey pocks, overlooking the proceedings with a proprietary gaze. If she does not approve of the festivities, will she fly down and make her displeasure known? Fortunately the frolicking appears to meet her standards and she merely smiles benignly upon the gathering.

Hallgerd, in the lady moon's honor, wears the dress of the

luminous Luna. It glimmers translucent in the firelight. The color does not rivet the attention like the golden splendor of sunlight, but it draws the eye irresistibly back to its folds in fascination, always changing, always new. I cannot decide which dress is more beautiful.

"I know!" Hallgerd grins with a blush of pride. "I could stare at the fabric all night and never end my fascination with it. This is joyous magic."

"You must remember your praise for Astrid when we return. She will be even more pleased than she was with your initial reward."

"Oh, I shall! She will tire of my compliments."

"Not the first few hundred," Grima argues.

"Come! We must get you into the party to work your own spell over the prince and his courtiers." We make our way through the dark shadows of the forest, circling once more around to the far edges of the gathering dancers and feasting. The mood of the celebrants crackles like the fires under the spits. Laughter and jubilant cries echo everywhere.

"Wish me luck!" Hallgerd whispers as she slips into the fray.

Once more the lively crowd swallows her form and I think fruitlessly of ways to see through her eyes, but realize the best way is merely to wait for her account. After all she has learned the art of story-weaving so well. I busy myself with devising a suitable distraction for later.

67

At the appointed hour I prepare for the distraction. Grima is right; there are so many more people here tonight! A small fox running through the dancing circles would do little to disturb the merrymaking. Instead I head over to the large enclosure beside the castle where the horses have been loosed to crop the grass shoots and to restore their strength for the journey home. The groomsmen appear to have abandoned their posts for the warmer environments of Grima's jolly kitchen with its hearty soups and ale to be drunk. I certainly don't blame them. And it is handy just now, too. Standing on my hind legs, I slip the loop tethering the gate from its place and slide into the enclosure. Already some of the horses raise their heads in alarm, busy nostrils working the wind for further clues. The two golden mares are nearest. They'll do.

I circle around the two, who eye me uneasily. With small feints and charges I force them toward the open gate. They skitter nervously, occasionally stomping hooves with warning, but afraid to come too close. I begin snapping at their heels and they move more swiftly. This is hard work! My admiration increases for the dogs who do such work daily. I must run faster and faster, from side to side, to keep them on track for the destination. They want to avoid the crowds, but I harry them on ceaselessly and they plunge headlong into the gathering amid shouts and curses and a general outcry. The assembled dancers part like the whale road before a sea-mare's prow. I hope it is enough!

Without a moment to catch my breath, I turn and run into the forest to meet my Princess. Again Grima has brought the warm fur cape and she throws it over Hallgerd, who can hardly contain her excited tale. "So much to tell you!" But we run inside without time for more than Hallgerd's delighted laughing at the disturbance.

"Those poor horses!" she exclaims. "They were far more frightened than any of the fine ladies and gentlemen who, it seems, were more surprised than anything else. I think some of them thought it was part of the entertainment! But it worked a like charm, Nanna. Everyone's eye was upon them and it was easy to slip away, though Mord certainly didn't want to let me go—"

"Quickly, now! Story later, hurry my dear. If Skapti shows up now…"

In a flash Hallgerd has the beautiful folds of moonlit dress tumbled on the floor and hastily dons her old breeches and dirty apron. "Hair!" Grima helps her to wrap her elegant curls in an unassuming rag. "There!"

Hallgerd hugs the dress before slipping it into the walnut. "Even I could hardly take my eyes off it, I must say. Enchanting! And the moonlight only made it sparkle more."

"I long to see it so for more than the few hurried minutes we had," I say. "Soon, soon…but in the meantime I think that's Skapti's step! Let me hide this time."

It proves a fortunate instinct. For before the haughty steward says a word, he stalks over to the closet and yanks the door open. I run out eagerly as if I had indeed been enclosed for hours, frisking around the kitchen before running out into the clearing, just far enough to be out of his sight. Grima gapes at him in genuine surprise. My innocence now established, I creep back to the doorway to watch the next step in our story unfold.

"There was a strange occurrence tonight. Horses interrupted the dancing, charging into the crowds. Three ladies fainted—and two men!"

"By the gods!" Grima cries.

Hallgerd tries to look shocked.

Skapti squints narrowly at the two of them. "There were those who claimed to see a fox behind the confusion. That there should be two foxes—in such a short time. Very odd. Very."

"Especially for the time of year," Grima concurs nodding sagely. "You just don't see that round these parts. Bodes ill for the pheasant hunting, no doubt."

"No doubt," Skapti grumbles crossly. His eye is on Hallgerd who stirs the simmering bread soup with a compelling air of meekness. "The prince shall want to do some fox-hunting quite soon. They are getting to be quite a menace to the realm." Hallgerd pays no mind, stirring the pot in silence.

"Stringy though," Grima says helpfully. "Not much good eating there."

Skapti exhales noisily in exasperation. "Never mind. But bring the prince his bread soup now, make haste—and no surprises."

"Again so soon?" Grima asks, feigning innocence. "Does the prince not enjoy his special festival? Seems such a shame—"

"The prince's pleasure is no matter for your concern," Skapti returns sharply. "Send up his soup and some fresh bread, and get back to work—if you wish to remain under his beneficence."

"At once," Grima says weakly with a bow.

Skapti turns and clatters his way up the stairs yet again. His anger seems almost to hang in the air with the more pleasant smells of cooking.

"Dear me," Hallgerd says laying a hand on Grima's arm, "I fear we are putting you in far too much danger. Nanna, perhaps we should not risk it."

"It is Grima's choice," I agree, coming back into the kitchen area, but I fear too that we have endangered our friend too much.

"Pish posh," Grima says at once. Though she looks frightened, her mouth is fixed firmly. "I am not afraid. Well, I am afraid, but I am not afraid of him. Hmph. That he should think he is so much—why when we were children it was he who needed protection from bullies, always such a small lad, always in tears. Threaten me? Threaten me! Ha. We shall do exactly as we have planned." Grima's looks defiantly at us both, daring our protests with folded arms and braced feet.

"Your courage blesses us all," Hallgerd says softly, hugging the feisty cook. "I shall repay, I swear, I shall repay your boundless courage." Grima says nothing but nods shyly as bright tears glisten unshed.

"Don't forget the token," I urge as Hallgerd fills Mord's shiny soup bowl. "We must continue the mystery. The prince's curiosity must be whetted."

"Oh it is," Hallgerd assures me, "but more of that later." She sighs and drops the little golden spindle into the soup. "Here's to Mord drawing out all his excellence. Well, away I go." She clatters up the steps with eager feet, disappearing from our view.

"Grima, you are brave," I say, "but do not risk more than you dare. We could not bear harm to come to you."

Grima remains silent for a moment, choosing her words with unaccustomed care. "I trust you two. I have to. For the first time in many years I can feel joy. I do not dread each dawn or wonder why I am still not dead. This is your doing. I owe you all I can give."

"We may yet fail," I caution her, "and would have to move on."

Grima shakes her head. "No, I feel such certainty. It's as if— as if all the flowers in the garden are blooming at once, beautiful, really beautiful. Or all the spices blending just right." She laughs. "I can hardly put it into words, but it's the way I feel. Now you'll call me a silly old woman, but I know what's right."

"But I believe it too. As much as I fear all the dangers, I cannot help but think that we will find the help we need here—as we have so far."

Suddenly Hallgerd returns, flushed, racing down the stairs. "Oh, so close, so close! I fear he knows all too well!"

"What happened?!"

"Well, as usual, I brought the soup to his chamber but after I set it down, he jumped up and snatched my arm—I was so glad I had taken the time to rub it well with burned wood!—and looked keenly into my face. I tried to avoid his eye as if frightened—I was frightened too! Frightened that he would recognize me. I contorted my face, trying to look imbecilic. At length he let go my hand and turned away. I thought to ask him what was wrong, but decided a real servant would just scurry away. So I did."

"He knows!" Grima's hands fly to her mouth.

"He suspects," I soothe. "He probably suspects everyone at this point. The curiosity must be devouring him—or at least intriguing him."

"I dread Skapti's return! Whatever will we say to him?" Hallgerd wrings her hands nervously. "Will he believe our pleading innocence again?"

Grima says nothing but looks fearful too.

"We can only do what we must—let us wait and see," I say. "We can all think on our feet. If we stick together, we are strong.

In the meantime, let us turn to and do our work. Busy hands—"

"Assuage a busy mind," Hallgerd finishes with a smile. "Let's forget our troubles in our toil. After all, there is much to be done for the final night of the festival."

Indeed there is, and it occupies our hands and soon our minds too: cooking, baking, cleaning—herbs to be spread to dry, dry herbs to be ground with mortar and pestle—kitchen magic still takes work! In fact a good deal of time has gone by before Hallgerd looks up from her grinding and says, "Shouldn't Skapti have been here by now, demanding to know what is going on?"

"Heavens! But you're right. I could hardly concentrate on my chopping for fear of hearing his step on the stairs. The waiting is the worst part!" Grima wipes her hands on her apron.

"Perhaps he is not coming," I say as the thought comes to me, "perhaps the prince has not told him anything was amiss."

"Dear me, you don't suppose Prince Mord swallowed the token unknowingly, oh dear, that would be very bad indeed!" Grima says and Hallgerd's eyes nearly pop out of her head with astonishment.

"Oh Nanna, you don't suppose—!"

"Now, now, come, let us think carefully. Were you the prince and found such a wonder in your soup bowl one night, would you not look very carefully the next night too? Remember too how he detained you, hoping for some kind of response from you?"

"True, true. He was quite intimidating. And yes, if I were he, I would check very carefully my next soup bowl—not to mention everything else too."

"But why has Skapti not come?" Grima asks.

"I suspect that the prince has not confided in his right hand this time. He got no results from Skapti's interrogation last night, so perhaps he is trying to be crafty himself. He knows a mystery is afoot and he has assured himself that no one will immediately admit to it. Prince Mord must unravel the puzzle himself. He is uncertain whom to trust."

"I see. I think you may be right, Nanna. It does make sense."

"Then will he try us all in turn?" Grima says, trying not to betray her nervousness as she continues to finely chop the leeks.

"Perhaps, but I think he rightly suspects our Princess, but has not figured out the link between her two guises."

"Are you sure? What if he has guessed?"

"Surely he would be here now, or Skapti would be bringing you before him. No, he does not know yet, but he has been hooked by Loki's curse all right."

Hallgerd nods. "I too would be curious. An enigmatic and beautiful young woman suddenly appears—and disappears before you can learn her name. Strange gold tokens appear in your supper. A terrific story, Nanna." Hallgerd laughs with delight, hanging her apron upon the hook.

"Speaking of stories my dear, you owe us one."

"Oh yes! Well, I suppose Skapti is not coming, so it should be safe enough now. Well, let's see—hmmm, the first thing was running into the other young ladies. I finally relented, as I put it, and told them I could not possibly divulge to them everything, but that I was in hiding and far from my homeland, where there was a terrible plot to kill me and well, it was all terribly exciting and I kind of drew it up as I went along, talking about all the hardships and sorrows, why, I barely escaped with my life! If it were not for my incredible luck and cunning mind, I would already be dead. Nanna, you would be proud."

"I am," I say, though I cannot stifle a bark of laughter too.

"I feel a little silly claiming full credit, but I thought it best not to have them even suspect that I had an accomplice."

"Wisely done, my child. They should not have any more information than necessary. You must have been the talk of the dance within no time."

"Oh yes! People kept coming up to me and greeting me, asking introductions, wanting to hear more of my adventures." Hallgerd hugs herself remembering the fun.

"And the prince?"

"Oh, he did not come to me at first, but I too did not go to him. I needed to test my hook, as it were. It did not take too long, and of course I pretended not to notice him immediately—nor did everyone else, much to his annoyance! Suddenly someone realised the prince was nigh and they began hastily to bow and curtsey. I joined them, giving the required curtsey. Mord looked at me even as he spoke to the others, so I was not surprised when he asked for my arm and led me to the dancing." The princess twirls about the kitchen reliving the steps. "We enjoyed a few hearty turns about the clearing then he asked whether I might like to continue our conversation from the night before as he had so many more things to tell me."

"Oh, you have captivated him indeed, my lady!" Grima claps her hands.

"I suppose. There were so many things to consider. I did not know at first whether my adventurous tales had made their way to him, but soon he began to ask me of them and I responded with a becoming modesty—I think!—so that it would seem as if I did not really brag that much of my supposed adventures, though of course I had to the others. But from the things he related to me, the stories were stretched out all recognition by the repeated tellings—one even had me fighting a dragon!" Hallgerd says with a wink at me. "But I finally got him to move on from my stories to his. I found that he too had lost his mother when rather young."

"Oh dear, child, I am so sorry to hear that. I didn't know. I would have gladly given you mine," Grima adds with sour humor.

"I told him that I had never even known her, as you know, Nanna—Nanna was a very dear friend of my mother too, Grima—and he told me had very little memory of his, just a few brief glimpses of warmth and sunshine and love."

"She was a very beloved queen," Grima says. "I seldom saw her but maybe once or twice when the King and Queen came out here for hunting parties or other such entertainment, or were on their way to distant lands. But stories of her kindness and beneficence are still common currency."

I nod too. "I have heard much of her goodness too. She and Queen Gunnhild would write to one another on occasion, sharing good news and kind hopes. She was by all accounts a fine Queen and a lovely woman. I know little of the King however."

"He was a good king," Grima says, "but the Queen brought a much greater kindness to the people. King Valgard was fair, but he wasn't always the most good-natured man. His temper was quite stormy as a young man—I've heard stories from my mama—but the Queen seemed to leaven his anger with her sweetness." She inhales the steam from the stewpot and after a moment's consideration adds more leeks and a handful of laurel leaves.

"Well, Mord didn't really go into detail about that, but it was nice to hear of his mother. He spoke too of his exile here after the disastrous trip where his brother's favorite was killed. He seemed somewhat bitter but also resigned. You know, I think that like his brother, Mord blames himself for Bjorn's death. And though he revenged himself upon many who were there, I do not think he is at peace. He does not know how to mourn his loss."

"Ah, so sad." I feel at once that Hallgerd has hit upon the truth. "Such sorrow carried in the heart darkens anyone's mind and mood."

"Yes, you need only look at me to see that it is so," Grima says quietly.

Hallgerd hugs her quickly. "But no longer! You shall have to be called Grima the Not So Grim now."

"Well, I don't know—" Grima says, but looks quite pleased.

"Mord needs friendship, too," I say. "He is too much surrounded with vulturous nobles whose only interest is entertainment."

"Too true, Nanna. The people who gather for this festival are a frivolous lot, their greatest concerns focus on their clothes—and the food! They are not bad people, but they are silly."

"A good leader leads the people in many ways—not only in war and government, but in values and deeds. The common folk will always emulate their leaders: good leaders bring the best out in all."

"Nanna, I'm getting worried. What shall we do for tomorrow? What if the prince has guessed my identity?"

"We have little choice but to continue in our disguising. If he were certain—he would be here now. But if he should uncover our scheme tomorrow, I think we will manage all right."

Hallgerd remains silent as she considers this, chewing meditatively on her lip. "I suppose that's true. Still, it makes me uneasy. I wish we knew for sure."

"There is no way to be sure—but I think it is safe to assume from Skapti's absence that the prince is thinking things over, deciding on a plan for tomorrow. He too wishes to set a trap. But in the end that is what we want him to do."

"Heavens, what if—well, what if—oh dear!" Hallgerd sighs. "Well, I suppose if he tries to expose me tomorrow night I shall have to think of something, and think fast."

"Would he try to unmask you in front of all those people?" Grima cries in sudden alarm. Her eyes widen and she slaps her hands to her cheeks.

"Now now, we don't know that he is certain of anything," I caution, "We can assume though, that he is going to be as sly as he can be, so you will need to be very careful tomorrow night. Give him some tantalizing hints, but nothing to put him off. After all we do want him to find you out eventually, and although I'm not sure tomorrow is the best time—we may not have a choice."

"Let's hope so."

68

The following morning dawns bright and cheerful. The air carries the scents of the early buds and the awakening land. Winter has folded her arms and retreated to slumber in the mountains until the cold winds wake her once more. Everywhere birds sing. Even our little chickens have caught the fever and merrily frolic outside the kitchen.

Hallgerd, despite her fears, has caught Dame Nature's joy and dances around the kitchen at her chores, sometimes grabbing Grima into an impromptu waltz. We all feel it. Such anticipation in the wind—excitement, but nervous perturbation too; will tonight be the end of our masquerade? I tell myself it is not the worst outcome—after all, we must unveil soon. And from what Hallgerd has said, the Prince seems charmed indeed. I think he shall help the Princess regain her land. All will be well, I scold my thoughts, but doubt lingers, whispering its cautions.

People begin arriving quite a bit earlier on this last night of the festivities, as if they desire to stretch out their pleasure for as long as possible. There is such wistful joy in the faces, a barely contained energy in their steps. They want to make the most of this final evening. Everyone seems to have a scheme afoot; between the early arrivals there is much whispering and laughter. How many hearts yearn for solace tonight? Intrigues, romances, perhaps even dreams more nefarious—who is to know? Many secrets twinkle in the eyes of those who idle in the clearing as the servants reconstruct the gaiety once more. More food, more musicians, more colorful banners—how else can the third night top those previous? And in no time too, rumor and legend will make the fantasy grow even greater, whatever the reality. All who were there will wax proud in their tellings—all who were not, will vow to come next time.

The kitchen area floats on an ocean of fantastic smells. My fox nose can hardly bear the intoxication. I have to run outside and gulp lungfuls of sweet fresh air, itself still redolent of all the new life growing. Poor fox, locked in the cell, how he must suffer! Deprived of the sharp senses upon which he relies, straining to sniff the air with my poor human nose, to hear the cuckoo's call—how he must long to be free. Only a little longer, my friend, only a little more.

When the band begins playing, we know it is time to ready our princess for her final dazzling entrance. Grima keeps a nervous eye on the stairs where Skapti might possibly appear, while Hallgerd rinses her golden locks in an infusion of chamomile flowers. How lustrous her hair will be! Even so, it will be nothing against the glittering of the gown of twinkling stars. Hanging in the dark of our little closet under the stairs, its luminescence creates a glow of surprising brightness. Again and again I see Hallgerd's eyes return to drink in its glory. Grima too can seldom resist snatching a glance at the shimmering fabric, shaking her head in wonder as if she cannot believe it really exists. Each dress has been more fantastic than the last. Bless Astrid!

In no time Hallgerd has made herself ready. From the top of her head to the delicate gold slippers on her feet, she is every inch royal. The stars in her dress twinkle convincingly enough for any astrologer and we three have fun identifying the constellations on the midnight fabric.

"Look! The little bear!"

"And the big one too," Grima adds with satisfaction, peering at Hallgerd's backside. "And the dragon as well. Goodness! You could make quite a game of this."

Hallgerd giggles. "I think I had better be going before I completely forget about the dance."

"At least you have something to entertain the other fine folk with tonight!"

"If conversation slows, I'll be ready!"

Despite our worries, we all seem to be in rare spirits tonight. It is as if all fear has been dispelled—whatever the outcome tonight, our hearts are full of joy now. Perhaps it should be taken as an omen, an augury of good fortune. I breathe a wish that it be so as Hallgerd, wrapped in her cloak of furs, steps out of the kitchen and scurries into the welcoming darkness of the forest's edge with a hasty wave back at us. I wait behind. I have attracted too much attention already—a third night with a fox is far too much coincidence for the gullible, let alone for a suspicious mind like Skapti's—and the prince's. We shall have to rely on Hallgerd's wits to find another way for her to sneak out of the festivities tonight. She will be all right, surely. But I chafe at the waiting nonetheless.

Grima and I busy ourselves. It will be hours before we find out what occurs tonight. In the meantime, there is always much to do in the kitchen and though I am small, I can help out. I carry my small basket back and forth, fetching herbs, and I can use my teeth to drag a larger basket of potatoes across the floor. Grima and I talk too, wondering aloud on occasion what will happen tonight, though we curb our talk when the coach drivers come by hoping for a bite and a glass of refreshing mead or ale. Fortunately they do not linger long—Grima does her best to grumble at them—as they must watch by their horses in case their lords and ladies should take it in their heads to depart, or send them off on some errand. One elderly gent tells us of having to drive off in the moonlight and search for scented rushes in the dark one year. Seems his lord wanted to impress a fine young lady. "Covered in mud up to my elbows and knees, shaking with cholera, and all he said was, 'Oh no—she danced most atrociously, never mind.' Passing fancy, it was—and near the death of me!" Grima gives the man an extra mug of the better mead and almost smiles at him.

So many people in and out, so much to do. Always, more food! More bread, more soup, more chickens to set aroasting—at least I could help catch them. Grima whirls to and fro, never stopping for a rest, never halting her constant mutter of ringing doom. "Well, no use, the chickens'll be too tough, like as not crack a tooth on them—stringy! And too much laurel there! Oh, why didn't I keep my mind on that while—heavens, the spigot is on! Turn that off or we'll be awash in it, waste of good ale!" But all the hand-wringing and doom-saying aside, this is surely the finest feast ever presented in the realm if only for Grima's better nature, though I must say my knowledge of herbs has helped a little too.

At last the rush of demands and visitors wanes. Grima wipes her hands on her apron and stretches her stiff back. I open my jaws for a satisfyingly wide yawn, which makes the old cook laugh out loud.

"Fenris himself couldn't gape wider, my friend. But I suppose you have earned it. Little as you are, you have indeed been a help."

"I try, I try. And it certainly is far more pleasant to be useful than to be idle—it surely helps pass the time."

"Oh yes. We shall no doubt have some time yet before—"

"Before I return?"

"Hallgerd!" We two stare at our princess in wonder.

"It is so early still!"

"Has something happened?" I ask, my thoughts quickly turning to foreboding.

"Oh, heavens, the moon has fallen, the doom is nigh, the Prince—"

"Now, now, Grima. Nothing terrible has happened," Hallgerd reassures her friend. "Though it is a bit odd. First let us get the soup ready, I have a strong feeling it will be called for very soon and I want to be sure it is ready." Hallgerd leans over the bubbling pot of bread soup and inhales the aroma. "Pinch of betony, I think."

"How did you get away?" I ask, worrying, for the princess looks somewhat concerned herself, confused even. "Was there any trouble?"

Hallgerd replies in a voice that seems very far away somehow. "No, no trouble. None. In fact it was very easy—which worries me."

"How so?"

"Well, Mord was very peculiar tonight. Perhaps he has lost interest...I'm not sure."

"Oh, but surely not!" Grima cries. "He is very interested, how could he not be?" The dear woman seems near to tears in her disappointment.

Hallgerd stirs the soup a little more. "I'm not quite certain what to think. Mord seemed very cool, almost like he was observing me. But he left early too, so I did not even have to come up with a ruse, at least not to fool him, and the others, well, there was little to fear from them. I merely walked away."

I run to get the walnut from the closet, calling over my shoulder, "We should be ready for the prince's summons though, just in case." I have no more than reached the closet, when we all hear the distinct clatter of Skapti's feet on the stair. I look to Hallgerd and her eyes widen in mute appeal. I duck into the darkness and grab the nut while the princess tries to hide as much as possible her twinkling sleeves inside the cloak and pulls the hood low over her brow. She keeps her eyes cast down upon the simmering pot.

"The prince wishes his bread soup," Skapti announces sourly.

"At once," Hallgerd mumbles grabbing the special bowl. "Grima, could you hand me the prince's spoon?"

"Of course—oh dear, look at this!" Grima pretends to see something marring its golden surface, drawing Skapti's attention as I creep back to Hallgerd's side. "Let me just rinse this off, won't do! The very idea, prince eating from a dirty spoon!" Furtively I drop the walnut in Hallgerd's upturned palm and slink a few feet away. "Here we are, clean enough for the Aesir."

Hallgerd's smile shines full of thanks for our friend. As she reaches for the spoon with her left hand, her right places the golden ring—the last of the tokens—into the bowl. Still trying to keep her head down, Hallgerd fills the bowl with the steaming soup then holds it before her.

"Well, come on!" Skapti growls. "Let's not keep the prince waiting."

I can see Hallgerd tremble. She has not had time to remove her sparkling dress of starlight. The furry hood barely conceals her golden hair. How to fool the prince now? But she must obey Skapti's command and meekly follows him up the stair. After a moment's hesitation, I trust my instincts and rush after her quietly. She must not face her fate alone tonight.

Up the stairs, through the large hall, we pass some of the revelers who have taken refuge in the castle. Up another flight of stone steps, where I have never been, Hallgerd treads in Skapti's steps as I silently pad in hers. We come to the prince's private chamber at last.

"Your soup, majesty!" With a low bow, Skapti presents Hallgerd, who curtseys just to be on the safe side. Mord stands at the small window, hands clasped behind his back and does not appear to notice our arrival. However, he quietly orders Skapti to leave. Heart pounding, I back into the shadows masking the corner outside the doorway and hold my breath. Skapti passes without looking down at all, muttering disconsolately to himself. When he has reached the end of the corridor and begun to descend the stairs, I creep back to the doorway and poke my nose around. One stealthy eye and then the other—good, they are not looking in my direction at all.

How rich the trappings of this room: thick woolen tapestries depicting deeds of champions, a massive oak chair, a bed carved from ruddy maple wood. Yet there is an air of comfort here too—though richly furnished, the chamber is not as opulent and gaudy as the great hall. Instead it seems the sanctuary of a powerful man. Here Mord seems more the prince—and that much more intimidating. Hallgerd stands meekly before him as, at last, he takes a seat in the carved wooden chair.

"Bring me my soup, lass," he growls amiably. Hallgerd hold the bowl out to him, her eyes still cast down. Mord seems to examine with care the little he can see of her face. Finally he reaches out and takes the bowl from her hands. Hallgerd at once begins to back away respectfully, but he tells her, "Stay. I wish to ask you something." Hallgerd tries to shrink further within herself, head bowed, arms drawn in tightly.

Mord stirs the soup idly, then scoops a spoonful from the surface. He inhales the aroma and smiles before sipping the hot broth. "Your bread soup is the finest I've ever had," he says with genuine warmth.

"Thank you, my lord," Hallgerd answers, throwing in another curtsey.

Mord takes a few more spoonfuls. "How do you like things here in my realm?"

"Well, very well, my lord. You are so very generous to allow me to stay."

"How are you treated here?"

"Extremely well, my lord."

"No one unkind to you?"

"Never, my lord."

"How is your little fox?"

"Just fine, my lord."

"Hmmm." Mord continues eating his soup, his eyes never leaving Hallgerd's lowered visage. He is unsure, but he is also fairly confident, I think. He is only playing the cat with us now, enjoying the game. What can be holding him back? Surely he does not fear embarrassing himself in front of a mere servant? Ah, but indeed he does—and should. Rumors also tarnish kings.

"What ho!" the Prince cries as his spoon clinks against the golden ring. This is the sign for which he has been waiting. The third token! Mord's smile conveys his triumph. He is willing to reveal his arsenal now. "What could this be?!" he asks, holding the shiny ring out to Hallgerd.

"I'm sure I don't know, my lord."

"Come, come! You cooked my soup, did you not? Poured it in my bowl? Skapti saw you do so, did he not?"

"Yes, my lord," Hallgerd agrees in a voice squeaking with suspense.

"Well, then? Who else could have put the ring in there? And these other little objects," he adds, pulling the bobbin and spindle from a pocket in the breast of his tunic. "Where did they come from? Hmm?"

Hallgerd sinks to her knees. "I don't know, my lord! I am nothing but a poor orphan kitchen maid, no one to care for me, good for nothing but to be beat about the head with boots, at the mercy of a noble prince like you—"

"Orphan, eh? Hmmm—I seem to recall that you had run away after your parents tried to force you to marry, what was it? Ah yes, a warty old man, wasn't it? That's the story I remember you telling the day we found you treed by my hounds."

"They died...just after making their wishes known...about the wedding," Hallgerd adds lamely, caught in her own story web.

Mord throws back his head and howls with laughter.

Hallgerd blushes crimson—at least the little bit of her cheek I can see under the hood—but she says nothing further.

"A gold ring, a bobbin and a spindle. What can they mean? Perhaps they are simply a gift from the gods, an assurance of their bounty. But I have no need of such things, they seem like the trinkets of a woman. Perhaps if I had my goldsmith melt them down—"

"You mustn't!" Hallgerd cries before she can think better of it, raising her head so even I can see her storm-blue eyes flash.

"Mustn't! Mustn't? The prince mustn't? And who says so, my little friend?" Mord stands now, the tokens clutched in his hand, his eyes brightly dancing. Yet, I cannot see any true anger in his face, no fury. Just a barely concealed sense of victory.

"I only meant, my lord—I only suggest—such valuable items…"

"Oh, and how do you know they are so valuable?" He does not even try to cover his delight now.

"They are gold—my lord," Hallgerd says at last.

"Ah, I thought perhaps it was because they were yours—"

"Why no, my—"

"Oh, we shall have to be certain!" Mord cries, jumping to his feet. "Let us see if they are yours."

Hallgerd draws back, genuinely frightened, but he is too swift.

Mord grabs her hand—ah, but with such tenderness I see—and slips the ring on her finger. "Why like the glass slipper on Aschenputtel's dainty foot, a perfect fit!"

Hallgerd does not seem to know what to say and stares at him open-mouthed.

Mord stands before her, hands now on his hips, and simply laughs.

I can see my princess' temper begin to rise, as she does too.

But before the venomous words can reach her lips, the prince intercedes once more. "And what have we here?" The hem of Hallgerd's sleeve peeps out from inside her cloak and stars shine brilliantly. With quick fingers Mord hauls the rest of the sleeve from its hiding place. "Ah, more secrets, more surprises! Come, reveal yourself, my secret friend. I think I know all too well what shining gold hair lies under that hood."

Mutely Hallgerd looks at him and then with a grand gesture, sweeps off her cloak of many furs. And here in the warm light of this chamber, in the glow of the many lamps, I see my princess in all her splendor, from her crowning glory of golden braids to the sparkling dress of twinkling starlight on midnight blue to the dainty slippers on her feet. So different even from the arresting vision we saw in the smoky half-light of the dark kitchen, Hallgerd is every inch a royal beauty. Unmasked at last, she stands proudly, defiantly and Mord—despite his boyish delight—seems awed as well.

"Please, tell me your name!" he manages to say.

"I am Hallgerd, daughter of Gunnhild."

Mord bows low before her. "I can't tell you how pleased I am to make your acquaintance—again."

"Charmed, I'm sure," Hallgerd says stiffly, but a smile creeps into her face as she takes in the absurdity of their greetings.

"Well, now that we are all unmasking—" I say as I trot into the room, "I suppose I can safely introduce myself as well."

"It talks!" Mord's mouth forms a small 'o' of astonishment.

"I can even sing, if need be," I say with unnecessary coyness. "But I haven't been called upon to do that too much lately."

"Well, Nanna, I guess we are found out."

"We are indeed. Which is quite a relief in the end, I must say. Poor Skapti, he may not think so."

"Talking foxes! Hidden princesses! There's something rotten in my province," Mord says with mock severity.

"There is something truly terrible going on in my realm," Hallgerd says, her face suddenly grave.

"And perhaps you can help us," I add.

"Gladly!" Mord's delight is evident. Despite the grimness of Hallgerd's demeanor, he can hardly contain the thrill he feels for a fairy tale come true. "Please sit—no! Take my chair!" Mord offers Hallgerd his own oaken chair carved with interlocking dragons. "And for you, little fox, uh—here! This little stool. See, it's very nicely padded." He pats the cushion to demonstrate. "Well, I suppose you have a name, too?"

"My charges have always called me, Nanna. It will do."

"She is not usually a fox," Hallgerd explains.

I laugh. "No, I am quite human. But it was easier for me to escape this way."

"Escape?" Mord takes Hallgerd's hand. "Please, tell me what terrible forces have caused you to hide in the woods—and in my kitchen."

So much to tell! Between the two of us though we spin the tale of Gunnhild's death, of Kormak's affliction, of Thomas' growing power, of brave friends like dear Unn, clever Astrid and the gallant twins. Mord listens with deep concentration. His face betrays his anger at the wrongs and his approval of the courageous acts. He seems so unlike the frivolous sporting rogue we first met in the woods. When Hallgerd gets to our clever machinations for the dance, Mord laughs out loud at how he was fooled, hooked and baited.

"You piqued my interest all right," he smiles at Hallgerd, "There was none more beautiful than you—and none even a hundredth as interesting. Your stories drew me in, as did your wit, your dancing, even if your stories weren't true—everything else was."

Hallgerd glows red as a coal fire and seems lost for words. I decide this is a good place to jump in. "We regret playing our games with you, my lord—"

"I don't."

"But we needed to know if we could trust you, ask for your assistance. I feel confident now that we can."

"I shall do whatever I can," he answers me, but his eyes never leave Hallgerd's. "Command me. I shall do your bidding."

"First, please, could I have the other tokens?" Hallgerd smiles but I know she is quite serious. "I hate to have them away from me for so long."

"Oh, certainly. What was I thinking?" Mord takes them out of his pocket and places them in Hallgerd's hand. "They are exquisite."

"They are essential. From my mother to me, from her mother, and her mother before her. How far back does the legacy go, Nanna? How many generations?"

"Oh, before even I came to the land, my dear."

"And you are even older than the hills, are you not, Nanna?"

"I am not so old as that," I chuckle.

"But far back, through the women of my realm. Reminders, tokens—they tie us to our responsibilities, to our duties, our charge. There is a poem—" and together we chant,

The bobbin for guidance through wisdom and sense,
The spindle for drawing out all excellence,
The ring for binding the oath to this land
To love and protect and be at its command.

Hallgerd smiles and takes my paw in her free hand. The three of us form a circle now—the symbol of strength.

Mord looks back and forth at the two of us. "I see now why you have been able to withstand your misfortunes with such fortitude. Your faith, your honor, is so strong. I am ashamed to say the same is not true for me."

"That was the past. Your future begins now."

"If only it were so easy—"

"It can be. Jump into the fire and see how quickly you learn! I was a spoiled child—now Nanna, don't disagree! I was protected and cared for with love, and then one day, I was thrust suddenly into intrigue, evil and hardship. It has not been easy, I will not lie, but I am so much stronger now, not to mention patient, resourceful and a good cook," Hallgerd adds, laughing.

"You too will find challenges worth taking," I say. "After all, Grima told us much of your youthful adventures and courage—"

"And the mistakes I made?" Mord says with bitter venom.

Hallgerd shakes his hand impatiently. "You have had too great luxury to replay your mistakes and wallow in self-pity. Mistakes are inevitable. Not learning from them is the greatest error. What would your friend think of your behavior since his death?"

It is the prince's turn to redden. He rises and stalks to the window, hands clenched at his sides. Hallgerd goes to him and takes a fist in her hand, gently uncurling the fingers. "I ask this not to anger or shame you, but to help you honor your friend's memory. Make him proud."

After a moment, Mord releases his other fist and holds Hallgerd hands. "I do appreciate it. I know you are right. I have castigated myself for so long over what I could have done or done differently or not done. Foolish! Bjorn would be full of scorn for the cowardly way I have retreated to this castle and such idleness. No more!" Mord claps his fist to his chest in avowal. "Henceforth I honor the sacrifice my friend made to keep me alive. I shall rise to challenges and put away my self-pity. I shall carry on his proud legacy!"

"Bless you!" Hallgerd says, pride gleaming from her eyes.

"Thank you, Prince Mord. Your help will be essential to returning Hallgerd to her rightful place. But it is late. We should get a fresh start in the morning." Mord and Hallgerd look fresh still, but I am so tired!

"I shall have maps and everything else helpful ready." Mord

looks ready to charge off anywhere and begin the battle. "And tonight, you shall not sleep in the lowly kitchen, but in the finest chamber of the castle. I shall call Skapti to prepare it—"

"Well, first," I say, "we need to go tell Grima what has come to pass, so she does not fear we have lost our heads up here!"

"Heavens, yes!" Hallgerd agrees. "Poor woman, she's probably worried sick—let's go tell her now."

69

It is wonderful the next morning to wake from sleeping on soft cushions and stretch with exquisite luxury and ease, rather than scurry at once to our chores. Poor Grima! She was indeed terrified as to what had happened to us and our reassurances brought tears of relief to her eyes. And soon too, more relief will be coming her way. Mord has promised to get some young helpers to join her in the kitchen and ease the heavy burdens on her shoulders. All will be well.

It was much fun, too, to see Skapti's face when he was called to arrange for our room. The persnickety servant did not wish to let on, but his eyes very nearly popped out of his head when he saw the "guests" to whom he was instructed to offer the finest hospitality of the castle. It was all we could do not to giggle out loud as Skapti quickly put the room to rights with a flurry of crisp linens and feather beds. A timid young servant arrived with a large bowl of dried apples decorated with early flower buds to brighten the chamber and garlands of fragrant rushes were looped over the frame of the bed to make Hallgerd's sleep more comfortable. She thanked all her attendants graciously, though Skapti seemed to find it hard to suppress his indignation.

This morning, though, we have much more serious matters on our minds. Hallgerd, Mord and I gather around the large table in his bookhouse, a large chamber at the top of the castle which appears to have suffered some neglect of late. As we enter, I see Hallgerd purse her lips in displeasure at the dust and the bound manuscripts lying open, face down. But she says nothing. Mord steps quickly around her to brush away the film of dust covering the large central desk. He blushes, telling the princess awkwardly, "I haven't been up here in a while."

"You are fortunate to have a wonderful collection. It would be a shame to see it damaged by neglect." Hallgerd smiles thinly but she cannot hide her disapproval.

"This was once my most treasured part of the castle. Before I fell into idleness and the indolence of easy flattery." Mord carefully closes a delicate binding of sheepskins and replaces it on a shelf. "I even had delusions of recording my own experiences for those who came after, but—" He shrugs.

"As you ought!" Hallgerd's smile warms once more. "And you shall, we can work on them together—after all this is done," she adds, sharing a determined look with me.

Oh, my princess, is that love I see growing in your eyes? Yet I only say, "Have you maps of the region?"

Mord nods and examines a collection of rolled pieces of vellum, at last selecting the right one. With a flourish he unfurls in on the desk. "We're here," he indicates, pointing, "and this would be your realm there," moving his finger toward the edge of the map.

"Ah! Yes, here is the forest where you found us." Hallgerd peers at the ink scratching on the surface. "Heavens! It is quite a long way. No wonder we were so tired!"

"It won't be so long on horseback. And far less perilous in the company of my troops."

"How large a force can you summon?"

"Oh, I should be able to draw on the surrounding areas and perhaps ask my brother for reinforcements—as it would only be for a short time—thus I could probably count on at least a hundred, probably more."

"Will that be enough, Nanna?"

"It should be enough to make Thomas afraid, but we cannot merely take the land by force. There are other considerations."

"What?" Hallgerd looks up from her perusal of the map, surprise evident on her features. "I thought we would simply oust Thomas and that would be that. What more need we do?"

"First, never forget the powers he has. He did not take your land with troops and there are other forces that hold it under his power. You need to deal with those forces as well. Your father may be in a very serious situation, and we can extricate him from it only with great delicacy."

"I'm afraid I don't understand," Mord says. His confusion is plain—and understandable. He did not grow up immersed in magic as my charge did.

Hallgerd answers him. "Thomas has charmed my father in some way—first to persuade him, when his mind was weak with grief, later to control him, and now, perhaps—" Hallgerd pauses and looks to me for help.

"And now to steal his very essence, his spirit."

Mord is aghast. "Is such a thing possible?"

"I'm afraid so. It is very dangerous and has serious repercussions. Some day he will be facing great spiritual retribution, but we cannot afford to wait for that day. So we must outsmart him—and that will not be easy."

"But you use magic too—why not use your magic against him?"

"A good question Mord, but I cannot without sacrificing myself and exposing the possibility of tragic consequences for you all. It is a long story—perhaps I will have time to tell it to you once day—but for now suffice it to say that the women of my line are forbidden to work magic against the men of his."

"All this magic! Your people: they are not of this land, nor that of Hallgerd's people, are they?"

"No," I smile as I think of the emerald hills of my homeland, as green in my memory as this morning's sunrise. "I believe you have referred to it as the Isle of Monks. It is known by many names to travelers."

"Ah, yes, I have been there. One of our more peaceful visits it was too. I shudder to think now what we might have risked from the seemingly gentle people." Mord laughs but I can sense the tingle of fear this brings him.

"Magic is not a tool wielded without great deliberation. In my land, when such a one as Thomas runs wildly, carelessly, endangering those around him, punishment is swift and terrible. That is why he is no longer in that land."

"I hate to ask," Mord begins hesitantly, but firmly, "But why are you no longer in your homeland?"

Hallgerd's eyes flash with temper, but I silence her with an upraised paw. "It is a legitimate question to ask, one I would expect of a thoughtful ruler. I was captured as a slave by the people of Hallgerd's realm, many a long year ago—"

"Many, many a long year ago," Hallgerd adds with a significant look.

"I could have easily eluded them with my magic, but I had a grief in my heart that made me desire to be far from the verdant meadows and dark forests of my land, to try to forget. Time and distance can help, sometimes, to heal."

"She has proved invaluable to me, to my mother before me, to her mother before that, and—well, just how far back, Nanna?" Hallgerd chuckles. "Can you remember?"

"I remember everything, but I would have to sit down and consider it for a little while. It's hardly important just now."

Mord looks at me with renewed awe. "I had no idea. I still cannot imagine what you look like as a woman. It will take some getting used to, I can tell you that!"

"Oh, I am quite an unremarkable old woman in many ways. You would think nothing of me, to see me."

Mord shakes his head. "I shall look at all older women in an entirely new light now."

"Very wise!"

"Nanna," Hallgerd says, tapping her chin, "many of the people still follow Thomas willingly. That's another reason too, not to take the land by force, isn't it? We want to win the people back as much as the land."

I nod. "Indeed. We shall have to wage our war with great consideration. The traditions must be adhered to if we are to retain the will of the folk."

"Traditions?" Hallgerd's brow wrinkles.

"A threat to the kingdom from without—when no woman sits on throne—can be met only by hand to hand combat between the ruling king and his challenger. A sensible enough tradition to save the lives of the warriors."

The princess gapes. "But the king cannot fight! Surely Thomas will step in for him, and then, why, then it will be easy for us to defeat him!"

"Perhaps, perhaps. But Thomas is clever. It should hardly be something as simple as that. We must be cleverer—for every scheme he plots, we must counter it. I will need to get into the castle ahead of time. And I will need help from our dear Unn if she is still in her honored place—and under Thomas' daily scrutiny. We must prepare to guard your father's spirit."

Hallgerd gasps. "You know where it is?"

"If her description is accurate, Unn saw it trapped in a bottle in Thomas' own chamber. We need to have it in our hands to keep your father safe from that one's evil intents. I shall have to go on ahead and work my way into the castle, then meet up with you and your forces as you approach."

"Thomas should not be expecting us, so we should be able to take him by surprise. He will not be able to plan then, simply to act upon things already set in motion."

"But if he is as shrewd as you say," Mord argues, "would he not already be planning for your possible return?"

"True," Hallgerd admits. "But would he guess that I would not come back alone?"

"Perhaps not. But Nanna is right—we must be ready for anything."

"How soon can you assemble your warriors?" Hallgerd asks.

"Within the week."

"Then we shall be ready, right Nanna?"

"I swear it, by all my people swear by."

I can hardly believe that our return shall come at last. Fraught with such dangers, it nonetheless brings pleasure to me, the hope of returning to my adopted home. I long for my divination ball of crystal, but preparation is what I need, not enigmatic views of the ever-changing future. There are herbs to gather and have ready at hand, amulets for dire circumstances—I do not wish to endanger myself, but if it is the only way to save my princess, I will not hesitate.

But most of my time is taken up with thinking, trying as I might to think like Thomas—though that is as alien to my nature as mine is no doubt to his. I fear too that, regardless of the schemes I contemplate, he will have others more nefarious of which I could not conceive. Evil, true evil, is far beyond the comprehension of the good. The king cannot fight a duel with Mord—what will Thomas do instead? Surely he will not risk his own foul skin. What then?

We spend my last evening in the castle with Grima. She is a much happier woman now with her two young helpers. Though she keeps them strictly in line, she is also quite kind to her new charges. We sit upon stools at the new table placed in the kitchen at Hallgerd's request. Grima may still spend most of her days on her feet, but now she has somewhere to rest.

"I cannot thank you enough, my lady," Grima repeats for the tenth time. "It makes such a difference, such a difference!"

Hallgerd laughs. "You deserve it! Not just for all the help and kindness you offered us, but as a busy woman you need help. It was ridiculous to require you to do everything yourself—feeding a whole castle like this, and at a feast time too!"

"Well, fortunately things aren't quite so hurry-scurry as they were during the dance. I don't know that we could have lasted one more day." Grima shakes her head. "Though certainly the fear and the anticipation added to that a great deal. Who could have imagined it would turn out this way? Not me, oh no. And not Skapti either. Oh, the sour face that one has these days!"

"How are your young helpers doing?" I ask.

"Oh, such a lot to learn! Seems like they're both as ignorant as puppies—but I was once too, or so I try to remember. That one," she points at a raven-haired young girl, "she's afraid to say 'boo' to a goose, but that other one," she indicates a red-head, all gangly legs and elbows, "can't seem to stop talking for a minute. Talking to me, to her, to the chickens, to the air—ah, well, no doubt they'll both pick things up quickly, they seem to so far."

"I did. I learned a great deal here," Hallgerd says, hugging the cook. "This is only the beginning of my thanking you for all the help you gave us. You shall be well-paid."

"By the gods! I can't say I'm accustomed to all this praise. I did nothing, my lady, nothing at all."

"Nonsense. You did a great deal, why—"

"No, it was you who did so much for me." Grima leans toward me looking into my eyes. "You gave me back my heart. There are not thanks enough in the world for that. But my blessings and well-wishings go with you tonight, and anything else I can do."

"It will be dangerous. Oh Nanna, I wish I could go with you. I hate to think of you all alone in that peril."

"I know, my dear, but no one will take notice of a little fox. And I need to find Unn and see whether we can get the bottle that I am certain holds your father's essence. It will be a delicate operation. I fear too, from what Unn told me, that Thomas may have further secrets up his sleeve. I have tried to think of all the likely tricks, but I cannot think like that one. I have prepared for as many dangerous possibilities as I can think of, but doubtless we will need to be ready to react to the unexpected."

"I trust you to do your best, Nanna, as will we all, and to advise me of the best action. Mord, too, promises to follow your wise counsel."

"I shall do my utmost to reward your faith in me."

20

I think of my promise later as I set out alone in the early morning dew. I shiver. The sun will not be up for some time yet and the chill dampens my spirits. Fear creeps into my thoughts. What has Thomas planned—for surely he has foreseen the possibility of Hallgerd's return—how will he meet our challenge? Without my magic, I will feel helpless but I must turn to it only when every other defense has been tried, for if it should fail...no, I cannot think of that prospect. I must keep hope in my heart.

It is a long journey. No spirit this time, flying high and low through leaves and branches, but only a small creature taking small steps, running between the trees, wading through the cold brooks. I steal naps as I tire, then run on in the dark and the light, hurrying along, so much to do. My thoughts I keep buoyant with happiness: I think ahead to Unn's gladness when I shall greet her, to the fox's joy upon returning to his skin, to the comfortable familiarity of my own body, old and stiff as it may be, and to the affection blossoming between Hallgerd and Mord. He will find purpose with her and she will find challenge in his strength. They will ask the best of one another and find it. If all goes well, if all goes well, I remind myself.

I see disturbing signs as I approach the castle of Hallgerd's family. The people I pass seem bewildered, angry or sullen. How quickly the land deteriorates under the reins of a despot. Fear clutches the spirit. As I approach the gates of the town, I watch a foursome of warriors, loutish and arrogant, make their noisy way along. A young woman up about her early chores shudders as they pass, trying to make herself small and beyond their notice. Her terror must have root in past deeds. There will have to be many changes here when Hallgerd returns. Many changes, indeed.

It is early yet, so I make my way around the back of the castle.

It proves simple enough—if very wet—to make my way through the water outlet in the gate behind the kitchens. I feel a shiver that does not come from the cold dampness of my fur, but from the knowledge that my body lies below me in the earthen chamber. Soon little fox, soon, your flesh shall be returned to you, I promise. Though the sun has not lifted its head from the horizon, the kitchen is a flurry of activity. A young woman calmly directs her charges, themselves quite young, too young. I knew the twins were sent away, but where are the others who worked here just a short time ago? So much bodes ill—so many friends gone. Thomas has made a thorough house-cleaning. I make a quick wish—let my dear Unn not be among the missing. That would be too much to bear. I slip through the smoky kitchen trying not to be seen. With any luck I should be mistaken for a dog if I am seen. I keep my head down and pad quickly across the stone floor. So far, so good. Up the stairs—no one there—down the corridor I run, claws clacking. I am nearer Thomas' lair; I feel his malignancy as a palpable thing. But I know too that Unn is near—or was. My nose finds her long before my eyes, blessed be its sense. Is she alone? I pause. The keen fox nose tells me she is. I venture to poke my head around the corner of the doorway. Unn sits in my old oak chair, Siur in her lap and a spindle in her hand. Her face, so beautiful to my eyes, shows her disquiet even as her fingers absently twist the thread. Siur sees me first, hissing and spitting in alarm. Unn grumbles something rude to her, then freezes in alarm when she spots me.

"Don't be afraid, dear friend, it is only me," I whisper, afraid that Thomas might be near.

The arch in Siur's back melts at once and she pokes her nose out, nostrils questing. She cannot seem to reconcile the smell and the voice but I think she realizes it is me. Unn stares. "You?" she finally manages weakly.

"Yes, my dear, remember when I came to you in spirit? I told you I was in the body of a fox—"

"Oh, indeed you did, you did! Oh, but by the heavens! I never expected to see you thus." Unn shakes her head. "Quite unexpected."

"Is Thomas about?"

"No, no, he was off even earlier today—such a ruckus!

215

Gathering those hooligans that he calls a troop, though they're no better than a pack of thieves!"

"Where was he off to?" Knowing we are safe I walk in and jump up on the bed, the better to see my friend. "Another rebellion?"

"Oh, very likely, my lady. Although there was something odd about it—what was it? Something he said—or did—made me take notice. It wasn't like his usual forays against the rebel forces. He was particularly gleeful. He even ordered poor Katla to pack up a great deal of the food stores, as if he expected to be out with the troops for some time."

"Does he usually go with the warriors on their forays?"

"Occasionally, but he has never sent them out with such amounts of food. Most of the time he makes them forage for their own edibles, which of course they steal from or beat out of the locals. And another thing! He packed a lot of herbs in his own pouch, healing ones too, if I recall your teachings, lady. He doesn't often waste his precious time with healing. Soldiers who are injured are sent away to languish."

I consider Unn's observations. What can it mean? A small rebellion in some corner of the land would hardly seem to warrant such preparation. But a more intense battle—"Oh heavens, Unn, didn't you tell me that Thomas carried a mirror in his hand? How could I be so stupid? How could I be so blind!"

"What, lady, what?"

"He has been keeping watch for Hallgerd's return! Oh, I cannot explain the hows and the whys of the magic, but he has set the mirror as a watcher at the bounds of this land. He must have known as soon as she crossed the border!"

"Oh dear! Then she is in danger!"

I nod. "We must ride to meet her—but first, this is our best opportunity to save the King!"

"We can restore his spirit?" Unn leaps up sending Siur and her spindle flying. "Oh, praised be, lady! How can I help?"

"Get that bottle from Thomas' chamber!"

Together we run down the corridor to the darkened room. I pause at the threshold, but can sense no magical wards. Hesitantly, I step into the room and Unn follows behind me, picking up my caution. Apparently Thomas trusts in the fear that keeps others far from his chamber. I look around. Bound volumes lay in disarray. Beakers and bottles jumble together on a table, some emptied of their contents, some unstoppered but full. None of them have what I'm looking for and I fear he has decided to risk carrying it with him. But no! There on the shelf I can see the bottle, glowing like ghost light over a bog. Surely I have guessed correctly this time. "Grab that bottle!" I tell Unn.

She pick it up gingerly, afraid it might bite. "What must we do with it?"

"We must take it to the King—and we will need some things, some healing herbs if there are any left, a knife, some peat, oh dear, what else, what else?"

To the end of the hall we hurry toward the king's chamber and Unn lifts the bolt from the door. "Good thing there are no guards today!" she smiles and we step inside. But the room is empty.

"No guards because there is no one to guard," I say, feeling as empty as the room.

"No, no! It cannot be," Unn wails, despair weighing in her voice. "Where would Thomas have put him? He has not been out of his room in such a long time, so feeble, so weak—"

"He has taken him to the battlefield," I say in a voice that rings as hollow as my hopes, "he has taken him to weaken Hallgerd's resolve, to fight her heart when she needs all her courage, to make her doubt, to make her fear. Oh, the evil in that black heart! I swear by all my people swear by that we shall vanquish him or I will die trying!"

"Yes, yes, lady, I swear the same, the very same, but now we must hurry to meet the Princess as you said. Let's not lose the cake for burning the tart!"

Anger crackles fiercely in my heart, but I know my sensible friend is right. There is still so much to do. We must get to Hallgerd as quickly as we can and warn her. "You are right; I must keep my wits about me. And we must be on our way. Wrap that bottle in your shawl—we must protect it with our lives."

"How can we get to the Princess to warn her?"

"On horseback, of course!"

"Oh lady, I haven't sat upon a horse since I was a wee tot, so high! I couldn't ever stay on one of those monstrous steeds like the ones kept around here, oh dear me, no!"

"You could for our Princess—for the realm!"

"Oh, oh!" Unn wrings her hands but starts to trot down the corridor. "The Great Lady protect me and keep me from falling! Let's go, before I regain my senses and think better of it!"

26

While the grooms in the stable look with amazement at the two of us as we demand a mount, they are too timid with fear to question us. While Unn finds an imperious voice to command the young men, all assumed authority leaves her when they bring out an enormous black charger who snorts defiantly as if daring her to climb him, Getting poor Unn up on his back is complicated. Spooked by our very real anxiety, he shies at every shadow. But once Unn finally scrambles atop the fence and eases herself onto the nervous horse, he seems to calm somewhat, though his head remains up, nostrils questing of signs of danger. I fear that he may bolt when I leap up into Unn's arms, but the distracted horse appears to take no notice of the additional rider. Unn clutches the saddle as if fearing she could be thrown from at it any moment. I take the reins up in my mouth, passing them to Unn who utters a harsh "gee up!" It is all the black stallion needs to set him off and we are galloping away from the stable area. If anyone tries to stop us, it will be now as we circle the castle. But there is only the young woman I had seen earlier in the kitchen, now stepping outside to gather kindling from the woodpile. She gapes at us, too surprised to consider any kind of alarm.

"Oh heavens, Katla! What will she think of her auntie now?" Unn gasps as the ragged gait throws her from side to side.

"That's Katla? Hopeless little Katla who can't do anything right?"

"She's improved," Unn admits. "Not without a lot of work though, I must say. Oh dear, my lady, I am so glad I haven't eaten yet this morning. I think I'm going to be ill!"

Despite Unn's predictions, she does not become ill and the charger, spurred on by his own agitation and the words of encouragement I pour in his swiveling ears, carries us swiftly across the land. In no time at all we are upon the heels of the more slowly traveling warrior troops. We circle widely to avoid their notice and press on to find Hallgerd and Mord. So little time, so much to do—if only, if only! Ah, but it is too late to berate myself with "if only." The question remaining is: what can I help to do now? What does that black-hearted one have up his sleeve? And how can we foil him?

At last we glimpse Mord's warriors through the woods. There's Hallgerd riding at the front in her cloak of many furs. Her face shows grim fortitude and an eager determination. The strong will of all her ancestors seems to radiate from her brow. She will not be defeated.

"Oh, blessed be! The Princess!" Unn forgets her fears in a moment of joyous recognition. Her grip remains firm though on the sweaty flanks of our horse as we turn him to gallop toward Hallgerd.

Hallgerd's expression softens into a welcome happiness and she spurs her own horse to meet us. "Nanna! Unn! You made it! You're safe!" She hugs Unn who careens between fear and felicity while attempting to remain upright on the charger.

"Oh my precious! Oh dear, I'm slipping—heavens!"

"You're fine, Unn. I wouldn't let you fall."

Their merriment delights me, but desperate matters are at hand. "Thomas is on his way, with troops. I should have known, but I did not—he was watching the border through magical means. He must have seen when you crossed it."

Hallgerd's expression returns to a fierce determination. "I am not afraid. We came here to restore my realm and we shall do it."

"But we must take care. He has your father with him. I am certain it is to cause you distress, to divide your thoughts."

"He shall pay for his evil. My poor father! Is there nothing we can do to help him, Nanna?"

"Oh yes! We can restore his spirit, but we will have to have him in order to do that, so we must get him safely away from Thomas. That will be the trick, I'm afraid."

Before Hallgerd has a chance to answer, a resounding blast from a battle horn cries out across the plain. Mord shouts to Hallgerd, pointing across the horizon. We all ride to his side and see what we had feared—and expected.

Thomas rides at the front of the troops, covered with a thick black cloak and leading a grey mare behind him. Lashed onto the mare is the King, his face a blank tablet. To my surprise, old Gunnar the Greybeard trots along beside him. Why would the old councilor join the troops of war? My heart leaps up—perhaps Thomas does not wish a war! But my spirits sink just as quickly—whatever he does want, it will surely not be good. Evil is at its worst when it smiles.

Indeed, behind the threesome rides Grim Eriksson and his men, armed for battle. Their halberds glint in the sun and their armor jangles in time with their horses' steps. Though Mord's warriors are equally prepared, I feel a shiver of fear. It has been a very long time since I was in the midst of battles and bloodshed—the horror never goes away. Can it be avoided this time?

Thomas raises his arm. The troops halt as he continues forward with the King and the old councilor. His expression is jovial—another warning sign.

"Greetings! What business have you in this land?" His enormous grin belies the maliciousness in his voice. "We shall have to assume your heavily-armed warriors do not betoken a peaceful visit."

"I come to reclaim my realm," Hallgerd states plainly. "Relinquish it now and save us all bloodshed."

"I?" Thomas' eyes widen in a parody of surprise. "I am but a mere functionary of the noble King Kormak. His majesty rules this land." Thomas bows and gestures to the king, who sits mutely upon his horse, eyes as empty as shaded pools. "You must bring your claims to him."

Mord puts a reassuring hand on Hallgerd's shoulder. But her face remains a mask of hatred and anger. "This realm is mine, as it was my mother's before me. Leave now and you will not have to suffer death."

"Ah, but I beg to differ! The realm has not been passed to you as you have not reached the appropriate age. Your father rules—is it not so, Greybeard?"

The old man shifts uncomfortably in his saddle. "It is indeed so."

"You would not wish the people to accept a usurper, would you?"

"They already have one," Hallgerd says evenly, though her contempt is clear enough. "You will leave this realm—now."

"Oh, I would indeed wish it, there is so much yet to be done elsewhere, but I'm afraid the King has said he cannot do without me."

"Then I demand the duel that the laws of this land grant. When no woman sits upon the throne, a challenge from without must be met by the ruler of the land. Consider Mord the challenger."

"Is this so, Greybeard?" Thomas asks with an air of considered politeness, while gazing upon Mord. "Is there such a provision in the laws of this realm?"

"Yes, sir. It is written thus."

"Well, then! A duel we shall have!" I cannot understand this one's delight. But at once Thomas turns to the captain of his guards and demands, "Prepare the king for battle!"

Hallgerd's mouth flies open. "The king? Surely he is not fit to fight in a duel. You cannot force an incapacitated man to lift a sword!"

"Oh but you'd be surprised! He perks right up with a weapon in his hand—isn't that so, Kormak?" The king's eyes do not even flicker. No wonder, when his spirit is in a jar strapped behind Unn on the saddle.

"Nanna!" Hallgerd turns to me, anger and fear battling for her heart. "What are we to do?"

"Nanna!" Thomas echoes. "Oh dear, don't tell me it's you? Oh, you have seen better days—how have you come to this? Eat a toadstool? Irritate a real sorcerer? How well your powers have served you!" He throws his head back for a hearty laugh. "This day just gets better and better!"

I ignore his gibes and meet Hallgerd's pained gaze. My decision must be swift—and secret. We cannot speak before this one or all will be lost. Oh, how sure I had been that there would be a proxy! How foolish of me not to guess that evil would be as evil always is—ruthless. Trust me, child, trust me—this will be very dangerous but it could just work, if that one does not guess our scheme. I fix my eyes upon Hallgerd's, willing her to trust my years of devotion, my sworn pledge to her and all the women before her. She must trust me, though I will ask her to go along with something that seems unutterably cruel. And Thomas—Maldachta! Let me call him by his true name—he must not guess what I hope for. He must assume us desperate enough to forfeit the lost king. Let it be so.

"We shall have the duel," I say simply, but send out my will to Hallgerd.

Her face contorts with anger. Thomas laughs aloud. Mord stares at me with shocked revulsion. Unn clutches me tighter. I match Hallgerd's gaze, no expression showing on my fox face. Trust me, I will her, trust me.

"What, no magic? No last-minute miracle? Not willing to pay for his life with your own? Oh, how the proud have fallen on hard times!" Thomas' voice rings jubilantly across the plain.

I pay him no mind but keep my eyes upon Hallgerd. I can see the struggle in her face. Trust me! I cannot say it aloud but she must think. She must know that I will do nothing but what I think will be best for us all.

Her expression becomes guarded. Her decision is made. "Proceed," she says coldly, turning away from me. I pretend to hang my head in dejection. Unn pats my back consolingly.

Thomas barks with laughter once more and rubs his hands together in glee. "Prepare the king for battle!" At once he helps the King down from his mare, signaling Grim to ride forth. Even the old warrior's face reveals his disgust at the thought of this engagement. There is no honor here. But he bows to his leader's will and removes his own armor and weapons, placing them upon the king. Kormak makes no movement himself but his arms and legs remain where they are placed, even when a heavy long sword is put in his hand.

Mord, too, prepares. He is already suited in his chain mail. His visored helmet sits upon his saddle—surely he will not need it. At each side of him hangs a sword, a short sword on his right, a long one on the left. Hallgerd helps to adjust the heavy plate on his chest and looks sadly into his eyes. Mord returns her glance and hugs her quickly, fiercely.

When I am certain that Thomas is occupied with outfitting the feeble king, I whisper hoarsely to Mord, "Pierce his heart, but do not go through it!" Mord stares at me in wonder and Hallgerd flushes red, hastily trying to conceal her renewed hope. Oh, this is dangerous indeed, but it may be our only chance!

"Are we ready?" Thomas asks, nearly dancing with joy. But the heavy lines on his face and the distinct stripe of grey in his hair do not seem to match his light-heartedness. Things have not gone well for him, despite his machinations. Running a realm is a great deal of work—it has drained him. Perhaps he tires of his game, and seeks an excuse to leave all this behind. I can only hope he has not considered my true powers—but he has always dismissed healing magic as "women's work," hardly worthy of mention.

Mord steps forward, his face grimly set. Thomas leads the horses away from the combatants and we all leave room. It is Gunnar who calls out "Let the duel begin!" and then steps away, out of range. The king stands, sword uplifted only because Thomas has raised his arm. Mord approaches him, but he makes no move—he barely seems to breathe. The young prince hesitates—this is no battle. He looks to Hallgerd, then to me. Nothing shows on our faces but deep in my heart I clutch hope. Let it be as I will. Mord turns back to his opponent and strikes his sword against the king's. The clash rings out across the open plain until the forest swallows the sound. There is no delaying now. Taking a deep breath, Mord steps back and plunges his sword into the king's chest. A tremor runs through the body and as Mord removes the blade, the king gives out a long sigh. Hallgerd screams in agony. At once rich red blood pours forth from the wound and the king keels forward into Mord's arms. He staggers with the weight and drops his sword. Hallgerd runs to them, helping Mord lay the king on the soft earth.

"Well," Thomas says with an evil chuckle, "I guess you win. The realm is yours! And all you had to was kill your own dear father!" His face shines with triumph. "I was sick of all the headaches anyway. I have much better things to be doing. Anon, witch!" Lifting his arm, he swirls the black cloak about him and the winds rise up as if they have come from the folds of the material. A bird flight! As I should have guessed! In a twinkling, he has shrunk in size, and the pleats of his cloak have become wings. The winds lift the newly-born raven up, above our heads, above the trees, and into the air. Too late, too late! We all gape helplessly at his sudden exit. Fortunately Hallgerd is the first to regain her senses, running to her horse and pulling the bow from its saddle. She only has time to get off one arrow, but it flies true and we hear angry shriek as Maldachta tumbles into the broad branches of an oak. At once Mord cries out, "Capture him! Climb the tree! Bring a net!" He rushes off to join his men in the capture.

Confident that they will detain him, I turn back to the most pressing matter. "Quickly, Unn! The bottle! Hallgerd! The herbs! And some earth, soft earth!" I jump down from the horse and run to the king. Old Gunnar stands by slack-jawed with horror. I command him, "Hold the edges of the wound together, we must slow the loss of blood!" Unn dashes over, the bottle held gingerly before her. "Remove the stopper and put it over the wound!" Unn does so and at once the wispy smoke-like essence is drawn into the body. The king gasps.

"Hallgerd! Knead the herbs into the earth, mix them well! All right, now, here, Unn take the bottle away and yes, Hallgerd, there! Pack the earth on top of the wound, yes, thickly—just there. Good! Now hold it, hold it." The king's eyes flicker and he groans. Hallgerd looks at me with tears in her eyes but I cannot think about happiness yet. "Take off his armor! We need to make him warm."

Hallgerd removes her cloak, wrapping it around the old king's body as Unn holds the earthen poultice in place. Blood seeps through, turning the mud scarlet. I have Hallgerd knead more of the mixture and replace the original.

We are on the third of these when the king's eyes no longer flutter but open widely in confused surprise. "Where am I?"

"Oh, by the gods!" Unn gasps "He's alive!"

"Of course I am alive," Kormak rejoins weakly, "But where am I?"

"You are in the southern reaches of the realm where there has been a great battle," Hallgerd says to him softly, tears running down her cheeks.

"But I was just in the great hall—I saw my beloved!"

"Mother!" Hallgerd gasps.

"Please," Kormak pleads with his savior, "Please, let me go. It is long since time."

"But father, I—I have not had a chance…I want to…" She cannot finish her thought but the king understands.

He smiles at her. "Child, I heard all about you, even in my prison. And I see you now, a fine young woman, with a proud warrior as your champion. There is little I can do for you, bent and weary—the years I could have done you some good are long past. I am ashamed of my weaknesses. Let me pass on. I am weary, and lonely for my loved one. Fear not, the dead may watch the living as she has told me. She watches you even now."

Hallgerd, overcome with emotion, lays her cheek against the withered one of her father. "Mother sees me?"

"Indeed. Please, let me pass on. I seek the great hall with the other warriors, to drink beneath its golden beams, to share the feast with your mother, to hold her in my arms again, and to ready for the final battle. Let me die."

Hallgerd weeps, but she nods. "A majestic burial cairn will be raised in your honor, filled with all manner of treasures—"

"No, no," Kormak shook his head sadly, "useless, such vanity. I was a foolish man, selfish and single-minded as an old boar past his prime. Let your treasure fill the people's bellies, fill the library with knowledge, fill the castle with music and dancing. Let my bones lie unmarked next to those of she whom I loved. Nanna, for I know it is you who saved me, restored my spirit, make her see the truth in what I speak. Can you not let me go?"

I nod. He sees me even in this guise. He is at the borderlands already. "If it is truly your desire, my lord."

"It is. Your wisdom, your loyalty will be rewarded amply by my dear daughter. Myself, I offer you my humble apology and thanks for protecting her, raising her, and teaching her so well." His eyes cloud with unshed tears. Turning to the other side, his look grows stern. "Gunnar, my old councilor, draw near and heed me well."

Old Greybeard kneels down, his joy for the king's return warring in his heart with the knowledge of the harm done. "My lord, my lord—"

"Let all know my final words, my joy, my pride in my daughter and in her great victory. Amend your shameful deeds with your firm allegiance to her. And never forget, law must always be subservient to wisdom—never the reverse." He coughs and blood stains his lips. "Now, release me, release me. I do not wish to tarry any longer. Reunite me with she who was ever in my heart and

226

forgive my weaknesses. I shall do better in the final battle, when we will all be together one last time."

With reluctance, Hallgerd removes the poultice and once more the blood flows freely. As we gaze sadly upon him, the king's eyes flutter and he sighs as his spirit departs. Hallgerd lays across his body, whispering, "Farewell!"

Mord sends some of his troops to find a wagon to transport the king's body and the captured raven back to the castle. Though he struggles mightily within the net, Maldachta does not return to his human form. "Are you sure it is really he?" Mord asks again, but Hallgerd's arrow makes us certain it is. We go slowly so as not to bounce too much, for fear of losing him, though the net seems secure. Unn, grateful to avoid another gallop, rides beside him, keeping an angry scolding pouring into his ear. It is nightfall before we return, but word has come ahead of us and the people gather before the castle to greet Hallgerd and Mord. There is evident relief in their faces as they wave to the pair, though sobered by the loss of the king. Hallgerd's own expression mirrors their dueling emotions, as she waves to the people while riding at the side of the wagon. Eyes quickly turn to regard Mord with curiosity, and I can see whisperings back and forth as many wonder about the history of the handsome young prince.

Within the castle the remaining servants assemble to welcome home the princess now queen and to prepare her father's body for burial. Such cries greet us! Everyone speaks at once as Hallgerd and Mord lay the king upon his bed and Unn takes command, ordering about anyone who comes within her reach, sending this one off for firewood, that one off for a restorative soup, and another for fine linen to shroud the king. It is easy enough for me to slip away unseen. I have a debt to pay.

My claws tick on the floor as I make my way to the cells below the ground floor. I hold the cold metal key in my mouth, warming it. How strange it shall feel to be human again! It is with a great deal of difficulty that I at last manage to turn the key in the lock. I have to use all my small strength to hurl myself against the door and move it on its groaning hinges. When there is enough room to slip through, I step into the murk and see my body hunched upon the bench. My head raises, sniffing the air with suspicion when suddenly the eyes widen in surprise. "You have returned! At last! Now free me from this terrible body. I want to smell the world again!"

"I need your help to do it. The fingers of my body are far more nimble than your paws." Patiently I explain how to extract the pouch of herbs from the hem of my dress and mix them with water in the palm of my hand. This is not done without a great deal of spilling and mess, but there is enough to make it work. "Now dip your finger—yes, there—in the mixture and draw a circle—ah, this shape," I demonstrate with my paw, toeing a circle into the dirt floor. "Draw this on my forehead and yours—yes, good—now take my paw in your hand—" and once more I envision the exchange. Again the energy shocks through me like a bolt of lightning and stars pop in my eyes. But when I open them, I am looking down at a little fox who yelps with pleasure.

"I can smell, I can smell! Now I want to run! How do I get out of here?"

I laugh too, sharing his joy. I lead him away through the castle, into the kitchen and out into the night. He leaps into the grass and rolls gleefully, rubbing his spine into the earth. Shaking himself thoroughly, he finally looks up at me. "I don't know how you can live in that body. I should never trade again."

"I know. It was a terrible sacrifice to ask of you, but I shall repay you as you asked. Under each full moon, I shall go to the grove of elders west of the castle and sing you the magical songs you enjoyed. I swear by all my people swear by, this shall be so for as long as I live."

The fox gazes up at me. "I shall look forward to that. And when I die, my children will be there to listen and wonder. Now I must hunt! I think I shall catch that rabbit over there!"

I watch him as he runs off, thoughts already fixed upon his meal. How simple, how true his desires, while we humans engage in complicated wars and intrigues. But we must be as we are— even in a fox's body, I was still human. Ah, but this body of mine! Oh, dear—so stiff, so dirty! It will be the best of rewards to sit in the steam of the bathhouse and be clean and warm all the way through.

The burial of the king takes place the very next night. The fires rise high into the black sky and many join in the lamenting dirges, singing his soul onto the great hall with regret and wishes for eternal happiness. Hallgerd's tears shine in the firelight, but her face looks grim and strong. Mord stands beside her, quiet but with clear emotion writ upon his face. When the ashes are consigned to the burial mound—the cairn where her mother's bones lie, as Kormak had requested—Mord lays his bloodied sword upon the remains. As the king had desired, it is the only treasure consigned to the mound. As men cover the bones once more, the people depart and we all carry our grief away.

In the Great Hall that night, many recite the deeds of King Kormak as they pass the harp and drink deeply of the horns of mead. Hallgerd and Mord sit on the dais, mostly silent but overseeing the remembrance with proper dignity. They are still so young, but trouble and sorrow lend them both wisdom. Though the people sorrow tonight, I can feel hope rekindled.

The land is not as it was before the troubles. Calamities affect a realm as much as individuals. But it is stronger now. Hallgerd looks more and more like her mother every day as she deals with the council and disciplines those who supported Thomas. Judgment is swift—and sometimes harsh. But equally speedy is the reward to those who remained true. The twins Thordis and Thorgerd have been returned to their rightful places here in the castle, while Grim Eriksson has been driven from the realm, his ill-gotten lands restored to their original owners. There is time now for a much-needed healing, but most of life has returned to normalcy.

Hallgerd will be crowned officially in a public ceremony in three days time, but she has already taken the reins of power and holds them firmly. We sit together, me sewing—trying to get my fingers limber again as I fight with Siur for the yarn—while she makes lists of the things to be done for her wedding to Mord next month. The tenderness between them delights us all. They will be great rulers for this realm. Already they are making plans for bringing scholars and artists to enrich our lives. Mord's sister Sæl has taken his vacated throne—Grima apparently finds that quite suitable. Hardly a surprise when Mord has made certain to tell his sister what Hallgerd and I owe that sweet woman. Apparently she now directs a full staff of workers, needing to do little toil herself. We even sent her the little walnut—perhaps it will help her with her chores!

Unn should be coming soon, to call us to dinner. That is if she's not too busy hanging over the shoulder of the very capable Katla and second-guessing every decision. If we want to have a peaceful kitchen, we shall have to find a new interest for Unn— perhaps she shall have to be put in charge of the flurry of visitors we shall be having soon. I suggest it to Hallgerd, who laughs and agrees.

"We shall be a very full house in the next month, it will keep her busy—and happy." Hallgerd looks up as the door opens, but it is not Unn. Mord enters. Hallgerd jumps up to welcome him, and the young prince puts a hand on her lovely face, mutely begging her forgiveness yet again. He has not yet reconciled himself to having struck the death blow of her father. Hallgerd's look softens at once and her smile reassures him mutely, yet again. He is loved. She is happy.

"They found this in the king's pocket," he tells Hallgerd, handing her a tiny scroll. Hallgerd casts a bitter glance my way—it is another of Thomas' amulets. We have found them everywhere. Hallgerd grinds it beneath her foot, tearing it to shreds. She picks up the pieces and casts them into the fire.

"He has not resumed his human shape, " she says. I know the thought has been on her mind since the day of the battle. "We cannot be sure it is he, can we?"

"Not unless he chooses to speak, or otherwise betray himself," I admit. "But I am quite certain it is he."

"What should we do, Nanna? If it is not he—even if it is…"

"We should just roast him for supper one night," Mord scowls. "Though I expect that anyone would choke upon such a meal."

Hallgerd laughs and takes his hand. "Yet I cannot just kill someone in cold blood—what if it is only a poor bird after all. But if it is Thomas, I do want to keep him from causing further harm. Is it right, Nanna?"

I sigh and shake my head. "We do what we can. Right? Wrong? We must follow our wisdom and sense. He is bound by the cage. Be assured, if it is he, then he suffers. Nothing could be more humiliating."

Hallgerd sighs, drops Mord's hand and paces before the fire. It is, I know, no comfort. "It makes me furious to think that his evil works could still be out there. There must be something we can do—"

"I will do what I can, find what tricks I may. I may find a way to scry the truth from this bird. But remember, child—evil exists. It will always exist. We cannot make it disappear. But we can always recognize good in all who fight evil."

Hallgerd smiles wanly and goes back to her lover's side. Mord takes her hand and she lays her head upon his shoulder. Smiling to myself, I set aside my needle to walk out upon the balcony and restore my heart with the beauty of this bountiful land. She will do well, he will always be her champion. Somehow we will deal with Thomas, wherever he may be— in the cage which stands in the chamber below, or winging his way across this dark sky. Yes, evil will always exist—but so too will good. I breathe in the crisp night air and know there is magic everywhere.

A matchless storyteller once taught me, "Nothing ever begins." Thus stories, having no beginning, can have no end. This story, too, goes on. Shall I tell you more?

Moggie

The scowlers come in and say Moggie where's our food an I say here it be an they are never grate full as it is a very mean feast indeed. They pay so ill. Not my fault tho it be they still blame. Moggie they say an tho it is not my name I must tell why is the food so bland. Sure enow I tell them I have no herbs to spare you take them for your speriments an they laff. Gold one day, Moggie, gold enuf for us all.

But only stink comes from their work room no gold an if I could find work else I would be gone but no one wants Moggie an her one eye an bent arm. Ugly I be but strong an no grucching when they use me ill. Brother Junius laff most an be cruel before others but happy enuff to slip under my bed clothes when he fancy a tumble in the deep night. I don't mind as he is a stout fellow an much warmer beside me than my moggie who gruch much when pushed out of her place. I always save me some of his spill as mama said, but I do not have love so I do not hold him, just keep it in case.

Some things they do be wrong I trow. When others come they get shy like horses, jumping at words, smiling like maids, so I kno what they do is not right enow, but I do not have care for their souls tho Brother Theodore some times say that they will be damned for certain when he mutters over soup. The others shush him and say 'more bread Moggie' so I do not hear them hiss at him like snakes.

Snakes kno too much.

Brother Junius told me of the snake who made the world, who tempted woman into evil an cursed man too because of her. Why is it her sin if he give in too? I ask him. Woman tempted man he says. Why is that her sin? He might say no. But Brother Junius is more eager to put his own snake to use than to tell me the old stories. Snake made the world but not fair to women. Even the abbess bows to the bishop. No one bows to Moggie.

Big doings up for the feast day. I can tell from the lilt in their talk as they chatter over porridge, pressing hands together like bairns on the way to the fair. Maybe it will be gold soon an Moggie can have a cottage an no more toil. Tho I try to ignore their gibbering I get the spirit too an feel tight in my gut as when I wait for papa to come home when small, tho often he strike us when we meet, tho not always as hard as the worst time, and he never come back an mama say he lies under the willow all day long.

Today the scowlers depart off to the woods to gather hidden treasures that must come now for their cooking. I watch them trot away, giggling like boys with grey hair and bald pates. I find my eyes lead me to the work room where I do not go, they do not want me to go, but I have caught their bee buzzing mood an want to kno more, so I see the big book an its gold an blue an red picture, an I am startled because a woman lies beneath a man an then I fear. Do they want Moggie for this secret rite? What do they do to me an will I end up tipped in the lav like all their bad work?

I shake like a poplar leaf an run to my closet where my moggie wakes with a start and purrs for my warmth tho I feel cold. I stroke her head an think what must I do. I hear mama's voice in my head tho she is dead many winters. I kno the way an I must get my own treasures in the wood but I need not go so far away as they. I kno they will be up late always dark of night when they work, when Brother Junius does not seek me. Too busy an no rising for matins, so I have time, an I find all I need, an I go to my pot, an fear I can not call to mind all mama said, but I put them in, an scrape some of Brother Junius spill for good luck. Must be of some use, tho mama not clear on why.

When they come from the wood they are tired but happy, still buzzing brother bees. I feed them stew an they say Moggie you've out done your self an I say feast day feast, an they laff. We have gold soon? I ask, an they say very soon Moggie. I try not to watch them eat the stew tho I am curious how long it will take. Mama never say.

Sun long down when the first one begins to moan. Then two then all. Moggie they say the stew was bad, Moggie get us

Pelzmantel and Other Tales of Medieval Magic

mustard, get us auntie money, but I listen not an shake my head as if I can not kno their meaning. Brother Junius begin to turn blue an I feel sad for him but kno they would have made me part of a speriment and so I can not feel too sad.

By first dawn light all is cold, all is still. I put my cloak around my shoulders an I trot to the abbess. The sister who lets me in is ugly as me an cross, but I plead to see the abbess an she comes at last and I sob an tell her my tale how all the brothers die. Do not tell her of my herbs. Her mouth a line that turns down at last. Are they damned abbess? I ask her an she sighs.

Men from the fields come to take the bodies away. They not buried in the abbey yard but off in the wood. New brothers will come, Moggie, the abbess say, but for now the scowlers hall is mine. Just us two moggies. Thank you mama, I say outloud, as I pet her head an she purrs too.

Walpurgisnacht

Walther knew. But he could not resist, what ten-year-old could? Every year was the same. Grandmother Dunkelhaus would shake her finger at him and warn, "Walpurgisnacht, the devil's night—you stay indoors. Devils, witches, ghosts—they come, they get little boys, eat you." Then she would snap together her shiny wooden teeth—clack!—as if she knew the flights of witches first hand.

But this year—tonight!—he would know, he and Elsa. "We must see," they had promised one another. Walther slipped out this afternoon, to sleep a while in the orchard as Elsa had suggested. The nap should help him stay awake tonight. He had put apples in his rucksack and a handful of matches—also Elsa's idea. She swore she would sneak away with a lamp. He looked around the room; never know what you might need. His woolen cap and sweater would keep him warm—spring was on the calendar, but not in the night air.

Downstairs his family gathered round the fire. Its crackles and sparks echoed up here in the garret, where they all assumed their youngest slept. But Walther waited for Elsa, his rucksack on his shoulder, his eyes eagerly seeking through the darkness. A movement: only leaves, caught by the tempestuous wind, they whirled and danced, begging someone to join their waltz. Walther cocked his ear back toward the group downstairs but heard only the familiar murmuring argument, Gran and Grandfather arguing still, as they had these sixty odd years.

Another whispering movement, this one with legs. Elsa beckoned from the oak tree, almost disappearing in its enormous girth. Walther lifted up the window silently, swinging himself over the sill, hanging for a moment, then dropping to the ground ten feet below and rolling as he hit the ground. The apples would be bruised.

"Wally. Here." Elsa swung a lantern by her side. A battered rucksack lay at the foot of the gnarled tree. "Did you bring the matches?"

"Yes, a lot of them. Good kitchen matches, wooden."

Her grey eyes caught the moon's bright glow and reflected it back to him despite the fading bruise below her left one. Elsa's face, wind-swept and tear-stained, tilted up at him, her decisive chin jutting out. "Let's go," she said, taking his offered hand.

The two children ran between the darkened trees, feeling the limbs bend down in concern as if trying to stop their flight. Out of sight of the house they slowed their pace, their breaths making curlicues in the night air.

"Did they suspect?" Elsa asked, wiping her dripping nose.

"No, no one even checked on me—not that they normally do," Walther hastened to add, a man after all at age ten. "And no one noticed that I was gone this afternoon either. I feel quite awake."

"I got this too," Elsa said and stopped to root through her rucksack. She pulled out a flask that had perhaps seen action in the Great War. "Coffee. Help us stay awake. It's cold," she added with regret, "But I think it will still work."

"I've never had coffee before. Well, once. I sipped my Gran's coffee. She said it would put hair on my chest."

"Did it?" Elsa shook the flask and the contents sloshed noisily.

"No," Walther kicked the ground, wishing he had thought to bring coffee. "But I did feel stronger."

"Come, we have to walk faster. It will be midnight soon."

"Did you bring a watch?"

Elsa halted and whirled around. "Damn!"

"Elsa, don't swear. God will punish you."

"God doesn't know I exist."

"God knows everything."

Elsa laughed. "Such a good little boy, a good little boy."

"Am not. I'm grown up."

"Oh, I don't know about that—never had coffee, never can swear."

"Do you think we should go back and get a watch?" Walther asked, trying hard to change the unpleasant subject.

Elsa pondered the question, pulling her wool socks back up

over her knees which looked bluish and cold by the light of the indifferent moon. "No, I'm sure we'll see them all. It should make quite a ruckus after all. Your Gran says she hears them all the way in your house."

"I think Gran fibs though," Walther admitted.

"Perhaps she exaggerates, but come on, it has to make a lot of noise, all that dancing and drinking and wild songs. I'm surprised that we haven't heard it in the past."

"We were too young," Walther said wisely. "Now that we are older we will go and see it for ourselves and we will be able to tell the others all about it. How envious Marta and Lulu will be when we tell them." Walther could see himself telling them, pretending to be bored by it all, as if Walpurgisnacht came every night and he had flown with the witches a thousand times or more.

"We're here," Elsa said quietly. Walther roused himself from his daydream, saw the cold granite wall of the cemetery before them and shivered. Suddenly the adventure seemed less welcoming than his warm goose-down bed.

"How do we get in? The gate is locked."

Elsa stared at him. One eyebrow arched upward in the derision he knew so well. "What? You can jump out a window but you can't climb a fence? Boost me."

Walther bent over dutifully and clasped his hands. Elsa put one ill-fitting shoe in his palms and vaulted up, giving Walther a brief glance of her switch-scarred thigh. "You should have worn trousers. You'll be cold."

Elsa regarded him haughtily from the top of the wall, but said nothing and swung her legs over. He heard her landing 'plop' on the other side. He shrugged off his rucksack and threw it as gently as he could over the wall. Elsa must have caught it, for he did not hear it land. Inhaling deeply, Walther gathered himself and leapt. In vain his fingers fumbled at the cold surface and he slid back down. One two three, and again inhale—this time his fingers caught and, feet pedaling like mad, Walther pulled himself up to the top of the wall. Down below Elsa waited, her hair touched by moonlight, her eyes grown large in the darkness. Someday we will be married, Walther thought helplessly, then threw himself down to the ground beside her.

"I know where we should go," Elsa hissed, whispering as if the dead might hear. She led him over to the Wahlberg crypt with its big angel and mourner's bench. They lit the lantern and sipped the coffee, which both declared delicious, so delicious that they would save it for later. Walther put his arm around Elsa to try to keep her warm and was almost at once asleep.

The sound that awoke them was neither a cry nor a scream, but a song. It was not a melody they knew. Suddenly conscious, Walther mistook the singing for his father's snores, reached for the covers he must have kicked off—and suddenly noticed where he was. Elsa's jaw hung low, her mouth forming an 'o' as she stared at the scene before them.

Witches, mad witches, gathered around a sparkling bonfire, chanting their happy praises to the night and waving sticks about. Corpses danced—a waltz, a mazurka, a reel of unknown origin, their wasted limbs carelessly free as they swung their partners high and laughed and bowed. Were they devils over there?—demons, maybe—that leaped about in some wild game, running back and forth, hiding behind the crypts, their shaggy hindquarters a curious surprise attached to their manly torsos. And there! In the sky, barely over the goat-men's heads, ethereal will-o-wisp women, seemingly made of little more than moonbeams and dust, whirled and swooped and shrieked in glee. The night was alive with shouts and motion. Everywhere they looked, some ghoulish creature jigged or crooned or guffawed with pleasure. Joyous music rose—from where did it come? There! The few spindly trees that usually hung silent and brooding over the solemnity of the graveyard, tonight rubbed spidery branches together for a cricket's song, a lively tune that led the dancers and lifted the spirits.

"Walther," whispered Elsa, breathless, "It's all true."

"Stay back," Walther hissed, grabbing her hand. Elsa turned in surprise, her eyes a-glitter with the dazzling scene before them. "You don't know what they'll do! Evil, Elsa, they're devils."

"Ha," Elsa shook off his grip, "They're not devils. Devils don't dance."

Walther stopped to consider this logic and she, laughing, ran from him to join the revelers. At once a space broke in the ring of dancers, hands reached out to welcome the little girl into the circle. Around and round the open grave they wound, throwing laughter and cries up to the skies, a merriment of sinless delight.

"Come back," Walther said weakly and even the gentle breeze did not carry his words far. But he could not make his feet move. The words of the Reverend Lochrie bound him fast—such beings were demons, they imperiled your soul. No matter that their raucous, giddy sounds beckoned in endless joy. Happiness was not to be trusted; the way of God was hard.

Yet Elsa danced—and laughed—imagine! Elsa laughing. The bonfire flickered in her face, her eyes—rapture flew from her lips as song. But still his feet were lead, were stone. Grandmother Dunkelhaus' words came unbidden, "They get little boys, eat you!" Walther realized he had clutched his rucksack protectively before him as if its battered sides could shield him from the devil's spawn. Elsa took no such precautions. Her rucksack lay behind him on the bench, abandoned.

Then the clock began to strike.

What time was it? How long had he stood transfixed by the spectacle? The second bell and the dancers stopped, dropping hands with a palpable reluctance and many wistful glances. A third chime and the witches stamped on their roaring bonfire, swatting at it with their sticks and brooms, still caught by their infectious laughter and dancing away from the lively sparks. A fourth chime—how many more could there be? Was that the dawn peeking over the edge of the world so soon?—and the goat-men and the whispering sprites sprinted for the cover of the woods at the far side of the cemetery. They called back and forth, promises of revels yet to be, stories of the night that was.

Fifth bell and the witches mounted, each testing the winds with a wet finger in the air, each choosing her own course. There! A very old witch, surely two or three hundred years by the look of her wrinkles and her grey, tasseled locks, but with the gentle face of somebody's grandmother—despite a leering scar that raked her kindly cheek. She offered a hand to Elsa, who took it gladly, without looking back.

That broke the spell. Walther's feet moved and he thrust his rucksack from him, running pell-mell to catch her, to stop her—maybe, just maybe, to join her. But the final bell was ringing and Elsa was waving, a grin lighting up her face as if the bonfire now burned within her heart. Elsa, Elsa; he couldn't even yell her name, it was too late, she was gone gone gone like the last echoing knell of the bell. But two words echoed back, two words of magic, flying from the receding spark of fire. Two words that gave him hope, that made his heart yearn and the dreams live yet in his breast. "Next year!"

Darkest Day

She was a sacrifice. Not because she was pure—though that she was—but because she was their best. Much fame to her family, for she would be their second offering. Many long winters before, her sister Sari had gone. "Sari is with the Winter Giant," Mama had often said to the little ones, smiling while her eyes sorrowed. And now Arja must go too, and add to the sadness in her mother's heart.

The village honored them all. The hunters insisted that Arja choose from the best of each kill. Old Pekka grumbled by with a skin of his berry liqueur, mumbling a grudging word of thanks to Papa before stomping off into the snow. Linne crafted a fine necklace of jangling bones and reindeer horn and shiny bright blue stones that lit up the twin gems of Arja's eyes. The elders had walked all together one night to present her with a fine bearskin cloak. Her papa crowed over its thick pelt, holding it aloft so Arja and her mama could trace the fine stitches embroidered on the inside. Three scenes told the story of Aino, the salmon maiden— her spurning of old Väinämöinin, and her watery death and final transformation. This cloak was her people's treasure. Arja thanked them humbly, blushing with terror and enjoyment, even as she wondered to herself how much good it would do her in the Winter Giant's realm. But she took it gratefully—such a prize! Papa swelled with pride. "Even Sari did not receive such a magnificent gift," he said, pulling playfully at her long braids. Arja glowed as if the fire reflected in her cheeks had caught and burned. She loved to clap the bear paws together under her chin and hear the claws clack.

That sound was less enjoyable as she waited on the frozen tundra, the many gifts surrounding her under the three-sided tent.

243

The open side faced north. He would come from there, Arja knew. After rising long before their men would stir, her mother and the other women had led Arja to the sauna for a careful cleansing. They had beat her skin with the birch twigs until she felt the pleasant glow of well-being, as the steam belched up with each ladle of cold water poured upon the hot rocks. Arja could almost forget why she was being so pampered. Mamma had woven red and white ribbons in her hair, braiding the colors into her waist-length plaits. The women had helped her slip into the beautiful red dress they had all had a hand in making—Mari's fine stitching, Linne's beads, Hanni's weaving—and pulled on the warm fur boots that had belonged to the eldest of the elders. Fine silver bells ringed the ermine tops and jangled when she walked.

These bells rang out across the plains as Arja stamped her feet to keep warm, and her little chimes were answered with further ringing from the north. She squinted into the darkness, trying to find movement within the white. If the sun were rising, Arja thought, I would be able to see him. But this day, again, the sun did not rise. Hiisi had taken it away, further and further, until darkness fell upon their land without respite—as he did every winter. *And I have been chosen to appease him.* Arja clacked the bear claws together under her chin and felt her heart beat faster.

Now she could see a shape against the drifts. The steady chime of the bells melted into Arja's thoughts until she could no longer hear it. The occasional crack of the whip, to urge the beast on, ran through her head and snapped through her body. Closer now. The animal drawing the sled seemed to be an elk of immense proportions, but there was something odd to it, too. As it plunged through the wind-sculpted banks layering the plain and covered the distance with surprising speed, Arja puzzled at the beast's strange silhouette. When it was yards away, she could make out the yellow eyes that twinkled like lilies on the pond's surface, the head like a stump rotted by winter's cruelty and crowned with a broken branch. The legs that ran so fast, leaping through the snow, and looked like saplings or maybe fence posts. The fur of this creature, now pulling up before her, appeared to be as rough as the bark of a fir, winter hardened and wind teased. Could such a thing live? This sorcery made her shudder.

But Arja's wide eyes had not even taken in the one who had

conjured such an alarming creature into being. He was taking her in, though. As he threw down his whip and shook off several layers of white bear skins, his eyes—dark as a night-flying raven—hungrily swallowed her body. Arja felt faint. He was so tall! And his shoulders hunched with power, like twin eels ready to spring. White hair rippled out the sides of his cap, but it brought her no comfort—this was no grandfather. The Winter Giant stepped down from his sleigh accompanied by a ringing as the massive elk shook his traces, pawing at the snow. Arja's body was a river of trembles that shook music from her boots and tears from her eyes.

A foot away now, he looked down upon Arja, then shifted his gaze to the goods behind her. At last, a smile. The Giant moved with surprising speed—and grace. He crowed like a small boy, delighted with the fresh-baked breads, the exquisitely smoked meat—Matti used special herbs along with the birch twigs to flavor the reindeer flesh—and of course, Pekka's berry drink. He lifted the skin above his head and squeezed the fermented juice into his gaping jaws. Such sharp teeth! And so many—Arja gulped, but her mouth remained dry.

It took him scant minutes to load the sleigh. It had taken half the village to bring all the gifts out here in the darkness, then leave one by one—Mamma holding on as if she might not leave, until she too had turned away and walked off into the night. The Winter Giant carried armfuls to the sleigh, piling them quickly, but with care, so nothing would get squashed in the ride back. He did not ask her help, so Arja stood silently by. The loading done, he rubbed his hands—paws? They were so rough, the nails so long and sharp—together with satisfaction and turned to Arja.

"Well, my bride, it is time we go."

Arja took his offered hand, her toes curling under as her small fingers were grasped by his frigid ones. Their cold was a new shock, even after the hours alone in the tent on the plains. A cold that came from within, from his cold heart, no doubt, Arja thought. *How can I bear this?* But she was already seated beside him and he was drawing the white bear skins over their laps. He paused to run his fingers over her own bear skin cloak. "Not bad for a little creature." Again he laughed, smiling down at Arja. The smile was terribly frightening. Arja could only think of how those teeth would feel in the morning.

"What are you thinking, my bride?"

Arja opened her mouth but no sound came out at first. She swallowed. "I was wondering what it will feel like to be in Tuonela."

Again the Giant roared with laughter. "You will not go to the Land of the Dead, child. When I eat you, I eat your spirit. Why do you think I am so strong? How can I pull the sun so far from your land? I eat spirits of human folk! Tasty they are!" His teeth scraped together as he spoke, like knives on bone.

Though warm under all the bear skins, Arja felt chilled to her heart. She had resigned herself to death. Someone had to die after all, for the good of the tribe—and there was honor in it. But to be consigned to oblivion! Trapped forever in the brutish hulk of this ogre—no, no, that she had not prepared for. Sitting next to the great giant as he urged on the huge elk with growls and whipcracks, Arja strained to hear the lost souls trapped within him. To be so cut off from the world of the living—she could not fathom it. There had been some comfort in the thought that Mamma would be able to call forth Arja's spirit from the grave already laid for her, the grave without a body. Only a lock of her hair, braided then cut off—only that was buried in the hollow with the other folk of their tribe. A scree of carefully chosen stones marked the place where her body would not lie. A shiver had run through her then, too, but it was balanced with the thought that her spirit might commune with family again at that spot. We go on, Papa always said. But Sari was always "with the Winter Giant." Had they known? Then why make her grave?

"You are silent," the giant said gruffly, pausing to wipe his streaming nose.

"I am unhappy," Arja said.

The big teeth gaped wide once more as he threw his head back laughing. When he stopped, the big grey eyes regarded Arja perplexedly. "Well, at least you are quiet." And without another word they rode for hours with only the elk's jingling traces to break the silence of the windswept plains.

The Winter Giant's home was a cleft in a cliff that opened into an immense cavern. One could never find it in the landscape's vast blankness without knowing just where to look. Arja watched as the giant released the elk, who shook his head and ran for the edge of the forest to make his dinner of what he could paw from the drifts. Just as easily as before, the great ogre carried all the precious gifts deep into the cave, motioning with a jerk of his head that Arja should follow within. A merry fire burned there, as if determined to cheer the poor girl, but still she shivered.

Here I will die, Arja thought glumly. She was too tired even to work up any anger or to fight. What could she possibly do against such a foe? Her eyes followed the giant. He was pawing through all the gifts with a child-like eagerness that somehow made his powerful frame that much more menacing. He could hurl her against the wall as easily as a boy might throw a snowball. And then eat her. It was too much.

"Here." The Winter Giant had opened all the packages and finally settled on the liqueur, some of the braided breads, as well as the pickled herring in the earthenware jar. He held out a piece of bread to her, ripped from a loaf. His claws held it fast. She hesitated. He laughed. "Yes, have some!"

Gingerly, Arja reached for the bread, sure the claws would dart out and stab her hand, but he released the piece of bread and it dropped into her tiny palm.

"Well, how do you like your wedding night."

"Will there be no ceremony, even?"

"What does it matter? You are only food, in the end."

"It matters to me. I am offered by my people as your bride— that I must perish after is not my concern. But the ritual is very important to me."

"Well, you may leap over the fire if you wish. I believe your people do such a thing." The giant chuckled as if this were very funny. "Then are we married?"

Arja stood up and felt the prickly skin of her legs as the blood began to flow sluggishly. "It will do."

It should have been such a joyful moment. Her family should have been around her, her village. Some young man should have been standing on the other side of the fire—not this great hairy beast of a creature, gnawing his way through her people's precious goods as the water sweated down the ice of the cavern. The fire should have been a symbol of blessing and fertility, filling her with the potential fruitfulness that their harsh life demanded. But here she was in the cave of the Winter Giant, his wife, his food. *Let there be some blessing in this*, Arja thought, eyes closed. Mother Sun, may your presence return to my people and this fire warm my heart and spirit. After a moment's reflection, she gathered her skirts and leapt over the crackling flames. The orange and yellow fingers reached up as if to caress her sturdy legs, and buoyed Arja with a warm pillow of heat. She landed on the other side, her mind buzzing with half-formed thoughts. *So I am married, so our souls entwine, until death claims one. Must it be me?* Arja regarded her husband without emotion. "It is done. Now you will return the sun to my people?"

"It is already done," the giant mumbled with a mouth full of herring. "The sun is returning, a little more each day." Again his raucous laughter echoed through the cave. "You can know my secret now. I do not control the sun. She moves on her own. Her yearly path takes her far from this land, but she always returns. Your foolish people! One very very bad, harsh winter, they believed the bragging words of this one," he thumped his chest proudly, "so now they pay me, and I eat when the sun is farthest and the nights are coldest and game scarce. I eat well—tender young flesh."

Arja burned, her eyes grew flames and her heart sizzled.

"None of the others asked, you know. Terrified they were. No wedding, no fire jumping. Just tears. Is it better knowing? No," he cackled, "I can see it is not."

Arja's blood raged through her flesh, her anger gathering momentum. But she could not strike out—what good would it do? Make him roar with laughter all the more? No, she could not attack him. In Arja's heart, the hot rage turned to cold tin. The questions inspired by her leap over the fire continued to whip through her thoughts. She did not even realize there was a smile on her face—grim as it was—as she turned to the giant once more. "Husband, may I ask a boon of you?"

"You know, you may call me Hiisi, as you are my wife—for now." He smiled over the skin of berry liqueur, his lips stained red. Arja felt a deeper chill, realizing how he would look with her blood splashed across his greedy mouth. "You may ask a boon of me—provided you do not ask to be spared death."

"I shall not ask that. But as I am never to rest in the land of the dead, may I at least be allowed to see Tuonela once before I die? Surely that is not so much to ask."

"Hmmph," Hiisi grunted. He was quite comfortable sitting cross-legged upon his bear skins, the many gifts gathered around him. Clearly he had no desire to make such a journey. "There is little to interest anyone there. And you could only stand on the shore. I could not take you into the land itself. My power is not such."

Arja controlled her smile. It must not look happy, only ingratiating. "This is all I ask. It is not so much. After tonight I shall see nothing. Let me have one glimpse of the land from which my ancestors speak to us."

Hiisi considered her request as he chomped on the salty fish, stopping occasionally to slurp at his claws. "I suppose there is no harm in it. But there is little of interest in it either. You will be disappointed." He looked at Arja, her chin jutted out implacably, and sighed. "But I cannot refuse a final request from my delicious wife."

He sighed and put down his treats, with a careful pat, as if to bid them wait his return. Arja bundled her cloak around her shoulders once more, her eyes brightly eager. Hiisi stretched, wiped his jaws with a huge paw, and belched noisily. This made him laugh even more loudly. His young wife smiled agreeably, but her thoughts already ranged ahead: Tuonela! Never would she have thought that so much hope could dwell in the Land of the Dead.

If her journey to the ice cliffs had been swift, then she had no suitable word for the speed of her second ride. Arja struggled to stay upright as the sled whistled over the icy banks. The white skins shifted with every bounce, and her teeth chattered with the cold and terror. But she must be brave. It had been her choice to come, to face once more the pallid expanses and the rattling winds, to risk what little life she had left. Tears flowed freely down Arja's cheeks. Even she could not tell whether they sprang from the whips of frigid air or from her fears. She was going to die, Arja knew it truly now. But the question still hung before her—how?

Just at the horizon, white turned to black, a darkness that was yet not so dark as that overhead. With alarm Arja saw that the first presages of dawn—not that they would see the sun that day—had whispered across the sky. The heavens were still black, but no longer the dark of a raven's wing. *Hurry, hurry*, she silently urged the bark elk, who—as if he had heard her plea—seemed to have saved a final burst of energy to reach this far-off goal. Through her tears Arja could see the dark lake, its sooty surface broken only by the gliding swan's wake and the whirlpool's hungry swirl. Tuonela, the land of the dead: beyond the mist she could not see, but she knew in the center an island lay. No one knew how big or small, even those who dwelled there. Some things could not be known.

"Well, my wife," Hiisi roared too loud for the silent shores, as he pulled hard at the elk's reins. "Here is your land of dead. We must hurry back now, it is time to eat!" But Arja was already clambering down from her seat, squirming out from under the bear skins. Hiisi stared, his mouth hanging open. Arja looked into his eyes. For the first time all fear fled from her heart, and she saw her own truth. He cannot guess. Aino, share your gift, she muttered, then turned and ran toward the clouded banks. Hiisi gave a yelp of surprise, threw aside his whip and hopped down from the sled. But he was not so fast this time. He would not catch her. She did not even try to shake off her heavy clothes, her beautiful boots, the clanking necklace that chivvied her throat. She only ran. Her feet felt light and swift. Arja spread her arms as she approached the water's edge, and the swan—as if in sympathy with her flight—spread its wings too, and hissed a threat to any who might stop her, raising up from the water and arching its neck.

From the bank, Arja jumped. Her body arced, palms together now; she hit the water like a leaping pike and plunged into the black spiral whirling down from the surface. Cold, so cold—and she had thought the midwinter air frozen! It was nothing to the glacial grasp of the midnight waters, fingers of ice that wormed through her garments and probed into her soul. *I am dying*, Arja realized. Her dive seemed to gain momentum, as if the whirlpool were greedily drawing her to its heart. Down and down she spun, losing all sense of direction, feeling her life slip away like her discarded clothes. Arja's eyes remained open, but she saw only her memories against the inky depths. It was all disappearing, washing away, trailing behind her, perhaps bursting at the surface. She did not even notice when the last bubbles of air left her nostrils, for the force of the water drew her on imperiously, until she saw nothing but blackness and felt no cold on her skin. Like a stone, Arja hit the bottom with a soft thump. Unlike a stone, she flipped and nosed her way toward the surface, her strong tail propelling her up once more. Long before she breached the water's skin, Arja could see vague clouds stretching across the sky. It was the first midwinter dawn.

Arja leapt from the water, droplets dappling her new scales. It was a shock to slam down on the surface, gasping for air, then remembering, diving once more to pull the rich liquid through her gills. It was cold and pure and invigorating. But she had to go up one final time. She twisted around, trying to get her bearings. There, over there! Arja paddled her fins vigorously to keep her head above the waves, and looked back at her husband. Hiisi had fallen to his knees at the very place where she had leaped. It was not anger she heard in his voice now, only a terrible sadness. *He would have eaten me*, Arja reminded herself as she plunged back into her new watery world. Yet his aching cry followed her down. "But you will tell them! And then I will be alone!" Hiisi wailed, "Alone!"

Author's Introduction to Medieval Magic

I wrote *Pelzmantel* while I was also writing my dissertation in Medieval Studies, an interdisciplinary degree that brings together literature, history, culture and language. One of my fascinations was Medieval magic. This interest influenced the story a lot, as you might guess. While many fantasy novels work with magic in a Medieval setting, it was fun to incorporate *real* Medieval magic into my story.

The picture most people have of "Medieval magic" can be a bit misleading: the necromancer with his staff summoning demons is part of the later clerical magical tradition. Ditto the alchemist with his cauldrons and scales; and those pronouns are chosen deliberately, because those kinds of magic were largely practiced by men. Scholar Michael Bailey has suggested that it was the conflation of that kind of learned magic with the more humble practices that led to the later witch hunts, which were initially efforts to stamp out heretics.

They were also more a feature of the early modern period *not* the Medieval. People tend to associate "witch hunts" with the Medieval, despite knowing the famous trials like those in Salem or the career of the infamous Matthew Hopkins, Witchfinder General, which date to the 17th century, the real heyday. While we're at it, let me also note that people in the Middle Ages knew well that the world was round, no one argued about how many angels could dance on the head of a pin and Vikings did not wear horns on their helmets. It was not a dark age at all.

The magic of the common people inspired the kind of magic I had my characters use in *Pelzmantel*. The practical magic of this time proves to be fascinating, though we generally only get to see it through the lens of Christianity. That lens does not always have to be a negative thing. Most medieval Christians were a lot more easy-going than modern ones. There's a famous 7th century letter from the pope to his missionary bishop, Mellitus, who was sent to convert the Anglo-Saxons back to Christianity. Britain had been Christianised under Roman rule, but when the Germanic conquerors came, they brought their own faiths with them. The pope tells Mellitus to ease the transition by not destroying the temples, altars and groves of the people, since that's where they were accustomed to going on holy days.

That's quite a contrast to St. Boniface who chopped down the Frisian's holy oak!

Most of the Medieval magic that comes down to us does so because it was written down by monks, which tells us so much about how differently magic was regarded in this time. Magic was a technology that had effective results. Sure, the monks were not going to countenance prayers to Odin or calling on Freya, but they had no problem with a lot of patently pagan practices once they were given a Christian re-booting. Sympathetic magic formed the heart of these rituals: the power of divinity made it effective (whatever name that power might have at the time).

Magic used everything: herbs, milk, ale, cords, butter, communion wafers, knives—just about anything that a normal household would have had on hand. They mixed potions and poultices, but the most important part of most charms was the words. I tried to capture a little of this in the protective charm connected to the golden tokens. The verb for a recited charm, *galdor*, often appears in compounds to describe the galdor-woman or galdor-man, those who practiced the galdor-craeft, the magic of words. The chanting of the charms gives protection, but they can also act as a mnemonic device, helping people to remember important information.

A good example of this is the Nine Herbs charm, which names the plants that work against different kinds of poison. It's an Anglo-Saxon charm that was written down around 1000 (though there's also a later Norse version). It's unique for its mention of both Christ and Odin (actually 'Woden' which was his English name), centuries after the reintroduction of Christianity into England. While the *Beowulf* poet avoids naming the old gods, the Germanic god appears in this charm as well as in the poem known as *Maxims I*, which collects a lot of gnomic wisdom.

The stanza refers to a serpent or dragon (*wyrm* is used interchangeably) who threatens but is unable to cause any harm because Woden strikes it with nine *wuldortanas* (glory twigs or branches) and it bursts into nine parts so it could never enter the house again. Christ appears in the later verse, standing over all disease, but it is the charm-speaker who claims the final power, the power of knowledge that she or he alone has of the plants guarded by the nine serpents in the running stream that hides the secrets (you'll have figure out that nine was an important number in Germanic mythology).

The final part of the charm, after the verses contains instructions to go along with the verses, including the necessity of reciting the charm three times over each herb before you prepare them as well as into the ailing person's mouth and ears before chanting the words over the wound and applying the ointment made from the herbs. But the words form an essential part of the process; the herbs aren't enough alone. Poetry is magic.

There are charms for all kinds of things, not just to fight poison. There's a beautiful charm for a swarm of bees that refers to them as *sigewif* or victory woman; you see, bees were a valuable commodity in the Middle Ages, because they were the producers of honey, of course. Honey was not only important as a sweetener, but also as the primary ingredient of mead, the warrior's drink of choice. The charm seeks to calm an angry swarm and coax it to stay.

There are charms against the loss of cattle, too. Your herd wasn't simply a source of food, it was the measure of your holdings; the word *feoh* meant both "cattle" and "wealth" in Anglo-Saxon times. It's also the first letter of the runic alphabet, known as the

Futhark because of the first letters (*feoh, ur, thorn,* etc.).

Before setting out on a journey, you'd be sure to recite a charm to keep you and all you traveled with from harm from the *grymma gryre* and the *sara slege*, which sound like companions of the Jabberwock, but mean the 'grim horror' and the 'sore slaying'. The speaker of this charm also calls for *wordsige and worcsige*, victory in words and deeds. It's wonderful to have this little window into the past; we're so accustomed to zipping around the world now, it's hard to realise that even a short journey in the Middle Ages would have been quite an undertaking, fraught with difficulty and danger.

The majority of charms have to do with healing of both humans and animals. Horses were valuable creatures and equine illness was not only alarming, but potentially devastating economically. Charms for human ailments cover all kinds of maladies, including difficult births, sudden stitches, or the variety of diseases caused by tiny creatures like wens and elves. While we may smile with superiority at these "superstitious" beliefs, people in the Middle Ages had a sophisticated recognition that diseases were caused by things too tiny to see that got into the body somehow: not a bad metaphor for bacteria and viruses.

The charm against a wen uses a combination of cajoling and threats to get the creature to go away. Apparently a wen causes a kind of swelling. The charmer sings a little verse persuading the creature to not build his home here (in the person's body) but to go farther off to the north where the wen has a brother. Given the importance of kinship and community in the Middle Ages, this appeal would hold a lot of influence. If the wen isn't convinced, the tone becomes darker, declaring that he will become smaller and smaller, like coal on the hearth, like water evaporating, smaller than a linseed, smaller than a "hand-worm's hipbone" and finally so little that he will be nothing at all. Surely, any decent wen will be convinced.

One of the most usual of the Anglo-Saxon charms has to be the one called "Æcerbot" which could be translated as 'remedy for a field'. Health is important not just for people but for the land as well. When crops fail, it's important to do something. This elaborate charm and ritual must have been deemed effective enough to be copied down carefully in the eleventh century.

You start this charm by taking four pieces of sod from the edges of the land before dawn. Into the openings you pour honey, oil, milk from every creature on the farm, leaves from all the trees, from all the 'named' plants and some holy water before bidding the land to be fruitful and multiply (in Latin, which tells us that a priest is likely carrying out this ritual). The pieces of sod are even taken to church to have mass said over them, then an appeal is made to the east. While many elements suggest that this ritual comes from the pagan past, the whole of it has been fitted into a Christian context, including recitations of the Pater Noster and the Lord's Prayer.

While the supplicant prays to "Erce" the "earth mother" he does so under the authority of the *ece drihten*, the eternal lord and all his holy ones. But there is within the ritual a poem of praise that cannot be shoe-horned into orthodoxy easily:

Hal wes þu, folde, fira modor!
Beo þu growende on godes fæþme,
fodre gefylled firum to nytte.

which could be rendered as:

Hale be you, earth, mother of men!
Ever may you be growing in god's grasp,
Filled with food, useful for folk.

The remainder of the ritual cleaves close to standard Christian practices; there are so many repetitions of prayers and the lord's name that one begins to suspect there was a little nervousness about the older stanzas. However, the importance of fruitful land would be paramount; if the charm worked, that's all that mattered.

While it's easy to romanticize this pagan preservation (as people like Margaret Murray did), it's worth remembering that much of this magic was not only approved by the authorities, but carried out by priests and monks. Of course, there were some kinds of magic that were forbidden, most of which fell under the heading of *maleficum*, magic with evil intent. It's not at all surprising that the mostly male authority figures looked askance at magic practiced by women when it challenged that authority.

The magic that caused the most anxiety had to be love and sex magic. Not that all of it was carried out by women; there are plenty of priests accused of coercing women with a little magic (keep in mind, if monks were so abstemious, there wouldn't have had to be so many reforms throughout the period). Yet there seemed always to be a great deal of anxiety about what women got up to in the home, particularly when it came to sex. There were strong prohibitions against adding blood or semen to potions used in sex and love magic, which had a lot to do with the depiction of women as more of the flesh than the spirit.

Of course a big part of this had to do with the Christian demonisation of women as all Eves at heart. We can see a lot of this through the handbooks that priests got to help them deal with confession and penance, called penitentials. While many people see the Middle Ages as a time when the Church controlled every aspect of life, for much of the era, the average person would head to church once a year at Easter to confess their sins and be shriven. The priests had their penitentials in hand to be sure they were giving the correct penance for the sins.

While many of the handbooks make for dull reading, the *Corrector et Medicus* of the early 11th century ecclesiastic Burchard of Worms proves a lively example of the penitential—and his direct concern with women's sins. The vividness with which Burchard questions the—apparently—well-known magical practices of women, suggest a specific concern on the part of that cleric. He worries that women are cavorting with satyrs or goblins or—gasp!—the pagan goddess Hulda (a Germanic fertility goddess who gave some of her qualities to Father Christmas). While he calls these practices "foolish" and the women "deceived" the fear he feels is palpable. He's ahead of the curve on the gendering of women as witches, which really gets going in the late Middle Ages and early Modern period.

While magic has never been an exclusively female practice, authority figures certainly assumed the worst of women's 'mysterious' actions. Scholar L.M.C. Weston has attributed this to the interiority of women's lives in the home in contrast to the public world of the meadhall, where all the warriors hung out (and later the great halls of courts where the knights did the same). The women's sphere is not royal, not ecclesiastical and not military, so the overarching male authorities had little participation in it. I make the most of this in the novel, turning Grima's kitchen into a kind of safe place and an entirely female domain. There is the same suspicion about what goes on in there from the men in the castle.

Perhaps the most interesting and enigmatic aspect of this view of women's places as mysterious appears in a strange injunction in the *Penitential of Theodore*. Section XV "Of the Worship of Idols" forbids a number of practices and we are warned "if any woman puts her daughter upon a roof or into an oven for the cure of a fever, she shall do penance for seven years" (198). A serious offence, but an obscure one in our time. The important detail is that it appears in the section about idol-worship. It's entirely possible that the misunderstanding about this having to do with idol worship comes from a reading of the Old Testament book of Jeremiah, but that's the kind of thing that brings out what must have been common misunderstandings.

Perhaps a cleric observing a not uncommon healing method, pondered his scripture for a solution (rather than ask the local folk?) to what he assumed to be the 'secret magic' of women. The presence of mother and daughter together may have suggested to him a kind of occult domestic rite. While another woman may only have seen a long-standing cure for fever, the cleric may have seen yet another frightening example of the rituals and magic of women, visible as one mother passed her forbidden arts to her daughter.

The breadth of medieval magic from poetic charms to complicated brews shows the amazing sophistication of a time too often dismissed as "superstitious" and a "dark age" (grrrr!). We may prefer our willow bark in a smooth white aspirin pill, but we still practice a lot of the same magic: it's part of our creative approach to the mysteries of life.

If you're intrigued, you can find more about medieval magic in the following sources:

Bailey, Michael, *Battling Demons: Witchcraft, Heresy, and Reform in the Late Middle Ages* (University Park, PA: Pennsylvania State University Press, 2003).

Cockayne, Oswald, ed. and trans., *Leechdoms, Wortcunning, and Starcraft of Early England*, 3 vols. Rolls Series (London, 1864-66; repr. London: Holland Press, 1961).

Collins, Minta, *Medieval Herbals: The Illustrative Tradition* (Toronto: University of Toronto Press, 1999).

Fanger, Claire, ed., *Conjuring Spirits: Texts and Traditions of Medieval Ritual Magic* (University Park, PA: Pennsylvania State University Press, 1998).

Flint, Valerie, *The Rise of Magic in Early Medieval Europe* (Princeton: Princeton University Press, 1991).

Flowers, Stephen, *Runes and Magic: Magical Formulaic Elements in the Older Runic Traditions* (1986).

Glosecki, Stephen, *Shamanism and Old English Poetry* (New York: Garland, 1989).

Jolly, Karen Louise, *Popular Religion in Late Saxon England: Elf Charms in Context* (Chapel Hill: University of North Carolina Press, 1996).

Kieckhefer, Richard, *Magic in the Middle Ages* (Cambridge: Cambridge University Press, 1990).

Laity, K. A., "Up on the Roof: Understanding an Anglo-Saxon Healing Practice." *Societas Magica Newsletter* 18 (Fall 2007): pp. 1-8.

McNeill, John T. and Helena M., Gamer, *Medieval Handbooks of Penance* (New York: Octagon Books, 1965).

Meaney, Audrey L., "Women, Witchcraft and Magic in Anglo-Saxon England," *Superstition and Popular Medicine in Anglo-Saxon England*, ed. D. G. Scragg (Manchester: Manchester Centre for

Anglo-Saxon Studies, 1989), pp. 9-40.

Storms, Godfrid, ed. and trans., *Anglo-Saxon Magic* (Halle: Nijhoff, 1948; repr. Folcroft, PA: Folcroft Library Editions, 1975).

Thorndike, Lynn, *A History of Magic and Experimental Science during the First Thirteen Centuries of our Era*, 2 vols. (New York: Columbia University Press, 1923).

Weston, L. M. C., "Women's Medicine, Women's Magic: The Old English Metrical Childbirth Charms," *Modern Philology* 92 (1995), 279-293.

Publishing History of the Stories

Pelzmantel was originally published in in 2003 by Spilled Candy Books.

"Darkest Day" was originally published as "Sun Thief" in *Marion Zimmer Bradley's Sword and Sorceress XXI* (DAW 2004) and appeared as "Darkest Day" in *Unikirja* (Aino Press 2009).

"Walpurgisnacht" originally appeared in *The Seeker Journal* *v*13 n5 (2001) and was reprinted in *The Pagan Activist* (Jan 2007).

"Moggie" is brand new and has never been published before.

About the Author

 K. A. Laity seeks a nimbleness in writing that will keep up with her myriad interests. At present she teaches Medieval literature, creative writing, film and New Media in the English Department at the College of Saint Rose in upstate New York. In addition to novels and short stories, she also writes drama, humour, reviews, academic essays and journalism, including a weekly column for BitchBuzz, the global women's lifestyle network.

Magic, myth and folklore infuse her writing. The short story collection *Unikirja* (Aino Press 2009) grew from the influence of her family's Finnish roots as well as the myths and legends of the *Kalevala* and *Kanteletar*. Laity's travels around Iceland, Finland and Britain ground her magical writing in very real places, and her studies in the Middle Ages inform the stories she tells. It has always been her aim to bring interesting if obscure knowledge from the past to a popular audience. Dead languages and dusty manuscripts may not sound exciting, but within them lies a magical world that too few know.

Visit her website, www.kalaity.com, for a complete list of publications and bookmark her news blog, be sure to bookmark katewombat.blogspot.com, for the latest projects, or follow her on Facebook or Twitter.

Did You Like What You Read?

The Thorn Boy by Storm Constantine
ISBN: 978-1-904853-69-5 /IP0028
£12.99/$21.99 paperback
New ed. of Storm's dark and erotic novella, including two stories not included in the previous edition. Set in the world of the Magravandias Chronicles, The Thorn Boy recounts to the stories of two king's favourites and the twisted fate that befalls them.

The Janus House by David Barnett
ISBN 978-1-904853-70-1 /IP0093
£12.99/$21.99 paperback
In a lonely, snowbound house, the insular existence of a writer and his wife is disturbed by the arrival of a girl with no memory... and reverberations from the past which threaten to unbalance the present...

Mytholumina by Storm Constantine
ISBN 978-1-904853-58-9/IP0023
£12.99/$21.99 paperback
The third volume in the author's collected short stories – these tales include Storm's SF work and also a few pieces that cannot easily be categorized!

A Dream and a Lie by Fiona McGavin
ISBN 978-1-904853-63-3/ IP0087
£16.99/$25.99 paperback
The omnibus edition of Fiona's highly praised fantasy trilogy: 'A Dark God Laughing', 'Dreams of Drowning' and 'The Fourth Cleansing'.

Find these and the rest of our current list at http://www.immanion-press.com

Lightning Source UK Ltd.
Milton Keynes UK

173530UK00001B/38/P